TARIQ

Born and educated in Pakistan and later at Oxford
University, TARIQ ALI is a writer, playwright and
film-maker. He is an editor of the *New Left Review*
and the author of over a dozen books on world
history and politics; his first novel, *Redemption*, was
published in 1990. It was followed in 1992 by
Shadows of the Pomegranate Tree, which has been
translated into several languages and was awarded
the Best Foreign Language Fiction Prize in
Santiago de Compostela, Spain, in 1995.
Tariq Ali lives in London.

Fear of Mirrors

TARIQ ALI

ARCADIA BOOKS
LONDON

Arcadia Books
15–16 Nassau Street
London WIN 7RE

First published in Great Britain 1998
© Tariq Ali 1998

A catalogue record for this book is available
from the British Library.

ISBN 1–900850–10–9

Typeset in Monotype Fournier by Discript, London WC2N 4BL
Printed in Finland by WSOY

Arcadia Books are distributed in the USA
by Dufour Editions, Chester Springs, PA 19425-0007

Published with financial support from
The London Arts Board

For Chengiz

One

WE LIVE IN A DREARY VOID and this century is almost over. I have experienced both its passion and its chill. I have watched the sun set across the frozen tundra. I try not to begrudge my fate, but often without success. I know what you're thinking, Karl. You're thinking that I deserve the punishment history has inflicted on me.

You believe that the epoch that is now over, an epoch of genocidal utopias, subordinated the individual to bricks and steel, to gigantic hydro-electric projects, to crazed collectivization schemes and worse. Social architecture used to dwarf the moral stature of human beings and to crush their collective spirit. You're not far wrong, but that isn't the whole story.

At your age my parents talked endlessly of the roads that led to paradise. They were building a very special socialist highway, which would become the bridge to constructing heaven on earth. They refused to be humiliated in silence. They refused to accept the permanent insignificance of the poor. How lucky they were, my son. To dream such dreams, to dedicate their lives to fulfilling them. How crazy they seem now, not just to you or the world you represent, but to the billions who need to make a better world, but are now too frightened to dream.

Hope, unlike fear, can never be a passive emotion. It demands movement. It requires people who are active. Till now people have always dreamed of the possibility of a better life. Suddenly they have stopped. I know it's only a semi-colon, not a full-stop, but it is too late to convince poor old Gerhard. He is gone forever.

These are times when, for people like me, it sometimes requires a colossal effort simply to carry on living. It was the same during the thirties. My mother once told me of how, a year before Stalin's men killed him, my father had told her: 'In times like these it's much easier to die than to live.' For the first time I have understood what he meant. Life itself seems evil. The worst torture is to witness silently my own degeneration. I really had intended to start on a more cheerful note. Sorry.

Your mother and I, she in Dresden and me in Berlin, moved towards each other, seeking shelter from the suffocation that affected the majority of citizens of the German Democratic Republic. We yearned for anarchy because the centre of our bureaucratic world was based on order. Gerhard and all our other friends felt exactly the same. We loved our late-night meetings where we talked about the future full of hope and kept ourselves warm by the steam from the black coffee and the tiny glasses of slivowitz. Even in the darkest times there was always merriment. Songs. Poetry. Gerhard was a brilliant mimic and our gatherings always ended with him doing his Politburo turn.

We were desperate for liberation, so desperate that, for a time, we were blinded by the flashes emanating from the Western videosphere, which succeeded in disguising the drabness of the landscape that now confronts us.

The old order possessed, if nothing else, at least one virtue. Its very existence provoked us to think, to rebel, to bring the Wall down. If we lost our lives in the process, death struck us down like lightning. It was mercifully brief. The new uniformity is a slow killer; it encourages passivity. But enough pessimism for the moment.

This is the story of my parents, Karl. It is for you and the children that you will, I hope, father one day. Throughout your childhood you were fed daily with tales of heroism, most of which were true, but they were repetitive. And for that reason, perhaps, you will hate what you are about to read. Just like the poor used to hate potatoes.

Ever since you became a cultivated and capable young man, your mother and I have found it impossible to draw you out, to make you talk with us, to hear your complaints, your fears, your fantasies. Now I know why you couldn't say anything to us. In your eyes we had failed, and to the young failure is a terrible crime. Whatever your verdict on us, I would like you to read this till the end. At my age the passage of time appears as a waterfall, and so please treat this request as the last favour your old fart of a father is asking of you.

It has been so long since we have sat next to each other, laughed at memories of your childhood, exchanged confidences. You were still at school, your mother was still at home, the Wall still stood. I did not feel we were just father and son. I thought we were friends. Gerhard, the only one of my circle you really liked and trusted, would watch us and say: 'Lucky, Vlady. To have a cub like Karl.'

We had our differences, of course, but I preferred to believe they were generational, even oedipal. In recent years, you have mocked my beliefs and, on one occasion, I was told you referred to me in public as a dinosaur. I was born in 1937. Not that old, is it Karl? It was your choice of epithet that surprised me.

Dinosaurs died out over a million years ago, but we are still obsessed with them. Why? Because the knowledge of how and why they became extinct has a lot to teach us about the life of our planet.

There is even talk of genetically reconstructing a dinosaur. In other words, my boy, I am proud to be a dinosaur. Your analogy was more revealing than you think. Perhaps deep, deep down we are still on the same side?

My parents were revolutionaries in the golden days of communism as well as through its bloodiest years. I was a child in Moscow during a war that is now a distant memory in Europe. I have lived most of my life in the twentieth century. You were born in 1971, and with luck you'll live most of your life in the twenty-first century. All you remember is the death agony of the Soviet Union, the final decadence of the state system they called communism, your mother and me working for a future that never arrived, and the re-unification of Germany.

And, of course, you remember your mother packing her case and walking out of our apartment. I know you hold me responsible for the break-up of the relationship and your mother's subsequent decision to accept the offer of a job in New York. You think it was my affair with Evelyne that was the last straw, but you are wrong. Helge and I were far too close for that to happen.

How does a marriage like ours come to an end? I think we were too similar in temperament, too like each other in too many ways. Our marriage had been an act of self-defence. She needed me to break from her orthodox Lutheran household. I needed her to get away from my mother, Gertrude. When the outside pressures disappeared, our lives suddenly seemed empty, despite the tumult on the streets. We were trapped in ourselves. Evelyne was a postscript.

Sometimes I feel that you also hold me personally responsible for the crimes that were committed in the name of Communism. And now you are angry because I have joined the PDS.[*] Why? *Why?* I can still hear the anguish in your voice when I first told you of my decision. I, who had never been part of their officialdom, was now joining a Party you saw as nothing but a cover for the old apparatchiks.

Was it just that, Karl? Or did you think it might affect your own meteoric rise inside the SPD[†] and your future career? Am I being unfair? All I can say is that I would be very surprised if my decision to join the PDS kept you out of an SPD government in the next century. Judging from what I read and what I hear, I feel you will go far. You are already an expert at making socialism 'reasonable' to its natural enemies, by purging it of any subversive charge. Better that

---

[*] Party of Democratic Socialism, which is the reincarnated version of the former ruling Communist Party of East Germany.

[†] The German Social Democratic Party.

than a turn to religion. If you had become a priest or a theologian, your mother and I would have excommunicated you from the church that is our heart.

Please understand one thing. By the time you are sitting in the ante-chamber of the Chancellor's office, memories of the Cold War will have evaporated. You will be faced with very different, real-life monsters. Europe and America are full of demagogues, each busy working on his particular version of *Mein Kampf*, even though the style will be different. The animal ferocity of the old fascists is giving way to the unctuous paternalism of their successors.

I joined the PDS to protest against the squalid situation in which we Easties find ourselves, to publicly declare the dignity of distress, to show people that there might be a collective way out of our mess. There have been more suicides in East Germany than anywhere else in Eastern Europe. We don't starve, but we feel psychologically crushed. It affects us all, regardless of the initials that command our allegiance and for whom we vote in the elections. I know many supporters of our gross chancellor who feel exactly as I do.

The Westies thought that everything would be fine once our past had been destroyed and all traces of the DDR[*] eliminated. How foolish they are, these women and men of the West. They thought that money, their money, was the magic solution. It is the only language they understand themselves, and I don't blame them too much for this weakness. After all, in the post-war period their motto was to strive for money, more money and only then would people recognize their own true worth. They became so preoccupied with this task that it served as a therapy which helped many of them to erase the memories of their own complicity with the Third Reich.

In our case it wasn't so simple. However awful, however grotesque the old DDR was – and it was that from the beginning till the end – it was not the Third Reich. The equation is stupid. It insults our intelligence. You know that as well as I, so please make sure that it trickles down to your new masters.

Over forty years we evolved different cultures. Take our language, for instance. We even speak differently. In the West grammar has been almost forgotten. Life in the DDR schools was stifling, but our kindergartens were really good and in the sixties and seventies the Prusso-Stalinist structures in the universities were beginning to reveal dangerous cracks.

Your children will never see *The Sand Man*. Wasn't it much better than the American rubbish they show the children in the West, or am I

---

[*] Democratic Republic of Germany: the formal name of the old East Germany.

just a pathetic old bore, who is beginning to get on your nerves?

Many of us are happy that our country is one again, but sad that everything here is being crushed. Their new Berlin, the official Berlin for the next century, is being designed and constructed to obliterate the past, to put the genie of history back into the lamp. Yet they are simultaneously creating the conditions to revive the old polarizations. The rich Westies are buying up all the real estate so that they can become even richer. And they bring their own towels and soap when they stay in our hotels. A new homogeneity is being imposed on us. Of course, we have the freedom to protest. This is good.

Gerhard's letter arrived the day after I had heard his suicide reported on the radio. A few lines. A former professor had hanged himself in his garden in Jena. That's all. I read Gerhard's letter over and over again. This was the voice of my closest friend. Less than a fortnight ago, we had spent an evening together. Like me, Gerhard had been dismissed from his post. He could not remain Professor of Mathematics at the university in Jena because of his political views. Here was a man who had celebrated the fall of the Wall like everyone else.

Alas, Gerhard's father had been a general in military intelligence. The Westies were purging us with a vengeance. Tell me something, Karl. What use is a Germany that sentences people like Gerhard to death? You wept when I showed you his letter. Do you remember that mild, beaming face, often dreaming, often filled with self-doubt, but never withdrawn or gloomy?

At first it's like an ember. Then it begins to flicker and soon there's a flame. It is this flame that penetrates the brain. The result? Constant pain. It's when my mind cannot contain the pain; when it overpowers everything – hope, love, pleasant memories, everything – it's when it brutally occupies the past that the thought first occurs. The pain refuses to go away. And then, on a beautiful sunny afternoon like today, I think of the best way to go. Why shouldn't I hang myself from the old oak in the garden? A semi-public act. The neighbours will report the event. Ultimately, Vlady, it is the only means of escape left to us. The Westies want to write us off completely. We never existed. Everything was shit. I cannot live in a country where human beings are once again being seen as rubbish to be swept aside ... Spiritual poverty is worse than death, degradation or suicide ...

The only image you have of us, Karl, is that of a vanquished generation whose entire legacy is poisoned. Telling you Ludwik's story may give me the opportunity to tell you more than you know about your grandmother and about myself. Don't panic just yet. Spare me your condescension and pity. This is not going to be a self-justification or an attempt to wean you away from the apparatus to which you have become so attached. Everything in this world is now relative. I rejoice that you are a Social Democrat and not a Christian Democrat, and one day you must explain what divides you from them today.

What I want, above all, is to rescue the people in this story from the grip of all those whose only interest in the past is to justify their version of the present. Those of us who have been formed by and survived the fire-storms of this century owe this, if nothing else, to ourselves.

If you don't want to read what I have to say, perhaps you'll drop it in a drawer somewhere and let it lie there till your children or their children take it out. Perhaps by the time I've reached the end, I might not want to send it to anyone. Much of what you will read is my imagination. The spaces between what I know for sure could not be left empty. With your permission, then, I'll start in the time-honoured tradition.

Once upon a time, in the village of Pidvocholesk, in the province of Galicia, in the last decade of the preceding century, there were five boys whose names began with L. They all swam in the same river, went to the same school, chased the same girls and grew up indifferent to the fact that their little village, situated on the border between the Austro-Hungarian lands and the domains of the Tsar of All the Russias, was subject to the vagaries of imperialism. It changed hands every few years. All this meant was that they learnt two extra languages instead of one and were taught to read Pushkin and Goethe in the original.

Your grandmother, Gertrude, used to talk of a photograph she once saw in Moscow. There they all were. Five boys, virgin and uncorrupted, dripping with water from head to toe, their faces full of mischief, caught by the camera in their knee-length swimming trunks.

It was not till they were older that Ludwik, Lang (whom they always called Freddy), Levy, Livitsky and Larin, realized that the Tsar's regime was far more oppressive. The Austrians had encouraged the building of a library and a reading-room where they could read all the German-language newspapers and periodicals. The reading-room had become a trysting place even for the less literate youth of the village and there was anger when the Russians closed it down.

Of the five Ls, three, including my father, Ludwik, came from Jewish backgrounds and spoke Yiddish. The other two were of Polish peasant stock. Everything was mixed. People spoke each other's languages. When it was time to mark their tenth birthdays your grandfather and his friends were equally fluent in German, Russian, Polish and Yiddish.

We all know the negative features of the old empires, but they did have a positive side as well. Their existence united the populations over which they ruled by providing them with a common language and a common enemy.

The young men growing up in little Pidvocholesk never suspected that, within the space of a few years, most of them would be decimated by the First World War. Not that they were unaware of the turbulent times in which they lived. Life in a border village is rarely serene. It attracts fugitives of every hue. Criminals, political exiles, deserters from various armies, young couples fleeing from parental tyranny and trying desperately to find a way to the New World.

The Ls were well placed since Schmelka Livitsky's father owned the village inn. In his black caftan and matching black beard, Schmelka's father inspired both awe and respect. He was a kind man and clothed even the basest of his visitors with a rare dignity. It was here that Ludwik and his friends first heard from Polish exiles that a revolution had broken out against the Tsar in St Petersburg. The year was 1905.

They understood that the revolt had been crushed when a new flood of exiles passed through the village, which was once again in Austrian hands. The five Ls weren't living in Essen or Manchester or Lille, though even there, despite the presence of trade unions and reformers, they might have been impatient with the pace of change. Pidvocholesk was a central European peasant village on the margins of two mighty empires, and eighty per cent of its inhabitants were Jews. They had initially greeted the news from St Petersburg with unconcealed delight, but had soon reverted to their normal mood of cautious pessimism.

One sunny day in March 1906, when the snow was beginning to melt, a diminutive man in his early thirties with horn-rimmed spectacles and tired eyes came to Pidvocholesk. He was a Pole. His name was Adam. He had spent many years in the Tsar's prisons. All he wanted was a rest. Ludwik befriended him and Adam was admitted as an honorary member of the five Ls' secret society.

He would join them for long walks by the riverside. He would listen to their chatter. The village girls were a central theme, closely related to crude gossip concerning the rabbi and other village notables. This was followed by a comparison of parental atrocities.

Adam was a patient listener. He smiled a great deal, asked a few questions, but volunteered nothing. It was only when they began to question him that they realized how different his life had been compared to theirs. Adam's story moved them. Then he began to question them, and events that they took for granted soon appeared in a different light. Pogroms, for instance.

Ludwik told Adam of how, some years ago, he had accompanied his father to an uncle's wedding in a neighbouring village. Pidvocholesk was almost entirely Jewish and usually under Austrian rule. It felt safe. But his uncle lived in Russia. The main street of the village where he lived was like a ravine. Jewish houses and shops on one side and everyone else on the other. As Ludwik spoke his voice grew hoarse as he recalled the fear he had felt on that cold, autumn night. It was the Sabbath. Candles had been left burning, and as they walked down the street the windows in Jewish houses were framed in a magical soft glow.

He described the congregation as it left the synagogue. Old men with bent backs, lowered heads and gaping caftans. Others, like Ludwik, were young, but trying hard to walk like men. Some of the old ones must have smelt danger for at one stage, and for no apparent reason, they all fell silent.

Suddenly, without warning, a group of peasants led by priests ambushed them. Ludwik remembered the whips, sickles, scythes and sticks falling out of the sky on their heads like bitter rain. An old Jew in his sixties felt the whip wielded by a strong young peasant with a moustache. Ludwik described a face disfigured by hatred, the eyes glazed over as if something had possessed them. It had: the old Christian hatred of the Jew as a monster from Hell, sent by the Devil to kill Christ and persecute the godly through trade and plunder.

Ludwik's father had grabbed him by the hand and they ran and ran and ran till they had left the evil far behind. In their rush to escape punishment they had not even noticed another group rushing into Jewish houses and setting them alight with the Sabbath candles. It was a small pogrom. Only two Jews died that night. As they walked the twelve miles to Pidvocholesk, Ludwik's father told him not to worry. Things were much worse in Lemberg and Kiev.

Ludwik and his friends, inspired by Adam, were determined to escape from Pidvocholesk. They had all done well at school. Their families had managed to raise enough money to send them to the university in Vienna. The year was 1911.

Freddy, Levy and Larin studied medicine. Ludwik, despite the strong objection of his parents, who wanted him to become a lawyer, was studying German literature, raving about Heine and writing poetry. Schmelka Livitsky was a mathematician, but spent most of his time playing the violin.

At first they met every evening to exchange experiences, talk about home, complain about how expensive everything was and feel sorry for themselves. Apart from Livitsky, none of them could afford tailored clothes, and they attracted attention when they were huddled round a café table noisily drinking their coffee and speaking Yiddish. They were all quick to detect imagined slights. They wanted to outgrow their provincialism overnight.

After the first few weeks their meetings became less frequent. They were working hard and beginning to find new friends. Soon their contact with each other became limited to waving at each other across tables in their favourite coffee houses.

Ludwik was bewitched by Vienna. He was caught up in the amazing whirl of history. Everything appeared to have its opposite. The anti-Semitic Social Christians were being confronted by the Socialists. Schoenberg had unleashed his ultra-modernist fusillades against the Viennese waltz and a musical establishment happily buried in the past. Freud was challenging medical orthodoxy.

Ludwik was excited. He could not then see that what he was witnessing was nothing less than the disintegration of the old order. Unlike their English and French counterparts, the Austrian bourgeois élite had been unable either to fuse with or destroy their aristocracy. Instead it fell on its knees and sought to mimic its betters. The Emperor's authority was unchallenged, except from below: protofascists on the one side and socialists on the other.

Unable fully to comprehend the dynamics of this world, Ludwik sought refuge in the cultural section of the Viennese press. He was attracted to the *feuilleton* style and its leading practitioners. These were guys who specialized in cultivating their personal feelings and making the readers feel they were getting insights into the true nature of reality. Ludwik was impressed. The literary tone appealed to him greatly, as did the narcissism.

Ludwik often thought of home. He missed his mother and her meat dumplings. He missed the little pastries his Aunt Galina used to bake for special days, and he even missed his father's bantering tone. Late at night, all alone in his tiny room, he would sit and write what he thought were clever letters to impress his parents, mimicking the style of the *feuilletonists*.

The flippancy and false tone depressed his parents. Ludwik's father was a private tutor who earned a little money teaching music to the children of the Polish gentry. His mother made bread and cheesecakes for the Pidvocholesk bakery. Both had worked hard to send their favourite son to Vienna. Ludwik's brother, in sharp contrast, had been apprenticed to a watchmaker uncle in Warsaw and was doing well.

How long this would have gone on and where the five Ls would have ended I do not know. Two things happened to end their obsessive self-contemplation and push them in the direction of reality. The first was Krystina. The second was the outbreak of the First World War.

Krystina entered their lives in the summer of 1913. The month was June, the days were long, the sky was blue and the nights were balmy. Freddy had sighted her one evening on the pavement where they were sipping iced lemon drinks. His attempts to engage her in conversation had failed miserably. Ludwik had noticed she was reading a pamphlet by Kautsky. He had walked up to her and asked if he could borrow it for the evening. This approach had been more successful. She agreed to join their table, but insisted on paying for her own tea.

She was a few years older than them and possessed a fierce and combative intelligence. She was also very beautiful, but in a distant sort of way, and she disliked flattery. She had grown up in Warsaw, but had studied philosophy in Berlin and attended the study classes organized by the German Social Democratic Party. When she returned home she had become a Socialist and joined the underground Polish party. Her authority had been conferred by the four months she had spent in prison. All this she told them, but every attempt to question her about her personal life failed. She never talked to them about her parents or her lovers. They were not even sure if Krystina was her real name.

They all fell in love with her. Yes, even Ludwik, though later, when his wife Lisa questioned him about Krystina, he used to protest a bit too vigorously and say: 'Of course I love her. How could one not? But I'm not *in* love with her. A very big difference.'

One evening after they had been attending her study classes for a few months, Krystina recruited them all to the cause of international socialism. It's amazing how quickly she changed their perception of Vienna and the world. She had taught them not to accept life as it was, but to fight against every outrage with their fists. In her book, there was no such thing as accomplished facts. Everything could and should be changed.

The five boys from Pidvocholesk were now a clandestine cell of the Polish Socialist Party in exile. Krystina's tiny room had become their true university. Not that she encouraged them in any way to give up their academic careers. The working-class movement needed doctors to treat poor patients free of charge. This meant that three of the Ls were fine.

Krystina realized that Ludwik was a gifted linguist. She persuaded him to abandon German literature and study the details of the German, English, Russian, French, Spanish and Italian languages. She wanted him to appreciate the nuance of each language, and for this he insisted that he must read the literature produced by the different cultures. For several months he could be sighted at his favourite cafés absorbed in European novels.

They had never met a woman like her. She was fighting for a better world and had subordinated everything else in her life to achieve that goal. She taught them the meaning of commitment to a set of ideals. She had brought a sense of drama into their lives, made them feel that they were not simply individuals, but actors with a part to play on the stage of history. How grandiloquent this all sounds now as we look at the world today, but it was not always thus and this is something your generation wants to forget. Krystina had altered the way they saw the world, forced them to reflect on the need to change the human condition. She transformed their vision forever.

It was she who gave them their new identities. 'My five Ls', she used to call them, and they willingly became five fingers of her hand. It was undoubtedly her strong personality that pushed the five Ls towards the revolution. The social disintegration caused by the First World War did the rest.

Think of it, Karl. Each one married to his time. Working patiently for the world revolution. In Galicia the choice had always been limited. Emperor or Tsar? Krystina pointed them towards a new horizon. In her room in Vienna they used to wonder whether it was all talk, whether Krystina's utopian vision could ever be fulfilled. Ludwik had witnessed pogroms. He doubted whether the oppressed could ever be united under one banner. Those poor Polish and Russian peasants had been so easily incited to kill Jews and burn their homes. Could they really emancipate themselves? It would require a miracle to wrench them away from the deferential stupor in which they lay engulfed.

Krystina would listen patiently and smile. Ludwik was expressing the very same doubts that had plagued her a few years ago. Even as they argued, they heard excited shouts in the streets. News had arrived from Sarajevo. The heir to the Austrian throne had been assassinated by a Serbian nationalist. Who could have thought then, my dearest Karl, that our century of wars and revolutions would begin and end with Sarajevo?

With the outbreak of war, Ludwik's uncertainties evaporated. Krystina's position was clear from the very first day. She felt no need to consult a higher authority. This was a war in which it would be criminal to take sides. Neither Tsar nor Kaiser. The European powers were fighting each other to determine who would dominate the rest of the world and using their workers as cannon fodder. Krystina wanted all the workers' parties to call a Europe-wide general strike against the war. She did not want British workers to kill or be killed by their German counterparts. 'Workers have no country!' she had shouted with shining eyes at the new converts.

At first, the Ls were not convinced. For them, the Russian Tsar was the greater evil. A German victory would aid the democrats, free Poland and other Russian colonies and . . . Krystina became very angry. Why should they exchange one ruler for another? True freedom meant the end of all the monarchies and their empires. They argued for several days. Krystina won the argument.

What finally convinced the Ls was the sight of Krystina weeping over a copy of *Die Neue Zeit*. The German Social Democrats had voted in the Bundestag for war credits. Only Liebknecht had voted against. The war hysteria had gripped the workers and their party had been too weak to swim against the stream. Perhaps, Ludwik had suggested tentatively to calm her down, this meant that German workers did have a fatherland. But the dark look that greeted this heresy forced an immediate retreat. Ludwik was influenced by people rather than ideas, and his philosophy would always reflect this. The realization would from now on dominate his existence.

Their choice meant that they had to leave Vienna immediately since a general mobilization had been decreed. Krystina took them to Warsaw.

Two

L ET MY FATHER LUDWIK and his friends wait awhile. Krystina is training them in the arts of political warfare and I will return to them soon, but there is something else worrying me, keeping me awake at nights.

More than anything else, I want to repair our relationship, bring some laughter back into our lives. I can see where the danger lies. Unspoken bitternesses and unresolved tensions have become lodged within us both. I want to find an antidote to this poison. I hope you agree, Karl.

Even as I write, it seems ridiculous to go so far back into the past instead of coming to terms with more recent histories. I mean your mother's decision to leave us, for which you have always blamed me. Perhaps if she had stayed and I had left, you might have censured her instead, though that would have been equally unjustified.

Everything seemed to go wrong after the death of your grandmother Gertrude. Your mother and I found we had less and less to say to each other. With our apartment empty I noticed her absences much more and began to feel that she had lost interest in me. She was spending more and more time in her clinic. Then one day while I was having coffee with Klaus Winter, he said something he shouldn't have said. You remember Klaus, don't you? He was a very old friend of Gertrude and was weeping a great deal at her funeral. He's the one who bought you a pair of jeans from the other Berlin on your fourteenth birthday.

Klaus told me quite casually that he had seen Helge with a friend at a concert two days ago and asked why I had not been present. The point being, Karl, that not only had Helge not told me she was going to a concert, she had explicitly said that she couldn't attend a meeting of our Forum that same night because of a patient, whose condition was such that his appointment could not be cancelled. Why had she lied?

I left Klaus Winter stranded in the hotel where we were meeting and rushed home. I was crazy with jealousy. Fortunately, or perhaps unfortunately, you were out with your friends. When your mother returned I confronted her with the facts. To my amazement she smiled and called me pathetic. I hit her. I felt ashamed immediately afterwards. I pleaded to be forgiven. She did not speak, but walked slowly into our bedroom and began to remove her clothes from the cupboard. I was paralysed. I could neither say or do anything to stop her. I sat silently on the bed as she continued to collect her belongings and then pack them in her faded green pre-war suitcase, which had once belonged to her grandmother. I remembered the day I had brought her home after our wedding and carried this same suitcase into our bedroom.

'I did not lie to you, Vlady. I never have. The man with me at the concert *was* a patient and it *was* part of his treatment. Your reaction is a symptom of your own guilt-ridden mind. I'm going. We'll talk next week when you're calmer, and then we'll both talk to Karl. Tell him I've gone to Leipzig to see my mother. And if you want Evelyne to move in, I have no objection.'

That's all she said as she walked out of our home. I wanted to scream, to run after her, to drag her back, to fall on my knees and plead with her to stay and give our relationship a last chance, but I did nothing except shed a few silent tears as she walked away.

Perhaps something inside me told me it was no use. We had grown apart and nothing, not even you, Karl, could bring us back together again. The rest you know. She came back and I broke away from Evelyne. The big break came much later and for reasons we both understand.

Helge was wrong about Evelyne. If I'd confessed to her, she would have been angry, but she would have understood. She found out by accident – a stupid letter from Evelyne to me which I should have destroyed. A letter in which she argued that the female orgasm was a male invention and that I should not despair at my inability to satisfy her. I only kept the letter because it amused me. Your mother read it differently and ascribed powers to Evelyne which that young woman, alas, never possessed. I suppose I should begin at the beginning.

This may come as a surprise to you, Karl, but I was a popular lecturer at Humboldt. Comparative literature is a field that permits a great deal of creativity in its teaching. Evelyne was one of the students in my special seminars on Russian literature.

I used to, for instance, talk of Gogol reading extracts from *Dead Souls* to Pushkin and the students would then write an imaginary dialogue between the two men. Evelyne was quick-witted. We were all smiling at her clever dialogue till it reached a surreal stage. She was allergic to the prevailing orthodoxy and, as her imagined exchange neared the end, she had included some savage references to Honecker and the Politburo. Everyone looked at me. I did not comment, but moved on to the next student.

I had never spoken to her after my classes. Our relationship had been restricted to regular and sympathetic eye contact and the occasional smile, especially when a student trying hard to move upwards in the party hierarchy posed a particularly uninspired question.

That same week it was my fiftieth birthday. Helge had organized a party. To my surprise, Evelyne showed up with a few of her university friends, none of whom had been invited. Helge welcomed them all.

It was a haphazard and disordered occasion. Evelyne alone remained sober that night, observing us all through a haze of tobacco smoke. That was when I first saw her as an attractive young woman. Medium height, slim, short blond hair and exquisitely carved. Her breasts were not voluptuous like Helge's, but small and firm. Overlooking them was a pair of sharp blue eyes and an intelligent, angular face.

A week later we made love for the first time in a tiny apartment overlooking the old Jewish cemetery. It belonged to her aunt, who was never at home during the afternoon. For a few months we shared everything: experiences, confidences, worries, fantasies and dreams. Our love grew like a wild rose. We would walk to the park and sit on the grass, holding hands and kissing like nervous adolescents. Just when I was thinking seriously of telling your mother, the affair died suddenly. What had pruned it out of existence? On my side, I guess, it was the knife of reason. One afternoon I couldn't take her. She was mocking and cynical.

'My stock is clearly going down and yours is refusing to rise. I think we've exhausted each other. Time to move on. You look surprised, Vlady. You're not bad-looking for your age. I was into you because of your acid tongue. You were different from the other robots at Humboldt. You used to make me laugh. I never intended a long stay at your station, you old fool. Anyway your signals need repairing and you need a more experienced engineer than me.'

I thought then that she was driven by pure ambition. Her overriding need to change lovers was determined by which of them could help further her career. I had introduced her to a film-director acquaintance and had seen her at work on him. I had no doubt that he would replace me. He did.

Perhaps I'm being unfair. Perhaps she had simply outgrown me, moving to a different phase of her life. I had spent a lot of time on her compositions, making critical notes and compelling her to rewrite and rewrite till I thought she could do no better. It was I who had read her short stories and poems. It was I who had noted she had a good ear for dialogue and pushed her in the direction of writing film scripts.

A few days after we had ended our affair, I saw her on the street with the film director. I behaved badly. I disrupted their talk and dragged her away. Her reaction indicated that it really was all over. She poured scorn on me. Hatred flowed out of her like molten lava. She threatened to ring Helge. Then she walked away. I was embittered. I felt I had been exploited. I wanted to confront her once again, but she had disappeared. She and the film director had fled to the West. One of her friends told me she had settled in Heidelberg.

It seemed pointless to tell your mother anything. It was over. But someone had recorded the episode. Unknown to me or Evelyne our summer trysts in the park had attracted the attention of Leyla, a Turkish painter from Kreuzberg who had been commissioned to paint a set of East Berlin landscapes. Her portrait of us had a surrealist flavour. We were buried deep in an illicit embrace in the park. She had entitled her painting *Stolen Kisses*.

Many months passed. Evelyne was happily ensconced in my unconscious. One day there was a rainstorm. Your mother, desperate for shelter, entered an art gallery. A coincidence, of course, but what wretched luck. She saw the painting, pierced through the surrealist mask, recognized me and questioned Leyla with some intensity.

Helge could not afford to buy the painting, but Leyla, observing her distress, gave it to her. When the exhibition was over, Helge brought the painting back to our apartment. A hurricane swept through our relationship. I am shuddering as I write this, Karl. It was a horrible day. Our relationship was probably doomed, but *Stolen Kisses* sealed its fate. She took the painting with her when she left, informing me that though the subject made her nauseous she really liked the composition and had become good friends with Leyla.

There are times in life when a single setback encourages another, like a small, dislodged rock triggers an avalanche. A month later I met Klaus Winter for lunch and he informed me that the State Security was getting regular and detailed reports from the leadership meetings of our Forum for German Democracy. He repeated verbatim remarks that had been attributed to me. His report was completely accurate. That was when Winter told me that he was a senior figure in Foreign Intelligence and that Gertrude, your grandmother, and he had both worked for Soviet Military Intelligence since the late twenties. After the Second World War they had been assigned to the DDR intelligence services.

I was thunderstruck, Karl. I had no idea that Gertrude was still involved in all that stuff. She had left no trace of it in her papers. I did not let Winter see the effect of the blow he had dealt me. Gertrude had encouraged the formation of our Forum. She had actually helped me write our founding document. She had attended some of our meetings. I had discussed our innermost secrets with her, including a plan to steal documents from the Politburo, since one of our supporters worked in that building.

As I walked away from Winter's apartment, I wondered how much Gertrude had told Winter. Everything? Nothing? A few bits and pieces? In which case why had they not arrested us and disbanded the Forum? They could have done it very easily. Perhaps they had reported directly to Moscow and the men around Gorbachev had counselled them to let us grow.

I wanted answers, but before I was ready to confront Winter I had to discover the real Gertrude and the ghosts that had possessed her. She was dead. I had to piece together the disparate strands that had made up her life. How had it interrelated with that of Ludwik? When did she first meet Winter and where? And who was she in the first place? Her life was now beginning to haunt me.

I remember, not long before she died, you asking her whether she had any photographs of her family. I used to ask her that when I was a child and she would shake her head quickly and change the subject. When you asked her, she began to cry. Do you remember? Do you know why, Karl? Because she had left home in such a state that all relations between her and the family were broken.

Gertrude's parents were third-generation German Jews. Her grandfather, who had done well in the tea and caviar trade, had built a large mansion in Schwaben, then a fashionable Munich suburb. Most of those old houses have long since been destroyed. Not by the war, but by developers.

Gertrude's father was a greatly respected physician. Her mother led a life of leisure. Neither of them was religious. If anything, young Gertie and her brother Heinrich learned about religion from their cook and the two maids, all of whom were good Catholics.

Her childhood was happy. She would talk sometimes of the big garden at the end of which was a little gate that led to a small forest where she and Heinrich used to pick wild strawberries every summer. There was an old cedar tree and a swing. She used to delight in pushing Heinrich higher and higher till he was screaming, half in fear and half delight. The maid would rush from the house and rescue the little boy.

They were brought up like any other Germans of their class and generation. At the gymnasium she was punished for her insolence for refusing to accept the casual anti-Semitism of her history teacher. The head of the gymnasium wrote a strong letter to her father. Dr Meyer refused to take the matter seriously.

'They are ignorant, Gertie,' her father would tell her. 'To show anger is to come down to their level. You must learn to control yourself.'

'If he is ignorant,' she responded, 'why is he permitted to teach us history?'

Her father would smile and finger his beard, but could not reply. When she recalled all this her eyes would light up. It was the first time she had won an argument.

'I have no answer to your question, Gertie. May I simply recommend that you learn what they teach, pass your exams and prepare to enter the university. Do you think I could have become a physician if I had responded to every insult or curse? Anti-Semitism is strongly rooted in their culture. They imbibed it with Christianity. Luther made that side of it only worse, but it doesn't mean anything. Nothing at all.'

Gertie did pass her exams, but during her very first year at the University of Munich she fell in love with a fellow-student with the name of David Stein. There is a photograph of them as students, which I found as I was going through her papers a few months ago.

He was of medium height, with a shock of dark red hair and twinkling eyes. The son of a railway worker, he was a rarity at the university and the object of a great deal of prejudice. A Jew, and from a poor family.

Gertie was impressed by his remarkable self-confidence and his ability to rise above the jibes to which he was continuously subjected. This might seem strange to you, Karl, but don't forget that the German universities were the strongholds of reaction. Long before Hitler became Chancellor, his ideas had already triumphed in the universities.

Stein was a brilliant mathematician and Gertie always felt that if she had not distracted him, he would have easily reached the pinnacle of his profession. Perhaps, but had fate not intervened in the shape of your grandmother, he might just as easily have ended up in Auschwitz.

The two of them became inseparable. Slowly they began to explore each other's emotions and bodies. Together they flouted Jewish orthodoxy. Gertie's household may have been secular in every way, but the kitchen was never defiled by pig meat. David's parents were staunch atheists. They were both active in the Social Democratic Party. Here too, the old taboo against pork was strictly observed.

David and Gertie cemented their love by walking into a non-Jewish butcher's shop and buying some cooked ham. They walked to the old Jewish cemetery, sat on the grave of David's grandfather and consumed the ham. Once they had finished, they appealed to the Creator to prove his existence by striking them dead. The sky remained still. The excitement proved too much for Gertie. She vomited in the street, but as David helped to clean her mouth they both began to laugh. They had cured themselves of all superstitions forever. It was only after this episode that David had dragged her off to meet his parents.

The Steins lived in a two-room basement with a tiny kitchen. A fading portrait of Eduard Bernstein was pinned to the wall. How times change, Karl. In those days Bernstein was regarded as the father of revisionist thought. A turncoat. A reactionary who had made his peace with the class enemy. Twenty years ago, this view was still widely held. Read a few of his essays now, Karl, and compare them to the speeches you write for your new Social Democratic masters. Bernstein now seems to be a die-hard, a dinosaur no less! Of course, times have changed. Why do I keep forgetting this fact?

Next to Bernstein's portrait was a framed sepia-tinted photograph of David's father and six other men, all of them dressed in their Sunday best, with watch-chains proudly displayed. This was the executive of the Munich railway workers' union. Gertie was awed by David's father. She became a regular visitor. The only subject of conversation in the kitchen was socialist politics. David's father was one of the local leaders of the SDP, but he was entirely devoid of self-importance. He spoke softly and was always prepared to listen to his political opponents, whose numbers were growing within the railway workers' union.

It was 1918. Germany had been dismembered by the Allies. Lenin and Trotsky were in power in Petrograd and Moscow. Ferment was sweeping through Europe. The Kaiser had been toppled and the

Prussian Junkers were talking to Social Democrats, seeing them as the only way to avoid the German revolution.

Finally the day came when Gertie felt she had to take David home. If they were going to get married she had to introduce him to her parents. Aware of the polar contrast between the two households, she was dreading the occasion. Gertie's parents did not even attempt to conceal their shock. David's twinkling, intelligent eyes made no impact on them. They were horrified at the thought of their daughter marrying a penniless pauper, whose parents were probably recent arrivals from the *stetl*.

They saw a totally different David. A young man in patched trousers and tattered shoes. Gertie had prevented him from wearing his only suit. They noticed that he spoke in plebeian accents and, worst of all, was not in the least embarrassed by his poverty. The kindly Dr Meyer and his even kinder wife decided that the boy was cheeky. What they really meant by this was that David was not deferential. They decided to teach him the rudiments of civilized behaviour by subjecting him to an insolent inquisition. Who were his parents? Where were they from? Was his father a socialist? Where did they live? How large was their apartment? How had David got into the university?

Gertrude was horrified. She could not see that her parents were simply expressing a fear of the other and worried about losing their daughter. She saw it as a display of decadent, bourgeois philistinism. She told me that it was a side of her parents that she had, till then, sought to ignore and repress.

David registered only mild amusement. He had replied to each and every query with impeccable dignity, while simultaneously trying to warn Gertie with his eyes to calm down and avoid a tantrum at all costs. It was no use. Your grandmother was too far gone by that stage. She was livid. Ashamed of her parents, ashamed of their house, ashamed at the presence of uniformed maids, who couldn't keep their eyes off David, and ashamed of herself for belonging to the Meyer family.

She never asked David to visit her again. Instead, she began to spend more and more time with his family. It was in the Stein basement, where she spent most of the days of her vacation that December, that Gertie learnt of the significance of the Russian Revolution.

David's father thought that Lenin was fine for Russia, which had no tradition of political parties and trade unions, but not for Germany. He had little time for the revolutionaries of the Spartakusbund who had split the great German Social Democratic Party, accusing even Karl Kautsky of treachery. When David pointed out that the great German party had voted war credits to the Kaiser while the Russian party had not simply refused to support the Tsar, but had instead suggested to the workers that their real enemy was at home, his father nodded sadly. He, too, had been unhappy with the SPD policy of supporting the war, but he remained adamant on the other question. Germany was not prepared for Lenin's revolution. The old tried and tested methods of the German party were the only hope.

'There is an old German proverb,' Herr Stein told David and Gertie one evening. 'A silk hat is indeed very fine, provided only that I had mine. But Karl and Rosa are a long way off yet...' For Herr Stein, the Spartacists lived in an unreal world.

David, not wishing to upset his parents, had refrained from telling his father that he and Gertie had started attending Spartacist study classes in Munich. This was not so much because of their differences. David knew how much his parents had sacrificed in order to educate him. They would be worried that his new-found interest in politics would take him away from the university and his career.

When, a month later, in January 1919, Rosa Luxemburg and Karl Liebknecht were murdered in cold blood by the Freikorps in Berlin, the whole Stein family went into mourning. Did you know, Karl, that one of the officers involved in the murder was a man called Canaris, later Hitler's admiral and someone greatly admired by certain Western leaders during the war? They thought they could have done business with him. They were right.

David's father wept loudly as he shook his head. He was sad and angry. He had heard Rosa and Liebknecht speak at many meetings before the outbreak of war. He had raised funds for them when they were imprisoned for opposing the war, but despite his admiration for the slain revolutionaries, he still could not defend their decision to launch an uprising.

'Crazy dreamers,' he told David and Gertie while the tears were still pouring down his face. 'That's what they were. The workers will miss them in the years to come. Rosa should have known better. We have to act now. We can't sit still. If we don't move, the Junkers will kill us all. Spartacists, Independents, Social Democrats. We're all the same for them.'

David embraced his father, but did not speak. Old Stein was wrong. The Junkers knew the difference between the groups only too well. And Field Marshal von Hindenberg knew that in Friedrich Ebert, he had found a German patriot who would not flinch from the task that confronted him. Without the support of the Social Democrat leaders, Ebert, Noske and Scheidemann, the Junkers could not have drowned the Berlin uprising in blood.

Perhaps, Karl, you should persuade the Ebert Foundation to fund a commemoration of the uprising and the murders in 2018. Your SPD can claim that Ebert is the Father of German Democracy. My PDS, if it is still there, will argue that the Berlin tragedy of 1918–19 paved the way for the catastrophe of 1933. Engels once remarked, in a letter to a friend, that history is the result of conflicts of many individual wills, who have been affected in different ways by a host of particular conditions of life. The final result is often something that no one willed. As a general statement I think he's right, but Hindenberg and Ebert wanted to crush the revolution in Berlin. And they did.

So you see, Karl, my century began with a tragedy and is ending on the same note. Our generation was brought up on stories of how it might have all been different if the revolution had triumphed in Berlin. You might think I'm still trying desperately to cling on to something, to anything, even if it is just the debris of failed revolutions. You might even be right but, if only for a few minutes, forget I'm your father. Let me assume the guise of a professor of comparative literature and suggest that you read one of the great novelists of this century.

Even though Alfred Döblin was not a favoured author of the DDR commissars, I often used him in my lectures at Humboldt. I read passages from his works and had the following proposition by him put up in large type on my noticeboard:

> The subject of a novel is reality unchained, reality that confronts the reader completely independently of some firmly fixed course of events. It is the reader's task to judge, not the author's! To speak of a novel is to speak of layering, of piling in heaps, of wallowing, of pushing and shoving. A drama is about its poor plot, its desperately ever-present plot. In drama it is always 'forward!' But 'forward' is never the slogan of a novel.

Döblin was not simply the author of *Berlin, Alexanderplatz*. He wrote two other epic novels. When you have some time you should try and read *A People Betrayed: November 1918: A German Revolution* and its sequel *Karl and Rosa: A German Tragedy*. I'm not alone in this opinion. Your very own Gunter Grass, the lyric poet of German Social Democracy, is in full agreement with me on the Döblin question. He has acknowledged his own debt to Döblin, putting him on an even higher pedestal than Mann, Brecht and Kafka. I'm not sure that Grass likes the two novels I want you to read. I've not read anything by him on them, but don't let that bother you.

Like Brecht, Döblin found refuge in Los Angeles during the bad years. He worked under contract to MGM, waiting impatiently for the end of the Third Reich. Brecht returned to the East, Döblin to the West. Much of this you'll find in *Schicksalreise*, his memoirs, which affected me greatly thirty years ago.

Read him, Karl. Read him. It will make a refreshing change from those interminable Bundesbank reports which are clogging your brain. Of course, you have to study them in order to feed the jelly-fish who employ you, but give yourself a break.

Gertrude and her lover, David Stein, were making plans to run away together. They were thinking lofty thoughts. Your generation does not understand this, but for most of this century there have been millions who thought lofty thoughts. In those times large numbers of people were prepared to sacrifice their own future for a better world.

David and Gertrude were obsessed by the fate of their comrades in Berlin. They knew that the survivors of the Berlin massacre were traumatized. People from other cities were needed to help rebuild the Berlin organization. People like them.

Even as they were mapping their future, a revolution erupted in Munich. The very thought is unthinkable today. Bavaria? Which Bavaria? The land of beer cellars where Hitler's audiences became intoxicated on hatred and which later became a fascist stronghold or, in our own post-war times, the fiefdom controlled by Franz Joseph Strauss? I'm talking of another, older Bavaria.

In November 1918, Kurt Eisner, leader of the Independent Social Democrats, proclaimed a Bavarian Republic and was elected its prime minister. Three months later Eisner was executed by Count Arco. Even the moderates, men like David Stein's father, wanted revenge. They pleaded with the SPD leaders to do something, but were told to leave the decisions in tried and trusted hands.

'Tried and tested in murder!' old Stein had shouted in anger as he walked out of his party offices in Munich. The workers were, without doubt, in an angry mood, but did they want a revolution? Eugen Leviné did not think so. He had been despatched to Munich by the Comintern* to help prepare and organize the revolution.

Munich was full of dreamers and utopians. Gertrude and David were

---

* The Communist (Third) International (Comintern) was launched with great fanfare in Moscow in 1919. Its aim was a World Revolution of which it was the General Staff. It laid down a set of twenty-one conditions for membership, the principal function of which was to split the existing Socialist Parties of the Second International and form new Communist parties. For the first four years, the heroic period of the Comintern, this aim was pursued vigorously. Later, the Comintern became an instrument of Soviet foreign policy. It was dissolved unilaterally by Stalin in 1943 to convince Churchill and Roosevelt that he was a reliable ally.

certainly not alone. There were several thousand others and they wanted to seize power immediately. Poor Leviné! He knew the attempt was doomed. Gertrude was half in love with him. She used to talk of how he would sit up the whole night trying to deflate their dream-filled heads. Leviné warned them that they were still isolated. He wanted the uprising postponed, but Gertrude and her friends outnumbered him.

When news reached Munich in March 1919 of the uprising in Budapest and Bela Kun's proclamation of a Hungarian Soviet Republic, David told Gertrude that this was their first real chance to make history, to avenge the deaths in Berlin, to move the revolution forward. And so it happened. To the great horror of the middle classes and the Catholic peasants, the Bavarian Soviet Republic came into existence.

Moscow was overjoyed. Lenin and Trotsky were hard-headed men, but they were also desperate. They knew the price of isolation. Lenin firmly believed that without a revolution in Germany, the infant Soviet Republic could not last for long. He was right, wasn't he, Karl? I mean, the historical space occupied by seventy-five years is next to zero. It's nothing. So Lenin and Trotsky sent Munich their solidarity in the shape of hundreds of telegrams. They were hoping that Vienna, too, would fall and had already instructed the Red Marshal, Tukachevsky – the Tuka whom my father loved so deeply – to investigate the military possibilities of a corridor from the Soviet Union to Bavaria. Their man in Munich suffered from no such illusions. Leviné bade farewell to his wife and new-born child and prepared to sacrifice himself for a cause that had no hope of success.

The Junkers could have taken Munich painlessly, but that might not have been a sufficient deterrent to the rest of the country. Blood had to be shed. It's the same today. Serbs and Croats could capture a village peacefully and spare their civilian opponents, but they rarely do so. Bloodlust. The animal instinct that still echoes in human biology.

General von Oven crushed the Bavarian Republic with exemplary brutality. Citizens were pulled out of their beds, then shot, knifed, raped and beaten to death. Gertrude fled to her parents in Schwaben. David was given refuge by his professor. Leviné went into hiding. He thought of his wife and child and then all he could think of was flight, but he was betrayed, captured, tried and executed. His trial was a big show. Gertrude, dressed as a bourgeois Fräulein, attended the court every day. Till her dying day, your grandmother never forgot Leviné's final speech to the court. She used to recite it to me when I was still a child, growing up in what they once called the Soviet Union.

We communists are dead men on leave. Of this I am fully aware. I do not know whether you will extend my leave or whether I shall have to join Karl Liebknecht and Rosa Luxemburg. I await your verdict in any case with composure and inner serenity. I have simply done my duty towards the International, and the World Revolution...

The words continued to haunt her long after the system to which she'd sold her soul had degenerated beyond recognition. They tell us now that it was always so, but I don't believe them, Karl, and nor should you. There was a nobility of purpose. It may have been utopian, but for a majority of the foot-soldiers it was never malignant. Otherwise it is impossible to understand the motives of those men and women who sacrificed their lives in those early years. People for whom the map of the world had no meaning if Utopia was not inscribed on each continent. These are the people whose lives I'm trying to reconstruct for you.

They executed Leviné early one morning. Two soldiers in the firing party had to have alcohol poured down their throats before they could pull the trigger. That same afternoon Gertie told her parents that she had become a Communist. She was never to forget the look of horror, mingled with fear, that transformed their faces. Her father left the room and a few minutes later she heard him being violently sick. Her mother simply sat down on a chair in the hall and wept.

A young officer, Otto Müller, who had been slightly wounded during the street battles, was bivouacked in their house. He came up behind her as she was staring out of the window at the old cedar and the swing and whispered in her ear.

'I heard everything. I greatly admire your decision. I wish I had been on Leviné's side. He refused to plead for mercy. His face was proud and held high just before they shot him.'

The initial shock gave way to amazement. If men like him, men on the winning side, could say things like that to her at such a time, then all was not lost. Strange, the trivial incidents that leave such an impact. Your grandmother was sure that the young officer's encouragement made up her mind for her. Many years later she met Müller in Berlin, where he was practising as a doctor. He was in a hurry. It was 1933 and he was helping to get his best friend's furniture to Denmark. The name of his childhood familiar was Bertolt Brecht.

When Gertie's father recovered he spoke to her in a hard but trembling voice. 'You are no longer my daughter.'

Her mother did not speak. Gertie went to her room and wept. 'Mutti, Mutti,' she sobbed. 'Why did you not speak? Why?'

Then she packed a few clothes, a framed photograph of Heinrich and herself, her books, and a tiny green shawl that had once belonged to her grandmother. Her brother was away on a school trip. She sat down at her desk and wrote him a farewell note: *My dearest Heiny, I have to leave now, but I will miss you terribly. Don't forget me. I will write and give you my address in Berlin. Many kisses and a big hug from your loving Gertie.*

She walked out of the house and down the drive. As she reached the bend after which the house became invisible she was desperate to turn round one last time, but she was proud and resisted the lure. Heiny later wrote and told her that their mother's tear-stained face had been pressed to the first-floor window, watching Gertie leaving her family house. She had told him so when he returned from his trip. I'm sure that none of them really believed in the finality of the breach, but then none of them knew what lay ahead.

Some years after the war, when she had returned to Berlin, Gertie wanted to return to Munich and see the house again. That was before the Wall was built. Travel between the two zones was easy. She took me with her. I was eleven at the time. I remember well our trip to Schwaben. The house was still there, just like it used to be. Gertie held me close and began to cry. She, a Communist, had fought the Nazis and survived. Her father, a staunch German nationalist, a man of the Right, perished in the camps with Heiny, her mother and the rest of the family. Gertrude and I were the sole survivors. We had been staring at the house from the driveway. Gertie was too frightened to go in. Slowly we turned round and as we began to walk out we noticed an old man on crutches who had stopped and was observing us from outside the gate.

'Who are you?' he asked Gertie.

She tightened her hand on mine. 'I used to live here a long time ago.'

The old man came close and stared right into Mutti's eyes. 'Fräulein Gertrude?'

She nodded.

'Haven't you recognized me? Frank. The gardener. I used to give you and little Heinrich rides on my back.' The old man's eyes filled with tears. Gertrude hugged him. When finally she moved away she was going to ask him what had happened, but he read the question in her eyes even before she spoke and shook his head.

'I was conscripted in '36. They were still here. The Doctor had many influential patients. Nazis who respected him, wouldn't change doctors for anything. When I returned in 1942 – I was one of the first casualties on the Russian front – they had all disappeared.'

We nodded. 'And the house, Frank?'

'You remember the young doctor who sometimes assisted your father. He joined the Nazi Party. This was his reward. He moved in with his family. Took the practice, the house, the furniture. Everything. A few years ago he got scared and sold the property. It's empty now. They're going to knock it down and build apartments. The garden will disappear completely. He's still in Munich. One of our distinguished citizens. He's set up a medical publishing house.'

We had lunch with Frank in a café. Gertie wanted to give him some money, but realized that she had none herself.

I thought of that visit, Karl, when, about two years ago, the inquisitors arrived from Bonn. I remember the date, because it was Helge's birthday. The sixth of April. These three men had come to investigate me and to decide whether I was a fit person to teach at the university. They were not in the least interested in the fact that I was opposed to the old regime, that I had shielded dissidents, distributed pamphlets, marched on the streets, helped bring down the Wall. They actually laughed when I showed them the manifesto I had helped to draft for the Forum for German Democracy.

'Marxist gibberish,' was the verdict of the man with red hair.

'You may have brought them out on the streets, but they voted for Chancellor Kohl!' his colleague informed me in a polite voice.

I never discussed this event with you before now Karl, because I was frightened. I thought you might agree with them. I was wrong. Forgive me. I wanted to shout at these hypocrites. Remind them of Schwaben. Ask when I could have Gertrude's house back. Ask why the Nazi who had stolen my grandparents' house was still thriving while they were making us all redundant. Instead I remained calm. I explained the volatility of the situation. Reminded them of how Turks and Vietnamese were being burnt alive in their homes while the citizens of the new Germany stood by and the Chancellor washed his hands.

'Why,' I asked them at one point, 'do you despise us Easterners so much? For us, not even a Treaty of Passau!'

They looked at me with blank impressions, none of them wanting to admit that they had no idea when or what the Treaty of Passau was. It was my only triumph that day. I explained that through the Treaty of 1552, the Lutherans had accepted a surly and grudging co-existence with the Catholic Church.

They questioned me for three hours, but it took them fifteen minutes to reach a verdict. They called me in to the investigation room, where, in the old days, I had often faced the hostility of our own ideological commissars.

'Professor Meyer, please sit down. After careful consideration, the Commission has decided that you are not fit to teach the course on Comparitive Literature at Humboldt University. We are aware of your gift for languages, your knowledge of English, Russian and Chinese. We are confident that you will carry on your translation work, which is of a high quality. But teaching. Now that, in our new conditions, is something different...'

I wrote you a brief letter telling you that I'd been sacked. I wanted to tell you how I was haunted by fear, tormented by insecurity, desperate for your mother to return. I walked around the city aimlessly for several hours. There was dust everywhere. Scaffolding on every main street. Hitler and Speer had wanted to rebaptize Berlin. Germania was their favoured name. Berlin will be a capital city once again.

At least it will bring you back here, Karl, away from the Ollenauerstrasse and quiet, old Bonn. That will be nice. I get the feeling that the architects are reverting to the nineteenth century, trying to forget that this century even happened. If they succeed, they will destroy Berlin.

I thought of our two cities in one. For too long, the Western half had been a forbidden zone. Did you know that sex shops have taken the place of churches and chapels? They cater for every taste. In Wedding, where Gertrude and David lived when they ran away from Munich, and which was a Communist working-class stronghold, the new entrepreneurs are trading in exotica. Rare tropical birds, powder from the horn of a rhinoceros, dried pigs' ears and a lot else.

Berlin is a shamelessly consumerist city. Art consists of the chassis of an old Cadillac fixed to slabs of concrete and wooden benches with carved breasts and penises.

To my own amazement, Karl, I began to miss the drab, dingy, prudish Berlin where both you and I grew up.

Three

K ARL MEYER stood at the window of his second-floor apartment on the Fritz-Tillman-Strasse in Bonn. He sometimes regretted his escape to this strange city. At first he had wanted to forget everything about Berlin. The Wall. The Fall. His parents. Gerhard. A beautiful teacher named Marianne. Grandma Gertrude. Everything. He loved them all, but when he looked back and remembered his father's petulance and blindness to reality or his mother's insistence on a monotone reading of the rich complexities of European politics, his anger returned. His parents were always delirious in their irrationality. The protective wall they had built around themselves and their friends had fallen at the same time as that other Wall. Now they complained bitterly of the miseries and lunacies of the new order. Karl held them responsible for their own failure.

Now, close to the centres of power in this dying capital, he was afraid of being forgotten by them. His mother was happy in New York, but Karl was often anxious about the state of his father's mind and health. He put on his dark-blue suit, found a matching bow-tie, and inspected himself in the mirror. He saw a very self-contained, slender, square-jawed young man. He nodded in approval, locked his flat and descended via the lift to street level. The café where he breakfasted was in the same block. As he sipped his espresso, Karl quickly flicked through that morning's *Frankfurter Allgemeine Zeitung*. Much speculation as to whether Kohl would last the course as Chancellor this time; reports of a dissident Muslim-Serb alliance in Bosnia; another crisis for the British Conservatives.

Karl was indifferent to the Balkans. Britain, in his eyes, was a laboratory experiment that had gone badly wrong, and the guinea pigs were on the verge of an electoral revolt. Perhaps, under a new government, it might be of some interest to Germany. Perhaps.

The fact was that Karl was interested only in the minutae of German politics. He knew, of course, that the United States, Japan and China were the major planetary players, but even this knowledge did not excite any real interest in the last two countries. Karl was a new German. He wanted Germany to play its part in the world. He did not believe that the crimes of the Third Reich annulled Germany's traditional position in the centre of Europe.

A few weeks ago, Karl, on the instructions of his leader, had spent a whole afternoon in concentrated talks with two pivotal Free Democrat members of parliament, one of whom had defied his party's instructions and failed to vote for the Christian Democrats' choice of Chancellor.

Karl's mission was as straightforward as his demeanour. He wanted Kohl dethroned, and the SPD leader crowned Chancellor in his place. His hosts plied him with questions about the future. How many posts in the Cabinet? What were SPD intentions on Europe? Could the young man assure them that Scharping was more than a creature of the apparatus?

Karl hid nothing. He told his astonished interlocutors that German stability required a Chancellor controlled by the apparatus. Better a weak-kneed provincial than a loud-mouthed populist who excited hopes that could never be fulfilled. Only under the SPD could Germany use its economic muscle and exert a political pressure commensurate with its new-found status in the post-Communist world. He added, for good measure, that only a politically assertive Germany could rebuild middle Europe. The two men from the Bundestag were impressed by the zeal and self-confidence exhibited by the young SPD apparatchik. Like them, he was interested only in power. They could certainly do business with him. They asked him to come and meet their colleagues in a few days' time.

The same evening Karl went to an early evening drinks party hosted by the local boss of CNN in honour of a visiting dignitary from Atlanta. At least three government ministers, numerous ambassadors, the SPD High Command and other denizens of the videosphere. A senior colleague introduced Karl to Monika Minnerup, a young woman who could not have been more than twenty-four or twenty-five years old. She smiled and her almond-shaped eyes lit up like oil lamps. Karl shook hands and looked at her. She had a wide, sensuous face framed by short, curly black hair, thin lips and was dressed in a loose grey silk suit, which made any speculation on the shape of the body that lay underneath a bit difficult. She was a systems analyst at a big bank and she earned a small fortune. Karl was impressed. If it had been any other occasion he would have stuck with her, but his eyes began to wander above her head, trying to glimpse the famous and the powerful. He wanted to go and join the group listening to the Foreign Minister.

'If you want to go and kiss arse, why don't you piss off? I loathe making polite talk with small town careerists. Goodbye.'

Monika walked away leaving him in a state of shock. His first instinct was to run after her, but she was already near the exit and, anyway, he told himself as he recovered from her impact, he really did want to hear what the Foreign Minister was telling the Americans.

After graduating, Karl had wanted only one thing: to run away, to get out of Berlin as quickly as possible. Helge's dash to New York had initially upset him. Bitterness had set in soon afterwards. He was angry with her for deserting him. She could have moved and set up a practice in Frankfurt. Why leave the country at such a time? Karl was genuinely puzzled by her choice of New York. Ultimately he'd convinced himself that it must be a lover. Fine, but why hadn't she told him?

He knew she wasn't pleased when, in one of her letters, she referred to him as an 'apparatchik on the make in Bonn, and working for an apparatus full of shit'. Her letter had made him laugh, but his sharp reply had led first to a ceasefire and then a total cessation on her part.

She no longer wrote. Instead they exchanged greetings and indulged in small talk on the phone, once, sometimes twice a week.

Karl sighed when he thought of his father. He was beyond redemption. Vlady was no bloody use at all. He lived in his own world, cocooned from reality. He had achieved nothing in his own life, apart from a few jargon-filled books on Marxist aesthetics which were no longer fashionable. In previous years, even though very few students had understood what he was trying to say, his books had been obligatory bookshelf decoration for left-wing intellectuals on both sides of the Wall. Nobody bought Vlady's books any more. Karl felt completely alienated from his father. Vlady's lifestyle – he still refused to dress properly – was a disgrace. His politics just left Karl speechless and angry. Why couldn't the old fool understand it was all over? Karl had stopped arguing, but Vlady still had enough intellectual power to provoke and irritate his son. On the last occasion Karl had struck back, his voice uncharacteristically high.

'It's all over, Vlady! Finished. Unlike the phoenix, your DDR will never rise again. And I'm glad.'

Vlady smiled.

'So am I, but what has any of that to do with Marxism?'

This time Karl almost screamed in dismay.

'Finished. Finished. Finished! A utopia flushed down with the rest. How can Marxism exist, when it has been abandoned by its subject – the heroic proletariat? Can't you and Helge understand? Marxists are nothing but flecks of foam on the dark blue ocean.'

He, who had once been so close to them, now wanted to disremember his parents. He was building his own career. He had a time plan. Success, he told himself, was the quickest way to erase DDR memories, which still haunted him. Karl intended to be a member of the Bundestag in 2000 and Chancellor by 2010.

This was ironic, given that he had never revealed any real interest in politics. His addiction was very new. He had chosen the SPD like one chooses a football team. There is a simple rule. If you stick with your team through bad times, there is a reward sooner or later. When he was young he had simply ignored the endless chatter about history and politics. He had loved his grandmother Gertrude. She had spent a lot of time with him, but not like the others. She always put him to bed with adventure yarns, stories of heroism during the last war and the resistance to Hitler in Germany. Perhaps some residue from that time had made him prefer the SPD to the Christian Democrats. Perhaps.

Karl wanted to start life afresh. He had seen an advertisement for a researcher's post and applied, never imagining that he would get an interview, let alone the job. The Ebert Foundation had advertised for graduates. They wanted bright young things in their twenties, whose brains could be attached to computers which would then churn out documents for the policy staff at SPD headquarters on the Ollenauerstrasse.

He had interviewed well. His cold-blooded critique of the DDR had impressed the two women who interviewed him. Unlike those of some of his competitors from the old East, Karl's presentation was emotionless. No grandiose proclamations of freedom had spouted from his mouth. His approach was clinical. He had concentrated on the inability of the state-ownership system to deliver the goods. For him, the collapse was due to material shortages, an insolvent economy which exposed an impoverished ideology. It was this, he told them, that triggered the Fall, rather than any great yearning for abstractions like democracy and freedom.

The women were impressed. They looked carefully at this tall young man in his dark-blue suit and grey bow-tie. He was clearly intelligent. His instincts were conservative. Everything about him – the way he took notes, the meticulous filing system in his briefcase – indicated a neat and systematic approach to work.

They kept him talking for nearly two hours, but the only time he had shown any trace of emotion was when they asked whether he would have been equally happy working for the CDU.

'Of course not!' Karl's voice was a note higher. 'I am a Social Democrat.' The older of the two women, Eva Wolf, a veteran of the sixties' student movement, would have preferred it if this young man had displayed just a tiny sign of rebelliousness, but he did not, and she had shrugged her shoulders. These kids were different.

In her written report on Karl to the Foundation, in which she recommended that he be given the job, Eva described him as the archetypal new model Social Democrat. She noted that he was 'a complete slave to power, obsessed with one idea: how to propel the SPD into power. If it means developing ideas that are acceptable to the Bavarians, he is ready to prepare a draft; if it means ditching old party shibboleths, even at the cost of annoying our friends in IG Metall, he is strongly in favour.

'When we asked him if he was prepared to move to Bonn within a few months, he smiled and said he was prepared to leave Berlin tomorrow. I think Tilman should have a long session with him and then we should make a final decision. Karl Meyer would be wasted as a researcher at the Institute. He should be given a position immediately in the Party apparatus. He thinks quickly but is not the sort who leaps to intuitive conclusions. Everything is thought out carefully. I am enclosing a copy of the speech he wrote when we tested him. You will notice a few original phrases. If Scharping can deliver speeches like this, who knows but we might even win.'

Eva's intuition on these matters was greatly respected by her friends at Party headquarters. Within a month of joining the Foundation, Karl was safely settled in the research bureau of the SPD.

One outcome of his move to Bonn was a strong personal friendship with Eva. Twenty-five years his senior, she had partially replaced Vlady and Helge in this crucial transition period of his life. She was the only friend with whom he could talk about his past. He told her about Gerhard's suicide, which had upset him a great deal. Gerhard, who understood him, but was worried by Karl's indifference to Marxist politics. Gerhard, who had taught him a song that began: 'From the devil's behind blows unrest/From God's backside only boredom...'

There were moments, Karl told Eva, when he used to wish that Gerhard had been his father. Perhaps it was Gerhard's closeness to Vlady, the fact that they were political siblings, that had created the confusion in Karl's mind. He had written to Helge several times about Gerhard, and she had responded warmly. To Vlady he had written nothing, and Vlady was the parent who really needed to talk about Gerhard. Karl sometimes wondered why he was punishing his father, but no satisfactory response was forthcoming.

Eva always listened sympathetically. She was startled by the contrast between her young protégé's emotional confusion and his political confidence. Last night, during dinner, she had both comforted and confronted him.

'Everything has its limits, Karl. Everything. What a couple does for each other, what a father does for his son or the daughter for her mother. The fact is, you love your father much, much more than you ever acknowledge. Gerhard's death has forced you to admit this to yourself. Yet you hesitate. Why? You're hurt that your father didn't help you when you needed him the most, but did you ever help him?'

'Does Matthias ever help you?'

Eva smiled. She often discussed her family with Karl. Even though she had separated from Andi, her film-maker husband, when she was appointed Head of Research in the German section of the Foundation, they remained friends. Matthias, her son, was a lead singer with an anarcho-Green rock band in Berlin. He was the same age as Karl. They had nothing else in common. Despite his awkwardness, Eva adored her son.

'No,' she said in reply to Karl's question, 'but then I don't need him

so much. Matthias is very close to his father. They have many defects
in common. Their financial condition is never stable, but they manage
somehow. I am never permitted to send either of them any money.
They help each other. Both of them regard me as a traitor. Matthias
has written a new song about a once-radical and uncontaminated
mother who joined the SPD and now thinks impure thoughts. I'm told
that Stefan Heym's supporters were singing it in the streets during his
campaign. Unlike you, Karl, my Matthias hates Bonn. Hence my
monthly trips to Berlin. Soon you'll be back in Berlin, too. I'll be left
all alone. Will Monika accompany you?'

Karl blushed. How the hell did she know about Monika? The SPD
headquarters were relocating to Berlin. Karl was dreading the move.
Monika was only one reason, but how had Eva found out? He asked
her.

'There's no mystery. I tried to reach you a number of times. Your
colleague said you were on the phone to Monika. Is it serious?'

'I don't know . . . She's very big in her bank, you know. They're
fearful that she might be headhunted and taken away by rivals.'

'Is she on our side?'

'I don't know. She's not interested in politics. All politicians are
liars, shits and scumbags. Her words. She spent a year in San Francisco.
Her grandfather was a colonel in the SS, a great favourite of Heinrich
Himmler. Her mother was a Maoist and is now a primary school
teacher. Her father? He died in Stammheim. Monika is certain that he
could never have committed suicide. She insists he was murdered. I
don't know.'

'I can see why she is removed from politics.'

'Sometimes she is cruel. When we row I'm just another shitbag
desperate to get into the Bundestag, tell lies and line his pockets. When
I remind her that she's making more money than any SPD member of
the Bundestag, she claims her loot is not gained through deception, but
by playing the market, without breaking any rules. I love her, Eva. I
want her to have my children.'

'And here I was, beginning to think you were just a robot and
fearful that your girl might turn out to be another robot. Some mouse
or the other from the apparatus on Ollenauerstrasse. You've really
surprised me. I wonder what she sees in you? Bring her to me next
week. Supper on Wednesday?'

'Fine. I do not speak for Monika.'

'Tell her my Matthias sings with a crazy rock band. It might make
me a little less unattractive. Tell her what you want but bring her to
me.'

Karl spent the whole day preparing a briefing paper on the possibility of a new coalition. He wanted the SPD in power. He wanted Scharping as Chancellor. He wanted to stay in Bonn till 2000. By then the scars would have healed. He could even begin to see Vlady again. He made a note in his diary. Last year, at the height of his alienation from the past, he had forgotten his father's birthday. There must be no repetition.

He realized how much he still loved Vlady. The discovery shocked him.

Four

VLADIMIR MEYER was on a high. Yesterday's *Neues Deutschland* had published a long piece by him on the new trends in Russian literature. It was a polemical essay, written with a keen sense of the comic, describing how 'socialist realism' had been replaced by 'market realism', and with equally disastrous results. A precious pornography had replaced the ritual references to various First Secretaries.

This was his first published essay since the dismissal from his post at Humboldt. The results pleased him. A minor triumph. A clear signal to the enemy that he would not take defeat lying down. He would show young Karl that they were more than flecks of foam. He was going to fight back with his literary fists.

Several old friends had rung to congratulate him. In the old days Gerhard would have been the first to call. But Gerhard was dead. He knew me well, Vlady thought. He knew exactly how to drag me out of my melancholy. His judgements were sober and reliable. Not a trace of envy in his make-up. Gerhard, soft-hearted Gerhard, had not asked much of this world, but he had ceased to resist. Fatal. Death, in the mask of the new German order, had claimed him.

Outside it was night and a blanket of mist covered the street. Vlady had decided to stay at home. Better to be surrounded by ghosts, he thought, than to engage in the forced frivolity of the tavern. He read, paced up and down his room, read old letters, talked to himself, to Karl, to Helge, to Gerhard and then, as the clock struck two in the morning, he fell asleep.

That was yesterday. Today it was already late when he awoke. The day was clear, but the winter shadows were already beginning to mark the landscape. In a few hours the light would vanish. He jumped out of bed, dressed quickly and walked out into the street. Vlady wandered aimlessly, and, at the end of an hour and a half, feeling sad and lonely, he found himself in a second-hand bookshop on the Ku-Damm. The sight of bookshelves cheered him a little.

'What are you doing here?'

Evelyne was standing behind him. Surprise registered on both their faces. She smiled and hugged him with real warmth. 'The same old overcoat. The same old Vlady. Why haven't you shaved?'

He smiled and shrugged his shoulders. For a moment his depression disappeared. The sight of Evelyne had despatched his anxieties to the future. They walked to a tiny art gallery which dispensed the best coffee in Berlin. Evelyne behaved as if nothing had ever happened between them. She treated him as if he were just her old professor, pressed him to attend the press preview of her first feature film that evening and join the cast and crew for a celebratory dinner afterwards. Vlady looked doubtful. He was on his guard, not at all eager to be rejuvenated.

'You can meet my husband and his boyfriend. Come on Vlady. It's obvious you're not doing anything. My movie is a comedy. Even you will laugh.'

He accepted her invitation, thinking to himself that he could always change his mind.

'Have you found a new job?'

Vlady shook his head.

'Or a new politics?'

He shook his head again.

'Stop living in the past, Vlady. Wake up. I'll see you later.'

After she had left, he ordered another coffee. The next hour was spent in deep contemplation. Only a few hours ago, Vlady had ignored the beautiful autumn sun as he thought of the desperately empty day that lay ahead of him.

Could Evelyne be the remedy to his ills? Vlady shut his eyes, remembering the time they had spent together, but it was of no use. The world he did not want to see was buried deep inside his head. It seemed as if it would never go away.

It had been shattered by reality, but it was still there in his dreams and nightmares. Intact. Untouched. The old Prusso-Stalinist DDR with its maze of bureaucratic laws; its own peculiar customs; its deeply embedded irrationality; its habitual cruelty; its distorted lens through which one could only see a disfigured world. He was now compelled by history to live in a new world which had deprived him of his dignity as a citizen. Many others thought like him. Once he had complained bitterly to Gerhard, who had become impatient.

Vladimir Meyer was not alone in thinking that there had been aspects of life in the old DDR that were preferable to what existed today. Many saw their problems as the temporary result of a painful transition from a state-ownership system to the free market.

Vlady differed. He refused to write everything off as an unmitigated disaster. When he expressed these thoughts to old friends, they would reply, 'Of course things are bad for us, Vlady, but here in Berlin we do not wake up every morning and wonder whether we will still be alive at the end of day as many do in Sarajevo and Moscow.'

Vlady did not like such arguments. The blind worship of accomplished facts always led to passivity. Why should one come to terms with the present? Such an attitude would never have brought down the Wall. He refused to accept what existed simply because happenings elsewhere were much worse. History became an alibi. It was a cursed history whose womb was producing tiny new republics. Monstrous creations. How could they be otherwise, deformed as they were by decades of unnatural confinement?

Men, women and children were living and dying for these new states. In the past they had done the same for the big empires, but with this difference: in the old days they had fought reluctantly and cynically. It could have been any old job. Today they went to war with a sullen obstinacy, their heads and bodies distorted by an intolerant zeal. It would end badly. Of this Vlady was sure. In the last few years, he had abandoned many certainties. The bureaucratic-command-economy system was over, but its demise did not mean that what survived was superior or preferable. Only last week, one of Vlady's star pupils, a poet whose verse had once been pregnant with promise, had been arrested and charged with attempted murder. His victim, a Turkish stallholder in Kreuzberg, had survived, but was now blind in one eye.

Now, as he thought about it, Vlady recalled that the poem which had impressed him the most had been an evocation of old Königsberg, where the boy's grandparents had lived before the war and from where they had fled after the defeat and just before Königsberg was renamed Kaliningrad. Even though the spirit of Immanuel Kant had been invoked, the poem was a subconscious yearning for old frontiers. Perhaps he was reading too much into it and all this was nothing more than the alienation they had all, to some degree or the other, felt from the structures of the DDR.

He paid his bill and left the gallery. His planned visit to the Tiergarten abandoned because of Evelyne, he caught a bus back to the East. When he arrived home, it was just four o'clock. The apartment was untidy. He cleared up the mess in the kitchen and cleaned the sitting room. His own room was tidy. He lay down on the bed. There were times he envied those who had retreated so deep into their own worlds that nothing else mattered to them. History was none of their concern. Take Sao, for instance. Sao, who had abandoned history and turned to commerce. Try as he might, Vlady could not escape from history. There was no retreat to the forest for people like him. His upbringing, his milieu, his premises were totally different from Sao's. Nothing was immutable. Society had to be changed. The painfully restrained fury of the poor could not be held back permanently.

In the midst of these lofty thoughts he fell asleep. He woke up after about an hour and was startled by the dark outside, but it was only five o'clock. No need to panic. He rose slowly and walked to the bathroom. The cold light hurt his eyes as he began to shave. He was a tall, well-built man. His swarthy complexion, high cheekbones and just a hint of a slant in his brown eyes had led to numerous taunts at school. He had put on weight over the last year. Otherwise he had the look of a man in an Italian fresco, darkened by age. His hair had turned grey many years ago. He put on his faded green corduroy suit, brushed his hair and left the apartment.

At one in the morning, the rest of the party wanted to move on to a new gay nightclub, on a side-street off the Kantstrasse. Vlady was worn out. A quiet pain had stirred his heart. He often thought of Evelyne and he had been pleased at their accidental meeting, but he was unprepared for the celebration. He had assumed it would be a small and discreet celebration in some well-appointed restaurant. Instead he was confronted with an absurdist fancy-dress dinner in a deserted film studio.

They were seated on medieval benches, eating off a table decked with Turkish delicacies and lit like a film set. The waiters wore multi-coloured cod pieces. From the edges of the studio they were observed by suggestively lit models of vampires, skeletons, Marx-Engels-Lenins, knights-in-armour and the proletariat.

He looked at the self-important faces that surrounded him. Were they real? Why were their energy tanks not depleted? Could it be just the difference in age or were they intoxicated by imagined successes? Bored by his immediate neighbours, bemused by Evelyne, Vlady's eyes began to wander.

She had been looking at him and was surprised when their eyes met. She smiled. She was dressed in a red silk waistcoat, with black and gold embroidered designs and loose black trousers. He smiled. Like

him, she, too, had turned down the invitation to change into cinematic
fancy dress after the preview. He felt they had met before. He tried to
recall her name. His memories were usually impressionistic, composed
of words and images. The people themselves, what they were wearing,
their physical features or peculiarities remained a blur.

Suddenly he recognized her: Leyla. Kreuzberg-Leyla. The painter
who had inadvertently wrecked his life. The first post-Wall exhibition.
Leyla's striking self-portrait, inspired by Frida Kahlo. Her hair was the
colour of honey. Her eyes were green. In the painting she saw herself
with black hair and brown eyes. Her paintings had an unreal quality.
They were certainly not decorative. The figures and colours were taken
from memories of her Anatolian childhood, but the setting was
unmistakably Berlin. Turkish children, their faces filled with longing,
peeping from behind their windows at German children playing on the
streets. Two cars on the road. One packed with anxious Turkish faces.
The other being driven by a fat German bourgeois with a turgid nose
and placid, complacent, self-satisfied face. Dancers pass them by, their
legs fantastically silhouetted on the windscreens. And then there was
Stolen Kisses, which Helge had seen one rainy day; she had come home
and finally walked out of his life. Helge would have hated this occasion.

He put on a pained expression, signalling to Leyla the desolate shape
the evening had taken. She nodded sympathetically. Perhaps she was
also bored with it all: the shrieks of insincere laughter, the loud, over-
keen voices greeting Evelyne's success, the fake bonhomie, the
triumphalist banalities. How Evelyne had changed. The audacious
student with shining eyes who had temporarily occupied his heart had
become an egocentric monster. Or had she? Perhaps she was just
trying to shock, in which case she hadn't altered a great deal.

As if dealing with Evelyne wasn't bad enough, Vlady was hailed by
a corpulent, clean-shaven man, who was vaguely familiar, despite his
silly costume. He was drunk and it was the swollen sensual nose that
reminded him that this was Albert, whose lean face and coal-black
beard had dominated many a clandestine discussion in the old days.
The same Albert who had written a wonderfully obscure philosophical
critique of the DDR and the whole system of social relations in Eastern
Europe. The manuscript had been smuggled to West Berlin and
published in Frankfurt. Albert had spent a month in prison.

Few in the West had understood him or the Marxist categories he
deployed with some skill against those who claimed to rule in the name
of Marx, but he had been drenched in prize money and, for a while, his
book, *Questions Without an Answer*, had graced every fashionable
coffee-table in Western Europe. The old fools who ran the country had

not allowed him to return from Frankfurt where he had been a guest lecturer, courtesy of the Ebert Foundation. Albert had become a celebrity.

Now he was back in Berlin in a new guise. Albert had become a leading Green ideologue, who believed in the civilizing mission of NATO bombs in the Gulf, the Horn of Africa and, most recently, the Balkans.

'Hello, Vlady. We've been changing the world long enough. Time once again to interpret it. You agree or not?'

Vlady smiled vacantly, giving the man a half-nod. He was about to turn away, but Albert's patronizing smile enraged him.

'You talk such high-flown shit, Albert. I suppose it's got to come out somewhere. We all heard that your liver was permanently pickled, but I never thought your brain would atrophy so much.'

Albert lunged in the direction of the insults, but Vlady had stepped aside and his old comrade was helped up by the waitresses. Vlady felt nothing, neither sorrow nor pity. Three days ago, a Turkish family had been burnt to death in a small town in Germany, while the police and the populace had stood and watched the spectacle, and now some idiot dressed as a Roman centurion was telling him that all was well.

Vlady was trying to catch Leyla's eye again when Evelyne's shrill tones silenced the entire table.

'Vlady!'

The leer on Evelyne's face was illumined by the harsh theatrical lighting and the grotesque make-up combined to make her look hard and ugly. She was wearing a short black leather skirt and a matching bra.

'Why are you staring at Leyla in that way? She's mine. Keep off. All these people here tonight are *my* friends. They appreciate me. They know I'm much more talented than the film-makers you worship. Everybody, answer me. Do you love me?'

Drunken faces smiled and waved at her, but verbal support was not forthcoming. Vlady smiled, but his eyes were hard and stern. He regretted that he had accepted her invitation. Evelyne had always been insecure, manipulative, wildly ambitious, but also intellectually sharp, receptive to new ideas, allergic to orthodoxy. Her energy, suppressed for so long in the DDR, had now exploded on the screen. Pity it was such a bad film.

In reality it wasn't such a bad film. Vlady, unable to break out of his melancholy, had misunderstood its aim and failed to appreciate the gentle self-mockery that underlay the film. He had been so busy wallowing in self-pity that he had missed the satire.

He looked at Evelyne and sighed. She had wanted so much to shock him with this absurd evening. It was an old tune, a parody of Weimar decadence. In a different mood he might have enjoyed the evening, but he was tired. He wanted to go home. He exchanged a last glance with Leyla, who smiled and waved. He left the party. Leyla must have her own plans, he thought ruefully as he put on his old Russian hat and pulled his overcoat tight around him.

As he breathed the freezing cold, misty early morning air, he sighed with relief. He had escaped. He was wrong. A horribly familiar voice disturbed the Berlin dawn.

'Vlady!'

He turned round and saw Evelyne framing the doorway. She had removed her top and her breasts were shrouded in the mist.

'Vlady, you old shithead!' She shouted; her reverberating voice cruelly disrupted the silence and brought a group of revellers to her side. With her audience in place she addressed her old lover again.

'Why are you so unremittingly solemn? Why are you leaving now? What's the matter? Don't you want a fuck tonight? It can be arranged, unless it's Leyla you want and not me. That would –'

'No thank you, Evelyne. Neither you nor Leyla tonight. Thanks for the offer.'

He had to admit she looked magnificent. A modern Cleopatra, who 'loved men's lusting but hated men'. Dante's Cleopatra, not Shakespeare's. He almost told her, but it was late to discuss the circles of Hell and nor was Vlady in a mood to hear Dante described as a Tuscan arsehole. Instead he bade her a friendly farewell.

'Please go back before you catch a chill. I hope the movie's a big success.'

As he walked out of the giant courtyard he heard the disembodied echoes of her voice.

'Dumbhead! Arsehole! Communist! Wanker! You even wank with a condom. That's how safe you've become. Fuck off!'

Vlady laughed. It was an old line she'd used when he had refused to sleep with her, just before their affair had begun. He began to walk briskly. What an awful evening. It was not just that the jokes were awful. That was bad enough. The fact was that the forced humour was all part of a mask worn by Evelyne's new friends. They were all trying desperately to hide their unhappiness. They were living empty lives. Bereft of hope, bereft of belief, bereft of loyalties. They could not understand this, let alone acknowledge it and, for that reason, lived each day as it came.

Slowly his concentration returned. The animated aimlessness that had gripped him when Leyla had entered his fantasies during dinner had receded. His head was clear. He began to enjoy Berlin. His Berlin. It was the only time to really feel the old city. Trafficless. A friend of his had recently written a monograph calling for all cars to be restricted to certain zones and the old Berlin tramlines to be rehabilitated.

As he walked back home, Vlady revelled in the solitude. It was almost two in the morning. A chill wind was blowing and the ground was partially frozen. There was still some ice on the pavements, treacherous in places, so he walked slowly. Vlady smiled to himself. He was fifty-six today. What had loomed in the distance like a giant iceberg had finally caught up with him, but he had survived the encounter. He was still alive. Despite everything, he had not thrown himself under a train. He was still there and that was enough reason to celebrate.

A grey dawn broke just as he reached the Tiergarten. It must have been a night like this that they killed Rosa Luxemburg on that fateful January in 1919. He paused, nodded sadly as he saw the memorial to Rosa overlooking the canal, then walked over to the bridge to the Karl Liebknecht monument. The Junkers had never forgiven Liebknecht for announcing to the world in 1914 that a patriot was nothing more or less than an international blackleg. None of this mattered to his son's generation. His son, Karl, who had, uncharacteristically, shouted at him on the last occasion he had mentioned Rosa. 'What do I care about your dead gods, Vlady? Surely now you must understand it's finished for ever. It was a bad dream. A nightmare. Try and forget. Please.'

All they cared about was the present. The cursed present. Vlady remembered a line Heine had written in the middle of the eighteenth century. 'What the world seeks and hopes for now', the poet had written, 'has become utterly foreign to my heart.' The problem was that young Karl was in the very heart of that which had become so foreign to his father.

As he put the key in his door, Vlady was, for once, not thinking about the past, but the future. Would Karl have children? Would Vlady still be alive? Could Karl end up as an SPD minister? Vlady shuddered at this particular thought, but it made him even more determined to make a supreme effort and build a bridge on which both of them could meet – at least halfway. Unlike many of his friends, Karl did enjoy reading books. Vlady would write an account of his life. A partial confession, partial explanation. Not for posterity. Just for Karl. Yes, that was the solution. He would sit down and write everything he knew.

Did Vlady know everything? There were some crucially important gaps in the chronology bequeathed to him by his mother, Gertrude. He knew little about his father except tales of heroism and the fact that he had been killed on Stalin's orders a few months before Vlady was born in December 1937.

He often thought of his father, but how much his mother had left out of her accounts. She belonged to a generation that had no difficulty in subordinating truth to the needs of Moscow or even her own personal needs, to protect her new post-war identity in the new Germany. He had never believed her rosy accounts of life in the twenties and thirties.

The truth, or at least a minuscule segment of it, lay in the KGB archives. He needed access and, amongst his circle of acquaintances, there was only one person who might be able to help him.

Vlady recalled his old friend Sao, the one-time Vietnamese guerrilla turned entrepreneur. A man who wore his custom-tailored Parisian suits just as proudly as he used to wear his black Vietcong pyjamas. Sao had contacts in the new Russia where everything was for sale. Nowadays the Russians were finding paintings in the Hermitage, incunabula in private collections, and KGB crooks hawked their memoirs at the Frankfurt Book Fair as openly as the Generals sold vital military equipment before they withdrew from Berlin. Uranium and missiles could also be bought if you had the right contacts. Yes. There was no other way. Sao was his man and Sao was arriving in Berlin tomorrow to take Vlady out to dinner.

Overcome by exhaustion, Vlady undressed and sank gently on to his bed. It was already dawn and sleep came quickly to the rescue. He might have slept through the day, but at midday he was woken by the persistent ring of the phone. Bleary-eyed and chilled to the bone, he put his head under the blanket, cursing the heating system, which had collapsed a few days ago. The phone kept ringing. The thought that it might be Sao sent an electric current through his head. He jumped out of his bed, draped himself with a blanket and lifted the receiver.

'Yes?'

'Happy birthday, Vlady. Are you there? I was beginning to get worried. Vlady?'

It was Karl from Bonn. Vlady was touched, but his voice remained aloof. 'Hello Karl. Thanks a lot. I'm fine. You well?'

'Yes, yes. What news on the apartment?'

'I'm still here, aren't I?'

'But . . .'

'I think the Heuvels will have to wait another few years before they can have it back. The scum actually offered me money!'

'How much?'

'Fifty thousand marks.'

'For that amount you could not buy an apartment anywhere.'

'At last we are in agreement.'

'I'm coming to Berlin next month, Vlady. I can stay in my old room?'

'You mean you will stay here and not with your boss in the...?'

'Vlady. Please.'

'Of course, of course, Karl. This will be your home till the Treuhandt throws me out. By the way, tonight I'm having dinner with your old Uncle Sao. Remember him?'

Five

IT WAS A COLD NIGHT in February 1982. Dresden, where Vlady and his wife Helge were visiting her ill mother, was drenched in rain. After a week looking after Helge's mother, who had suffered a severe stroke, and comforting her eighty-year-old father, Vlady had insisted that they accept an invitation to dinner. The evening had passed off well. Over a dozen dissidents had been assembled in the tiny flat where they had exchanged experiences, discussed the situation on the Politburo and consumed a great deal of beer.

As they were walking back, Vlady had caught sight of a dapper Vietnamese with an attractive young German woman on his arm. Helge had wondered whether the Vietnamese was a student or a slave-worker, indentured to a local factory. Suddenly three or four figures had emerged from nowhere and surrounded the couple. Sao was flung to the ground and while one of the assailants held the girl, three pairs of boots descended on Sao. Then two of them sat on his chest, while the third pulled down Sao's trousers and brandished a knife.

At first neither the assailants nor Sao and his friend had raised their voices. Vlady and Helge had been paralysed by this silent tableau, which from a distance appeared as a grotesque display of shadow puppetry. Then the girl had screamed for help, and Vlady and Helge had rushed across the street screaming abuse and calling for the police. The assailants had run away. Vlady helped to lift Sao, whose nose was bleeding. Helge undid her scarf and used it to stem the flow of blood. The young girl was sobbing.

'Are you OK?'

'My balls are still here,' Sao had replied, managing a weak smile. 'As for the rest, you can see. Thank you.'

'Who were they?' inquired Helge.

Sao's friend spoke for the first time. 'Young Communists!' she hissed. 'One of them's been after me for months. When he found out I was seeing Sao, he threatened to kill him.'

'I hope you will report this to the police,' Vlady said somewhat pompously. 'I would be happy to be a witness. Do you know his name?'

Sao laughed. 'The boy who wanted to castrate me? Of course, but do you know that his father is the party boss in this town? If you complain, I am the one who will suffer. They will deport me.'

'How can you be so calm?'

'I am not at all calm,' Sao replied, keeping his anger under control. 'I am very angry, very embittered and filled with thoughts of revenge, but I am also powerless here in your very Democratic Republic. If I lost my self-control, I would be dead within a few weeks.'

A bewildered Vlady indicated that he could not follow Vietnamese logic. Sao smiled through the blood. 'I'm a trained soldier. A war veteran. I was taught to kill the enemy silently. I could have broken their necks if you had not arrived. And then the Stasi would have engineered an incident in my factory. Something heavy would have fallen on me. A small accident, another foreign worker dead. So you see, my friend, you saved my manhood and my life. Now please, we must go home. She to her mother's apartment, I to my dormitory.'

Helge insisted on taking Sao back to her own home. There she treated his wounds, none of which were severe, and overcame his reluctance to impose on them any further. Sao had a bath and, later, after an improvised meal, Vlady drove him to the Vietnamese dormitory, an ugly prison-style structure on the edge of the town. They arranged to meet the next day. Thus was their friendship born.

A year after the Dresden incident, Sao disappeared. Nobody knew where he had gone. One day a letter arrived from Moscow. Sao wanted Helge and Vlady to know that he had settled there and was happy. He had cousins, friends, fellow veterans from the Vietnam War dotted all over the Soviet Union. He was in constant communication with them all and travelled a great deal. He hoped Vlady, Helge and little Karl were well. He would see them soon. That was all the letter said.

Over the next few years they received the odd postcard; on occasion a visitor from Moscow would bring them a present from Sao, usually a large unmarked tin of caviar with a note from their friend informing them that this was a caviar specially designated for the Politburo. After tasting it, Vlady and Helge realized that Sao was not joking. They talked of him often, speculating as to his activities and whereabouts.

Vlady now recalled his many conversations with Sao. After a while he had begun to ignore his friend's endless fantasies, all of which revolved around making money. The two men could not have been more dissimilar. Their contrasts reflected their conditioning and origins.

Vlady Meyer had imbibed German idealism. Despite his addiction to many aspects of Marxist thinking, he was, deep down, a romantic agonizer. A living example, if not a parody, of why the German vocabulary current in the world language, English, has to contain words like *Weltschmerz, Angst, Zeitgeist*.

Once an ardent Young Communist, Sao had almost lost his life in the war, and seeing what was happening now he was impatient with abstractions. He came from a middle-peasant family. His father had fought in the French Army. For a long time, Sao had obliterated memories of his origins, but in the deprivation and gloom of the post-war years, he remembered his mother and uncles and how important verbs like buy, build, exchange and sell were to their everyday life. Increasingly alienated from the state for which he had fought, Sao moved backwards in time and forward simultaneously. He now appreciated the merits of the old peasant economy and pre-urban family relations. These could not be recreated, but the memory was important in helping him to reconstruct his own social status. He did not want to deaden the shocks produced by the new order that existed in the world. Whereas Vlady's instinct was to see the new realities as a depressing intrusion, Sao was determined to take advantage of them. It was this side of their family friend that appealed to young Karl.

Vlady was a useful counter-balance. Their regular exchange of ideas and experiences laid the basis for a relationship that had become fruitful for both of them.

Ten years passed. One day in 1992, Sao turned up without warning and knocked on the door of Vlady's apartment. At first Helge did not recognize him. Then she screamed with pleasure, bringing Vlady and Karl to the door. All three were taken aback. The old slave-worker was attired in a three-piece designer suit, a black silk fedora sat uncomfortably on his head and he was loaded with presents. He looked like a fifties photograph of Bao Dai, the deposed emperor of Vietnam, in his Parisian exile.

The reunion was joyous. He had insisted on taking them all to a small island off the Baltic coast, a seaside resort that was once the exclusive holidaying preserve of Party bigwigs. Sao, who spent a lot of time at the Casino in Nice, had assumed that there would be some luxury facilities, but he was a few years too early. His obvious disappointment had amused Helge, but it was a relaxed week. Vlady and Helge had not realized how much the continuous political activity of the last six months had exhausted them. Meetings, street demonstrations, all-night discussions had taken over their lives. Poor Karl had been virtually ignored. Now, thanks to Sao, they were all together again.

The poor citizens of the DDR were about to be orphaned, shell-shocked and raped, but few of them realized this in the heady weeks before reunification. Vlady was one of the few. His doubts had been aired in the press and on television. In those days, the little cabbages, mimicking the Big Cabbage in Bonn, used to respond in a friendly, albeit patronizing, fashion.

'Professor Meyer, you and your friends belong to the old world. We know you will always be a socialist at heart, but we don't hold that against you. We are ready to forgive and forget. You can still render some services to democracy. Come with us. Let us build the new Germany together.'

Sao knew that Vlady's thoughts were elsewhere. Vlady had shown only polite interest in the story of his friend's transformation from slave-worker to property-holder. Vlady and Helge had begun to feel guilty after a few days in the sunshine. At night Sao would hear them whispering to each other. He couldn't hear them properly but certain words and phrases indicated that they were obsessed with the future of their country.

It was young Karl who had followed every curve in the story. How Sao had exploited the quickened pace of history to transform his own life. The adventures of a Vietnamese entrepreneur and how he made his first million was just more exciting, thought Karl. He had been alienated from his parents and their recent activities. The big demonstrations in Berlin and Dresden had left the young man unmoved. He was, by temperament, a creature of the committee room rather than the street. Displays of public emotion embarrassed him. The passions of the multitude frightened him. Vlady and Helge were reduced to exchanging looks of despair or resignation as they watched their young cub grow.

Sao's odyssey had excited Karl. It was as if Sao had cast a spell on him. He listened carefully, his eyes sparkling, and occasionally he interrupted the story-teller to get exact details. It was Karl's interest that alerted his parents and compelled them – against their will, because all they wanted to think about was the precarious condition of the Politburo in Berlin – to pay serious attention to the tales being told by their Vietnamese friend.

Sao had fled to Moscow. Compared to Dresden and Berlin, he told them, Moscow was a cosmopolitan paradise. He had immediately established contact with the Vietnamese community and found a bed in a two-roomed apartment, which he shared with only five other people. Two of these were always travelling and, of the rest, there was one who came from a neighbouring village. Sao asked them about his cousin in Kiev, whom he hadn't seen for several years. They had no knowledge of him. When Sao asked if they would take a letter from him on their next trip to the Ukraine, they laughed and took Sao along instead. Travel documents and money posed no problems. It soon became clear that the two travellers were unofficial businessmen, involved in the task of primitively accumulating capital. They ran a growing black market for Vietnamese communities throughout the Soviet Union. Their distribution network was both efficient and reliable.

Sao was staggered by the scale of the operation and by the fact that the only currency they used was dollars or deutsche marks. On the train to Kiev, he thought of his own country. Since the fall of Saigon in 1975, the leaders in Hanoi had found themselves at the head of a ruined country. Its ecology had been severely damaged by chemical warfare; its bombed cities needed to be rebuilt; its orphans had to be found homes; its demobilized soldiers, traumatized by the war, had to be found jobs; surplus labour had to be sold to the Soviet Union and Eastern Europe in return for badly needed equipment and essential commodities.

The United States had promised reparations, but reneged on each and every promise and imposed an economic embargo instead. Sao knew that his country was being punished. They had dared to resist and win. Now they had to pay a price for their sensational victory against the most powerful country in the world.

The war years had been full of tension, anguish, fear, but also a sense of excitement at the thought that they would one day win and reunite Vietnam. That was all over. Peace had brought few dividends for the common people. Sao was bitter. He had fought hard. He knew that paradise was only a dream, but surely, he had thought, the immediate future would bring some relief.

Hope, struggle, hope, betrayal, hope, revenge, hope, collapse . . . no hope. He had said all that at a party meeting in Hanoi. Many heads, too many, had nodded in silent agreement. Within three weeks they had packed him off to a new front, the DDR, a misnamed country ruled by misled bureaucrats. What a life.

He felt he had come to the crossing of ways. He was travelling on shifting ground. His life could take many routes. He looked at his compatriots, busy working out what they would buy and sell in Kiev, and decided to join them. He felt the network should be extended to every major city in the Soviet Union and that they should develop links with Vietnamese workers in Eastern Europe.

'Commodities needed to be circulated,' Sao had laughed, 'and who better than us to circulate them? For centuries we had been ruled by the Chinese. Then it was the French. Then came the Russians. Now, we thought, let us work for an economic system.'

Sao and his friends developed a tried and tested network of middlemen, which straddled the whole country. Their money became a mountain. With the beginning of the collapse, they insisted on being paid in dollars or marks. Some of the money they filtered back to Vietnam. Many a new motorcycle or television/video set in Hanoi was the result of such activities. Hanoi actually experienced a tiny boom as it began to catch up with Ho Chi Minh City, which was still really Saigon.

'In the early days,' Sao continued, 'we had to share our profits with party bureaucrats big and small, starting with party officials of the *oblast* and ending up with members of the Central Committee. Then they decided to change the system. At first we panicked: could this be the end of us? We were small fish in a medium-sized lake. Now we would become minnows in the sea. The sharks would get everything. How wrong we were, my friends. How wrong we were.'

He stopped at this point and laughed. And laughed. There was more than a trace of hysteria in his laughter.

'What's so funny Uncle Sao?' Karl inquired in a puzzled voice.

'What's so funny is that we were the only ones in a position to exploit the collapse. Nobody had imagined that the Soviet Union would disintegrate so quickly, but it did. It did. Yeltsin was in a hurry to dump Gorbachev, and if he had to dump the old Soviet Union first he would do so. And he did. The Russian mafia was caught by surprise. Anyway, their connections were neither as extensive nor as efficient as ours. They had relied too heavily on their links with party officials. The old system was paralysed. Distribution collapsed. We Vietnamese came to the rescue, but at a price, just like they had come to the rescue during our war. At a price. We established a chain of command. We moved goods. We developed our own transport system. We stepped into the breach, my young Karl. And now your Uncle Sao has an apartment in Paris and a French wife. I can travel anywhere, but Vlady and Helge are my two best friends. Real friends. There is nobody like them anywhere else. Remember that Karl, always. OK?'

And then he was gone again.

A week or so ago he had rung Vlady to warn him of his imminent arrival in Berlin on important business. They had agreed a date for dinner. Vlady was on his way.

Nguyen van Sao, son of Vietnamese peasants, was submerged in a foam-filled bath in a luxury suite on the third floor of the Kempinski. He was in a foul mood. It had been an awful day. The flight from London had been delayed. Berlin immigration had inspected his French passport with too much care, but, biggest disappointment of all, he had failed earlier in the day to acquire a seventeenth-century silk condom, with an embossed *fleur-de-lis*, which had once been used by Louis XIV, though with what success was not made clear in the catalogue. Had it really impeded the pox which might otherwise have felled the Sun King?

Sao had wanted the object as a gift for his father's seventieth birthday, but at the Sotheby's auction he had been outbid by a determined, fur-coated Chechen, probably acting for some big dealer in Moscow or Berlin. At least, Sao mused, as he rose from the tub and wrapped himself in a comforting bathrobe, I forced the sonofabitch to pay fifty thousand dollars for the privilege of feeling the King's silk. Since more dollars were being printed in Russia than in America these days, he hoped that Sotheby's had been paid in forged currency. Sao felt remote and isolated from the world in which he had become so successful.

The problem remained. What should he buy his father? In previous years Sao had sent the old man silk shirts, handmade shoes, antique Vietnamese gowns, crates of champagne cognac and much else besides. Most of these presents ended up on the Hanoi black market.

This year, for the first time, his father had expressed a wish. He had read in a magazine that a Louis XIV condom was being offered for sale. For some deep, mystical and, to Sao, totally incomprehensible reason, it had become an object of desire for his father. Sao felt guilty. Perhaps he should have fought the Chechen to a standstill. It was the first time that his father had ever asked him for anything and he had failed. Sao loved his father.

Sao *père* had fought at Dienbienphu – a small town in Northern Vietnam occupied by the French, who imagined it to be impregnable – in 1954, but on the French side, though this fact was long forgotten and never mentioned. Family history claimed that he had always been a communist agent. This was not true.

He had been a uniformed menial, a batman who served and was well treated by an aristocratic French colonel with a large estate near Nîmes. Old clothes, discarded boots, generous tips, dregs of cognac and the odd kind word had kept the simple Vietnamese soldier happy. And all this because the Vietnamese, a skilled barber, shaved his master with great care every morning.

So pleased was the Colonel that he had offered to take him back to France. And so it might have been if history had not proved so awkward. One morning in 1954, Sao's father woke up in the besieged town of Dienbienphu and realized, even though he was no great military strategist, that the unthinkable was about to happen. His side was on the verge of collapse. The chief of the Vietnamese resistance army, Vo Nguyen Giap, the 'Bush General', as the French called him, was on the eve of a sensational victory. The élite corps of the French Army had only two options: abject surrender or annihilation.

Cruel disillusionment set in. Sao's father deserted to the winning side. He wasn't the only one. Two days later the French army surrendered. The second Vietnam War was over.

Old Sao was sure that his old master would die rather than yield. Despite the belated conversion, it turned out to be an astute move, politically and emotionally. The French were defeated. They withdrew from the Vietnamese peninsula, never to return. The Colonel had confirmed his native batman's instincts and shot himself in the head.

And, most important of all, Sao's father had met Sao's mother. Thu Van, twenty years old, already regarded as a veteran by her guerrilla comrades, had participated in the siege of Dienbienphu. It was she who had first sighted her future husband, in French army fatigues, crawling underneath the barbed wire and waving an extremely clean white handkerchief on a stick. For some reason the sight of him had made her laugh. She had debriefed him thoroughly, reported his defection and handed him over to her political officer, and returned to the front-line.

After the surrender, he did not give her a moment's peace. He followed her everywhere till she admitted to herself that she, too, loved him. Thu Van was a deeply committed Communist. She took her lover's political education very seriously. It was only after she felt that his education was complete, that he was a new man, that she deigned to bear him a son. Young Sao.

After the accords of 1956, when the country was partitioned, pending a general election, Sao's father stayed in the north with Thu Van and the Communists, abandoning Hue to the catholic priests and his cramped living quarters to a cousin.

Even though he regretted having served in the French army, deep in his heart old Sao missed the ways of the French. And, if the truth be told, he missed the dregs of the colonel's cognac and the tinned *grenouilles*. He missed the songs they used to sing. He missed the photographs of beautiful French women and curly-haired children. He missed the French colonial epoch. All the expensive presents and foodstuffs his son sent him from Paris did not taste the same. Their moral flavour was repugnant to his senses. Elections never happened in Vietnam. Why? Because the Americans, who had replaced the French, were scared that the Communists would win. The Third Vietnam War began. Thu Van, whose knowledge of the terrain in the south made her invaluable, left her young son and husband in Hanoi to join the newly organized National Liberation Front in the south.

'You must eat properly while I'm away, Sao. When you were a baby you were plump and round like a sweet flour candy. Look at you now. A scarecrow! Promise me you'll eat your meals.'

Sao had promised and she had lifted him off the ground and kissed his eyes. Her own eyes had filled with tears. As she bade farewell to her husband and son something told her she wouldn't see them again.

'Look after him well,' she whispered in his ear.

She was killed a few months later in 1962, during the battle of Ap Bac, when the Americans suffered their first serious reversal. The encounter itself was minor, but in it was written the war's future.

One day young Sao came into the dirty barber's shop in Haiphong where his father now worked and where the main customers were sailors on leave. It was late and there were no customers. Sao looked into the blinded mirror. His father's intense gaze suddenly gave way to tears. Sao hugged him quietly.

'The Americans are really stupid,' Sao's father said in a soft voice which indicated that he had been thinking of Thu Van. 'Can't they see that if the French couldn't beat us, nobody will?'

Sao always carried a photograph of his mother with him. It was one of those formal photographs designed for posterity and political propaganda. She was dressed in black pyjamas, a straw hat and was carrying a rifle. Her face, full of hope, was wreathed in smiles. It was the last photograph ever taken of her and he had carried it on him all his life. When he went to join the struggle he had shown it with pride to his comrades.

How could she have been so full of hope? Sao envied her this more than anything else. His world was the settled, comfortable one of a wealthy man, but it was devoid of an apocalyptic view of the future.

He was now completely dry. He picked up his watch, realized he was getting late and began to dress quickly. Just as he was putting his wallet in the inside pocket of his jacket, the phone rang. He let it ring for a few seconds while he tied his shoelaces.

'Excuse me, Herr Sao, there is a Professor Meyer waiting for you in reception.'

'Send him up, send him up,' said Sao excitedly as he laughed and threaded his gold cufflinks.

Vlady had walked to the Ku-Damm and the cold wind had given his cheeks a gentle flush. He felt refreshed, more alert in mind and body. As the lift ascended to the penthouse floor, Vlady smiled as he thought of the changes of the last decade that had transformed Sao's life and his own since the night of their accidental meeting in Dresden, in the old DDR, nearly twelve years ago.

Sao was waiting outside the open door of his room. The two friends embraced.

'My first question to you, Professor,' Sao spoke with a mischievous gleam in his eyes. 'Are the workers contented now?'

Both men laughed.

'Not all workers can live like you, Sao.'

'That is a pity,' laughed the Vietnamese as they descended to the ground floor and headed towards the Lobster Bar. He ordered caviar, lobster and champagne, while bemoaning that the seafood in Halong Bay was much superior. Vlady contented himself with a steak and salad. Two good meals in two days. His stock must be rising in this new world.

Later, back in Sao's suite, they shared a bottle of cognac and Sao, feeling maudlin, offered his friend money, a flat in Berlin or Paris, an institute of his own in Dresden, a new publishing house in Munich or Vienna or, indeed, anything else that Vlady desired.

Vlady smiled gratefully, but shook his head.

'Listen to me carefully, Vlady. You saved my life. Can I ever forget? Now I am rich. More money than I ever dreamt of. My children, my wife will have enough after I am gone. The money still keeps coming. I want to help you. What's the problem, Vlady? A moral dilemma? Yes? Why?'

Vlady was touched and his expression softened.

'The dilemma is existential, not moral. *How* to live is far less important a question than *whether* to live. Gerhard resolved the problem by hanging himself in his garden in Jena, but I . . .'

'But not you, Vladimir Meyer.' Sao gripped his friend's arm as if he were a prisoner of war. 'Not you. I will not, I cannot believe that you can just give up. So you've been sacked by a bunch of bastards from the West. Fight back with both fists. I'll fund your counterattack. Remember the line from Brecht you taught me so many years ago: "Were a wind to arise I could put up a sail; were there no sail I'd make one of canvas and sticks."'

Vlady smiled.

'Not only is there no wind, but the whole sea is occupied by giant ships with only one shanty to sing. Not Brecht, but "Deutschmark, deutschmark uber alles". The reunification has gone to their head, Sao. Do you know what some of them are saying? Unless we grow even greater, we shall become less.'

Sao grinned, pleased to see Vlady angry again. 'What about the snails?' he asked, referring to the SPD. 'Young Karl is doing well, which is good for me. If I have a friend in the Chancellery my business will prosper even more. You just calm down, Vlady. The new Germany is not an embryo of a Fourth Reich. Some idiots may dream of that, but the German bourgeoisie will not make the same mistake twice. Never. I'm sure the SPD will win again.'

'Not for some time. They need a brain transplant to halt the decline. But enough of dead politics and living-dead politicians. I want to know where your money is coming from, Sao. And I want the truth.'

Sao smiled. 'You mean you've forgotten? I told you everything. About myself, my family, my money. Everything. Remember the week we spent together. The week before reunification. You have forgotten. You were very drunk on freedom and democracy. My life story, by contrast, seemed insignificant. Never mind. You were right. It is insignificant. Vlady, I must go next door and call the West Coast. Business. I won't be long. Have some more cognac. There are many things I have to tell you.'

Vlady was indignant. He looked at his watch. Thirty-seven minutes past midnight.

'You can make your filthy phone calls later. First I want the truth. And, by the way, I've forgotten nothing. It's just that your life story has acquired a new instalment. Am I right or wrong?'

Sao settled back in his chair again and sighed. 'Well?' said the Vietnamese, refilling his glass.

'I still want my answer, Sao. Where's it all coming from *now*? Drugs or weapons?'

The two men looked at each other. Vlady saw a troubled look cross his friend's eyes. Then an oppressive silence. After what seemed an eternity, Sao began to talk.

'I could never be involved with drugs, Vlady. Never. Though it is true that my former partners holiday a great deal in Pakistan and Colombia. Not me, Vlady, not me.'

'So you're gun-running?'

'Gun-running?' Sao roared with laughter. 'So old-fashioned, Vlady. Tank-running, missile-running, fighter-aircraft-running, yes. Gun-running, no! I buy and sell. The Chinese want missiles. I fly to Alma Ata and do a deal with the Kazakhs. The Serbs want tanks. Iraq needs spare parts for its MIG fighters. I make sure they get them. Supply and demand, Vlady. Market rules. The capitalism you hate so much has conquered the world.'

'Your world, perhaps, but there is another world out there, Sao.' Vlady was trying hard to keep the bitter edge out of his voice. 'It may be submerged for a while, but it will rise again. I'm amazed that you, of all people could forget. After all the sacrifices made by ordinary people.'

'When the sands run against people, the people they should go away. Old Chinese proverb, Vlady. Sacrifices? We Vietnamese know more about that than anyone else. I joined the Communist Youth Brigade in Hanoi when I was sixteen. A year later I was fighting in the south. I saw all my close comrades die. I was given up for dead myself. I only survived because a peasant family scavenging for valuables saw I was still breathing. They took me in and informed the nearest NLF* unit. I was taken to a hospital in Cambodia, but returned to see the fall of Saigon. We deserved that victory, did we not? Sacrifices!

'I sometimes wonder whether it was worth it. We lost two million people, Vlady. What for? To build a better future? Even children don't believe that now, and few teachers think it worth repeating. I remember when I was twelve years old. Our towns and villages were being bombed day and night by American planes. We used to be so proud when our teacher marked our homework in downed US warplanes. So proud, Vlady. Why were we so proud and even happy, despite the deaths and destruction? We believed in something. It wasn't because we thought we'd end up as slave labourers in the old Eastern Europe, let alone the new world market. I mean, if we'd known that it would end like this, we could have done a deal with Washington a long time before 1975.

'All the speculators and parasites who fled with the Americans are slowly coming back, the same exploiters we fought against for thirty years. So I ask you: Was it worth it?'

Vlady, realizing that no glib rebuttal was possible, decided to return to the offensive. 'What about plutonium-running, Sao? Surely you have no moral inhibitions? I mean if the market rules, then why not supply plutonium when there is clearly a big demand? Give everyone the bomb!'

'You're angry, my friend. Please, Vlady, don't misunderstand me deliberately. I am not a freak or a monster. I work to live and I live well. That's all. Would it have made you happier if I'd returned to

---

* National Liberation Front.

Hanoi or Hue and opened a small book shop or become a party bureaucrat or a pimp or a street vendor? Don't tell me there's no living space in between soiling your hands and cutting your throat. And no, my friend, I don't trade in plutonium or chemical weapons. My arms business is strictly non-nuclear and non-chemical.'

Vlady gave him a cold stare.

'Do you believe me?'

'Yes,' Vlady replied. He felt strongly that Sao was telling the truth.

'But why are you here at the moment?'

'The old Red Army's still here, isn't it? The generals want to sell. I want to buy. There is a large order from Iraq. Payment is in dollars. At least one Russian general will be staying on in Berlin. That much I promise you.'

Sao stopped suddenly. His friend was far away. Vlady was wondering whether anything that had happened this century had been worth the trouble. The Russian Revolution and the epic resistance of the Vietnamese had finally ended up prostrate before the New York Stock Exchange. He was computing the lives that had been lost in Russia, when Sao's voice interrupted him.

'Now I've told you everything, Vlady. Why don't you let me buy you a publishing house? No? Books are now a commodity, just like tinned salmon. Do you want to go and live in the States, like your friend, Christa Wolf? Yes? It could be arranged. I have friends at the University of California.'

'No! Christa was hounded out, you sonofabitch. She was fine for them while the DDR was alive. They needed her then. She was a noble savage. Now they have to destroy her in order to convince themselves that everything in the DDR was tainted. Everything. And this from men who hired ex-Nazis by the thousands to run their new state after the war. Nazi war heroes are still celebrated in the Luftwaffe. Everything they do here stinks of double standards.'

'What are you going to do with your life, Vlady?'

'I don't know. One can carry on living in the present till one drops dead. Most people do that these days. For me it's like living in a jungle. Gerhard, whom you knew, decided he could no longer live in these conditions. And you, Sao, have changed so much...'

'You were never short of friends, Vlady.'

'But friendship meant something in those days. Now one meets people and discards them like autumn trees shed leaves.'

Sao smiled. He was partly fond of Vlady because he saw the absurdity of his political position. Absurd, but also admirable. Since Vlady had been expelled from his academic life and his dream of a non-western, non-Soviet East Germany had turned into a nightmare, it seemed to Sao that his friend had kept on fighting the dialectical battle that history had recently concluded. He could not tell Vlady that what he, Sao, wanted most of all was to smash the mirror Vlady kept gazing into only to peer further in the mirror behind him. He wanted Vlady to do the job himself.

'Let me help, Vlady. Please.'

A long pause followed before Vlady, after careful reflection, spoke again, but this time the tone was subdued. 'There is one thing you can do for me, Sao.'

Sao, who was lying on the sofa, sat up in surprise.

'What?'

'My father. I want to know how he died and who killed him. With your contacts in Moscow, could you get me his file from the KGB archives?'

Sao grinned with pleasure. 'Absolutely. The German mark can buy anything. These are times when whole cities are being bought and sold. All you want is pieces of paper. No problem at all. It is easier to buy history than real estate. The mafia is not interested in archives. I'll get you whatever it is that you want. Give me the details. Do you have a photograph?'

Vlady nodded.

'Fine,' said Sao. 'Bring it to me tomorrow.'

'If it's that easy,' said Vlady with a sigh, 'could you get my mother's file as well? Might as well have the whole story.'

'It's a deal,' Sao laughed, 'and if you think of anyone else, let me know. And Vlady, please let me help you in other ways.'

Vlady stood up and made a mock bow to Sao. 'Till tomorrow.'

Sao rose and hugged his friend. Vlady was gently disentangling himself from the embrace, when Sao whispered, 'You saved my life once. Let me save yours.'

Vlady's eyes smiled and he gave a tiny nod. It was a gesture of gratitude. Then he left Sao's room. Outside the Kempinski he surprised himself and took a taxi home. It was two-thirty in the morning. Inside his flat, Vlady undressed but he was gripped by a dull headache and sleep, cruel sleep, evaded him.

He thought of his former colleagues in the former Soviet Union and the former Czechoslovakia. He had not heard from them for a long time. How many had fallen off the feverish merry-go-round that was the new Europe? Newly rich. Newly free. Could any of his old friends be in the vanguard of this repellent and chaotic *fin de siècle*? Or had they, like him, sought refuge from this spectacle and become internal exiles? The important thing was to survive. To cover one's head with a blanket and wait till the polluted downpour was over.

He now began to have second thoughts about his request to Sao. Did he really want to know more? Perhaps the past was better protected and preserved. What difference would it make if the man he regarded as his father now turned out to be someone completely different? What was the point of it all? It would change nothing. Yes, it would. It would end the painful torment of memory. The century was cursed, but he still wanted to know. Try as he might, he could not simply write off the past or completely cut himself away from the present. The contradictions in his head finally exhausted themselves. He fell asleep.

Six

THE YEAR IS 1913. Vienna, the capital of an empire on the eve of extinction, appears unchanged. Its citizens show no overt signs of panic. The New Year celebrations are as frothy as usual. The Strauss waltz maintains its popularity in bourgeois and plebeian circles. Schoenberg's new music is heard by a small minority and appreciated only by a vanguard far removed from everyday realities. Or so it seems. The coming conflict between the Great Powers will change all this, but in *belle époque* Vienna the thoughts of the many do not entertain notions of a destructive war.

Students from the outer reaches of the empire were still being admitted to the university. That's how Ludwik met Lisa. Neither of them had celebrated their nineteenth birthday. She was sitting with friends in a café when he saw her features transformed by a smile and then heard the ring of a deep, throaty laugh. She had a strong, well-formed face, large forehead, raised cheekbones, piercing blue eyes and luxuriant, dark brown hair, bunched together in a bun. She was wearing a black dress and a silk scarf with a silver brooch.

He was looking for someone else, but could not take his eyes away from her, till she caught his glance and frowned. At first sight he was not particularly attractive. He had nice eyes, but was a bit too short and plump. The perfectionist in her preferred slim and sculpted figures. His crop of black hair was already beginning to thin and she thought he would be bald in another few years, and turned away. Ludwik persisted. It was his voice that entranced her and it was when he spoke that she felt the force of his personality. Still she resisted. Still he would not accept defeat.

They began an exhausting courtship, which seemed to last forever. It left them drained of energy and feelings at the end of each week. All the streets in Vienna acquired new meanings for him. They walked for hours, mute with emotion, each waiting for the other to break the silence till it was time to part and not a word had been spoken. Later he would replay the lost day in his mind and the streets would come to life again. Here she had laughed, there they had held hands and just as they had reached the Zentrale, another quarrel had erupted. Consumed with passion, he had been unable to eat anything, while she had ordered cakes with her coffee.

He had declared his love for her in the very first week after they had met. She had resisted, her instincts warning her that this one could be overwhelming and dangerous. She told him that she did not and could never love him. His face had paled, but he had said nothing, just stood up and walked away.

For a fortnight she went into hiding, avoiding all the cafés where they might see each other, and spent a few miserable days with an old boyfriend. It was when he tried to seduce her that she realized how much she was missing Ludwik. She thought of him all the time. Further resistance seemed useless. She parted from her old friend and went to find Ludwik.

They made love in her room one joyous afternoon, which had turned to dusk and then night. Lying in her arms, he had started to say something, but she had covered his mouth with her hand.

'Shh. No talk of pain tonight.'

'Why?'

'I think grief-filled days have ended for us.'

Ludwik was sated, but the melancholy broke through. 'Who knows what tomorrow will bring?'

'It is *this* night that truly matters, Ludwik. Let's imagine we're gods in heaven.'

They had blotted out all anguish-ridden memories, blotted out the dividing line between yesterday and tomorrow. There were to be no tears and lamentations for the past. Her ultra-romantic mood had surprised and infected him at the same time. He began to laugh at the sheer pleasure of it all.

Lisa dragged him back from the window where he was threatening to inform the world of his happiness. He kissed her eyes and she comforted him. 'What's the point of pining over what Fate might or might not bring? Does that make you happy?'

Both of them felt relieved. Both of them were intoxicated with each other. Both of them were still very young. Something had changed, but just as he thought that their relationship had reached a new and higher stage, she set up new emotional barriers and became withdrawn. She did not wish to be beholden to him or anyone else. It was still too soon. She needed time to think. She suggested that they part for a few months to see if they could survive without each other.

'I'm scared of falling in love with you, Ludwik. I don't know why. I just am. Please be patient.'

At first he exploded. Hurled insults. Abused her in Yiddish, which she did not understand. Then in Polish and German, which she did. Calm returned. They decided to split up. Ludwik had made a superhuman effort and distanced himself from her.

One night, after the others had left the meeting in Krystina's room, Ludwik confided in her. 'I've built a brick wall round my heart. I need to strengthen the fortifications before her artillery begins to open fire. She doesn't want to capture my heart, you understand, she only wants to break down the wall.'

Krystina understood only too well. She advised total rest, a change of air and concentrated political work. Krystina was a great believer in the theory that revolutionary ardour always triumphed over the other sort. And so Ludwik went to Warsaw. Here he was trained by an old Jewish printer in the art of forging documents, passports, but not banknotes. For that, his mentor told him, a special skill, which Ludwik, alas, did not possess, was required. After a month's intensive training he returned to Vienna. He had brought back instructions and a set of false passports which Krystina had requested from Dzherjhinsky. Ludwik proudly displayed the passports he had worked on himself. Krystina congratulated him, but, determined to keep him busy, she assigned him a set of urgent tasks and a grateful Ludwik immersed himself in underground political work.

'Is the cure working, Ludo?' Krystina asked him one day.

Ludwik shook his head in silence.

Lisa realized within a few weeks that she wanted him more than anything else. She began to yearn for him. She felt as if a light had gone out of her life. She laughed at his old jokes. She recast their conversations. She reread his letters and wrote new ones to him every day. Still no reply. Something told her one Friday morning that he was back in Vienna. She began to stalk the Café Zentrale every day. She knew his café hours and was convinced she would ambush him, but, unknown to her, Ludwik and the four Ls had stopped coming during the day.

Late one afternoon, in a despondent and desperate state, she stayed longer than usual, drowning her grief with black coffee. Perhaps he was still in Poland. Perhaps her imagination was overpowering reality. The Zentrale was built on the model of a cathedral. Pillars everywhere. Lisa used to sit at a corner table near the front entrance, which was virtually sealed off from the rest of the café by twin pillars. From this vantage point she had a clear view of the table usually occupied by Krystina and the five Ls.

Anyone observing Lisa from a distance would have seen an intense and beautiful woman scribbling furiously, and assumed she was a writer. In fact she was doodling; her fountain pen was moving in circles, reproducing the depression occupying her head.

When she came out of her reverie, she looked at her watch and suppressed a curse. Five to nine. It was dark outside. Just as she was about to leave, he walked in on Krystina's arm with the other four Ls in attendance. They were all laughing. Lisa was livid. Tears poured down her face. Anger, frustration and jealousy mingled with relief. They were so absorbed in each other that none of them had seen her. They sat at their usual table.

She was staring at Ludwik's back, while at the same time she could see part of his face in the wall-mirror. Why didn't he look sad? What had Krystina just said to make them all laugh? Anger was once again beginning to temporarily displace love and Lisa thought of walking out without attracting his attention, when, all of a sudden, he turned round and stared straight at her. For a moment they looked at each other in disbelief. Then he stood up, as if in a trance, hurried to her table and sat down facing her. Their faces were taut with emotion. Neither of them could speak. Far from abating, the fever now had both of them in its grip. She nodded. He understood. They walked out together, closely observed by Krystina and the four Ls.

They went to her room. The heaviness began to lift, their passion erupting like a tropical storm, clearing the air of mutual recriminations and making them laugh at their own stupidities. Whenever one of them started to speak and half apologize, half explain, half analyse the ebb and flow of their emotions, the other would interrupt at an early stage. Lisa did so by kissing him, the movements of her lips and tongue making further talk unnecessary. Ludwik decided to imitate her. He had woken up in the morning feeling excessively tender. He stroked her head, then kissed, stroked and nibbled her nipples.

'I love you, Lisa.'

She looked at him and gave a distracted smile. His heart sank. Were they going to go through yet another cycle of emotional conflict?

'I'm just a bit worried about my essay, you know. Professor Loew should have returned it last week. It's on the nervous system and –'

'Lisa!' he shouted. 'My nervous system can't take any more rejections from you.'

This made them both laugh and they had made love again. Sweet memories flowed like the Danube.

'The Landtmann! Remember, Ludo?'

He smiled. Lisa grinned. The first time they had met, 1913. The Archduke had not yet visited Sarajevo. On the surface, Vienna appeared as solid as before. Underneath, however, the cracks were beginning to show.

Lisa is sitting with a lover, a fellow medical student in the Café Landtmann. Their coffee cups are half full, the glasses of water lying on the table have not been touched. A stern young man, wearing a torn jacket, check shirt, trousers which are too short for him and black socks, walks in clutching a copy of *Arbeiterzeitung*. From his appearance it is obvious that he is a student, but they have never seen him before at the Landtmann. He is staring straight at her now and smiling. Lisa is amazed at how a smile can transform a face so completely. Her lover whispers in her ear: 'He's trying to pick you up. How do you think he will try and start a conversation?'

Before Lisa can reply, Ludwik has walked up to their table. He addresses her in German, but with a strong Polish accent.

'Excuse me, Fräulein. In weather like this even two-headed eagles can melt.'

The opening is undoubtedly original. Lisa bursts out laughing and finds it difficult to stop. Her companion joins her, but is more restrained. Ludwik's smile disappears. Lisa is now out of control. Suddenly a voice from an adjoining table interrupts their first meeting.

'To melt an eagle requires more than a newspaper.'

Ludwik turns round as if hit by a bullet. A woman in her late fifties, dressed in a black cotton blouse and long skirt, a beautiful white silk shawl covering her shoulders and wearing a red straw hat is inspecting Ludwik closely. Her eyes are boring holes in him. He blushes. (Yes, he actually blushed.) Apologizing hastily to Lisa and her friend, Ludwik escorts the older woman out of the café.

They laughed now at an incident which was very recent but seemed an eternity away.

'If it could always be like this, Lisa. What more do we need?'

'And the revolution? Forgotten? I hope you're not as fickle to me,' she teased.

It was getting dark outside. They had spent the whole day in bed. The realization made them feel decadent and happy.

Seven

I WAS FOUR YEARS OLD when Hitler invaded the Soviet Union. Your grandmother Gertrude and I were in Moscow at the time. Gertrude had asked to stay on in the Soviet capital and help with the German language broadcasts of Radio Moscow. Friends pleaded with her to let them take me out of the city. At one point she had weakened and was on the verge of surrender, but I refused to leave her. I threw a tantrum, broke glasses, threatened to jump out of the window, and so on. I put on such a frightening show, and it worked. They were scared. And so I stayed on in Moscow as well.

You know something, Karl, most of the people we met were not scared at all. Hitler had united us and we had forgotten the horrors of the purges and the murderous collectivization drives. And even though I was very small, I can still remember the looks on people's faces. Perhaps it is not all memory. Perhaps my own memories have become intertwined with what Gertrude told me then and later, after the Nazis had been defeated. You might find this strange, but there was a great deal of laughter in Moscow during the war years. It was as if through this bigger catastrophe we could transcend the tortures imposed on us by our own rulers.

The Germans were on the outskirts of the city. Stalin had to arm the population. I had older friends, aged ten and over, who were actually given rifles and joined the irregular defenders. I was desperate to go with them, but my mother wouldn't let me out of her sight.

I was dragged to the radio station with her and had to sit through interminably dull, heroic broadcasts to 'German people, to all German patriots'. Yes, patriots. Stalin's own broadcasts were now very nationalist in tone, but the fools did not understand that most German 'patriots' were willingly or reluctantly backing the Nazis and hoping for a victory in Moscow. Where Napoleon had failed, thought the German high command, Hitler might succeed.

Stalin, too, was obsessed by Napoleon. The Tsar's victory against the French general who sought to extend the Enlightenment through the bayonet was seen as a heroic and patriotic precedent. Those Red Army generals who had not yet been executed were released and sent to the front.

When Gertrude came home at night she would talk to me about her childhood and why she had fled Germany. In normal times I would probably have fallen asleep, but the excitement of the war, the charged atmosphere, the real heroism of ordinary people who lived in the same block – all this made me sit up and listen.

Years later, when I had forgotten some of her story, I would question her again and again till it became part of my own memory. I think she used to talk to you at night as well when you were in bed. You must have been about seven or eight at the time, but she would tell me laughingly, 'Your Karl will turn out to be a bourgeois. He always drops off at the wrong moments.'

She, of course, knew everything about being a bourgeois. It was the summer smells that would draw out her childhood experiences, and Munich, a city she always loved. She told me about the big garden of the old family house in Schwaben. Her excitement when the first wild strawberries were sighted, the invigorating scent of pine needles.

A few nights before she and her lover David left for Berlin, they went to the theatre to see Ernst Toller's revolutionary play *Masse-Mensch*, which was a call to arms. Gertie, in particular, was hypnotized by the story much more than the performance.

I've read the play, Karl, and it is truly awful. Reading it as a citizen of the DDR, I was repulsed, but not your grandmother. Till the last, she remembered the iron revolutionary will embodied in the words of the mass chorus which had gripped David and her simultaneously by the heart and the head:

> We, from eternity imprisoned
> In the abyss of towering towns;
> We, laid up on the altar of mechanical
> And mocking systems. We,
> Whose faces are blotted in the night of tears,
> Who from eternity are motherless –
> From the abysses of factories we cry:
> When shall we work in love?
> When shall we work at will?
> When is deliverance?

Toller's play only strengthened Gertrude's resolve. She would never be like the woman in Toller's play. She would never flinch from violence. She would never let humanist prejudices gain the upper hand.

It was in Berlin that she met my father for the first time. She told me the story so often, never missing a detail. Always exactly the same. Her tone became slightly high-pitched and artificial when she recounted the episode. I sometimes wondered what lay behind the anguish.

Gertrude first saw Ludwik in the bar of the Fürstenhof on Potsdamer

Platz. A cold November night in Berlin: November 7, to be precise. For some reason that last phrase always irritated me. November 7, to be precise. I mean it could never be 'November 7, to be imprecise' could it? We all knew it was the anniversary of the Russian Revolution. Perhaps it was the religious undertone that annoyed me.

She was tense, nervous, overexcited. Ludwik was an emissary from the Communist International and the Fourth Department of the Red Army. Military intelligence. She was only one of the six members who had been selected for clandestine work by the Berlin leadership of the German Communist Party. All six dropped everything. Personal identities, nationalities, formal membership of the party were repressed. They saw themselves as the eyes and ears of the world revolution, operating behind enemy lines. Ludwik permitted her to retain her first name purely on the grounds that he had never met a Communist called Gertrude. He was like that. Quirky, funny and someone who was loyal to his friends, even when loyalty clashed with the party line.

'Fräulein,' Ludwik said, bowing to the barmaid in an exaggerated fashion, 'two glasses of your finest Riesling, please. Today is November 7, our child's sixth birthday. And please join us.'

'Thank you kindly, Ludwik. Your child's name?'

For a moment Ludwik was flummoxed. Then he smiled and raised his glass.

'To Vladimir. We call him Vlady, you know, after his father.'

Gertrude had been too nervous to laugh and, anyway, wasn't it a bit undisciplined of him, making jokes about Lenin and the Revolution? Not that the barmaid understood, but Gertrude felt the sacrilege.

Her instructions had been to dress well. Pseudo-proletarian garb was not encouraged in her new field of work. This posed no problems for Gertrude. For her first meeting with Ludwik she was dressed in a dark brown check jacket and matching skirt, black tights and a beige blouse, fastened at the neck with an old amethyst brooch, which had once belonged to her grandmother. Her smooth, black hair was gathered in a knot and rested gently on her alabaster white neck. Her spectacles lay on the table and they were ugly. He made a mental note to recommend a new optician.

Ludwik noted that she spoke frankly and pleasantly, with a smile in her eyes, which were deeply shadowed. Why were they shadowed? What miseries was she living through in her life? He had read her file thoroughly. He knew about Munich and the break with her family. He knew about the short-lived marriage to David Stein in Wedding, but he did not know the reasons underlying the heavy shadows below her eyes, which neither the make-up nor her spectacles could conceal.

Gertie, for her part, wondered how Ludwik, who did not seem much older than her, had become such a senior figure in the Comintern. He looked very ordinary. Could he really be an intellectual? For her the face of an intellectual was symbolized by Rosa Luxemburg, Eugen Leviné, Karl Radek, Leon Trotsky.

She stopped mid-stream in her thoughts. Ludwik was a Slav, not a central European Jew. She was only half right. His mother was a Russian, his father a Galician Jew. From his mother, Ludwik had inherited a large forehead and dark blond hair. His eyes were blue, like his father's, and when he smiled his face was wreathed in wrinkles. Gertie noticed that he had thick, peasant's hands but beautifully manicured nails. No tobacco stains. No disfigured edges.

During dinner, Ludwik suddenly became stern. His face hardened, his eyes turned cold and piercing. He told her she was being recruited for one reason: her ability to speak English, French and Russian made her invaluable. He explained that her job would not be easy. It meant a great deal of travelling within and outside Germany. She was to leave for Moscow within two weeks for technical training; after that she would be given a new passport. She had immediately to break all links with the German party and return her membership card. She was not to be seen with sympathizers.

'Do you have a lover?'

'I don't see how that affects anything.'

'Is he a comrade?'

'No!' her tone was defiant.

'Well?' Ludwik was persistent.

'He's a photographer, if you must know. A Social Democrat, but not active. I mean he...'

Ludwik smiled.

'Fine. Excellent. Can he be trusted?'

'To do what?'

'To take some photographs we might need from time to time?'

'Will he be paid?'

'Of course.'

'Then he can be trusted.'

'Why did you break with David Stein? A wonderful human being, a good comrade. Why?'

'Is this relevant?'

'Everything I ask is relevant.'

'Well, if you must know, David fell in love with someone else. A social-democratic doctor!'

'I know.'

Gertrude started laughing, but Ludwik's face remained stern.

'Sorry. It was the way you said "I know". His new woman is called Gerda. He always wanted to be a doctor. The Bavarian revolution stopped him. Gerda was his route back to medicine. They're in Heidelberg now and she is paying for his studies. True love. I'm told he's no longer politically active.'

'You've been misinformed,' said Ludwik coldly.

That's how it all began, on the seventh day of November in 1923. If anyone had told her then where it would lead and how Ludwik would meet his end, she would have laughed in his face and thought him insane.

And yet there were people, even then, like that embittered old Karl Kautsky, who warned over and over again that the Bolshevik experiment, isolated from world realities, could only lead to disaster. Lenin and Trotsky, master polemicists that they were, had penned their replies to him. Party members all over Germany had roared their approbation and taunted Social Democrats by thrusting *The Renegade Kautsky and the Proletarian Revolution* and *Terrorism and Communism* in their faces. Yes, literally. And yes, it had felt good.

And Ludwik? As Gertie came to know him – his jokes, his sudden changes of mood, his luminous intelligence, his psychological insights into the strengths and weaknesses of Communist leaders in Moscow and Berlin – she began to appreciate how and why he had risen so rapidly. He was something very special. Half poet, half commissar, tender-hearted and ruthless.

I remember a beautiful summer day in Pushkino. We were staying with friends, Aunt Yelena and her husband, Uncle Mitya. Their son, Sasha, was my age and we went to the same school in Moscow. Uncle Mitya was a physicist working on splitting the atom and so he had this special dacha, where he could work in peace.

Sasha and I were carving our names on the birch tree when we heard Gertrude's joy-filled voice as she ran towards us followed by Sasha's parents, who were dancing with delight.

'The Red Army is on its way to Berlin! Do you know what it means, Vlady? We've won the war!'

Sasha and I stared at the three adults.

'Is it really true, Mutti?'

'It's true, my boy.' Uncle Mitya spoke in a gruff voice as he stroked his beard in a self-satisfied fashion. 'The Germans are finished. The hammer and sickle will fly over Berlin.'

'But we're Germans,' I remember myself saying, and I got angry when they all started laughing, just like you used to get angry when your mother and I laughed at some question you had asked. Sasha got worried by what I'd said.

'Will our generals kill all the Germans?'

'Of course not, you idiot,' his mother reprimanded him, 'only the Nazis.'

We got tired of listening to the grown-ups and ran to our favourite hide-out in the river-fields. Here we used to lie down on our bellies, our faces resting in our hands and stare for hours at the river flowing by, engrossed in our fantasies. The only noises were those of chirping birds and the humming of a small stream as it flowed out of ancient Jurassic clay and rocks, making its way to the river below.

We used to climb on the slippery rocks, covered with dark green lichen which changed to a reddish brown when the sun shone on them, and jump into the stream, even though this was forbidden because the stream was very shallow. It was idyllic. Here one forgot that the Soviet Union was at war, that millions lay dead, hundreds of cities and towns were empty shells, and even as we stood on those rocks, the Red Army was on its way to Berlin. I never forgot that afternoon in Pushkino. Never. And years later I would still remember that bewitched landscape. How tranquil everything seemed. Gertrude told me many years later that she felt the same. All her bad memories were temporarily frozen. She was overcome by lofty thoughts, utopian desires, dreams of my future as she floated with the river. She always went on her own.

Gertrude knew what Stalingrad and Leningrad looked like. She had interviewed General von Paulus and his defeated Sixth Army soldiers for Moscow Radio. She began to wonder what Germany would be like when she returned. Memories of Schwaben flooded back and she wept as she thought of Heiny and her parents. I rushed to hug her. We were always very close, much closer than you are to your parents. I often wonder why this is the case. What did we do wrong, Karl? After all neither of us were apologists for the old regime. Both of us were fighting for change, but not the shock therapy, the forced decollectivization they have inflicted on us, disregarding our status as human beings. Even you and your friends at the Ebert Stiftung must see that it could have been done differently.

I remember Gertrude sending me back to the dacha to get some cold lemonade, but nothing else. That was a day of good memories for me, but Gertrude told me later of how the day had ended. I rushed back without the lemonade shouting at her.

'Mutti! Mutti!' I ran towards her and as I drew closer she saw my tear-stained face and hugged me tight.

'Three men to see you,' I told her, trying to regain my breath. 'Army men. They want to see you.'

'Calm down, calm down. I'm coming. Why are you so upset, my Vladimiro?'

'One of them, he has black hair and a moustache like comrade Stalin. He grabbed me tight, so I couldn't escape. Then he threw me in the air and they all laughed. They spoke to each other in some other language. Then he told me, 'You go and get your mother. Tell her if she doesn't get here soon, we'll chop her German head off.'

Gertie's face had paled; she knew. Holding me tightly by the hand to stop her own from trembling, she walked back to the dacha. She knew who it was and why he had held Vlady in his animal-like grip. She felt sick.

I did not go inside the house with Mother. From the outside I observed their silhouetted gestures, caught echoes of their raised voices and was pleased that Gertrude, too, seemed not to like the man with the moustache. The man caught sight of us spying, and he raised his fist to threaten. Sasha and I ran into the woods and hid. We only came out when we heard the noise of a command car driving away.

'Who was that man, Mutti? Why was he here?'

'Quiet, Vlady! Quiet. I worked with him many years ago.'

'He's cruel,' I replied. 'He's a cruel man.'

Gertie flinched, startled by the accuracy of a child's instinct. 'I hope you will never meet him again.'

Eight

MOSCOW IN JANUARY 1924 was experiencing its coldest recorded winter. It was forty degrees below zero on the day Lenin died. Everything was frozen. Bonfires were lit in squares. People gathered as the news began to spread. Comrade Lenin is dead. Comrade Lenin is dead. From every part of the city and its suburbs, slow crowds, clothed in black and red, were moving towards the Hall of Pillars where the dead leader was lying.

The smoke from the bonfires was tar-laden and had reduced visibility to such an extent that even the trams, their bells ringing, were proceeding at a snail's pace. Covered in ice, carriages appeared stationary because the people on foot were moving at a quicker pace.

From Lubianka Square, Ludwik could hear the music. It was the *Funeral March*, punctuated by explosions of dynamite. Even in death,

Lenin was not allowed any peace. They were breaking up the earth to dig his grave. It was dark now. Moscow and its citizens were engulfed by the polar night.

They moved towards his body in total silence. On the raised bier, surrounded by flowers and red flags, Lenin's tired face was hidden. Tears slid down Ludwik's face. Lisa gripped him by the arm tightly as they walked past the dead man with the bulging forehead and tiny hands. They had heard him speak many times. Ludwik had observed him from close quarters at meetings of the Comintern, spoken to him on a number of occasions. Lisa stroked her distended stomach and spoke to her unborn child.

'This is the centre of history. Do you understand?'

As they were walking out, Ludwik saw Gertie, dressed in black, her head covered by a red scarf, her tear-stained face distorted by grief. He took her by the arm and they walked away from Red Square. What other generation had experienced what they had been through – war, revolution and civil war? In their tiny room lit by candles, they drank vodka and talked about Lenin.

Ludwik told Gertie and Lisa that there were ugly rumours. Stalin had insulted Lenin's long-time companion, Krupskaya. Lenin had broken off all relations with Stalin. Lenin had appealed to Trotsky for a common bloc against Stalin. Lenin had left behind a last testament asking the Party to remove Stalin from his post as General Secretary. Stalin had poisoned Lenin.

'Is it true?' Gertie had asked, breathless with emotion.

Ludwik shrugged his shoulders.

The next day, at the funeral, Trotsky was absent, lying indisposed with a high temperature far away from Moscow. The Politburo had advised him to get better before travelling back to the capital.

'We vow to thee, Comrade Lenin ...' began Stalin's funeral oration. This language was alien to Ludwik and most party members. Ludwik was repelled by the strong undertones of religion and superstition. But why Stalin? He accepted that Trotsky was absent, Trotsky whose oratory had held Petrograd spellbound in 1917 and who, as the Commissar for War and leader of the Red Army could, through persuasion and example, convince soldiers to fight better than anyone else, but anyone else would have done better. Bukharin. Zinoviev. Kamenev. All present and able. Why Stalin? Even ordinary people were perplexed.

'A new war has begun,' Ludwik told Lisa that night, 'a war for the succession, and I fear our friend is already out of the running. He should have got up from his sick bed and boarded a train. I have seen him lead men into battle with a high temperature.' Ludwik had never spoken to the Commissar for War, but he had fought under him during the civil war and fallen under his spell.

'Do you think more blood will be spilled?' asked Lisa. 'Will we too devour our own, like the French?'

Ludwik's eyes betrayed his anxiety. He had been unhappy when the Party, egged on by Lenin and Trotsky, had decided to cross the frozen waters and take Kronstadt by force, disband the sailors' committees, denounce the rebels as 'objective agents of the counter-revolution', meaning that no matter what their motives, the state was entitled to treat them as it would treat conscious and deliberate enemies.

It was Thermidor, Lenin had explained. Remember the fate of Robespierre and Saint-Just. This is our tragedy, Ludwik had thought, every new revolution haunted by the fate of its predecessor. Lenin was obsessed with Thermidor. Power must be held at any price. The Mensheviks and Left Social Revolutionaries had been banned, together with their newspapers. Factions within the Bolshevik Party had been disbanded. All in the name of the cursed Thermidor.

He remembered Radek's account of his conversation with Rosa Luxemburg three days before her murder. 'Their terror,' Rosa told Radek in Berlin, 'never succeeded in crushing us. How can *we* rely on terror?' Radek had puffed on his pipe in silence, waiting for Ludwik or the others to ask for his reply, but no one had spoken.

Radek, irritated and impatient, had told them anyway. 'I told her bluntly. "Rosa," I said, "the world revolution is at stake here. We have to gain a few years. Terror is powerless in the hands of a doomed class against the rising tide of a new class, but it becomes powerful when applied by our side against a class which has been sentenced to death by history."'

Five voices in unison, unimpressed by the sophistry, had confronted Radek: 'What did she reply?'

Radek had glared at them. He knew all of them, knew they were veterans of the Polish underground. They had served spells in prison. They loved Rosa. Radek did not reply, but stood up quietly and left the café.

Lisa's face was shining in the soft light of the lamp. Looking up, Ludwik read worry in her eyes. They hugged each other, an embrace that owed more to despair than passion. Ludwik cupped her cheeks in his hands and kissed her lips, then her eyes. Their child was due this month. Would it find any warmth in Moscow?

He was worried about the future, yes, even at that early stage of the Revolution. They had been banking so hard on a victory in Germany, but it remained elusive. Ludwik was now almost convinced that a German revolution was impossible. The socialists were far too strongly entrenched in the factories. The countryside was hostile. The universities were dominated by German nationalism. The intelligentsia was divided and the middle classes had been scared off by the Russian Revolution. These thoughts, in the year 1924, bordered on heresy.

But what of Gertie? On the train from Berlin to Moscow, Gertie decided that she wanted Ludwik, not just for the journey, but forever. They had just seen in the New Year on the train with other passengers. Now they had retired to their compartment. Their passports showed them to be man and wife. She proposed that they become lovers.

Gently, very gently, he declined her offer, pleading emotional commitments – his wife was pregnant with their child in Moscow – and professional rules. It was bad practice, and dangerous in the extreme, for people in their field of work to get attached to each other. Lives could be put in jeopardy. Comradeship was all he could offer. Gertie tried to hide how upset she was by becoming flippant.

'You mean you aren't even a "glass-of-water" man?'

Ludwik smiled. Lenin had told Clara Zetkin – or was it Kollontai? – that sex was like drinking a glass of water. Nothing more. Nothing less. Overnight this throwaway remark had become a convenient orthodoxy for many Communists all over Europe. In consequence much water was consumed throughout the world.

'No,' Ludwik replied with a smile. 'In any case Vladimir Ilyich was only referring to his relations with Krupskaya. It was never a glass of water with Inessa, or some others I could tell you about.'

Gertie was hurt by the rebuff and angry with herself for being hurt. Once they arrived in Moscow, she became immersed in an intensive training programme. Slowly, her passion for Ludwik receded. They remained friends and after Gertie had met Ludwik's lover, Lisa, it became clear to her that any serious affair with him was permanently excluded.

Gertie had become a Comintern loyalist, a follower of Grigori Zinoviev, and would brook no challenge to the prevailing orthodoxy. She quarrelled fiercely with Ludwik in private and at party meetings to discuss the 'situation in Germany'. She would pounce like a tigress on the mildest display of what she denounced as 'petty-bourgeois pessimism'.

'Do you think the proletariat are always optimistic?' teased Ludwik, but Gertie was intoxicated, drunk on hopes and possibilities, driven by an energy that she never knew she had possessed. She was living in the capital of world revolution, meeting comrades from all corners of the world, revelling in the fear the revolution had struck in the hearts of the bourgeois and imperialist leaders in the West. She had little time for more ordinary pursuits.

One day an English journalist from a radical newspaper had come to interview Zinoviev about a letter he was supposed to have written to trade unionists in Britain. The document, known as the 'Zinoviev letter', had been crudely forged by British intelligence to embarrass the minority Labour Government. It had succeeded. Zinoviev had not been angry, but amused and, if the truth be told, flattered by the incident.

The journalist, a tall wiry man called Christopher Brown, had been impressed by Gertrude's skills as an interpreter. He invited her to dinner. She talked and talked. He listened. Her enthusiasm began to infect him. She introduced him to her friends. She took him to hear Mayakovsky, the poet who loved to step on the throat of his own poems. He was in great form that night: *'In the Soviet melting pot lies / A thin layer of mould / And from behind the back of the USSR / Peeps out the bourgeois' snout.'*

Once Brown had been sufficiently softened, it was Ludwik's turn. He spent a long time with him, questioning him in detail about the situation in Britain and in India. Brown, who had planned to spend a fortnight in Moscow, ended up staying for three months. His reports to his newspaper at home became more and more fevered.

Then two things happened. Gertrude took him as a lover and Ludwik recruited him as an undercover agent.

'We are not the foot soldiers of the world revolution,' Ludwik told him, 'but its eyes and ears. When you go back you must break publicly with us, say you were repelled by some aspects of what you saw. This means you won't have to lie. We can help with some material. I want you to leave the *Manchester Guardian* and get a job on *The Times.*'

Brown was stunned. He was not a good actor and was nervous about how he would handle his friends. He had not been prepared for duplicity on such a scale. Gertie convinced him that it was necessary. He had fallen in love with her, proposed marriage and suggested that she return with him to London. Ludwik had considered the idea seriously, but rejected it. He needed Gertrude in Germany.

Gertie and the Englishman made love every day, but when he declared his love for her, she could not contain herself no longer. Her own romantic meandering with David Stein long forgotten, she now affected to loathe all sentimentality and romance in personal relations.

'Love!' she said to Brown as they were getting into bed one night. 'Love! What does it mean? It's a disease that lays siege to the mind. It makes you irrational. I despise the very word. What a joke. Love for people like you means a nice house, children and a healthy bank balance. Love is a bourgeois concept. You've read too much romantic poetry. It's an old German disease. That is why I understand you. It's an affliction, Christopher. Get it out of your system, for heaven's sake. Poets and novelists who write just about love and tender feelings, do so because they shut their eyes to the baseness of this world. Now turn over so I can fuck you.'

Brown was shocked by her outburst. Even though he was filled with the ardour of a new convert, he knew she was wrong and he wondered what really lay beneath the eruption. But her casualness had excited him and so he did as she asked. The following week he returned to London.

Gertie had tried hard and become friends with Lisa. They talked about everything. Their early lives, their families, the break with the past and their lovers.

It was from a heavily pregnant Lisa that Gertie had first heard the story of Ludwik and his four friends.

It was a quiet Sunday. Outside it was freezing underneath a clear blue sky; the temperature had dropped again. Ludwik was due to return from Prague in the afternoon. Lisa's child was restless inside her. She felt it was a boy and imagined him as a miniature Ludwik trapped in her stomach. The thought redoubled her tenderness and she began to stroke her stomach gently and sing an old Ukrainian song her mother had sung to her as a child.

She was relieved when Gertie, wearing a Red Army greatcoat and an astrakhan, arrived well stocked with provisions. Black bread, cheese and chocolate. Soon the talk turned to Ludwik.

'When I first saw him,' she confessed to Lisa, 'he struck me as very ordinary.' They laughed at the ridiculousness of such a notion.

'That's why he's so good at his job. An average-sized small businessman from *mittel* Europe. You know in Prague he meets his agents above a tavern, which is also used as a brothel. The tavern keeper is convinced that he's a pimp!'

Gertie suddenly noticed a small, framed photograph on the mantel-piece. Five boys, dripping with water from head to toe, their faces full of mischief, caught by the camera in their strange knee-length swimming trunks.

'Can you recognize Ludwik?' Lisa asked her.

'Which one is he?'

'Guess!'

Gertie guessed. Lisa smiled.

'Have you met the others?'

Gertie shook her head.

'I think you must have. They're all in the same department as you.'

'But that's impossible. All of them?'

Lisa nodded. Just then she felt a contraction and clutched her stomach. Gertie put down her glass of tea and began to gently massage Lisa's neck and shoulders.

'It seems close, Gertie. I really need Ludwik. I want him now. You're sure he'll be back today?'

'Yes, of course. Where did you first meet him? Were you from the same village?'

'No!' Lisa gave a rich, throaty laugh. 'I was a Lemberg girl. I met him in Vienna at the university. All five of them were there, each studying something different. Ludwik was studying literature. He was the funniest, made me laugh a lot. Those were carefree days, just before the outbreak of war. We lived in a safe world – or so we thought. The Dual Monarchy had been there forever. If someone had told us that soon there would be a war that would trigger a revolution that would destroy the Tsar, the Kaiser and the Emperor, we would have laughed and sent him off to see Dr Freud.'

'Is Ludwik his real name?'

Lisa smiled, but did not reply. Gertrude knew she could go no further. One of the first lessons she had been taught in the Department was that she was never to reveal her true identity, even to her closest friends. It was vital for her own security in the field. She had to forget the past.

'Whatever happened to Krystina?'

'Died in Baku last year. Typhus. Her five Ls carried the coffin. You should have seen them that day. These men are veterans of the revolution; four of them are heroes of the civil war. They wept like children, loudly and for a long time. I have never seen Ludwik in such a state. I think it was the death of innocence – a farewell to their youth. Poor Krystina.'

'You didn't like her, Lisa?'

'Not really. She had such a hold on Ludwik. I was jealous. I knew their friendship was not physical, but it was deep. Too deep for me. Yes, I was jealous and it showed. To be honest, I felt nothing much when she died. It made me sad to see how upset they all were, but secretly I was relieved. There, I've got it off my chest. I think it was mutual. She always kept me at arm's length. She disapproved of our relationship. It was too much like a marriage.'

'A "glass-of-water" woman?'

'Probably. I know that none of our five men slept with her. She was put on a pedestal and worshipped, a true Bolshevik madonna. I doubt we would have agreed to have a child if Krystina had still been alive. She was strongly opposed. When I told her once that having a child would help, since Ludwik and I would be accepted anywhere in Europe as a bourgeois couple, she looked at me with such anger that none of us could speak for several minutes. Then, her face pale with rage, she said: "We are revolutionaries, engaged in dangerous work. We are trying to banish fear from our hearts. A child stops us doing that. We worry too much, we become cowards." Her voice was full of contempt.'

Lisa stopped suddenly and clutched her womb. Her waters had broken. There was a midwife in the building who had already been alerted, but where was Ludwik? As Gertie went to fetch the midwife, she heard the big entrance door to the barracks heave open and in walked Ludwik, looking cheerful and loaded with packages of different sizes. He smiled on seeing her; his eyes asked her whether he was too late, but Gertie smiled.

'Not yet, but soon. Just in time, Ludwik.'

He grinned. 'I always am.'

Little Felix was born a few minutes before the clock struck midnight.

'I knew it was a boy. It had to be a boy,' Lisa said a few minutes after giving birth and just before demanding a mug of hot chocolate. Later, as she sipped her drink, she told them why.

'If it had been a girl, he would have insisted on naming her Krystina. I don't like ghosts.'

'Look at him. Look at Felix,' crooned Ludwik, ignoring her remark. 'He's just like the Revolution: ugly and insolent!'

Gertrude, who lived a few kilometres from the old barracks where Ludwik and other Fourth Department operatives were housed, was walking back to her room. Outside, behind the black birch trees, a full moon was in motion. The ground was covered with snow. She walked slowly, very slowly, trying to keep pace with the moon.

Seeing the joy in Ludwik's eyes as he held his newborn child had awakened suppressed passions in her. She did not feel any guilt. Does a volcano feel guilty when it realizes that it is no longer dormant?

Nine

I N 1928, Ludwik had been awarded the Order of the Red Banner, the highest military honour of the Soviet Republic. The citation had referred to the services he had rendered to the world revolution –

services that could not be listed for reasons of security. Lisa knew that he had established networks in several European countries, but the Red Banner was for something very special.

For a moment she wondered if he had killed an important enemy. He denied that strongly. Till now, he told her, he had not killed anyone. Not that a single death mattered too much. This was a generation that had known the First World War, when the Germans alone had lost nearly two million people. The Great War had devalued death, devalued human lives to such an extent that killing the odd individual did not pose moral problems for either side in the interwar years. If not a strategically important murder, then what else could it be? Lisa was genuinely puzzled.

'What did you do, Ludwik? Please tell me. Was it dangerous?'

He never did tell her. Ludwik concealed most of his exploits on special missions from her. He did not want her implicated if they were ever arrested by the other side. Lisa understood the reasons for his caution, but that did not prevent her from being irritated by his secretiveness. There had been a time, she told herself, when they had no secrets from each other. Throughout the years of civil war neither of them had felt the need to hide anything from each other. She often pestered him for details of the affair that had led to the medal, but he had always refused.

Years later she discovered that the events had taken place while they were in Amsterdam in 1927, the only time when the three of them had come close to leading a normal existence. Ludwik had set up a stationery shop to establish a cover. Lisa had run it so well that the wretched enterprise had started making a profit, much to their surprise and to the great amusement of Berzin and the rest of the gang in Moscow.

It was Hans the painter, one of Ludwik's oldest comrades and agents, who had told her last winter, while visiting Paris. Hans had been genuinely surprised that she had not been told. They always assumed she knew everything.

'You mean he never told you?'

Lisa shook her head and frowned. Hans lit his pipe, and in his Dutch-inflected German told her the whole story. 'Your Ludwik always made everything sound so simple. One day he came to my studio. "Pack your bags, my friend. We're off on a trip." The next thing I knew we were in London, where we stayed with Olga. You know her? No? It doesn't matter. We stayed for three days. On the first day, Ludwik took me for a walk: Trafalgar Square, Buckingham Palace, the House of Commons. You know, the usual tourist jaunt. Then he showed me their Foreign Office. "Look at that building carefully, Hans." I did. To me it was just like the others. Imperialist architecture. I shrugged my shoulders. "Forget the aesthetic side for a minute, comrade. This is the centre of their International. World counter-revolution is planned and executed from that building. We've got to get someone in there." I laughed at the joke and so did Ludwik. I forgot about it all till we returned to Amsterdam.

'The following week we had dinner together at your house. Suddenly he said to me: "You know, I wasn't joking." I couldn't even remember what he was talking about. I really had forgotten the whole episode. He reminded me. I thought he was going mad. How could I, a Dutch painter, with very bad English, get anyone into any place in London, let alone their Foreign Office? But Ludwik, as always, had a plan. It could easily have been a disaster. In fact, I was convinced it would fail. Instead it succeeded. Are you sure you don't want to go out and eat now?'

'No, you idiot,' Lisa almost shouted at him. 'Finish the story first.'

'It was a simple plan, so simple that any old fool could have thought of it, but your Ludwik was never any old fool. Was he? Behind the simplicity of his plans there is always a touch of genius, which is more than can be said for my paintings.'

'Hans,' Lisa pleaded, 'just tell me.'

'It was a three-stage operation. I'm beginning even to sound like him now. First I was to go to Geneva and set up a studio. During the day, he told me, I could paint or fornicate or both. My evenings were in the service of the Fourth Department. Are you wondering why Geneva?'

'The League of Nations?'

'Exactly. And in the League a British Delegation. And in the British Delegation a few cryptographers. I was to find one of them and befriend him. It wasn't easy, what with my poor command of English, but Ludwik showed up and soon obtained a description of two of the cryptographers and where they drank in the evenings.

'For two weeks I observed them closely. I decided – don't ask me why, pure instinct, I guess – to go for the older of the two, a very intelligent man from a lower middle-class background, fluent in German, French and Russian. That solved the communication problem. We became good friends. First stage was complete.

'After a few months I confessed my communist sympathies, discussed the Russian Revolution and all that sort of business. Then I introduced him to Ludwik. Within three weeks, Lisa, your husband had recruited our English friend to the ranks of the Communist International. He was an intelligent fellow, grasped the arguments very quickly. He really did know the English ruling class. The stories he told us about Curzon were funny and vicious. He had a real contempt for the men who ruled his country. One day Ludwik casually popped the question. Just like that, you know, and David agreed to work for us. We now had someone at the very heart of their world-wide operations. It had cost us not a penny. Pure politics. All that has gone now, but in those days...' Hans paused to clean and relight his pipe.

'And stage three, Hans?'

'Simple,' he said, his voice devoid of emotion. 'When David had ended his tour of duty in Geneva he went back to the Foreign Office in London. Ludwik transferred me there as well, but this time as a photographer. I set up a tiny shop and studio in Fleet Street, specializing in portraits. I earned more money than I ever had from my paintings. Ludwik always told us that whatever cover we used, it must be real. To be a complete fake was a serious risk.'

Lisa laughed, remembering their stationery shop in Amsterdam. Hans guessed the cause of her amusement.

'Your shop, eh? Exactly! I had always been interested in photography. Ludwik made me a professional. I started selling photographs to newspapers in England and on the Continent, but always to serious bourgeois papers. He told me never to contact any left newspaper. And some of the pictures I took were good, really good. So I became a fixture on Fleet Street. Everyone knew how I earned a living. Once a week, the cryptographer, David, would arrive from the Foreign Office. We would meet in a restaurant or café. He would take out a sheaf of papers. I would take them back to my studio, photograph every single page, and then rush back to the café and return them to him. He would breathe easily and depart. That same afternoon I would process the material and that same evening, a courier would collect the stuff and off it would go to Moscow. There were occasions when Moscow read the documents before they reached the Foreign Secretary or Downing Street. For that master-stroke, they gave Ludwik the Order of the Red Banner.'

'What happened to David the cryptographer?'

'You won't believe it,' Hans's eyes disappeared as his face creased with laughter. 'David was transferred to the British Embassy in Moscow!'

Ten

'**W**HY IS HE ALWAYS LATE, Mama? Why?' Felix's voice, as he stood there with his freshly cut, washed and combed light blond hair, had a desperate ring. It was his tenth birthday. He had demanded and been promised a celebratory meal at the Sacher, and Lisa had ordered a special cake to mark the occasion.

Felix was dressed in a dark brown three-piece suit – his first – and a red tie. He had now perfected the art of tying his own knot in the shape and style he wanted, although it had taken him an hour in front of the mirror. Felix was excited, but where was Ludwik?

Lisa too, was smartly attired in a cream silk blouse, a long beige skirt and matching jacket. Her fur coat was resting on an armchair, ready to protect her from the cold outside.

'Will he come today, Mama?'

She smiled at her son and stroked his head lightly, trying to conceal her own worry. It had always been the same. Whenever he was late, she imagined the worst. Death. An unmarked grave. The torment of not knowing if he was dead or alive! During the civil war when Red and White detachments had fought hand-to-hand battles, death, compared to the survival of the Revolution, had been of little account. More importantly, she, too, had been on the front as a Commissar. Both of them had faced similar dangers, and this had made the separation bearable. In fact, the problems she confronted with her detachment had meant that she barely had time to think of Ludwik.

Now her task was to keep up the appearance of a good mother and wife. And there was Felix. She recalled Krystina's warning about how children adversely affected one's revolutionary commitment. Lisa permitted herself a wry smile. Clever Krystina. She knew.

Everything had become much worse since the fascist victory in Germany. Berlin, for so long a city on which so many dreams and hopes had been pinned, had gone over to the enemy. Ludwik and Gertrude had been there for over two weeks. He was reorganizing the clandestine networks, finding out how many of his agents were in prison, meeting those still at liberty, to ascertain in the most delicate fashion possible whether any of them had, in some way, been touched by the Brown flood which was sweeping the country.

Lisa missed Ludwik more than she had thought possible. There were times when her entire being was filled with an overwhelming longing for him. She recalled his voice, his body-movements and gestures, felt the touch of his hand on her face, smelled the scent of the coffee at the Zentrale where they had met in the first few days of their courtship. At moments like this she became paralysed, incapable of doing anything, and distracted from her Ludwik-thoughts only by the insistent voice of her son.

'Mama?'

'My child, listen to me. We shall wait ten more minutes. Then you will escort your mother to the restaurant. We shall eat, drink a toast to your health and enjoy ourselves.'

Felix's eyes filled with tears. Lisa knelt down and hugged him tightly to her bosom.

'Wherever your father is, and I'm sure he's on a train nearing Vienna, you can be sure he's thinking of you. Let's not wait any longer. Let's go.'

Mother and son walked out of the apartment block arm in arm. Outside it was cold and dark. They had to wait some time for a tram; both of them were shivering. As the doorman outside the Sacher held the doors open for them, they sighed with relief. The warmth was welcoming. Felix looked up at Lisa and smiled. They handed their coats to the cloakroom attendant and made their way into the restaurant. As the head waiter was accompanying them to the table, specially reserved in Felix's name, the boy's eyes lit up. Decorum disappeared.

'Papa! Papa!'

Ludwik put down his newspaper and rose from the table to embrace and kiss his son. Lisa stared at him, trying hard to control her emotions. He was safe.

'Well now,' said Ludwik in his most paternal voice. 'Trust the pair of you to be late. I thought we were due here at eight precisely. You have kept me waiting.'

Felix laughed with delight. His father handed him a small parcel. Felix undid the string, his pleasure unrestrained: a new stamp album and several little brown envelopes bursting with stamps. The collapse of the Hapsburgs had led to the birth of new countries, and this meant new stamps. Felix specialized in Central and Eastern Europe. His father's never-ending travels had one positive feature – they helped to enhance the stamp collection. Felix began to inspect the swastikas and brown shirts on the new German stamps.

'How was Berlin?' Asked in a normal voice, Lisa's question was anything but banal.

'Not good. Most of our friends have disappeared.'

Nothing more was said. They were sure that Felix, even though he asked very few questions, took in much more than they ever realized. He was no longer an infant and so, over the last few years, their conversations in his presence had become more and more coded.

Lisa leaned over and stroked Ludwik's face. His eyes smiled. He took her hand and kissed it. They had been in Vienna for just over a year and had scrupulously avoided old haunts and most of their old political friends. But it was impossible to seal off the past so completely. Too many old memories lay hidden in Vienna. Both of them were thinking of the old days and smiling. Felix brought them back to the present.

'Mama, can I have another ice-cream?'

'Of course,' replied his father, 'today is your day. Eat whatever you like.'

'Ludwik,' said Lisa, 'did I ever tell you why I used to sip coffee at the Landtmann?'

'Because it was near the university, because you were not interested in politics, because your stupid boyfriend insisted, because you wanted to study how Alma Mahler preserved her beauty?'

Felix laughed.

'No, you fool,' Lisa rapped Ludwik lightly on the knuckles with a dessert spoon. 'It was to catch a glimpse of Sigmund Freud.'

'At the Zentrale, my boy,' Ludwik told his son, 'we could watch something of far greater interest than Dr Freud. We used to watch Adler and Trotsky playing chess!'

'Who won?' inquired Felix.

Later that night, after Felix was sound asleep, Ludwik unburdened himself. He told Lisa that the situation in Germany was irretrievable in the immediate future. 'We have suffered a defeat that will change the map of Europe. Of that I'm sure. It could have been avoided if those fools in Moscow had understood that...'

'Trotsky was right.' There was anger in Lisa's voice.

'Yes, that too. It's too late now. Communists and Social Democrats are being taken in trucks to prison camps. Now they will unite against Hitler. A unity imposed by the graveyard.'

'And Gertrude? Is she still in Berlin?'

'No. I sent her to Munich, to find out if our organization was intact. I got one message from her before I left. Our people are still in place, but her father is losing most of his non-Jewish patients, even though he supports Hitler.'

'Ludo...?'

'What?'

'You and Gertrude. Did you . . . ?'

'What?'

'It's obvious she finds you very attractive. I just thought you might . . .'

'You thought *what*? You big idiot. Do you think she's my type? You might as well ask if I've been making love to an aubergine with spectacles!'

'It's not a question of types, Ludo. Comradeship. Loneliness. Many other things suddenly become important for our people. You know that well. I just want to know the truth.'

Realizing that she was serious, Ludwik changed his tone. 'By now you should know me better. I'm not Richard Sorge. Or am I?' Lisa smiled. Sorge's promiscuity was the subject of never-ending gossip in the Fourth Department headquarters in Moscow. The intelligence chiefs regarded Sorge as their most capable agent, but were worried that his sexual delinquency coupled with his vodka habit might one day let in the enemy.

'Ludwik, don't play games.'

'She made me a proposition.'

'I thought as much.'

'I refused.'

'Why?'

'Because it would have meant much more to her than to me. And there is no physical attraction on my part. None whatsoever. Is that clear? Or do you wish to carry on the interrogation? If so, I suggest you call in two other Ls. They're better at it than you.'

'I love you, Ludwik.'

'I know, so please stop this business now.'

Later still, after they had made love and Ludwik, exhausted and happy, was half asleep, Lisa returned to the subject.

'Wake up, Ludo. I haven't seen you for weeks. You can sleep as long as you like in the morning.'

He groaned and opened his eyes, protest written all over his face. Pleased that he had obeyed her, Lisa asked in her most innocent and beguiling fashion, 'If someone is in a strange land, working very hard, and suddenly feels thirsty, surely a glass of water is permissible.'

'Oh, not all that again.'

'Answer!'

'Yes, it is permissible.'

'For women as well as men.'

'Of course!'

'No restrictions.'

'A few. If the water is polluted, the use of a filter is essential.'

She laughed. 'That's all?'

'I think so.'

'What if drinking from the same glass regularly becomes a habit?'

'Then one has to ask whether the drinker is satisfying a thirst or whether he has become addicted to the glass.'

'Thank you, Herr Ludwik. Let me know if ever you become addicted to a glass. Agreed?'

'I vow to thee, comrade Lisa,' said Ludwik mimicking Stalin.

'Stop. You're not in a state to discuss anything serious tonight. Let's go to sleep.'

'I was asleep,' moaned Ludwik.

After Felix had been despatched to school the next morning, Ludwik sat down at his typewriter, his code book in front of him, and began to tap out a detailed but controlled report on the situation in Germany. He restricted himself to the bare facts, avoiding the temptation to savage the crazed sectarianism unleashed by Moscow at the Sixth Congress of the Comintern. The leaders of the world revolution had declared social democracy to be the principal enemy and called for an unremitting struggle against its organizations.

And fascism? 'First Hitler, then our turn' had been the flip response. Even a hint of how he felt would have led to his recall, disgrace, perhaps even execution. There was work to be done in Europe, especially now that Hitler was in power. Austrian independence was likely to be the first casualty. The situation was getting worse. Ludwik knew they would have to move to another city before the end of the year.

The sky was cloudless and there was no breeze; the warmth of the sun indicated that spring was not far behind. The report safely delivered to the Soviet Embassy for immediate transmission, Ludwik breathed the crisp mid-morning air and walked briskly towards the Zentrale to keep an appointment. Teddy, one of his Hungarians stationed in Vienna, had sounded excited.

'You'd better meet him for yourself, Ludo. He'll be working under you. If we're about to make a mistake, it had better be your mistake. Otherwise Bortnotsky will say: "You mean you took the Hungarians at their word?"'

Ludwik smiled. The rivalry between the Poles and the Hungarians working for the Fourth Department had given rise to jokes on both sides. He wondered about the Englishman. Why were they all so impressed?

As he walked into the Zentrale he saw them sitting at a corner table.

Ludwik ignored them and went and sat at a distance from where he could observe them without being seen himself. The woman was clearly a Hungarian. She had those slightly wild Magyar eyes and was probably one of Teddy's mistresses. Most men had glasses of water. Teddy believed in drinking straight from the jug till it was drained. This jug still seemed to be half full. The affair was not over.

He examined the Englishman closely and was instinctively pleased with what he saw: a conventional type, properly dressed in a three-piece suit. He didn't seem to be saying very much, which was also good. Was this the famous English reserve or was he of a withdrawn and introvert temperament? How ridiculous, Ludwik told himself. Instincts are notoriously wrong. This fellow may be none of these things. He may be a loud-mouthed drunk on his best behaviour. Impossible to tell at a first sighting, but the appearance is positive.

When Teddy looked at him, Ludwik nodded and walked towards their table. The two men embraced.

'I'm Ludwik,' he said, shaking hands with the woman and staring straight into the Englishman's eyes.

'Hannah,' said the woman with a smile which revealed a set of perfect teeth.

'Philby,' said the Englishman with a slight stammer, as he proffered his hand to Ludwik.

Eleven

'THEY WERE SO YOUNG,' a middle-aged woman from Hanoi kept repeating. 'So much hate written on their faces. So young, so evil.'

A pregnant woman, barely twenty-five years old, told Sao of how she had been kicked in the belly.

'And all the time he kept talking about the old days. "All you foreigners should be gassed, just like the Jews." They haven't forgotten the past, you know. They think of it all the time, with affection.'

The voices kept reverberating in his head.

Sao was sipping tea in Vlady's kitchen. His relaxed and well-groomed face was tense; he had been listening to horror stories for one whole day. His cousin, her friends, women old and young, schoolboys, had told him in great detail what had happened on that night over a year ago, when their hostel had been set on fire by a fascist mob. Sao had read about the affair in *Le Monde*, but that had not prepared him for the tales they had told him in Rostock yesterday. 'I can't tell you any more, Vlady. You talk.'

Vlady looked at his friend. 'Why are you surprised? You were almost castrated in Dresden one night and that was during the DDR days. What a strange sound. DDR days. If they could do it then, it was only a matter of time before the explosion. Rostock is by no means the worst. At least no one was killed. In Sollingen they burnt the Turks.'

Sao shouted at him, his voice becoming squeaky, a sure sign that he was both tired and losing control. 'What are you trying to say, you deluded arsehole? That the Westies are more beastly than the Easties? It was pure luck that nobody was killed in Rostock. Our sense of solidarity saved us! Everyone helped each other.'

'I know – and not just Vietnamese. German families gave shelter. Calm down, Sao. Please. You come here after a long absence and are shocked. I live here. Of course it's horrible, but no worse than France or Italy. There they burn Africans. The new fascists are a European phenomenon. The pattern is the same in England and in Sweden. That doesn't mean it's less nasty here, but please don't join in the chorus of Germany on the brink of a Fourth Reich. We are not a few decades away from fascism. They don't need it any more. History repeats itself the second time as farce.'

'That's a joke in itself. A clever but thoughtless remark by the old philosopher, Karl Marx trying to be Oscar Wilde. A stray sentence transformed into an eternal truth by the party faithful. Spare me your homilies, Vlady, as my uncle in Louisiana is forever telling me. Not today. Let's talk about something else.'

For a minute neither of them spoke. Vlady sighed, but did not say anything.

'Do you miss lecturing?' Sao asked him.

'There were times when I found it more wearying to give a single lecture than making love three times over.'

'What if you had made love four times or five or six, would you still have felt less tired? Surely the tongue is busy in both cases. It's the signals from the brain that are different. Sometimes I just don't understand you at all, Vlady.'

Vlady laughed. Normal service had been resumed. Sao was his usual self again. And yet the visit to Rostock had clearly unnerved him. 'What was it that really upset you, Sao?'

'The fire.'

'I understand.'

'No, you don't Vlady. When I was sixteen years old I had a sweetheart, a girl called Dua. She was a year older than me. Her father was fighting in the south. We had been evacuated from Hanoi to a small village, twenty kilometres from Haiphong. When we had finished our work in the village, Dua and I would walk a few kilometres and sit on a rock. Below us we could see the sun set on Halong Bay. The dragon-shaped rocks reflected the sun for a few magical moments. It was as if they had become a real dragon. And then the sun disappeared and for a few minutes we basked in the twilight as the water changed colours. "Nature's paintings," Dua would whisper, and we would hold each other tight.

'It was the height of the war, but it was the most beautiful moment of my life. Everything seemed pure. After the war, I used to say to myself, I will travel the world with her.' Sao became silent, overpowered by the memory. Then he resumed his story.

'I went to Hanoi for the New Year that February to see my father. There was a two-day ceasefire. On my way back I heard the bombers. For two whole days I couldn't approach the village. We were hiding in caves. The third, I managed to get back. There was nothing left, Vlady. Nothing except the charred remains of our homes and friends. Dua had been burnt alive. She had been sitting in a jeep with some friends. The human cinder was still there and recognizable. Her flesh was petrified, but I recognized her, Vlady. I recognized her.'

Vlady wanted to hug his friend, console him, tell him about how Gertrude's entire family had perished in the camps. Sao and I have more in common than he imagines, thought Vlady, but he could not speak. His eyes filled with tears. He rose and walked slowly to the window. The faithful old gnarled pear tree was still there. As a child, when he was feeling upset, Vlady had found the old tree strangely reassuring. The memory brought a smile to his face and he returned to the table. Sao was smiling again. He was in a more philosophical mood.

'I don't think the gods ever intended humanity to be happy.'

'Is it really as bad as that, Sao?'

'It's worse, Vlady, much worse. Look at me. I have wealth, a beautiful French wife, two children. I can go where I please and do what I want. Money is my global passport. I am content, but am I happy? No.'

'Why not?'

'You of all people ask me that?'

'Yes. You were never a very political person. Can't you see that your life is a paradise for the majority of our citizens, East and West? If they had even a tiny percentage of what you possess, there would not be burnings in Rostock. And another thing, Sao. You're looking much better than ever before. This new life suits you. All your

Today, in Sao's presence, he had been unable to repress his father-anxieties, which had tormented him since he was a child. Sometimes, Vlady would imagine what his relationship with a father might be like. Whole conversations would be constructed. His views on fatherhood were derived largely from fiction and, as a result, were not fixed. The opening pages of *The Radetsky March,* Joseph Roth's masterpiece, were enough to put him in a truculent mood, banish all sentimental thoughts, and get him thanking history for depriving him of a father. Today his mood was different. Roth's corrosive cynicism did not enter his thoughts at all. Instead, he was thinking of his son, Karl, and wondering to what extent his own failure as a father was related to his not having had one.

He sat down at his desk, cleared his typewriter and decided to write a letter to Karl. He might or might not complete the memoirs. They would probably remain a set of disjointed, chaotic memories of his life. Karl would understand; the boy had always been good at deciphering puzzles. In the meantime, thought Vlady, I owe him a letter.

My dear Karl,

After you rang on my birthday I was filled with remorse. Why hadn't I been more warm? We, who were once so close, can only speak to each other in formal and strained tones. This pains me and hence this letter to you, my son. What can I write to you after a four-year gap? There is so much to tell you — and yet I don't know where to start. Should I begin where it hurts the most? You think your mother left because I was having an affair with Evelyne. This is not true. Helge never elevated the personal above the political. This is a fact, Karl. It was an article of faith for your mother, your grandmother and myself.

In any event I want you to know something. Your mother's departure was the worst personal blow that I have suffered. I lost something very precious. After Gerhard's death, it was Helge who was my closest friend and companion. We talked about everything (yes, including Evelyne). We consoled each other over the political and personal losses we suffered. Her decision to go to New York was so sudden, so extraordinary, that it left me speechless. I wanted to go down on my knees, to plead with her to stay, to tell her that life without her was unthinkable, but before I recovered from the shock she had gone.

There was one occasion when I felt so depressed that I contemplated following Gerhard's example. Except that he parted company with our world for reasons of state and I, low in self-esteem and extremely lonely, was simply feeling sorry for myself.

When you were ten or eleven, we took you to see Brecht's

Threepenny Opera. *You loved the actor who played Macheath. He was an old friend of Gertrude and afterwards, when we went to his dressing room, he sang 'Mac the Knife' especially for you. Remember? He won't be singing again. Like Gerhard, he too, took his own life. He had been in a state of depression ever since the return of the old order. Personally he had no problems — he had received acting offers from Hamburg, and was not short of money. He had no connections with the Stasi and nobody even accused him of that, but he was unhappy. He simply could not bear to live in the new Germany. What he hated most was the undeniable fact that our people voted for the Christian Democrats, that everything had changed so quickly and there was no space left, at least in his lifetime, even to hope. So he decided that there was no point in living. Even in the darkest years of this century, when it seemed that the Third Reich might prevail over Europe, few people of our persuasion took such an extreme step. Why now? Because a heavy greyness is gnawing at our soul and some of us find it difficult to sing our swan songs to the bitter end. This century has been one of pain, ugliness and anguish.*

Christian mythology regards suicide as a sin. Secular systems today treat suicide as a crime, which is ridiculous, for if the 'crime' is successful the perpetrator can never be punished. Christian fantasists are, at least, more consistent, since they believe in the migration of souls.

Their most gifted poet places 'The Wood of the Suicides' in the Seventh Circle of Hell, close to the centre of the Inferno. The trees and bushes in this wood have flowered from the souls of the suicides on earth and for Dante even the souls are polluted, for his wood has 'No green leaves . . . no smooth branches . . . no fruit, but thorns of poison.'

Why should we accept all this rubbish? Taking one's own life is an extreme step and, of course, there are numerous examples of people driven to self-destruction by a momentary fit of insanity or a deep shock from which they imagine they could never recover. They need help, treatment, whatever. But there are others. Gerhard and Macheath, for example, who have thought about the matter long and hard and have come to the conclusion that they would rather die than live in this world. However painful it is for us, their survivors, they have a right to decide their own future. Individual self-determination! Do you agree? Will your children-yet-to-come agree? Who knows. Are you surprised that I think like this now? Do you think my rationale is intensely solipsistic and too existentialist? Do you think it runs counter to my socialist instincts which should compel me to regard people as part of a community, a network? Perhaps it does, but this is an emergency, Karl. They have deliberately destroyed our self-respect, our dignity as human beings, and that has also rent our community asunder. Sometimes existential choices are the only solutions for individuals.

Try and understand your parents, Karl. You owe us at least that much. I know you're angry. You feel wounded. You think that Helge and I were obsessed with the Idea, that it finally imploded, and this has made you suspicious of all ideas. And yet you know full well that our Idea was not the DDR. You can make many criticisms of Marx, but to hold him responsible for our so-called socialist experiences is unfair. Leave that to the demagogues.

I can imagine you reading this. DDR: the initials make you flinch now. And yet there were many who were prepared to try and make even this wretched system work. Your grandmother, Gertrude, for one – but not just her. Hundreds of thousands of ordinary working people who hoped that after the horrors of the war, they could build a decent house, with decent furniture. Alas, this was not to be. The foundations of the DDR were laid on the shoulders of the Red Army and the furniture which Ulbricht and Honecker found was third-hand junk – cast-offs from the Lubianka prison in Moscow. And yet, I ask myself: would they have permitted the Vietnamese or Turks to be burnt alive? I don't think so, if only in order to preserve their law and order. Our sad country has made itself known for sending millions to the gas chamber during the fascist period. Burning foreign workers and their families is a new democratic privilege. I suppose we must get used to it, like everything else. Your leaders say it is a crime, but what of the police who let it happen and, worse, our citizens who stand idly by or cross the road just like their grandparents did on Kristallnacht in the thirties or when they saw Jews being carted off in trains to the camps? When ordinary people lose their humanity, it reflects badly on the state whose citizens they are.

When the demonstrations began in Dresden and Berlin, Helge and I were filled with joy. We believed that we could remove the filth from here without importing the muck from where you are now, but it was utopian. Bonn's inevitable hegemony was predetermined by its economic strength. That we, of all people, should have failed to register this reality was an indication that we were stuck on the ninth cloud, loving the whole world. Your mother was always a pillar of strength for me, a tree trunk I could lean against. We talked about everything. There were no secrets, except one, and that destroyed us in the end. I will tell you about it after we have become friends again. To tell you now would be to lose you forever and I don't want that to happen. I feel lost without Helge, crippled, functioning with only half an engine, and could crash anytime. Do you understand what I'm saying?

There are times when I wonder whether I could ever have been the *father you needed or wanted. I remember once when I hit you really hard on the face. I can't remember now what you'd done and that alone indicates it must have been something trivial, some stupid challenge to my patriarchal authority. But I can remember the horror written on your face. You were about twelve. My unexpected violence was an act of total betrayal as far as you were concerned. You would not speak to me for a week. I really had to plead with you to forgive me. I often wondered where that blow came from. You see, not having known a father, my points of reference are limited. Paternal brutality is passed from father to son till the chain is broken, but I was not brutalized as a child and Gertrude insisted that Ludwik, your grandfather, was the kindest person she had ever known. I will tell you his story one day, when I know it all myself. Your Uncle Sao is helping me to trace the last details through his contacts with Moscow. Perhaps your son will be the one who will really be able to understand this century, from the distance of the next.*

On the phone you invited me to visit you in Bonn. It's not my favourite German city. Why don't we meet in Munich next month? Leviné is buried there. I would like to see you, and also visit the Jewish cemetery. Pay a belated tribute to a good man, by-passed by history. I know how that feels. Except for the difference in time. Leviné lived when there was still hope. My generation has given up 'all hope of ever seeing Heaven'. We are being led 'into eternal darkness, ice and fire', though I'm sure you don't see it like that from your apartment in Bonn. Do you think this is just another of my romantic illusions: a utopia missed in a bygone decade? You may think you're right, but you're wrong. Are you laughing?

I am.

Write to me soon.

Love,

Vlady.

(Your father!)

After he had typed out Karl's address on the plain brown envelope, Vlady had second thoughts. Perhaps the letter would only annoy his son further, but Vlady was in no mood to confess everything. Not yet. Perhaps in a year's time. Should he tear up the letter? Drop him a banal postcard instead? Pity Sao had left, or he could have asked his advice. In desperate situations like this Vlady consulted his bookshelves, in much the same fashion as those who are more mystically inclined approach an astrologer who usually tells them what they want to hear. Vlady decided on a poet. Pushkin. He climbed on a stool and gently removed a copy of the *Collected Works* from the top shelf, where the

Russian poets all lived. He sat on the edge of his desk and opened the book. He was in luck today and began to read aloud:

> a crowd of oppressive thoughts
> Throngs my anguished mind; silently
> Before me, Memory unfolds its long scroll;
> And with loathing, reading the chronicle of my life,
> I tremble and curse, and shed bitter tears,
> But I do not wash away these sad lines.

Pushkin's advice was followed. The envelope was sealed, stamped and posted. As he walked back from the letter-box, Vlady's thoughts shifted to his mother.

'Mutti, when did you fall in love with Father?'

She had been startled by the question, but had recovered immediately. 'I think in Berlin. Yes, definitely. In a the bar off the Fürstenhof in Berlin.'

'And did you travel together a lot?'

'So many questions, Vlady. I never seem to be able to satisfy your curiosity. We travelled everywhere. Moscow, Paris, Berlin and, of course Vienna. I remember I had to deliver an important message to him in Vienna in 1934. We met at the Zentrale, even though it was packed with Nazi spies and Mussolini's agents. Ludwik thought it was safe because they were mainly spying on each other, trying to find out whether the Austrian Nationalists would opt for Italy or Germany...'

Yes, Vlady thought, she always had a good story to divert his mind from what he really wanted to know. One day after he had been questioning her persistently, she told him that his father had first made love to her in Vienna, in her hotel room on a cold February morning, and they had stood naked at the window and watched the snow on the pavements.

The details had convinced Vlady at the time, but not now. Now he doubted everything she had ever told him. His mind was permanently engaged in an attempt to decipher what was true and distinguish it from the falsehoods which he now knew had dominated his conversations with Gertrude.

The world that had made his mother tell lies, the world that had compromised him morally, made him feel sick in himself, that world now lay in ruins. This fact alone should have made him feel happy. But he was not happy.

Twelve

I T WAS FEBRUARY 1934. Gertrude spent many months in Vienna that year, working directly for Ludwik and Teddy. She never forget what happened there and, of all her stories, this one never changed.

Vienna had begun to turn nasty. The Germans used to joke that the 'Austrians were bad Nazis but good anti-Semites'. Gertrude once told me how a Jewish and non-Jewish member of the Socialist party were captured by some Brownshirts and locked up in a tiny room. Every half hour or so, the captors would rush into the room, stand on the table and piss on the heads of the two men. The Jewish socialist was forced to repeat rhythmically: 'I am a stinking Jew', while his friend was forced to repeat in tandem, 'And I desire to become a German'. This went on for the whole night. Then the men were released.

David Frohmann wasn't so lucky. Like his father and grandfather before him, he was a watchmaker. One morning he noticed a group of young Brownshirts hovering outside his shop. One of them was the son of an old friend, a shopkeeper a few doors down. Frohmann was just about to open the shop. Before he could do so the Brownshirts kicked in the glass door and entered the shop. They smashed the display cabinets, grabbed Frohmann by the neck and rubbed his face in the broken glass. One of them, drunk on hatred, shouted 'Let's kill the Jew'. Frohmann, his face bleeding, writhed on the ground, trying to avoid their kicks. A bystander finally gave the alarm and the young thugs ran away. What they could not steal, they had wrecked.

Felix, wearing a fur hat with ear muffs, the top of his face covered by one of Ludwik's old brown scarves, rushed home from school the day after this incident in a state of considerable agitation. His best friend, Erich Frohmann, who had missed school yesterday, had arrived late today and been tearful throughout lessons. On being teased by the school bully he had lashed out wildly.

Felix, upset for his friend, had fetched their teacher. During the lunch-break, Erich told Felix what had happened to his father the previous day. In hospital where he was being X-rayed and his wounds treated, he had suffered a heart attack. His condition was serious.

Erich's mother had insisted he go to school while she kept vigil at his father's bedside. After school that day, Felix had pleaded with his friend to come home with him, but Erich had refused, saying he was needed at the hospital.

For the first time Felix realized that the swastikas sprouting on almost every Viennese street meant danger and death. When Lisa opened the door of their apartment to let him in, Felix put his arms round her and burst into tears. She let him cry and gently stroked his head. When his sobs had subsided she questioned him gently and in a few short bursts Felix recounted the tragedy that had befallen his friend.

Lisa put on her coat and gloves. In Ludwik's field of work it was an iron law that the family must not attract attention to itself or become too involved in local friendships, but she felt it was important for Felix that she behave like a normal human being and not conceal her maternal reflexes. Their son's formative years could not be totally determined by the exigencies of the Fourth Department. She took Felix by the arm.

'Come. We're going to see Erich and his father at the hospital.'

It was too late. Erich's father was dead. Erich and his mother had already gone home. Lisa and Felix took a tram to Helengistadt.

Erich and his family lived in the Karl Marx Hof, apartment blocks designed for workers and constructed by the Socialist administration of Vienna. People stuck together here, looked after each other. There was a strong sense of belonging to one community. Solidarity prevailed against the other world, the world of profiteers and swastikas, the world of enemies. Otto Bauer, the Socialist leader, often boasted of this little oasis in the Austrian desert. Socialism in one locality. Its popularity with working-class families irritated the clerico-fascists. The bourgeoisie perceived 'Red Vienna' as a threat. If ever you go to Vienna, Karl, go and see these apartments and you will understand that public housing did not necessarily lead to urban squalor or socialist giantism, replete with 70-foot statues of Marx or Lenin.

News had spread and small groups of workers were standing at the entrance to Erich's block, talking in hushed voices, their faces covered with sadness. Lisa and Felix climbed the stairs to the second floor, where the watchmaker had lived. The corridor was like a railway station. Human bodies everywhere. Erich's apartment, too, was crowded.

One of the faces was only too familiar. At first, Lisa thought he was one of Ludwik's old friends, but as she moved towards him she saw with a start that it was Julius Deutsch, the Commander of the Schutzbund, the volunteer defence force of the Austrian Socialist Party. His photograph often appeared in the right-wing press where he was portrayed as a Judeo-Bolshevik monster.

If only he were a monster, thought Lisa, as Deutsch made his farewells and left the apartment. As Erich saw Felix, he rushed through the crowded room and hugged his friend. The two boys disappeared. They were still wearing their school uniforms, white shirts, a tie, dark shorts that just reached their knees, and jackets that covered their shorts. Long stockings travelled to the knees from the other end. They went into Erich's room and sat on the bed, staring at the wall in silence.

Lisa introduced herself and offered her condolences to Erich's mother. The watchmaker's wife was distraught, her face distorted by grief. In a state of total shock, she received condolences with a tiny nod, unable to do more than reiterate her refusal to accept that she would never see her husband again. Lisa asked if Erich could come and spend the weekend with them. His mother was touched, but shook her head.

'I need him by my side now. Things will get worse. I don't want my Erich to live here any more. My sister and her husband are in London. They appear to be happy. For a whole year she wrote and pleaded with us to join her, but my husband was obstinate. "I was born here and I will die here."' She began to weep. Tears sprang to Lisa's eyes. She hugged the bereaved woman and gently stroked her head.

'For Erich's sake I will go to London. This country has no future. The rumours are that once the Prussians have captured Vienna, it will be difficult for Jews and Socialists to get passports.'

Lisa nodded. There was nothing more she could do today. She disentangled her son from his friend and observed another silent tearful farewell. As they left Erich's apartment, more people were arriving. Felix took her hand and held it tightly all the way home, even while they were on the tram.

'Where is my father today?'

Lisa's two-handed gesture indicated that she did not know.

'What work does he do?'

'You know very well what he does. He travels. He sells fountain-pens all over Europe. He gets new orders, which enable us to keep this stationery shop here and in Amsterdam.'

'Then how come he couldn't tell me the price of a pen the other day? I'm not a fool, you know. What's the point of not telling me the truth?'

She looked at his flashing eyes and smiled. 'You must ask him yourself. Tonight if you like, if he's not too late.'

'I'm sure he's at the Zentrale, talking to his friends. Should we go and find him?'

Lisa shook her head. 'It's too cold to go out again. Please go and wash, and then do some homework. I'll prepare some food. Your father promised to be home for supper tonight.'

Felix's instincts had been accurate. Ludwik was at the Zentrale, where an animated conversation was in progress. News of the watchmaker's death had spread and this latest tragedy had become intertwined with the permanently polarized political situation in Austria. Ludwik was listening quietly, while the two Englishmen questioned Ernst, the columnist from *Arbeiterzeitung*, the Socialist Party newspaper. Philby spoke quietly. His tone was ultra-polite. He was interested in the details, and had been interrogating Ernst for nearly an hour, demanding information about the concrete relationship of forces inside the police and the army.

'I suppose what I am asking boils down to this: does the Socialist Party have cells in the police force and the army, or is its military work confined to its own defence force, the Schutzbund?'

Ernst smiled, an irritating, self-important smile, the aim of which was to indicate that he knew, but would not tell. Philby felt instinctively that he did not know, for the simple reason that there was nothing to know. The Socialists had deliberately kept aloof from the police and the army for fear of provoking repression. Ernst was trying to conceal this fact. Philby exchanged the briefest of glances with Ludwik.

He is asking the questions I would ask, thought Ludwik. He has an analytical mind. Philby's compatriot, a young Oxford-educated socialist in his early thirties, was more aggressive, but less incisive. He had arrived at the café with the man from *Arbeiterzeitung*. The Austrian had been trying to convince his English friend that the tactics being followed by the Austrian Socialist Party represented the only possible alternative to the Nazis and the clerico-fascists.

'These are your views, my friend; others have expressed contrary opinions.' Hugh Gaitskell, a visiting English social democrat, spoke in a loud and excited voice. 'You speak as if there was only one possibility, but I think you're on the wrong track.'

Gertrude, who had arrived in Vienna that morning with vital new information from Berlin, smiled with her eyes at Ludwik. She was impressed by young Gaitskell's lack of tact.

'Come, come, Ernst. Enough of this hogwash.' Gaitskell had no intention of stopping the argument. 'Let's have some straight answers to a few simple questions. One: if the fascists are armed and brutalize the workers, is not the only way to resist them by force of arms? Or do you and Otto Bauer really believe that the threat will disappear by a mere show of strength?'

'We are engaged in a delicate game of chess, my dear English friends,' replied Ernst with a weary smile. 'And you want *us* to trample all over the board. We can never do that because the workers would not accept it.'

Everyone sitting around the table understood the reference to chess. You will, too, Karl, although your employers would find Bauer too radical. His 'Chess Editorial' in the *Arbeiterzeitung* had become notorious and led to excited debates all over Europe. Moscow, of course, had denounced it as an abject capitulation to the bourgeoisie, but elsewhere it was taken seriously. The Austrian fascists, in polar opposition to Moscow, had seen it as a threat and accused Bauer of fomenting revolution. In the editorial, the Austrian leader saw democracy as a game of chess with its rules, the most important of which was that the beaten opponent must be given a chance to defeat the victors. The problem was playing with the Nazis, because their player said: 'I don't believe in the game or its rules, but I am going to take part in it till I win. Then I shall kick over the chess board, burn the pieces, guillotine or imprison my enemy and declare it high treason ever to play chess again.' To permit such a player to play the game was tantamount to suicide. The preservation of democracy required the exclusion of the Nazis. This was what Bauer had written.

What do you think Karl? Too ultra-left? Or a realist who understood the German events only too well, unlike Stalin and his sycophants in the Kremlin?

'The real problem,' insisted Gaitskell, 'is that it's not just the pro-German Nazis who threaten you. It's that little rascal Dolfuss. He and his clerico-fascists, as you so quaintly refer to them, won't play according to your rules. Dolfuss loathes the Germans. He knows they see him as a tool, to be used and discarded. But he is frightened of our side even more. He wants to show everyone that he's a tough leader, just like Mussolini. He will remove your queen, knights and castles, leaving you only the pawns. What price chess after that? Eh?'

Ernst was irritated by this exchange. He had assumed that his British friend would support him. He frowned, looked at his watch, informed Gaitskell that they had a dinner appointment, and rose. The others followed suit. Ludwik arranged to meet Philby the following day and shook hands solemnly. Gertrude followed him out of the door, leaving Philby absorbed in a week-old copy of *The Times*.

Outside the night sky was streaked with clouds. The snow which had begun to thaw earlier had now turned to ice. The night was cold and the pavement treacherous. Gertrude took his arm. She knew instinctively that he was walking towards Bakerstrasse and to his wife and son. For a few minutes she walked alongside him in silence. Then she made a weak attempt to distract him.

'Should we go and eat somewhere?'

'Not tonight. I promised Lisa and Felix I wouldn't be late. The watchmaker died today. His son was Felix's best friend. The boy will be very upset.'

Gertrude hid her disappointment. It was always like this, she thought to herself. Every time I try and drag him away, he has an excuse. Aloud she said, 'Of course, of course. I understand. My love to them both. And, here. I almost forgot. I know he likes them.' She dug into her bag and produced a box of neatly wrapped chocolates.

He smiled as he accepted the gift and kissed her on both cheeks. 'Half of these usually end up in my stomach,' he said.

Felix, crying, was waiting for him as he entered their apartment. Ludwik lifted the boy off the ground and hugged him.

'Why, Papa? Why? Why do they hate the Jews so much? Erich's grandmother told him it was all the fault of democracy. She said that if the Emperor had still been on the throne, things like this could never have happened.'

'Perhaps,' replied Ludwik. 'Perhaps, but under the Tsar in Russia it was much, much worse. Should I tell you a story tonight? Not a story my grandmother told me, but something I saw with my own eyes in Galicia?'

'What was it Papa? What? Are we Jewish?'

'Both my parents were orthodox Jews, but your mother is not Jewish. This means that for the real Jews, the believers, you are not a real Jew. But for the Nazis and anti-Semites it makes no difference at all. For them you are a Jew.'

Felix trembled slightly.

'Don't frighten him, Ignaty.' Ludwik's real name had slipped from her mouth before she could control herself. Ludwik glared at her, but Felix, who had noticed, did not say anything. Tonight all he wanted to know was why his friend Erich was without a father. And now he also wanted to know whether the men in brown shirts would one day kill his father. Lisa had done her best to shield her son from the horrors of the real world, but now he had encountered history at first hand. He needed to be given some answers.

'What did you see in Galicia, Papa? Papa?'

Ludwik's eyes filled with sadness. He hugged his son and began to talk about the pogrom he had witnessed and how Jews were killed for no other reason but that they were Jews.

'What did you do, Papa?' asked the boy.

'Nothing at the time. A few years later, when I was sixteen, I became a Socialist. I would peer into the future with excitement and passion. We wanted a change so desperately. You see, my son, for the poor, the choices of how they wanted to die were restricted – through indifference and neglect in peacetime, or through violence in wars. The First World War cost everyone millions of dead. The life of a human being was worth nothing to these generals who paraded around in their fancy caps, being saluted and fed with truffles and the best cognac.

'Seneca, in ancient Rome, first raised the question: "What if the slaves were to count themselves?" We began to do just that. Hundreds of thousands, including people like me, non-Jewish Jews, sought refuge in the Revolution. We thought this was the only way to bring the filth to an end.'

'But why, Papa? Why do they hate so much?'

'There is no single answer. From the beginnings of our world human beings have possessed an infinite capacity to do mischief to each other. It still goes on. Deep down we are still imprisoned by biology. It is the animal in us. You know the way a herd will sometimes expel or kill one of its number which looks different or poses a threat, usually imagined. Why does that happen? For animals it is an instinctive fear; in many ways it's the same when human beings become frenzied and maniacal and start killing each other.'

'Except for one simple fact, Ludwik,' interrupted Lisa. 'Humans have brains capable of understanding. The power of reason distinguishes us from the animal kingdom.'

'Does it? Tell that to the Germans fleeing from Hitler.'

'Will we ever go to London, like Erich?'

'Perhaps,' replied his father, 'but first you must go to bed.'

For a long time that night Ludwik did not speak. He was sitting hunched in an old armchair, staring at the mantelpiece. Lisa knew these moods of old and made no attempt to breach the silence. She knew he would talk before the night was out, but she was tired and hoped it would not be a long wait. When he stood up to pour himself a large brandy she sighed with relief.

'I hate this apartment. Look at it. Filthy curtains. The chair has no springs...'

'Ludwik,' she interrupted, 'is it time to leave Vienna?'

'Yes,' he replied in a tired voice.

'Was the Englishman depressing?'

'No. He was quite sharp. I was depressing. Moscow is depressing. The Comintern is depressing. He questioned me in detail about the debacle in Germany, the Comintern's role in paving the way for Hitler's victory. I agreed with him, but had to defend the line. Always the line. "Have you been reading Trotsky's pamphlets on Germany?" I asked him, just to put him on the defensive. He denied it strongly. I was aching to tell him. "You should. He got it right. Moscow got it wrong", but the shock might have been too great.'

'Did you see Gertie?'

'That was depressing. She wants to leave the party and renounce Moscow. She's in a suicidal mood.'

'That may have nothing to do with Moscow or the insane policies of the Comintern!'

'Meaning?'

'Meaning she wants you. It's your refusal to sleep with her that is driving her to suicide.'

'Cruel! That may be mixed up in it, but she's in a mess. And it is political. Never forget that she's a German communist and her party's on the edge of extinction. I don't like any of my agents to be in such a state. It's dangerous for everyone.'

'You calmed her down?'

'Politically! I told her I agreed with her, but...'

'But?'

'But that we could not spit in the well from which we might have to drink water.'

'So you think Trotsky's wrong to denounce the Comintern and call for a new International?'

'The timing is wrong. There will be a new European war, of this I'm sure. The Soviet Union will be involved. Stalin will not survive. The party itself will find it essential to remove him.'

'Is that what the Fourth Department thinks?'

Ludwik nodded and attempted to rise from the chair, but sank down again, a very tired man. Lisa laughed and pulled him up.

'And Vienna?'

'The clerical thugs are preparing to wipe out the Socialists. After Dolfuss and the Heimwehr have destroyed the Left, the Nazis will get rid of Dolfuss and take over Austria.'

'But the Socialists are armed, unlike the Comintern in Germany. The Schutzbund will resist.'

'The Schutzbund's tactics are totally defensive. They are waiting for the government to choose the timing of the battle. For victory you have to be capable of going on the offensive. But you know that well, don't you, my commissar? These people lack the instinct to win. I would give them six months at the most. Then the Right will teach Otto Bauer how it plays chess!'

Are you still there, Karl? Or is your stomach turning slightly acid at the conversation you have just read? This is what it was like when political people on the same side were on their own. Ludwik and Lisa lived under a terrible strain. They lived a double lie. They were working for Soviet military intelligence and pretending to run a small business. They received orders from Moscow which was under the control of a despot whom they loathed. There were very few people with whom they could be frank. This was the cement that held them together.

Gertrude stressed this factor, but looking through her notebooks I also know what she didn't tell me. Ludwik and Lisa loved each other as well. They had a very close relationship. Even as I write I feel it in my bones that Gertrude was not Ludwik's mistress and that he was not my father. Why did she lie? I'm not sure. I'm awaiting information from the archives in Moscow, which Sao has promised to get for me.

Ludwik gave them six months at most. He had got the timing slightly wrong.

As he was walking to his shop near the university the next morning, he noticed a queue of idle tramcars on the Ringstrasse. At first he thought there might be a power breakdown, but then another empty tram pulled up. The driver got out and joined his circle of comrades. Ludwik walked up to them.

'Are you on strike, comrades?'

They replied with a collective shrug of the shoulders.

'You don't know?'

'No,' replied the youngest of them. 'We've heard the fascists have shot workers in Linz. There's a general strike. We're waiting for instructions from the party.'

Ludwik shook hands with them and began to walk briskly. On street corners he saw lines of battle-ready soldiers flanked by steel-helmeted policemen carrying rifles. Heimwehr units were on their way to the Rathaus to arrest the mayor.

Ludwik walked up to an officer. 'Excuse me,' he said in his best imitation of a bourgeois Viennese accent. 'What is going on?'

'Who are you?'

'A businessman.'

'The Socialists have launched a revolution. The government has declared martial law. You had better go home.'

Ludwik accepted the advice and began to walk back. He saw the tram-drivers. All of them were on the ground cowering. Above them stood a unit of Heimwehr men. The workers were being kicked and whipped with rifle butts. Ludwik felt sick. As he hurried away, he saw barbed wire barricades being constructed by soldiers all round the

Ringstrasse. Machine-gun units were being placed at regular intervals.

Otto Bauer had waited too long, and the counter-revolution had taken the offensive, thought Ludwik, as he walked back to his apartment. He was sure that it would be bloody, and he was equally sure that Hitler would swallow Austria. The Prussians would soon be in Vienna.

Later that evening, just as they were sitting down to eat, they heard noise of dulled explosions from the direction of the working-class suburbs. Socialist Vienna was being shelled by howitzers and trench mortars. The chess game was over. Felix was staring out of the window, hoping that Erich was safe. In the background he could hear the voices of his parents discussing the fate of Austria.

Dolfuss was strutting around trying to mimic Mussolini, but it would not last. By destroying the Socialists, the only party that could have resisted Hitler, he had effectively ordered his own execution. Ludwik was convinced that Hitler would strike soon and incorporate his native Austria into the Third Reich.

'At least,' muttered Lisa with a sigh, 'this is one defeat for which Moscow can't be held responsible.'

'Not directly, perhaps, but if we had not handed over Germany to Hitler, could this have happened here?'

'How many do you think there are in Moscow who talk as we do?'

'Too many, as far as Stalin is concerned.'

Three days of violence in Vienna. Three days in which the Schutzbund was incapable of effective resistance. Three days in which working-class Vienna lay in ruins, its leaders in prison or in exile. *Arbeiterzeitung* was being published clandestinely. Five years in prison for anyone caught in the act of distribution. Dolfuss triumphant.

Hitler, irritated by Mussolini's factional games in Austria and his apparent triumph, sent the following message to the defeated workers: 'I am convinced that the Austrian workers will stand now behind the Nazi cause as a natural reaction to the violence which the Austrian Government has used against them.'

Ludwik screamed in rage and quietly resumed his work. This man possessed five of the six attributes required of a great spy: an incredible memory for faces, names, conversations; the gift of languages; inexhaustible powers of invention; secrecy; capacity to engage in conversation with the most unlikely strangers. The sixth attribute – a freedom from conscience – always managed to elude Ludwik, and the men in Moscow were only too well aware of this, their spymaster's only vulnerability.

The following week he met Philby. It was a long meeting. Ludwik was pleased with the results and informed the Fourth Department of their new recruit. It was to his diary, in which he scribbled only irregularly, that he confided his innermost thoughts.

For a long time Ludwik had resisted writing a diary, regarding it as a manifestation of narcissism and individuality, but Lisa had snorted at such a suggestion and warned him that he was in danger of losing his humanity. How right she had been. Now he used the diary as a means for isolating himself from the noise of the surrounding tables in a café or the other passengers in a train. The sight of a blank page invited him to enter a tranquil world, an island of self-imposed solitude in a sea of noise.

20 FEBRUARY 1934:

I met P. again today, but we agreed to avoid the cafés, which were thick with intrigue. Instead we met on the bridge, near the Schottenring. I had suggested we walk alongside the Danube. It was cold but sunny, and after three-quarters of an hour we found a bench from where we could see the scarred façade of the Karl Marx Hof. We sat down and observed the wreckage that was Socialist Vienna. The events here have convinced P. of the correctness of our cause. His demeanour was calm. No trace of emotions or excitement in his voice. His decision was final. He is on our side. I asked him about the other Englishman, G. He smiled. Told me that G. had been affected in exactly the opposite fashion. The destruction of the Socialists had convinced him that the state could never be challenged effectively. 'Very English reaction', was P.'s epitaph on the affair.

P. said that he had met an underground leader of the Schutzbund who had boasted that his men had been disciplined. No plunder or looting. They had been very proper. Perfect gentlemen. That's why they lost, I said, and he nodded. I told him of one episode that had been reported to me by a Viennese Communist. As the Heimwehr were advancing near a park, the Schutzbund leader gave the order to surrender. Why? Because he would have had to walk on the grass in a park and violate the law that stated: Betreten Verboten! P. laughed at this and accused me of manufacturing the whole incident, but it was true.

P. then told me that some years ago he had been at a dinner party in London. Here a retired Austrian general was holding forth at length on the crimes of the Austrian Socialists. P. recalled his exact words: 'One day we're going to put a stop to all this nonsense by fair means or foul. Parquet floor and showers for the workers? Might as well put Persian carpets in the pig-sty and feed the animals on caviar!'

P. commented that it was odd how they always equated workers with pigs. Burke, he told me, had referred to the 'swinish multitude', and the radicals had responded by accepting the nomenclature and naming their newspapers The Swine, The Pig's Trotter, *etc.*

We talked then about the collapse of liberal bourgeois values in Austria. He was surprised by my suggestion that it was all to do with an élitist view of culture. I then gave him a brief lecture on the subject of the Viennese bourgeoisie. Brought back memories of all the discussions with Lisa and other friends before the war. As students at the university we used to stand for hours, look up at the ceiling and discuss the meaning of Klimt's painting Philosophy. *Was it truly a victory of light over darkness, as the Ministry of Culture had insisted? Or was it something far more ambiguous? Earth was dissolved into a fusion of Heaven and Hell. Suffering humanity was floating aimlessly in the universe. The painting had excited Lisa. I loved the painting, but hated its mysticism. Lisa was angry. The face at the bottom of the picture,* Das Wissen, *showed a conscious human mind. This face, she told us, was the real heart of the painting. Klimt was saying that* Das Wissen *was vital for all humanity. And so the debate had gone. We too had been caught up in the excesses of the Austrian bourgeoisie.*

P. laughed, but commented that this did not sound like a materialist explanation for the weakness of the Austrian intelligentsia. He put on a schoolmaster's expression and voice and said: Do try again. We both laughed.

I told P. that in Austria, the bourgeoisie had been unable, like its French and English counterparts, either to destroy or fuse with the aristocracy. Therefore it remained dependent on the Emperor and the court, always an outsider, and denied any real share in the monopoly of ruling the country. Denied power, it sought refuge in art, which acquired the status of a religion. I reminded him of Karl Kraus's withering comment about the sphere of action of Viennese liberalism being constricted to the parquets of theatres on opening night.

Liberal abdication had left the path clear for the clerico-fascists. The Emperor had defended the Jews against the anti-Semitic campaigns of the Catholics. Later, the Socialists had defended traditional liberal values. Now there was no holding back the fascists. Europe could only resist if it fought back.

A Europe-wide civil war? P. asked. I nodded.

He then questioned me in some detail about the German débâcle. Why, he insisted, had the leaders of the German Communist Party not resisted the suicidal instructions from Moscow? For the first time I saw P. quite agitated. Even though it was indiscreet, I told him about my conversation with one of the central leaders of the German party and a founder of the Comintern. I had known that this leader was in private scathing about Moscow's policies. Why don't you go public? I had asked him. Let the world know why the German workers were virtually handed over to Hitler by the Comintern. His answer, still imprinted on my memory as if it were yesterday: I cannot do what you want because of the existence of the Soviet Union. I know perfectly well that we sacrificed the German movement to avoid a struggle with Stalin. We may have to sacrifice the movement in many other countries as well. In the end Fascism will be victorious over the capitalist world. Then there will be a titanic struggle between Fascism and the Soviet Union.

P. was amazed: Did he really say that? I nodded. Doesn't the madman understand that if Fascism is established in the whole of Europe, let alone America, they will have enough resources to smash the Soviet Union five times over?

He then asked if he could go to Moscow. I told him that was impossible. His task was to work in the West. We needed information from the top circles in Germany and Britain. Therefore he had to abandon all his connections with the Left. He had to cultivate a new personality: arrogant, condescending, patronizing – and also a tiny stutter. He had to mix in the right circles. Otherwise he would be of no use to us. That's easier than you think in my case, he says. My father has excellent connections.

We shall see. I told him that this was the last time we would meet in public.

Thirteen

EVELYNE WOKE UP feeling angry. Angry that Vlady had not really liked her film. Angry that he had lacked the courage to say so to her face. And, above all, angry that he had turned down her totally serious offer to sleep with him.

She jumped out of bed and walked briskly into the bathroom. She turned on the light and viewed her naked body in the full-length mirror. 'Not bad at all,' she muttered to herself and frowned.

What's wrong with him? Does he really believe that I've gone off men? Menopausal fool! Or is it that I no longer matter?

As she brushed her teeth she suddenly felt like confronting Vlady in his lair. At first she thought she would ring and warn him, but she put the receiver down before he could respond. No. This wasn't a good idea. I'll surprise him.

It was Sunday, and the clocks in her three-storeyed house had just struck seven. Evelyne slipped on a pair of loose, grey silk trousers and a black cashmere sweater. As she passed the kitchen she paused, tempted by the fragrant steam of her special mix of coffees. She knew what would be on offer in Vlady's apartment. Should she have some coffee before she left? It would take too long. Lust overpowered greed. She rushed down to her car.

Evelyne loved Berlin at this time of morning. The streets were virtually empty. If she had not been feeling so angry with Vlady she would have walked. Instead she drove her Mercedes through the Ku-Damm at eighty kilometres. Within ten minutes she was outside Vlady's apartment block. But she did not jump out and race up the stairs. She sat clutching the steering wheel. Why had she come here? An inner voice responded: To lay a ghost, to lay a ghost.

Evelyne laughed. She sometimes visualized their relationship as a prematurely lanced boil, but not today. Anyway, she had never regarded her affair with Vlady as dead for all time. Could she be wrong? Was she deceiving herself? Was Vlady just a ghost then, a five-year-old memory that still haunted her because it had gone so disastrously wrong? What was she doing here?

It had been so different at the beginning. He had been so different. Full of fun. She remembered the very first time they had talked.

'Let me ask you something, Evelyne. Do you want to wreck my marriage?'

'No,' she had replied, taken aback but amused by his directness.

'That's fine. We can have an affair, but I must explain the ground rules.'

Several months later she had told him that she wanted a child.

'Why?' Vlady had asked. 'It's a crazy idea. Do you realize what it will do to your life?'

'I want one, Vlady. It will be a revolution in my life.'

'And a counter-revolution in mine!'

In those days the tension between them was always defused by laughter. Could that be the reason? Was she trying to relive the good memories?

Her inner voice interrupted once again: It's Sao isn't it? The Vietnamese moneybag from Paris. You just want cash for your next movie. Vlady is simply a conduit. Isn't that right?

No, Evelyne told herself. No! I'm not that cynical. I still feel something for him, but I'm not sure what or why.

Just as she had opened the door and was about to step out, she was overwhelmed by a memory and began to laugh loudly. She had only slept with him once. Then nothing for two weeks. Their failure to repeat the experience had made both of them irritable and bad-tempered with each other. Evelyne had broken the deadlock by entering his office at Humboldt wearing a long brown army coat with nothing underneath. She had locked the door, discarded her coat and asked in the sweetest voice imaginable: 'Herr Meyer, are you capable of something more than a one-night stand?' It was the look on his face, incredulity mingled with horror, that had made her laugh, then as now. Their relationship had prospered for a while after 'the happening', as he called it, and she had become attached to him. She still missed the old Vlady. The dissident leader with the venomous eye and the acid tongue; the polemicist who wielded his pen like a sword, producing pamphlets which panicked the regime; the enthusiastic professor who could infect his students with a love of Russian and Chinese literature. Having inspired herself, Evelyne began the long climb to the third floor. She pressed the bell. No reply. She began to knock on the door.

Vlady had been checking the proofs of a Chinese translation of Adorno's essays for most of the night. It was paid work and he enjoyed it a great deal. A very deep sleep had claimed him some hours ago and he did not hear the noise at the door. A desperate Evelyne was banging harder and harder and simultaneously pressing the bell. Slowly the loud and persistent rings penetrated his unconscious. Who? Why? He grabbed at his wrist watch on the side table. It was seven-thirty. Vlady cursed his tormentor as he got out of bed and stumbled towards the door.

'Evelyne! Why in God's name...?'

'Don't try too hard to be inhospitable, Vlady. You look a complete wreck. I'm desperate for some coffee.'

'Evelyne,' Vlady's tranquil voice was deceptive. 'What are you doing here at seven o'clock in the morning?'

'I felt like seeing you. Isn't that sufficient reason?'

This time anger breached the surface calm and he shouted. 'Not at this hour, damn you! Couldn't you wait till the afternoon? Please leave.'

'No.'

'Why?'

'Because the urge that brought me here is overpowering. I'm glad you're angry. I hate it when you pretend to be calm. You're still the same. Why don't you go back to bed, and I'll make some coffee.'

'There isn't any.'

'I don't believe you,' Evelyne shrieked in disbelief. 'What do you drink in the morning? Your own piss?'

Vlady grinned and walked out of the room. She followed him through the corridor to his study-bedroom. He got back into bed and held the quilt tightly around him.

'I'm going back to sleep. You can stay if you like. Read. Listen to music. Masturbate. Anything, but let me sleep. We'll talk later. Or you could go back home and return with a flask of coffee or you could have a shower, go for a walk and come back later. Anything you want, but just let me sleep.'

'Please be quiet. You're beginning to repeat yourself. I won't let you sleep. I barely slept myself.'

'Why? On your own?'

'I usually am. I felt like a change.'

She took off her clothes and got under the quilt with him. Vlady froze. He realized that a confrontation was inevitable. Till that ghastly dinner party he had neither written to Evelyne, nor thought of her and hadn't, no, not even for a moment, wanted to see her. She belonged to a tarnished past, mixed up with their hopes and illusions and Helge's departure, even though he knew that Evelyne was not responsible. He looked at her clouded face. The mask had disappeared. She was once again the troubled student, who had touched his heart five summers ago.

He got annoyed with her because he knew that she was faking. The frantic, post-modern hothead constantly longing to shock was a total fiction, part of her plan to make some money, to build a new career in this wide-open country where the fastest growing industry was pornography, but he wished she wouldn't try it all out on him.

Evelyne, for her part, was irritated by his self-righteousness and a solemn longing to have everything in order, *alles in Ordnung*. How ironic for a Jew born and brought up in Moscow to be so German. Helge's flight to New York had traumatized Vlady, and Evelyne had thought it was best to leave him alone to nurse his dented pride. If he thought she was wrong he should have told her. Why couldn't he let her make her own mistakes now? She wasn't his student any more. Sometimes, she told herself, the strongest emotion this tight-arsed fool feels is disapproval.

The last three months before they finally separated had been painful. They had slept together, but like two corpses, never making love. It had become a grotesque and obscene ritual. Evelyne would feel a terrible twist in her stomach after every night spent in this fashion. Finally she ran away.

As she observed his rigid frame the bad memories flowed through her once again and she cursed herself. Without saying a word she got out of bed and dressed. Vlady watched her in silence. It was not an unfamiliar scene.

'Don't go, Evelyne. Let me shave and get dressed. We'll go for a walk.'

A sad look crossed her face. 'What is it about us, Vlady? We were so close.'

Instead of replying he went to his desk and returned with Suhrkamp's 1980 edition of Adorno's *Gesammelte Schriften*.

'I was checking the Chinese translation of this last night. Look what a gem I found. They'd left it out of the earlier editions. God alone knows why. Perhaps it touched a sensitive chord in Adorno's own life.'

He left her holding the book, while he went next door to take a shower. So obscure, she thought, translating Adorno into Chinese. There must be more practical things he could do. Losing the job at Humboldt could be good if it drags him out his ghetto. He could easily become a columnist, or host a radio show – anything to stop him scrutinizing his own entrails.

'Have you finished? What do you think?'

She slumped back on the bed and read the recommended extract.

Post festum Pain at the decay of erotic relationships is not just, as it takes itself to be, fear of love's withdrawal, nor the kind of narcissistic melancholy that has been penetratingly described by Freud. Also involved is fear of the transience of one's own feeling. So little room is left to spontaneous impulses that anyone still granted them at all, feels them as joy and treasure even when they cause pain, and indeed, experiences the last stinging traces of immediacy as a possession to be grimly defended, in order not to become oneself a thing. The fear of loving another is greater, no doubt, than of losing that other's love. The idea offered to us as solace that in a few years we shall not understand our passion and will be able to meet the loved woman in company with nothing more than fleeting, astonished curiosity, is apt to exasperate the recipient beyond all measure. That passion, which breaches the context of rational utility and seems to help the self to break its monadic prison, should itself be something relative to be fitted back into individual life by ignominious reason, is the ultimate blasphemy. And yet, inescapably, passion itself in experiencing the inalienable boundary between two people, is forced to reflect on that very moment and thus, in the act of being overwhelmed by it, to recognize the nullity of its overwhelming. Really one has always sensed futility; happiness lay in the nonsensical thought of being carried away, and each time that went wrong was the last time, was death. The transience of that in which life is concentrated to the utmost breaks through in just that extreme concentration. On top of all else the unhappy lover has to admit that exactly where he thought he was forgetting himself he loved himself only. No directness leads outside the guilty circle of the natural, but only reflection on how closed it is.

She was reading it for the third time when Vlady re-emerged, wearing a black polo neck sweater, faded blue jeans and a pair of decrepit running shoes.

'Well?'

'It's dense, Vlady, just like you. Which bit turns you on?'

'The fear of the transience of one's own feeling.'

'I get the message.'

Vlady laughed. 'The problem with you, Evelyne, is that you take everything personally.'

'The problem with you, Vlady, is that ever since the DDR collapsed you've become slightly pathetic.'

'In more ways than one.'

'Meaning?'

'On the first death anniversary of the Wall, there was an unfortunate episode . . .'

'It's not like you to be so coy, Vlady. Not even in your present state.'

'I tried to make love and . . .'

'With who?' interrupted Evelyne.

'With someone whom you certainly don't know.'

'One of Adorno's transients, I suppose. Anyway, what happened?'

'That's the whole point. Nothing happened. Don't laugh, Evelyne. It's not funny.'

'You've never tried since?'

Vlady shook his head.

'You mean for the last three years you've lived like a monk?'

'Not exactly. Monks, as you know, have always led a full and frequent sexual life. Unlike them I have become truly celibate. It worries me. I thought of you a great deal, but I had no desire to see you.'

'That's reassuring, Vlady. I think I know what your problem is, my friend. You've stopped loving yourself and you've forgotten how to accept love. A surfeit of narcissism sickens, but none at all? Unnatural. You've been sinking in a pond of self-pity, Vlady. Your martyr complex has gained the upper hand. All this could be ended by one, nice, long, relaxed, fuck and I accept the challenge, Vlady, Berlin Wall or no Berlin Wall. Now, please, off with your clothes.'

Vlady laughed. 'OK, then. Why not?'

Clothes came off. The bed creaked with the extra weight.

'I'd forgotten your body,' he murmured as his hands fondled her, feeling her forgotten and familiar warmth.

Afterwards he looked at her expectantly. She sat up and laughed.

'There. It wasn't so bad, was it? Three out of ten for performance. Ten out of ten for effort. We will do this more often.'

He smiled. 'I think we should go for a walk, Evelyne. Just look at the sunshine.'

'You'd better get something warm. It's still cold out there.'

They dressed quickly. He lifted his faded, dark green overcoat from the chair and draped it around his shoulders. Evelyne laughed.

'You've still got this old DDR antique. Why not sell it to one of the Pakistani stallholders at Brandenburg Gate? You might get more for it than the portraits of Ulbricht, Honecker and DDR flags.'

Vlady smiled again. 'Don't mock, Evelyne. I often stop and talk to those stallholders. We share a cup of tea. I asked one of them, a guy in his thirties, why they sold all this stuff. Do you know what he said? "My mother's fucked. I'm fucked. What else is there to do but sell the remains of a fucked-up country?"'

'Good, Vlady, even though I know you made it up.' Evelyne roared with approving laughter. 'All I'm saying is that your coat, too, is fucked-up.'

'I did not make anything up, Fräulein, not a word. And leave my coat alone. Some things one must never throw away. This old rag doesn't protect me against the cold, but it brings back many warm memories.'

She saw him then as she had the first time. A packed lecture theatre on a cold November afternoon. It must have been seven or eight years ago. The lecture hall was heated, but Professor Meyer had not removed his overcoat. What made that day memorable was not Vlady's clothes or his demeanour or his body movements, but his subject. He had spoken about Heine, with an intimacy that had at first startled his listeners and then excited them. Not Heine the poet, but Heine, the historian of German culture. It was Heine, author of *Religion and Philosophy in Germany*, the book Vlady had taken as his text.

One effect of DDR conservatism was that it kept education in a pre-video phase with a habit of paying attention to long words. One of the first benefits of the Western victory was the influence of the videosphere in breaking down the old-fashioned central European respect for high culture, including the cynical devaluation of those very writers the West respected so much as long as they were dissidents against the Communist regimes. These same authors are now begging to be translated and beginning to understand that their long rebellion against socialist realism has left them disarmed against the new enemy: market realism.

Vlady remembered how after he had finished there had been a long silence and then uncharacteristic applause, which had taken him by surprise. He had smiled and then she had noticed everything else about him, including the green coat.

'Vlady,' she was thinking aloud, 'do you still remember that passage from Heine?'

'Which one?'

'On German abstinence. You know, where he explained the beginning of the Reformation as a revolt against the sale of indulgences, implying that our collective libido was frozen.'

Vlady grinned, took her by the arm and whispered Heine's words in her ear.

We Northerners are of colder blood, and we needed not so many indulgences for carnal sins as were sent by Leo in his fatherly concern for us. Our climate facilitates the practice of Christian virtues; and on the 31st October, 1516, as Luther nailed his theses against indulgences to the door of the Augustin Church, the moat that surrounded Wittenberg was perhaps already frozen over, and one could have skated on it, which is a very cold sort of pleasure, and consequently no sin.

Evelyne stroked his head.

'At least your memory hasn't gone.'

'Did you ever read the book?'

'No,' confessed Evelyne. 'There was no point. Your lecture told us everything. We all felt we knew the book. Intimately.'

'Philistine fools,' came the appreciative reply. 'How could I convey the beauty of the language? You might have even picked up a few phrases to enliven your film scripts.'

'Vlady, did you hate my movie?'

'No. It wasn't strong enough to hate. That was the problem. You're still a novice, aping Western fashions to catch their attention. Aren't you Frau Direktor? I want you to start hearing your own voice. *Our* voices, Evelyne. That's what is needed. I think you can do it. I'm sure.'

Evelyne did not reply. At first she was gripped by a mute rage. What an arrogant shit, she thought. I hate him.

They walked in silence for nearly fifteen minutes till Evelyne realized that he was right. For a few seconds this realization annoyed her even more. Then she gave him a hug.

'Thanks, Professor. Useful advice.'

Vlady was surprised and relieved by her response. For a moment he had thought she might start her act again and denounce him to the passers-by. Before he could mollify her further, a familiar voice startled them both.

'Evelyne and Vlady. Isn't it a beautiful morning?'

Kreuzberg Leyla, enveloped in an intricately woven, dark red shawl, laden with easel and box of paints, stood in front of them. She smiled, expecting a reply. None came. Finally, Vlady nodded vaguely and managed a weak smile. Evelyne hugged Leyla.

'This is not far from where I sketched *The Stolen Kiss*. You two were always lying on the grass, just underneath the willow. Your position was perfect for me. Every August afternoon that year. You could have been posing for me. The same body movements, and then the longest kiss I'd ever witnessed. Is this an anniversary visit? I've asked you several times before whether you liked the painting, but you never reply.'

'If I didn't like the painting, why should it be hanging on my bedroom wall?' inquired Evelyne dispassionately.

'I know that, Evelyne. I was asking Vlady.'

Evelyne's admission had startled Vlady.

'You had it all the time?'

'Yes.'

'Why didn't you tell me?'

'Herr Professor Meyer! Has your memory deserted you completely? Have you really forgotten how you walked out of my room saying I disgusted you and you never wanted to see me again? Hardly the best moment to inform you that I had acquired a work of art in which your reclining figure was prominently portrayed.'

'A work of what?'

'So, you didn't like it, Vlady?' came Leyla's plaintive voice.

'I am not an art critic, Leyla, but even I could see that your style was confused. You cannot marry Schiele and Picasso. They are –'

'Quiet, Vlady!' Evelyne screamed. 'You're just saying that to punish me. Why hurt Leyla? I can still recall your first reaction to the painting. "Hmm. It's rather unusual. Rich colours. The lines are a bit clumsy, but it's good. I like it." What's changed your mind?'

'I can't handle this today. Please excuse me, Leyla.'

He began to walk away slowly.

Fourteen

KARL HAD READ VLADY'S LETTER several times, but always on his own just like he was now in this hotel room. He was in Munich to meet a publisher. Karl would join him for dinner later.

He was suddenly overcome by an overpowering desire to justify himself. This had never happened before. Why did he want to defend his record to Vlady? Why did he want to justify himself? Was it because he was suddenly feeling politically insecure? There had been a change of leader in the Party and the new man was not to Karl's liking. He was far too rumbustious, unstable, incautious to make a good Chancellor. Karl was worried that power would elude the SPD again. He felt they needed power in order to struggle against the oblivion of time. He wanted to clarify his thoughts and, at times like this, he missed Vlady. Dinner was an hour away. He unpacked his laptop.

Dear Vlady,

I'm glad you wrote. I'm writing to reassure you that I do not hold you or Mother responsible for breaking up. I was upset, but it's all in the past. Remember how you used to mock my lack of motivation, my inability to make up my mind about my ultimate destination? Well, now I have made up my mind, but you're still angry because you don't agree with my decision. Do you want a son or a clone?

What drives me crazy about your generation is your refusal to accept history's verdict. Once, history was moving inexorably forward, towards your utopias. Then you saw it as a process with a subject: the great, invincible world proletariat united by class against its enemy. Now, history has become a whore. Look at the world around you, Vlady. Just look. Poor peasants in Rwanda killing their poor neighbours in the name of a tribe. Russian Orthodox Serbs killing Bosnian Muslims and Catholic Croats killing and being killed by the other two. Progress?

I don't grudge you your memories and your past, my father, but please don't grudge me my future. I don't want utopias. I want a quiet life, a decent government, a woman I love and who loves me, two children, a functioning public transport system and a sturdy bicycle – in that order. Boring? Perhaps, but I would rather be bored and live an ordinary existence than be excited and see millions perish. Reason must replace dogma and ideology. I refuse to compete for a history that destroys 'lesser' histories.

You're angry. You think I'm stubborn. You regard my views as a childish act of rebellion against you and Helge. You believe that alien beings have usurped my brain. You imagine that I am consumed by careerist impulses. And for all this you have come to despise my politics. You think that you and you alone are right. You refuse to accept any responsibility for this fucked-up century which was dominated by 'the Idea'. In reality, my dearest Vlady, the utopias for which you and Grandma Gertrude and my grandfather Ludwik (who you now tell me may not be my grandfather – the only one who fought and died for real ideals may not even be related to us!!) fought – all of you were really tilting at windmills. This will annoy you, but that's how I feel. Your past is not unimportant to me, but it teaches me nothing. Despite all this I feel very close to you and I need you. We can argue face to face.

I will be in Berlin soon. I'm glad the old apartment is still there. Please don't worry on that score. We can go and look for a new apartment together.

Helge has written to say that she might return to Germany. She is beginning to find New York 'very difficult' – at last! I'm really pleased. And you? Please write or ring soon. Better still, get a fax and an answer-machine. It will make communications a lot easier. When the telephone spread, people thought it would be the end of letter writing, but then the fax arrived and we're back again, that is, the rest of Europe apart from yourself. Where do you get your typewriter ribbon these days? I heard the factory had closed down.

Love,
Karl

Fifteen

IN SEPTEMBER 1936, the civil war in Spain was several weeks old. The land of Cervantes had become the cockpit of Europe. I was in two minds, Karl, whether or not to write about Spain. It seemed so long ago and I was fearful that I would really be taxing your patience. Then I went and saw *Land and Freedom* by Ken Loach, an English film-maker.

Strange irony. England is the most backward and insular country in our continent, and yet it produces Herr Loach. Later I noticed in the credits that most of the money came from Europe, which was reassuring, but still we must give credit to them because the idea germinated in England. The cinema was packed with young people and

I was wishing that you were sitting next to me. It is a flawed movie, but it brought back all the old memories and debates that I had heard from Gertrude and her friends in Berlin, many of whom had fought in the Thaelmann Brigade.

Gertrude often used to talk of Collioure, a French seaside resort. Once, when I was seventeen, Walter, an old friend of your grandmother, was stationed in Paris at the Trade Legation. We went to stay with him and all of us went to Collioure.

Later I was told of its significance. Ludwik had decided on Collioure as a rendezvous point. It was very close to Spain, without being a border town and all that entails. It had been sleepy, even at the height of summer, when Ludwik had come here with Lisa and Felix for a short holiday. Felix had pronounced it heaven.

Now Lisa and Felix were back in Paris, and Collioure was deserted apart from the locals, Ludwik and the two men from Moscow, his old friends, Freddy Lang and Schmelka Livitsky. They presented themselves to the locals as business friends, obsessed with fishing and good food. Outsiders always imagine that locals everywhere are easily deceived. This is rarely the case and the fisherman of Collioure were no exception. They liked the three Ls. They accepted that Ludwik and his friends were fond of fishing and passionately keen on the local wines and the French Catalan cuisine, but they never believed that the trio were businessmen just there for a good time. They knew that the foreigners were in some way connected with the civil war raging in the country next door.

Surrounded by a crescent of strikingly beautiful rock formations, Collioure was swathed in wisps of cloud that day. Ludwik's routine was simple. The three Ls would walk out of their hotel early in the morning. They would stroll down to the beach and sit silently watching the fishermen return with the night's catch, a motley collection of moray eel, John Dory, sea bass, angler fish and combers. This haul determined the character and quality of the bouillabaisse that would be served that night.

Freddy would light a pipe, the signal for them to stand up, smile, exchange a few pleasantries with the fishermen and walk briskly to the edge of the beach for their cliffside walk.

An hour later they could be seen breakfasting in the café opposite their hotel, immersed in the morning papers. Then they would disappear for the day in Ludwik's black Citroën.

Usually he drove them to Port Bou for assignments with agents from Spain. Today he was taking them to a village in the French Pyrenees, where the entire population of just under three hundred people were loyal to the Republican cause in Spain. Ludwik's organizational skills had transformed a minuscule mountain hamlet into a crucial, clandestine nerve centre linked to the battlefields in Catalonia.

Here there was a medium-sized workshop which manufactured French, Swiss and British passports, German and Italian identity cards and currency. Next door was a tailor who specialized in uniforms, and in the concealed attic there was a radio operator through whom Ludwik maintained contact with Spain and the Fourth Department in Moscow. Just outside the village was a large farm. Ludwik had chosen this bucolic location with great care. The outbuildings appeared to be decrepit and empty, but inside Ludwik had supervised the creation of a specialist armoury. Machine guns and revolvers were repaired, improved, tested and then returned to the agents of the Fourth Department in Spain, France and Portugal.

Freddy and Livitsky, impressed by the operation, looked at Ludwik and exchanged a smile; both of them were thinking of their schooldays in Pidvocholesk, where Ludwik had been the most undisciplined of them all.

'Come and drink something. Then we must work.' Ludwik's voice sounded tired.

His friends rose from the bench and extinguished their pipes. Slowly they walked to the outbuilding. Ludwik was standing outside and he grinned as they approached. He remembered Schmelka Livitsky's mother shouting at them for having thrown her only son into the river with all his clothes. For a whole week Schmelka had been barred from playing with them. Instead he had been sent for special lessons to the rabbi.

Ludwik explained the logistics of the operation and left his two colleagues from the Fourth Department to speak to the specialist workers on their own, so that he did not influence their first impressions. Freddy and Livitsky took detailed notes on how each of the sections functioned.

A few hours later, during a lunch of freshly baked bread, goats' cheese and locally brewed red wine, the three men exchanged information. Ludwik had been out of the Soviet Union since 1929. For the last three days they had been discussing the European crisis and the disposition of their agents. Ludwik was desperate for news from home. Later he must have briefed Gertrude on this meeting. The exchange below is one of the fragments from her notebooks. I have added explanatory sentences for your benefit, Karl, but a voice inside my head tells me that you won't get this far. If you do, please try and understand that what you call 'historical communism' was everyday life for these people. They were the human material and would not believe that the Idea could ever be defeated, except temporarily.

'It's our last chance,' volunteered Livitsky. 'If the fascists win in Spain, Hitler will take Europe and Stalin will consolidate his regime.'

Freddy spoke in a quiet voice, but his authority was unmistakable. As one of the chief controllers of the Fourth Department, he knew almost everything. 'If Hitler takes Europe, Stalin will do a deal with him.'

'No!' Livitsky's tone expressed his horror. 'You go too far, Freddy. Not even Stalin could get away with that ... the party would –'

'Don't talk to me about the party. It's become his instrument. I've seen German intelligence reports. They've established contact with us. Two of these reports imply that Marshal Tukachevsky is working for them.'

'Obvious forgeries,' said Ludwik contemptuously, 'and yet I'm sure that one person in Moscow desperately wants to believe them. Am I right or wrong, Freddy?'

'You are right, my friend.'

'Stalin!' Livitsky was genuinely shocked. 'But why, in heaven's name? Tuka is the best we have.'

'That's why Hitler's boys want him out. He knows their military strategy inside out. Early this year during manoeuvres, he mapped out how and where the Germans would attack the Soviet Union and how they should be resisted.'

'I know all that, F-F-Freddy,' Livitsky sometimes stuttered when he was over-excited, 'but why does our great leader want to get rid of him?'

'He's jealous of Tuka's standing in the Red Army, and deep down he's worried that in a crisis Tuka might move against him,' replied Ludwik. 'And he's never forgiven Tuka for refusing to denounce Trotsky. For these reasons our greatest military commander will, no doubt, soon be arrested and accused of being a German spy. Frederick?'

'I fear so. And he won't be the only one. They want to purge all those who worked under him as well.'

'I wish I'd died during our civil war.'

Freddy re-lit his pipe and studied his friend's face. Ludwik's eyes were filled with sadness. For a while none of them spoke. It was always the same when they discussed Moscow.

'Ludwik,' said Freddy, 'they want you to return to Moscow for a debriefing session.'

'Why?'

'On the face of it, the request is not unreasonable. You've been out of the country for seven years. Spain is crucial to the future of Europe. You know it better than anyone else.'

'But . . . ?' inquired Ludwik.

'But,' Freddy responded, 'you should decline the offer. One of Stalin's new boys was asking about you. Wanted to know why your brother had fought with the Poles against the Red Army in 1921. I think if you return they will keep you there.'

'If I have to die, I would rather go down fighting the fascists.'

'I agree,' interrupted Livitsky. 'Ludwik is needed in Spain. He is the only one who knows the location of our spies working on Franco's side.'

'I have a better idea,' said Freddy. 'I will report that for the moment, your presence in Europe is indispensable. We could out-manoeuvre them if you send Lisa and Felix to Moscow for a short holiday to see friends and relations. It would be a clear indication that your conscience is clear and that you have nothing to fear.'

'If something happened to them Freddy, I would not be able to live.'

'Nothing will happen if they come soon.'

'You're sure?'

'As sure as one can be of anything.'

'I'll think about it.'

As they were driving back to Collioure, the sky cleared. Ludwik stopped the car near a bend and all three men jumped out to see the last few minutes of the sunset.

'Frederick,' asked Ludwik as they got back into the car, 'I have been waiting three days for both of you to tell me something.'

'What?'

'Why have neither Schmelka nor you talked about the trial? Is it true you interrogated Zinoviev and Kamenev? Could this be true?'

Heard of these names before, Karl? The Rosencrantz and Guildenstern of the Russian Revolution. Founders, with Lenin, of the Bolshevik Party. His closest comrades. Kamenev was also a very close personal friend and Lenin, thinking he might be killed, left Kamenev his manuscript of *State and Revolution*, a very un-Leninist pamphlet.

Both these men were opposed to the October insurrection, regarded it as an adventure, were close to the Mensheviks, went public with the date the Bolsheviks were planning a seizure of power. Lenin was livid. Demanded their expulsions, but was outvoted by the Central Committee. Later he forgave them, but he did not forget.

After Lenin's death they linked up with Stalin against Trotsky, but then joined the latter in a united opposition to defeat Stalin. Naturally, the dictator never trusted them again. When Stalin decided to wipe out most of Lenin's Central Committee, they were first on his list. One more thing. Kamenev wrote an excellent essay on Macchiavelli, which was used against him during the trials. The Prince consumed them all.

Neither man replied. Then Livitsky, his face distorted by the memory, began to speak.

'Freddy and I interrogated them in turn.'

'Who was the hard man?'

'I was.'

'You!?'

Ludwik was really surprised. Schmelka Livitsky was the least hardened of the old gang. He must have been totally unconvincing. This must have been Freddy's idea, his way of telling the two old Bolsheviks that the whole thing was a farce.

Freddy knew instinctively that Ludwik had guessed his motives. The two men looked at each other.

'It was a horrible business,' Freddy confessed to his old comrade. 'You know, in the old days, we used to laugh at them because they always agreed with each other. Siamese twins. They were not as bad as all that. Zinoviev looked me straight in the eye and said: "You know better than most that all we are accused of is a pack of lies, so why are you doing this to us? At least do not insult our intelligence." Kamenev nodded in total agreement. Even in the Lubianka their character had not changed. I wanted to tell them the truth. I wanted to scream that whatever happened they should not confess, but I could not even reply to Zinoviev. Everything was being taped for Stalin and we were being observed. I just carried on.'

'How did you get them to confess? Why did they confess?'

'Simple. I told them that if they challenged Stalin's will in court, he would have them executed in any case, but would also punish their families. If they pleaded guilty their families would be left alone. In their case it worked.'

'Simple, was it, comrade? Simple? You said that to them? You? You told Lenin's oldest comrades to die with lies on their lips? For what? Why? Why?'

'I had no choice. You would have done the same if you had been in Moscow, Ludwik. Or else suffered their fate.'

'He hasn't told you everything, Ludwik.'

'Tell me, Schmelka. Everything.'

'It would take too long and before I could finish we would all be dead.'

'We learn nothing from the past,' Ludwik mused as he started the car and began to negotiate the mountain bends. 'When our revolution was born, we talked about nothing but the French Revolution. How we should avoid its mistakes. When they started killing their own people, their days were numbered.'

Freddy laughed. 'Our leaders were never too worried about that, Ludwik. Surely you remember the Tenth Party Congress. You were there, weren't you?'

Ludwik nodded grimly. 'Yes. I was there and I marched behind Tuka to Kronstadt.'

Kronstadt, my dear Karl, was an island fortress near Petrograd, as it was then called. A naval base. It had been a revolutionary stronghold in 1917. Trotsky had won the sailors over to the Bolsheviks. Now the sailors wanted bread and freedom. That was fine. Everyone did, but they threatened the Bolsheviks with arms. The Tenth Party Congress decided unanimously to crush the revolt.

'I thought so,' said Freddy. 'Do you remember Lenin's speech?'
'Which bit?'
'The bit where Lenin talked about Thermidor,' Livitsky interjected. 'Remember? We had to crush the Kronstadt rebellion because otherwise it might become our Thermidor.'

'That was the lesson we learned from the French,' muttered Freddy. 'Avoid Thermidor at all costs.'

Ludwik's anger flared. 'Stalin is Thermidor, resurrected Thermidor with a Georgian moustache and murder mass-produced. A Tsar in a Communist tunic, but with no ruling class to restrain him.'

'Bukharin used the same words to me. The pity is that he hasn't even an ounce of Napoleon's intelligence,' replied Freddy.

'But far more cunning,' said Ludwik, 'and an addict's taste for the blood of imagined enemies.'

No more was said till they reached Collioure. Later that night, after they had sampled the fish caught in the morning, Ludwik turned to Freddy.

'Till today I really believed that if we won in Spain, Stalin's position inside the party would be weakened and they might even get rid of him. But from the way you talk, I'm no longer so sure.'

'You're too pessimistic, Ludwik. Mediocrity thrives on stagnation and defeat. A victory in Spain would alter the overall balance of power in Europe. A wave of optimism would spread, reach Moscow and who knows what might happen. Even some of Stalin's followers are discontented. Don't give up just yet.'

'Schmelka?' asked Ludwik.

'Freddy may be right. He knows the inner circles better than me, but . . .' said Livitsky and shrugged his shoulders.

'The real question is whether we can win in Spain and here you are our most experienced operator in the field. Your sober and meticulous reports are appreciated by almost everyone in the Department. So my friend, what is your answer?'

'I'm not sure,' replied Ludwik.

'Why?' pressed Freddy. 'We've got the green light from the Big Moustache for weapons and money.'

'Yes, I know,' said Ludwik, 'in return for which he's asked the Republic to ship its entire gold reserves to Moscow for safe-keeping. This is internationalism with a vengeance. In any case, weaponry alone will not be sufficient. We need a leader who can unite all the forces of the Republic and who understands both military and political strategy. You know the POUM[*] asked the government to send for Trotsky from his Mexican exile.'

Freddy roared with laughter. 'It would be the quickest way to unite Stalin, Hitler, Daladier and Chamberlain.'

'Yes, it's funny, but the problems are real. The anarchists are bent on burning down churches and shooting priests. The Poumists are not strong enough to control this stupidity. The government is weak and the Spanish section of the Communist International understands the Popular Front as a strategy to destroy its opponents on the Left. On the other hand the Right is more or less united and its objectives are simple: defend the Church and its property against atrocities; defend Spain against the Bolshevik threat and pledge Spain to fight alongside Hitler and Mussolini in Europe. It's working. Many on the Right mistrust Franco, but they hate the Republic.'

'But, Ludwik,' Schmelka Livitsky moaned, 'you're far too pessimistic. The majority of the people support the Republic.'

'Probably. But for how long? The debate goes like this: The only way we can win the civil war is first to make the Revolution. Expropriate the expropriators. This is the view of the POUM, the anarchists, the left-socialists and many other decent people. Moscow's men, our so-called comrades, the social democrats and honest liberals reply: Until we win the war there can be no revolution.

---

[*] Unified Marxist party, strong in Catalonia. It was sympathetic to Trotsky. Its leader, Andres Nin, was assassinated by Stalin's agents.

'Both are right. Both are wrong. The counter position is stupid and dogmatic. Undialectical. Lenin or Trotsky might have understood that, but not this bunch. They imagine that history is like a powerful river. Unstoppable. On its way to the sea. If that were the case, there would not be any need for us. You try telling them that history is a collection of streams, and which of these flows to the river depends on many factors. Our stream could dry up, but this possibility is forever excluded.'

'Ludwik, we have new orders. Direct from the Kremlin.'

Something in Freddy's voice alerted Ludwik that the new instructions could test his loyalty. Schmelka was looking shifty.

Ludwik looked straight into Freddy's light grey eyes. 'I'm prepared for the worst.'

'A special unit has been set up, outside the Fourth Department, with only one purpose: the elimination of the POUM leaders in Spain and the assassination of Trotsky in Mexico.'

Ludwik was stunned. He looked at their faces in silence. Could they still remain silent? Like him, they had fought under Trotsky. Freddy had been attached to a special unit on Trotsky's train, whose sole purpose had been to keep the leader of the Red Army alive. Freddy and Schmelka knew what was preoccupying Ludwik.

'Perhaps the time has come,' said Ludwik in a whisper.

'No!' both men shouted in one voice.

'Why not? Whose interests are we serving by carrying out Stalin's murders?'

'It's not as simple as that,' said Freddy, 'and you know that better than both of us. If we win in Spain it is a blow against Hitler! You've been sending us reports for over three years with one overriding demand. A bloc against Hitler with anyone and everyone prepared to fight fascism. Now you want to exclude Stalin from your united front.'

'Stalin paved the way for Hitler. Trotsky was right.'

'Of course Trotsky was right on fascism, but he is, alas, powerless. It is Stalin who controls the Red Army and this army can fight fascism. That's why any romantic notions of breaking with Moscow are foolish. Understandable, but wrong. Don't think we haven't talked about all this in the Department.'

'Meanwhile we murder the old Bolsheviks, execute anarchists and Poumists, allow Trotsky to be killed, and watch silently while Stalin frames Tukachevsky, the most brilliant military strategist in Europe. If we do all this we might not be able to defeat fascism. Our methods will have become the same.'

'We won't sit still. Why should we? Trotsky should be warned that there is now a serious plot to kill him. You can do that via your contacts in Amsterdam. Your good friend Sneevliet is close to Trotsky's son. In Moscow we'll try to warn Tukachevsky and the others.'

'No doubt. Like you helped Zinoviev and Kamenev. Freddy, don't you understand? It's too late. Unless ... unless. Prepare for a heresy.' Ludwik paused for a moment and then his voice dropped to a whisper. 'Unless Tukachevsky seizes power!'

'Unthinkable. Bonapartism would kill the Revolution.'

'The Revolution died a long time ago, my friend.'

'I agree with you Ludwik, but it's too late.' muttered Schmelka.

They carried on talking till it was nearly light. None of them knew whether they would see each other again. They remembered the *élan* of the early twenties. Things had been bad, but hope had not yet been obliterated. That was before the victory of the degenerates; before the world had begun to be coloured by the blood of innocents; before the Austrian house-painter had found a new profession and for them, the most important of all, before the former seminarist from Georgia had captured the apparatus of power in Moscow.

It was a time when the thought of death as an escape from the ugliness of the world had not yet entered their thoughts. Freddy admitted that he kept on working for the Fourth Department because to resign would be suicide, an acknowledgement of guilt, which in their profession meant execution.

'I know,' said Ludwik in response, 'but surely you realize that none of you will be left alive. You're witnesses to what is happening. After the murder, the killer turns his attention to the accomplices who witnessed the act.'

'What then?' inquired Livitsky. 'The only way to stay alive is to give oneself to the West. That would be a life worse than death.'

'There is another alternative,' said Ludwik. 'To disappear completely. Change our identities. Live and fight in a different way.'

'Simple-minded utopianism,' replied Freddy. 'The only one who's managed to do that is Trotsky, and Moscow is going to kill him. If we do the same they'll kill us too. The more important question is how to defeat fascism. You agree on that, Ludwik. Let's remain single-minded. First defeat fascism and then Stalin. Sorge agrees with that too.'

'Where is Sorge? Still in China?'

Freddy shrugged his shoulders. Richard Sorge had been seconded from the German Communist Party to join the Fourth Department. His grandfather had been a friend of Marx and Engels. Sorge's self-confidence bordered on recklessness. He had infiltrated top Nazi circles in Germany, acquired impeccable credentials, and judged purely from the vantage point of acquiring secret information, Sorge was the Soviet Union's most brilliant spy.

'Come on Freddy. I want to know.'

'He's safe in Tokyo with his geishas and an incredible network. He has penetrated the German Embassy.'

Ludwik laughed and clapped his hands. Sorge's promiscuity was a subject of much ribaldry throughout the Department.

'Penetrated?' Ludwik smiled. 'Who's the lucky woman in the Embassy?'

'Nobody in the Embassy. For once he is being a total professional, not mixing work with pleasure. He is sending us such incredible reports that the Moustache thinks he is being duped.'

Ludwik had become pensive again. 'Stalin is an odd monster. Like others who use their cunning to outwit more intelligent opponents, he cannot believe that there are other dictators even more devious than him. Stalin believes he can outfox everyone. Hence his refusal to accept intelligence reports which go against his own limited instincts.'

His friends nodded in agreement. They were leaving that night and Freddy tried to lighten the mood.

'Remember our river at Pidvocholesk, Ludwik? When we stood on the bank waiting to jump in the cold water, we always knew we would reach the other side. Didn't we?'

'Yes,' Ludwik replied in a sombre voice, 'but water flowed down that river, not blood.'

Ludwik moved in the thought-channels of his century. He wished that the eclipse that had blighted his life would disappear, that the sun would shine again. He wanted the Spanish Republic to triumph because he understood, better than many of those who fought for the Republic, the international impact of such a victory. If his work made such a triumph possible, then it would be worth hanging on for a few more years.

As the train began to move he thought of Freddy and Schmelka. How had they managed to survive in the furnace? How?

He began to dream again. Franco crushed and humiliated, fleeing to his refuge in Rome. The red flag flying defiantly over Madrid and Barcelona, Burgos and Valencia. A set of chain reactions. A popular uprising in Italy. Mussolini toppled. A democratic Republic in Rome. Hitler on the defensive. Splits inside the very heart of the German élite. Perhaps even a Junker *coup d'état* in Berlin. And then a revival of the German workers' movement. Socialist and Communist unity against the fascists. Strikes against the Nazis.

The dream always ended in Moscow. The spider in the Kremlin

dislodged, his cobweb dismantled. A new leadership which united the old guard and the best of the new. Trotsky recalled from his Mexican exile to take charge of the Red Army. The release of all political prisoners. And Stalin? Stumpy, stocky Stalin would be in the dock, charged with murder. His face ashen, his low forehead lower than ever before, wearing his grey tunic and grey breeches, but his boots would no longer be shining because there would be no one to polish them. And the sentence?

As the train approached Paris, where Felix and Lisa anxiously awaited his return, Ludwik sighed and listened to his inner voice. Cold, hard and realistic. Always realistic. Intolerant of sentimentality or romanticism:

If only it were so, but it will not be. Don't wait. Don't hope. Scatter. Disappear. The Terror rages in Berlin and Moscow. A frenzied delirium has gripped Spain. Everywhere the monotonous beat of merciless hearts, immune to all pleas. Pitiless eyes which pierce everything like a cold Siberian wind. Young lives prematurely truncated.

It was past nine in the evening when Ludwik found himself, tired and out of breath, pressing the bell on the front door of his top-floor apartment. He had been away for nearly five weeks. Lisa peered through the hole, sighed with relief and unbolted the door. He let his suitcase drop to the floor and embraced her in silence. Tears of relief slid down her cheeks. He wiped them and kissed her eyes, then her giant forehead.

'Papa!'

A pyjama-clad Felix rushed into the corridor and was lifted off the ground by two strong arms.

'I was worried you would never come back.'

'I promised you I'd be back this week, and here I am. Now, let's go back to your bed.'

As he entered his son's tiny bedroom, Ludwik noticed a French edition of *War and Peace* on the table, near the glass of water. Felix had already read *Anna Karenina*, but in Russian.

'It's difficult enough in Russian. Why read it in French?'

'Mama helps with the more difficult words and I skip all the boring bits myself. I love the battles.'

'And the love scenes?'

'They're all right,' Felix answered, averting his head slightly. He then told his father how the teacher at school had not believed him when he told the class that his favourite writers were Tolstoy and Shakespeare.

'I told them the story of *Anna Karenina* in French and recited Mark Antony's speech from *Julius Caesar* in Russian.'

Ludwik laughed.

'Did he apologize?'

Felix shook his head.

'They never do, do they?'

'Papa, is it true that Tolstoy hated Shakespeare?'

'Alas, yes.'

'But why?'

'I'm not sure. Perhaps the old Count was simply jealous of a superior talent.'

'I still don't understand.'

'When you're twenty-five or even thirty, read Tolstoy again. You'll understand. I used to read and re-read Tolstoy and every time I learnt something new about him. He was a deeply moral man. I think he was offended by Shakespeare's irony, his mocking of life, his cynicism. He thought Shakespeare was amoral. Didn't understand that this was part of his creative genius as a writer. Just as much as his own sense of morality. Tolstoy used to say that Harriet Beecher Stowe was far more talented than Shakespeare!'

'Who is she? What did she write?'

'A book about the lives of American Negroes, *Uncle Tom's Cabin*. It's good, but to compare it to Shakespeare? Ridiculous, even though the Count was serious. Now, lights off, and sleep.'

Father and son exchanged kisses. Felix made a mental note to find a Russian edition of *Uncle Tom's Cabin*.

Later that night Lisa told Ludwik of Gertrude's phone call. 'She sounded hysterical. Someone from Moscow had told her how the old Bolsheviks were being tortured in prison. She wanted to break now. I calmed her down, but you'll have to see her tomorrow. She even talked of suicide.'

'Things are bad in Moscow. They want me to go back. Schmelka says I must not, but to make them less suspicious, he suggests a brief trip by Felix and you. I'm not sure.'

'I am,' said Lisa. 'Felix cannot stay here on his own. So we will go. Not another word. That's settled. If we don't do it, it means a break before we're ready and that's even more dangerous.'

Nothing was settled. They argued for most of the night. At one stage, unable to make any headway through what he considered to be rational argument, Ludwik lost his temper and shouted at her, calling her an obstinate Ukrainian beetroot, insisting that he would not risk Felix's life for anything in the world, demanding that she obey him.

'I am no longer requesting, Lisa. I speak now not as your lover, but as the head of our entire intelligence operation in Europe. I order you not to take Felix with you to Moscow.'

Lisa remained calm and refused to capitulate. 'Anything could happen to you here. The enemy could kill you. Our own people could order your liquidation. And then what would happen to Felix? I will feel safer if he remains with me.'

It was well past three when Ludwik acknowledged defeat, turned his back on her and fell asleep.

Sixteen

To: Professor Vladimir Meyer,
Berlin
From: Sao,
Moscow, 1994

Dear friend,

I have suffered a terrible blow and I want to share the pain with you. None of my other friends will understand, perhaps because none of them are friends like you and I. Before I start, I want you to know that I've been thinking of you a great deal for the last few months. I have not forgotten your request, but I have been out of Moscow for most of the time since we last met. Buying and selling. Helping the flow of commodities from one market to the next. Does anything else really matter these days? Please don't reply to this question. I'm not in the mood.

I wanted to write from Beijing, but your refusal to let me buy you a fax machine made this impossible. Letter writing is so boring these days and such an effort. Only the fax machine has revived this lost art, but your hostility to new technology means that I will fax this to Suzanne in Paris and she will post it to you.

When I return to Berlin, I will give you a detailed account of my adventures in Mongolia and how the North Koreans wanted to pay me in bags of heroin ... Incidentally Pyongyang, too, is full of prostitutes. I wanted to try one just to see whether she would commence her activities by citing some 'on-the-spot guidance' she had received from the Great and Beloved Leader Kim-il-Sung or his son and heir, the 'Dear Leader', Kim Jong Il, but you will be pleased to hear that I resisted the temptation.

And now for my story. I returned to Moscow a month ago. Three days after my arrival, I went to the old flat which I had shared with my friends.

We had never relinquished this flat, partly out of sentimentality and partly because it was still used to house visitors from other towns. The lift wasn't working. I climbed up five flights of stairs. The front door was unlocked. I knew immediately that something was wrong.

I went in and saw their dead bodies on the floor. No blood. No trace of a battle. Two of my oldest and closest friends, with whom I had first started on our business enterprise, had been murdered. Think about it, Vlady. We survived the war. The Americans couldn't kill us with all their bombs and napalm. Russian gangsters walked in and strangled them. Took them by surprise. Nothing was taken from the flat, not even the dollars hidden under the mattress. Nothing was touched. The killers must have been expected. They were obviously men my friends had traded with. Who were they?

At first I was scared. If them, why not me? I thought of my two children in Paris. My friends, especially you. I wanted to get a taxi to the airport and get the first plane out, leave this sick, dying town forever. All the good memories evaporated. Then I began to feel ashamed at my own cowardice. I felt angry.

I remembered the heavy insurance we'd paid Yeltsin's gang over the last eight months — dollars and yen to help speed up the 'reform process', you understand. Why should I let them get away with murder? I went straight to the top. Tsar Boris was busy with other things. He was confronted with a parliament which is in permanent opposition. Solution? Destroy it and gain more power for the President. You must have seen it all on television. Amazing how they destroyed their White House, backed by the Western leaders. Remember the US major who defended the destruction of Ben Tre, a small town by saying: 'The only way we could save Ben Tre was by destroying it.' Yesterday's war. That's exactly how Yeltsin is saving Russian democracy. I watched it on CNN in my hotel room, but I couldn't concentrate. I kept seeing the two dead bodies in the flat. My friends. Finally I switched off the TV and began to ring everyone I knew in Yeltsin's entourage. Most of them were in hiding, unsure of the outcome. This did not surprise me.

Late that night I finally got hold of Andrei K., the Tsar's private banker. He was not so busy. He asked me to come over to his office in the Kremlin. I had always wanted to see the inside of the Kremlin, but not at two in the morning. I went anyway and spent three hours with Andrei. When I knew him in the old days, when he was a reform Communist who couldn't believe they had someone like Gorbachev in power, he used to dress in blue denims and a sweater. That night he was wearing a tweed jacket, grey flannel trousers and a bow-tie. His hair was well groomed, his absurd little moustache was disgustingly neat. He was in an exultant mood, constantly refilling his glass, and the whisky was talking.

'We have made Russia safe for the free market,' he told me. 'Democracy has won. Better a horrible end than a horror without end, eh, Sao? You agree, eh Sao? We're teaching our people that it is sometimes necessary to pay a high price in order to gain the benefits of civilization.'

It was obvious that Andrei had known fear, and now wanted revenge against those who had reduced him to this state. His desires, hidden below the surface, were now uncontainable. He talked a lot of nonsense. I let him go on for a while. His inner emptiness was now combined with an anger, but this only served to render his banalities even more commonplace than before. I wanted to tear off his silly, little bow, dip it in whisky and stuff it in his mouth just so that he would stop talking. His voice was beginning to drive me mad. At last he paused and opened a new bottle of whisky.

I looked straight into his eyes and asked who had killed my colleagues. The look on his face changed. He looked uneasy and moved his eyes away from mine. He expressed his sorrow. He made no attempt to pretend that he wasn't aware of the killing. You see, he knew my friends very well. In emergencies they used to hand over thousands of dollars to him.

I shouted at him. I demanded an investigation. He said there was no need for one. My friends had been killed by a gang of army officers who resented our role in the arms trade. The same people, he said, who were trying to seize power. He warned me to be careful. 'We are in transition, Sao. You know that well. At such times nobody is safe. I am truly sorry that your friends are dead, but please don't grieve unduly. Save yourself. I suggest you leave Moscow tomorrow.' I slapped his face hard. I couldn't help myself, Vlady. He slumped into a chair. I asked him once again, but this time in a soft voice: 'Who killed my friends?'

At first he claimed that they were part of the anti-reform wing of the army. When I asked for names, he shrugged his shoulders. I knew he was lying. I told Andrei that if nothing was done, I would go public. I warned him that if anything happened to me, my lawyers had been instructed to publish everything. 'This includes your name and those of five others in the President's entourage. I have everything. When you were paid, how much, and even the numbers of your bank accounts in Zurich.'

At this point he collapsed. I was promised a private inquiry. I told him all I wanted was names, and left.

Within two days he told me that his earlier information had been wrong. He had been told that the murderers were drug-traffickers, who had already been arrested and sent to prison. They had told the police that the Vietnamese had owed them money. I stared into Andrei's frightened eyes. He knew as well as I that we never traded in drugs. He started crying. He swore that none of them knew who was responsible for the killings. He had given me false information just to get me off his back. I felt this was *probably the closest I would get to the truth, but before I left I warned him that unless I got a name I would expose his whole gang. I also pointed out that killing me would ensure that the information would appear in* Le Monde *the next day. My lawyers had very clear instructions.*

I tell you all this so that you will understand that when I asked Andrei to secure me the files you wanted from the KGB archives, he was only too eager to help. History means nothing to them any more. They would sell anything. But I did not even have to pay. I was received by a KGB general who wanted to discuss the whole business with me, but I told him the papers I had demanded were for a friend. He shrugged his shoulders and handed them over. I have all the files you wanted with me, and even the belongings of the man Ludwik. Extraordinary, how much material they kept on file. They really meant it when they stamped on people's files: TO BE PRESERVED FOREVER. *There's even a suitcase. I will hand them over to you when I return to Berlin in a few months' time. At least I have made you happy, my friend.*

I have never felt so sad in Moscow as on this trip. Not just because my friends are dead. Ever since the collapse, people here have been living in a vacuum. The intelligentsia no longer seems able to defend the best of the old culture. The culture that exists is badly damaged. No attempts to reclaim or even invent a common past, except, of course, for the idiots who glorify Tsarism and the Church. This is a crushed people. Like Germany after the Treaty of Versailles. My old friend Zinaida burst into tears in the middle of a conversation last week. This is not so unusual in Moscow and so I held her hand to comfort her. I thought it was because she was poor and needed money and food. I was preparing to offer her some dollars when she looked into my eyes and said: 'You don't know why I'm crying, do you?' I shook my head. She dried her eyes, took out a crumpled newspaper clipping from her handbag and handed it to me without a word. It was the result of a survey. Izvestia, *a much-liked daily paper, had asked sixteen-year-old Russian girls in all the big towns what they wanted to do when they left school. Forty per cent answered: 'Hard-currency prostitution.' Zina told me that in the Baltic States the figure was much higher. You know, Vlady, that after the war in my country conditions were bad. There were many young women who became prostitutes in Hanoi, but they were ashamed.*

Later that night, after many glasses of wine, Zina confessed that one of these young girls was her eighteen-year-old daughter, Irina. I was very shocked, Vlady. I know the young woman. She's attractive, intelligent, well bred. She doesn't need to think of prostitution. A girl like her in Hanoi would be aiming to become an interpreter attached to the Foreign Office or something like that, but not Irina. When Zina shouted at her, the girl screamed back: 'And why not, Mother? It's non-taxable income! And why are you shouting at me Mama? Look at our country. When you go for shock therapy you must be prepared for shocks.' Zina could not think of a reply.

The sky today was a beautifully sharp, clear blue, but I don't think I will ever return to Moscow again. I find this city too full of menace. It scares me. It will explode one of these days. It is better to stay well away.

I have just looked out of the window. Even the full moon looks like a turnip.

I hope you're well and not feeling too gloomy, though this wretched letter is unlikely to raise your spirits. You have to learn how to rise above the neurosis that afflicts the whole of the old DDR. Understand? I will see you very soon, my friend. Keep calm and don't panic.

Your friend,

Sao

Seventeen

FOR A LONG TIME after the 1930s, and even after the death of the paranoid tyrant, Joseph Stalin, in 1953, when Lisa tried to remember her last trip to Moscow she could never see it in a straight perspective or an ordinary light. It wasn't only the tide of adrenaline pumping through her system, the dry throat, the copper taste of apprehension – she had felt all these before. It was as if a tangible distillation of the terror suffered by its citizens had been vented into the Moscow atmosphere, converting sights and sounds into the fabric of an Expressionist film – pools of black shadow, a background of croaks and whispers, faces worn like masks. She remembered the visit as a series of episodes whose logic belonged so specifically to that time and place that she could not re-create it elsewhere.

Remember, she kept telling herself, never betray surprise or fear or anger. They are holes for death to creep through. It was May 1937. The border-crossing at Eydkhunen in Latvia had passed without any problems. It was the moment Lisa always hated. Soviet border guards were under strict instructions to question foreigners. Perhaps they had been notified. They must have been or else they would have been questioned. Anyway she had not been bothered, despite their fake Czech passports. Even the luggage hadn't been searched.

Felix, innocent, unsuspecting boy, was fast asleep as the train approached Moscow. It was early morning and Lisa was greeted by sunshine and a clear sky. Outside the birches and poplars were standing guard as always, faithful sentinels of the Russian countryside.

She lowered the window and put her head out, shutting her eyes as she breathed the clean air. It reminded her of more indolent times and suddenly she felt light-hearted. But the mood lasted less than five seconds. She thought she saw the trunk of a birch tree splattered with blood. She raised the window again and sat down, her pulse quicker than before.

'Wake up, Felix. We're almost there.'

In Moscow itself, thought Lisa as she grimaced, life must be normal. Innumerable bureaucrats, spies, secret policemen, ordinary people trying to be good citizens, Party members with a misguided sense of loyalty, all working continually in the background, sometimes out of sight, but never out of the mind of the country as a whole.

The Leader had wanted every good citizen to be a spy and now they kept watch, they wrote reports, they competed to see who could denounce the largest number of 'enemies of the people'. If their hard work resulted in an interrogation, they would smile to themselves, but if the interrogation resulted in a prison sentence, not to mention a trial and execution, they felt elated, imagining themselves totally safe. Poor fools, thought Lisa. Poor, poor fools.

The train stopped. She wondered whether Freddy had got her telegram. Then, looking at the sea of faces, she wondered whether there were any human beings left in the country – people so good that they could not even think of evil.

'Lisa! Lisa! This way.'

It was Freddy. His face comforted her. She grabbed Felix's arm, and mother and son suddenly found themselves lifted off the ground by a laughing giant in a greatcoat. Next to him stood his son, Adam, who was the same age as Felix. The two boys had been inseparable when Ludwik was stationed in Moscow. They would have a lot to talk about, but in the presence of parents they exchanged smiles.

'Welcome to Moscow! Felix, how you've grown. Adam you've been left behind. It must be the food in France!'

Adam groaned. Felix grinned. The predictability of the adult world depressed both of them. Freddy ignored the boys as he continued.

'If only you had come ten days ago, I would have taken you to the big May Day parade.'

'Was Trotsky there?' asked Felix.

Freddy's face clouded.

'And Zinoviev?' Felix continued. 'Kamenev? No, of course not. Enemies of the people. Sorry, Uncle Freddy.'

Adam gave his friend a look full of awe. Freddy sighed. Lisa was amazed. This was the first time that Felix had ever said anything of this sort. What had taken hold of the boy and why here, in Moscow, where people were sent to Siberia for asking less pointed questions?

She glared at her son in silence. He raised his eyebrows in mock surprise. She pinched his arm as Freddy bundled them into a black Zim and drove away from the station. There was hardly any traffic, but Freddy still drove slowly. How different it still is from Paris or Berlin, thought Lisa as she looked with affection at the man who was driving them to their hotel. Despite her knowledge that the city was gripped by fear, she found it impossible to resist the Moscow summer.

Once they were safely settled in the car, Lisa decided it was the time to find out which of the old gang were still around.

'Are any of our friends still in Moscow?'

'The fewer people you see, the better.'

'Ludwik instructed me to follow your instructions on everything, Freddy but ... I know Livitsky's in Paris, but Levy? Larin?'

'Levy is dead. He warned Bukharin that Stalin was out to get him. Suggested to Bukharin that he should not return to Moscow after his next trip abroad. That alone would have been enough, but Levy went further. He told Bukharin to go to Mexico. Someone in Bukharin's circle talked. Levy disappeared. No interrogation was necessary. He admitted everything and cursed the Moustache. I think he wanted to die quickly. They shot him three nights ago. As a result we're all under suspicion. Especially Ludwik.'

Lisa's face was pale. Misha Levy was dead. He had been a fresh-faced youth when she had first met him in Vienna. Tears brimmed in her eyes. She wiped them ruthlessly away. A tear-stained face would arouse suspicions at their Moscow hotel.

Misha was the first of the five Ls to die and Ludwik did not even know that he had been arrested. She spoke in a choked whisper. 'It's too horrible for words, Freddy.'

'I know. He wanted to go. He told me last year that he couldn't stand the trials and killings. He was desperate to go abroad and see Ludwik, but it was difficult to organize. As you know, he spoke only Russian. Larin is in Moscow. He will come and see you tomorrow evening.'

The car pulled up outside the Savoy. Lisa and Felix were to pretend they were here as tourists.

'I'll pick you up in the morning, Lisa. The Boss wants to see you for a few minutes. Felix can come as well. He and Adam can play chess in my office while you're debriefed. And Lisa, one more thing. Be very careful. The dictatorship is now totally ruthless.'

'And the proletariat?' whispered Lisa.

'Crushed,' replied Freddy, 'and yet I'm sure it will all turn out right in the end.'

'Are you really, Freddy?'

'Of course! This muck cannot last forever. The Moustache cannot destroy the Soviet Union.'

Felix and Adam had heard the entire conversation in silence. As they left the car, Felix pressed Adam's hand as if to say, 'I know. Don't worry. I won't let you down.'

'I will see you tomorrow,' Adam told him as he got out of the back seat and joined Freddy in the front of the car.

The hotel was half empty. Stray businessmen, a delegation of American Communists. They stared at her and Felix, trying to place the newly arrived pair in the order of things. A single woman and her child could not be here for business. Was she a visiting dignitary? A few of them smiled and waved a welcome. Lisa nodded politely and went straight to the lift. They all looked slightly tense, despite the vodka they appeared to have consumed. How different it was from the Hotel Lux that time in 1926, when the International meant something and when comrades from all over the world were still full of hope, arguing and shouting at each other. Everything had not been crushed then, even though all the signs pointed in Stalin's direction. Ludwik had told her that Stalin was bound to win. The civil war had made people on both sides sullen and demoralized, uninterested in politics.

She diverted herself by telling Felix to go and have a shower. As she dried his hair she began to think of the time she had first met Ludwik. She found herself remembering Vienna. Felix's eyes were sparkling again as he got into his pyjamas.

'Father told me there was one poem by Pushkin they all used to recite regularly when they were boys.'

'Which one? Let me think.'

'It had something to do with chains...'

'Of course,' Lisa shouted with delight. Then she raised her voice for the benefit of those listening. 'It was a poem against Tsarist tyranny, *Message to Siberia*. I can't remember it all, Felix, but tomorrow I will get a copy from Uncle Freddy and —'

'Please try, Mutti. A few lines. I'm sure you can if you try. Sometimes I think I've forgotten a poem and the teacher tells me to think and think and I do, and then I remember.'

'I'll try, but you get into bed. We've been on trains for two days. Sleep. Come on.'

Felix snuggled under the blankets and looked at her expectantly.

The boy was right, thought Lisa. Some of Pushkin's words had begun to creep into her consciousness and she began to recite in a soft, but firm voice.

> The sister of misfortune, Hope,
> In the under-darkness dumb
> Speaks joyful courage to your heart:
> The day desired will come.

> And love and friendship pour to you
> Across the darkened doors,
> Even as round your galley-beds
> My free music pours.

Felix sat up in bed, his eyes shining, for he, too, had now remembered the last verse which Ludwik had recited so often only a few years ago. Mother and son spoke in harmony.

> The heavy-hanging chains will fall,
> The walls will crumble at a word;
> And Freedom greet you in the light,
> And brothers give you back the sword.

Lisa remembered Misha and wept silently. She kissed Felix and turned out the lamp, but the darkness could not drown her sorrows. Sleep would not come to her, and after an hour of tossing and turning she got out of bed. Felix was fast asleep. Lisa was exceedingly perturbed. She knew Freddy must have been shattered by Misha's execution just as much as she was, but he had spoken of it casually, almost as if Misha had lost a game of roulette. And if even Bukharin was under threat, how could anything change?

Freddy and Adam joined them while they were having breakfast.

'I have a surprise for you, waiting in the foyer.'

'Larin?'

'No, he will come this evening. An old friend of yours, Lisa, and her son, who used to play with Felix and Adam about five years ago, when you were in Berlin. Remember? Her husband was killed by the Nazis.'

Felix's eyes lit up. 'Hans Wolf?'

'Correct. And his mother, Minna.'

Lisa was pleased and surprised.

'How long have they been in Moscow?'

'Since Hitler came to power. It was bad enough being a member of the KPD,[*] but having been married to a Jewish poet, even a dead one, meant the camps and death, sooner or later.'

As they left the dining room, Lisa felt a shiver of excitement. She and Minna had been very close. They had discussed everything with each other. Once, in Ludwik's presence, Lisa had confided to Minna how ugly and unattractive she found Stalin.

'Why,' she had said, 'he has no forehead.'

Both women had laughed, but Ludwik had looked round nervously in the restaurant and told them that remarks like that could lead to immediate expulsion from the Party. They had laughed at him then, but now Lisa felt frightened. If Minna were ever to pass on the remark of several years ago, she might not be allowed to leave Moscow.

'Lisa! Felix!'

Minna rose and hugged Lisa, kissing her warmly on both cheeks. Then it was Felix's turn. The boy winced slightly. He turned to Hans and they shook hands as if they were grown men. The mothers exchanged smiles.

'So you've made friends again, eh?' said Freddy with a wink, but he was subjected to such a withering gaze from Adam, Felix and Hans that he went and hid behind the two mothers.

'Lisa! You look well. Frederick tells me that you are wanted by the Department. We would like to borrow Felix and Adam for the day. If you're finished by three or four, come and have tea with us. Otherwise we'll bring him back here.'

Minna's tone was subdued and somewhat artificial. Lisa looked at her son. What was being suggested was perfectly normal and yet her heart was beating faster. She looked at her boy.

'Is that OK, Felix?'

'Yes, fine,' he muttered.

'Great, that's settled, then. I will bring Lisa to your flat between three and four. If we're delayed I will make sure to ring you.'

In the safety of the car, Lisa began to talk openly to Freddy.

'Now that the boy isn't here, let me tell you a few things. Did you know that Moscow has hired a band of killers whose only task is to wipe out Communist oppositionists? Navachine was killed while taking his morning walk in the Bois de Boulogne in January. He was only going to make a speech!'

'I know,' replied Freddy, 'but what a speech! It was the most brilliant demolition of the trials. Better even than Trotsky, because he knows much more. The Boss read the speech himself and ordered him despatched.'

---

[*] KPD: Communist Party of Germany.

'Slutsky?'

'No. Stalin.'

'So you know all about it?'

'Of course.'

'And?'

'And nothing. We are wading in shit and blood, Lisa. Ludwik knows that well. It cannot last much longer. There will be a new war with Germany. Stalin might be removed.'

'But by whom? He's removed everyone who could have removed him. And now Bukharin, too, is being made ready for the executioner's bullet.'

'He doesn't fear Bukharin. Plays him like a piano. But he feels Bukharin could be the figurehead if there was a more concerted rebellion. So Bukharin will follow the others.'

'And us, Freddy?'

'You two must try and stay alive. Tell Ludwik to avoid any heroic gestures. Someone must write one day about what happened to our own people. Before we go in, I just want you to be very careful. Listen, but say little yourself. Reply only to direct questions. Do not volunteer any information. The fact that you've come here with the boy has disarmed them. They have stopped asking me stupid questions about Ludwik. Understand?'

Lisa had met Slutsky before, but never in these circumstances. She could barely conceal a smile when she was shown into his room. He was wearing navy blue uniform, adorned with brass buttons. He could have been the doorman outside the Metropol. So this was the uniform worn by the Head of Foreign Military Intelligence. How he's changed, she thought. His demeanour is so official, but he's trying a bit too hard. A part of her wanted to burst out laughing. He looked like a clown in this stupid uniform.

Slutsky was aware of her presence, but wanted to keep her standing for a few minutes. He pretended to be absorbed in a file marked TOP SECRET. Lisa understood the game. She was tempted for a moment to take the empty chair opposite his desk and stare straight into his face, but Freddy's warning stopped her. Instead she coughed delicately.

'So you are here. Please take a seat. You have many friends in our Department. I hope they are looking after you?'

Lisa smiled and nodded.

'For myself, I would have preferred to have your husband sitting in front of me, not that he is as pretty as you...' Slutsky stared at her breasts and gave a sinister, throaty laugh. Then he lit a cigarette. Lisa remained silent. She was startled by the sound of a cough from a darkened corner of the room. She had no idea that someone else was present in the room. As she turned, she saw a pimply-faced man, probably in his late twenties, rising from an armchair.

'This is Comrade Kedrov.'

'I think we've met before. At the rest-home, about six years ago?' Kedrov nodded.

'He is now our top interrogator. It was he who broke Radek. Didn't you, Kedrov? That filthy cosmopolitan thought he could play games with us. Didn't he, Kedrov? You soon put him right, didn't you?'

Kedrov smiled, avoiding Lisa's eyes. And this boy, Lisa thought, is the son of two old Bolsheviks who worked closely with Lenin in Switzerland. Slutsky suspected she might be thinking something like that. He pounced on her to put her on the defensive.

'What did Ludwik think of Radek's trial?'

'I don't know. We never discussed the matter.'

'Come now, my dear. You mean to tell me that your husband, who knew Radek well, remained silent?'

'I said he never discussed the matter with me.'

After another hour of inconclusive fencing, Slutsky indicated that the audience was at an end.

'When do you return to Paris?'

'Next week.'

'Tell Ludwik I want him back here. This Spanish business will end badly. Tell him to forget about Europe. I want our most experienced men back here. To defend our Soviet fortress.'

'I will tell him, Comrade Slutsky. Thank you. And best of luck, Comrade Kedrov.'

'Please tell Ludwik that we admire him greatly,' Kedrov spoke in a soft voice. 'I look forward very much to meeting him.' Kedrov's smile froze Lisa. She stared at him. Ambition oozed out of him so effortlessly. He will go far before his fall, she thought.

She rushed straight into Freddy's room, but before she could speak a word, he put his finger on his lips to remind her that the office was unsafe.

'Well, how did it go?'

'Very well. Comrade Slutsky was very kind. I had no idea that Kedrov had interrogated Radek.'

'He was part of the conveyor belt, but it was he who finally broke Radek. He is most skilful.'

She shut her eyes in pain. Freddy put on a jovial voice.

'Lunch?'

The minute they were in the car, Lisa exploded.

'That boy, that spotty bastard. He boasts about his successes. As for Slutsky, he's degenerated beyond belief. I want to get out of here, Freddy, and I want you and Larin out as well.'

Freddy stroked her face. 'Better to die here, my Lisa. Abroad one will always live in permanent fear of them. What's the point of life if you're constantly in fear of death? By the way, don't judge Slutsky too harshly.'

'How can you say that? He was never sweet and inoffensive, I grant you that, but to wallow in Kedrov's glory. It makes me sick. If Ludwik ever came back they would kill him, wouldn't they, Freddy?'

Freddy nodded. 'By the way, Slutsky will be joining us for lunch.'

'I don't believe you.'

'You should.'

Lisa was so shocked by the casual tone that she sulked for the rest of the journey. Freddy sighed as he parked the car near the Writer's Club. He took her by the arm and whispered.

'You don't live here. You can't understand what it's like any more.'

They were shown a small, private room, where a table with three chairs had been prepared for their lunch. On it were placed a host of delicacies, which included caviar, smoked fish of several varieties, cold meats, salad and a bottle of vodka. Before Lisa could comment on this unusual arrangement, Slutsky entered the room. He went straight to her and kissed her on both cheeks.

'Let me guess. You were confiding to Freddy how I had changed. Where once I was a filthy skunk, now I had become a sewer rat. Yes?'

Lisa smiled despite herself.

'You see, my dear,' Slutsky continued, 'there are still a few intelligent people left in Soviet intelligence. Despite ten years of good conduct, I have still not been able to win the confidence of Comrade Stalin. Only last week in Leningrad, three dozen young Communists were executed for asking too many questions. Every time they asked a perfectly normal question – normal, that is, for a Communist – they were denounced as Trotskyite saboteurs. So just before they were shot they shouted, "Long Live Trotsky." These were kids, who had probably only heard of Trotsky from their parents. Vodka?'

Lisa was amazed. Freddy tried hard to conceal a smile as he noticed her astonishment. He turned to Slutsky.

'Our friend was disgusted by your performance in front of Kedrov.'

'Good, good! I agree with her. It was a good performance.'

'Perhaps,' said Lisa, slowly realizing that the earlier scene she had participated in was a charade, 'we should have booked a table at the Actor's Club.'

The two men laughed. They can still laugh, she thought, even while they are living through unimaginable horrors every day. Aloud she asked: 'And Kedrov? Was he part of the act?'

Slutsky's face changed. 'That young man is a true believer. Stalin sees Kedrov often these days. He likes to hear of how his old enemies behave during interrogation and just before they are executed. So Kedrov now believes in the divine right of interrogators. He really believes that he will end up a member of the Politburo.'

'He might. After all, there are others like him...'

'My dear Lisa, Kedrov knows too much. Most of the oppositionists didn't confess to anything. Instead they denounced Stalin and the apparatus. They detailed his crimes. Kedrov has heard everything. His turn will come soon. And he will be shot. The fact that he hasn't realized this himself indicates the limits of his intelligence.'

'Do you really want Ludwik to return?'

'Are you mad? Tell him to stay outside as long as he can. If possible, forever. Within a year the Kedrovs will be in charge of everything. Ludwik is a legend in the Department and old legends have to be destroyed so that new time-servers can build themselves. How is he?'

'Well.'

'I don't mean his health, Lisa. His brain. What is he thinking?'

Lisa looked at Freddy for guidance as to whether or not it was safe to reply to Slutsky's question. Freddy nodded.

'He's very depressed. The trials have shaken us to the very core. Ludwik says that we should never have banned the Mensheviks. He traces the decline to that decision, but I'm not so sure. The only thing that keeps him going is Spain. If the fascists are defeated, he imagines it might start off a chain reaction in Italy and even Germany. If that happens, Ludwik argues, then Stalin, who's a monster born out of the defeats in Europe and the depoliticization of Soviet workers, will fall as well.'

'It must be nice for him, eh, Freddy?' said Slutsky with a sad smile. 'Ludwik is still able to dream. All I see is even worse nightmares. I hope he's right and I'm wrong, but I fear the opposite. Has Freddy told you of how we got Smirnov and Mrachovsky to confess?'

Lisa stared at them in horror. 'It was you?'

Both men nodded.

'Ludwik was convinced that neither Mrachovsky nor Smirnov could ever be broken. For some reason he was very sure. He wept when he read of their confessions. And it was you?'

Freddy looked away. Slutsky told her the story.

'He wept, Lisa? He wept? What do you think it did to us? When I began the interrogation, I had a full head of hair. Look at me now. I questioned him for ninety hours.

'He had walked in limping – a civil war wound. I served under him, but he'd forgotten. "Comrade Mrachovsky, I have been ordered to question you."

'"Have you, you sonofabitch?" was his first reply. Then, looking at me with pure contempt, he just carried on. "I will not speak to men like you. Scum of the lowest order. You're worse than the Okhrana. The Tsar's men were better than you. How dare *you* question *me*? Two Orders of the Red Banner, eh? Did you steal them? You call me comrade. The man before you called me a reptile and counter-revolutionary. Me! I was born in a Tsarist prison. My parents died in exile in Siberia. I became a Bolshevik at the age of fifteen. Do you want to see my decorations?"

'At this point, Lisa, he rose and bared his chest. It was criss-crossed with scars of every shape and size. I was on the verge of tears. "Comrade Mrachovsky, I fought under your command on the Tashkent front. That's how I earned the Order of the Red Banner." I had to send for my biography from the archives before he was convinced. He stared at me. "So you were once a Communist and a revolutionary. How have you degenerated into a police hound? Let me tell you something, Slutsky. They took me twice to see Stalin. On both occasions he tried to bribe me. I spat in his face. I reminded him of what Trotsky had called him to his face: Gravedigger of the revolution. That's when you were called in, Slutsky. So finish your job. I am not going to confess.'

'I talked and I talked, Lisa, reminding him of the revolution, the civil war, the fact that we were surrounded by a hostile world, Hitler's rise to power. I told him that the question was no longer Stalin, but how long the Soviet Union could survive. We both began to weep. Then he said, "If my confession would strengthen the Soviet Union, I would consider it seriously." I felt like saying "Don't, don't," but everything was being recorded. Later that day he met Smirnov, who talked him out of it, but we carried on. When Smirnov realized Mrachovsky had confessed, he broke down.'

'Though at the trial,' Freddy spoke for the first time, 'Smirnov tried on several occasions to retract his confession. Each time he was stopped by the prosecutors.'

Lisa looked at both men. Their eyes had filled with tears.

'Tell Ludwik to stay away, Lisa,' said Slutsky, 'and warn him that a new man is being sent to the Embassy. A friend of Kedrov, by the name of Speigelglass. His job is to spy on Ludwik.'

Lisa had never liked Slutsky, not even in the old days, but now, as he rose, she hugged him.

'Goodbye, Lisa. Remember me to Ludwik. I doubt whether we'll ever see each other again.'

After Slutsky had left there was a tense silence. Lisa still could not believe that Freddy, one of the five Ls of Pidvocholesk, a childhood friend of her Ludwik, was the man who had broken Smirnov. She looked at him. To avoid her gaze, Freddy lit a cigarette and then shamefacedly offered her one. Lisa declined.

'Take me to Minna's apartment, Freddy.'

She did not speak to him in the car, but as they neared the Embankment, Lisa screamed at him.

'Stop the car, Freddy. Now!'

Freddy braked and looked at her.

'Isn't that Krupskaya, walking towards the Kremlin? Can't I just run after her and exchange greetings? She knows Ludwik and –'

Felix paled. 'Yes, it is Lenin's widow. But look now. She's being followed. She's never alone. He hates her. And if I were to let you run up and kiss her, you would never leave Moscow. Anyway she's a stupid bitch.'

'Freddy!' Lisa had begun to tremble with anger. 'How dare you speak of her like that! She suffered even when Lenin was alive. And now . . .'

'Listen. She was the only person who could have denounced the trials and been heard at home and abroad. Of course he would have had her poisoned and our doctors would have diagnosed a stroke or heart failure or whatever, but at least she might have had an impact. Instead, she did her pleading in private.'

'What are you saying?'

'One day last year, Slutsky and I were both called in to Stalin's office. This was not unusual. Zinoviev and Kamenev were on trial for terrorism, espionage and all the usual shit. He wanted to know what they were saying about him. Therefore we did not regard the request as unusual.

'When we went in, he told us to sit in the corner. "I want you two veterans of the civil war to observe in silence. You will learn a great deal." After five minutes, Krupskaya was shown in. He stood up and received her courteously. She fell on her knees. "Josef Vissarionovich," she said in a broken voice, "Zinoviev and Kamenev were Lenin's oldest comrades. I beg of you. Spare their lives." She spoke of the two men, their strengths and weaknesses, their contribution to the Party. He heard her in silence.

'When she had finished he helped her to stand up. "Comrade Krupskaya, I am not the Tsar. Please do not petition me in this fashion. It disturbs me." He then denounced the two old Bolsheviks as traitors and reminded her of what Lenin had said about them on the eve of the Revolution. "It was Vladimir Ilyich who then demanded their expulsion from the Party." After several exchanges, Stalin convinced her that he would spare their lives, if she, Krupskaya, denounced them in public. And she did. And they were executed. And she should have known better. And that's why I called her a stupid bitch. I'm sorry for that. She, too, is a victim, and it must be very painful for her. She must be constantly thinking what it was meant to be and what it has become. And she knows that in the months before he died, Lenin realized what was taking place.'

'It's all over now, isn't it, Freddy? He has destroyed the revolution.'

They had arrived at Minna's apartment. Freddy bade her farewell. 'Don't forget, Larin is taking you and Felix home for dinner tonight. His room is safe, but best to be careful. I won't come up now. Tell Adam I'm waiting for him.'

Minna burst out laughing as she let Lisa into her flat. She laughed again on seeing the bewildered look on Lisa's face.

'Pure relief, my dear,' she said by way of explanation, while both of them were still outside the front door. 'You're back. And in Moscow that's wonderful. The boys have been playing happily. Come in.'

The two women exchanged smiles and retired to the tiny kitchen. Neither of them could be sure whether or not microphones had been hidden in the rooms. Both were careful and so they ensured that their conversation did not move in dangerous directions.

'Hans and I are happy here. We would not have survived in Germany. When Michael was arrested, we thought it would only be for a few weeks, then friends said it might be a few months and then one day we were told that Michael had been shot while trying to escape.'

'And Hans. How did he . . . ?'

'It was three years ago. He understood what had happened. He was nine then, but he felt he had to look after me. At night in his bed I used to hear him cry and call his father's name, but never in front of me. Michael and he were very close. His last set of poems was written for Hans and read out to him at bedtime. He still keeps them under his pillow.'

Lisa took out a pen from her handbag and scribbled a note on a piece of paper and put it in front of Minna: *This city is not safe for you. Ludwik is sure that Stalin is negotiating secretly with the Nazis. We have met some of the agents who have taken messages to Germany. I don't want to frighten you, but this place is dangerous.*

Lisa knew she had taken a risk, but she did not want Hans to suffer any more. Minna read the note with a sad smile and a grateful nod and set the paper alight. She took Lisa's hand and held it tight. Then she whispered softly in her ear.

'Thanks. Some German exiles here suspect something big is about to happen. A whole group of German Communists have already been arrested as enemies of the people. Kippenberger and Hirsch were actually tortured. I have to pretend all is well. I don't want Hans to worry. He was so happy last November, seeing all the tanks and soldiers marching past Stalin on the anniversary. He saw them as our protectors against the Nazis.'

The two women looked at each other in silence. Then Lisa spoke in a loud and carefree voice. 'It's a beautiful day. Why don't we take the boys for a walk by the river?'

The boys had returned and started a new game. They were not keen to be taken outdoors, but a combined effort by the mothers finally succeeded. The apartment was abandoned.

The day was beginning to decline towards sunset. They walked in the golden brown shadows of late afternoon. Hans and Felix had dropped all pretence of being grown-ups. They would throw twigs in the river and then race ahead to see which stick was winning.

'If I could leave this place I would do so tomorrow,' Minna confided to Lisa. 'I have cousins in Baltimore, but if I even tried to correspond with them in this atmosphere, I might be arrested.'

'I could write to them on your behalf.'

'I'm not sure. They might want to help, but even though Michael is dead, he was a Communist. Would the Americans let me in?'

'I think they might. I'll happily try if you want me to.'

'Too risky. If the attempt fails, I'll end up in Siberia and Hans in an orphanage.'

The two women talked till the sun had set. It was time to part. Hans and Felix shook hands warmly. Lisa and Minna hugged each other. Lisa was now sure that none of them could ever return while Stalin was in power.

Later that night in Larin's room, she questioned him about his wife and child, whom she had never met. 'Where are they, Larin?'

'With my mother-in-law in the country.'

'Tell me about them.'

'Look Lisa, forget them. Forget all of us. You make sure that Ludwik, Felix and yourself survive. Here it's just a question of who gets whom. A war of survival. If only *he* were to die. Disappear off the face of our world. Do you know what I mean? Then some of us might live. Livitsky, Ludwik, Freddy, me, the others. We would survive. Tell Ludwik that in Moscow we dream of dying in battle against our enemies ... Hitler, Franco, Mussolini. Who wants to be executed by our own people?'

Larin's face was suddenly disfigured with hatred. She had never seen him like this before. He was the only one of the five Ls who had not fought in the civil war. Larin had always been a moralist. He possessed more vitality than the revolution needed, but he hated violence. Like Ludwik, he was too independent-minded to tolerate any theory that forced life to conform to it. Dogma repelled him.

'I'll tell you something, Lisa. We all know he's going to kill us. We are witnesses to his crimes. Why ... why doesn't one of us have the guts to kill him? There are cases when individual terrorism is justified. Are there not, Lisa?'

'Perhaps. But look at it another way. He'll die one day. Will his death alone change what needs to be changed? Marxism would be in a sorry state if we believed in the powers of an individual. Ludwik thinks the problem goes deeper, much deeper.'

Felix was fast asleep on the sofa.

Larin began to talk of Ludwik and their life as children. The little town in Galicia began to come alive once again and as Lisa half shut her eyes listening to Larin's chatter, she could picture the river and the trees on its edge and imagine her Ludwik as a boy, jumping in and swimming to the other shore.

'Go home now, Lisa, and never come back.'

'This used to be my home, Larin.'

'I know. Keep yourself and one day tell the world how we were killed by our own people. And Lisa, tell Ludwik. Tell him never to come back.'

As the Prague-bound train began to move away from Moscow, she felt like Orpheus emerging from Hades. She felt she was under observation. One look back would be a fatal gesture. A steadier heartbeat, a sigh of relaxation, lessening tension in her shoulders would prove her to be an enemy of the state.

I used to love this city, she told herself.

Eighteen

I N GERMANY, you will agree Karl, everyone has a political family tree: history's poisoned legacies, which we forget at peril to ourselves as individuals and human beings. Everyone has something in their past that angers or embarrasses them.

There are things I have to tell you about Gertrude. Are you reading this a few months from now, or some time in the next century when you've scattered my ashes over the Wannsee and opened the sealed package, typed with human hands, copied on acid-free paper and, I hope, still intact? Are you reading it on your own? I'm trying to tell you this story in the order things happened, not the order I learned them, so you can share the ignorance I started with. There is artifice in the telling, but you get the whole story in the end. Don't turn straight to the last chapter. I want you to share the way I felt while I was trying to find a voice you might listen to.

Ten days before New Year's Eve in 1956, Helge persuaded me to organize a party in our apartment. At first I resisted, but Gerhard and other friends joined in and the pressure became irresistible. The apartment was large. Gertrude was away in Moscow. Her supply of Russian vodka and caviar lay untouched. The entire country was in a state of anticipatory excitement. Khruschev's speech denouncing the 'crimes of Stalin' at the Twentieth Party Congress in Moscow was only a few months old.

The Hungarians had responded to the Congress by a celebratory insurrection. They wanted a free and democratic Hungary. Their greatest Marxist philosopher, Gyorgi Lukács supported them and became a minister in the new government, but Khruschev, nervous lest the disease should spread, sent in Russian tanks. Lukács sought asylum in the Yugoslav Embassy. The rebellion was crushed.

Despite the brutalities in Budapest, hope was still alive. People east of the Elbe were yearning for a thaw. They were desperate to cease being human toys of some grand design, tired of being bit-players in a gigantic fantasy, which was now beginning to overwhelm its creators.

It had been an exciting year, but I wanted to spend New Year's Eve with your mother. I loved her so much that nothing else mattered and it was not often we had the apartment on our own. It seemed a pity to fill it with friends at this time.

She laughed when I said all this to her, a throaty, infectious chuckle.

We were lying in bed, late in the afternoon, overcome by post-coital torpor. It was always more relaxed when Gertrude was out of the country. I buried my head in her breasts, revelling in her body scents.

'You're lovely. Fragrant. Like a plucked lily.'

Helge would not be distracted.

'We can spend New Year's Day together. All on our own. In bed. But we must have a New Year's Eve party. All the signs are auspicious.'

'Meaning?'

'Suddenly we aren't frozen with fear.'

'Tell that to the Hungarians!'

'Vlady! No excuses. Yes or no?' She was now sitting on me, her hands moving towards my neck as if to strangle me. I surrendered. Helge laughed. We embraced and made love to seal the agreement.

'Vlady . . .'

'Hmm.'

'You promised you would let me read it one day. Why not now?'

'Because it's clumsy, it's unfinished and you won't like it.'

'So what?'

I sighed, got out of the bed and went to the desk. My hands explored the disorder till they uncovered a handwritten sheet of paper. I handed it to Helge and went in search of my clothes.

She put the piece of paper on her chest as she watched me dress. Then she jumped out of bed, found her thick blue trousers and her knitted black jumper and dressed herself. There are times, Karl, when I miss her more than she could imagine. She read my poem twice.

FOR B. B.

Long sleepless nights with inspiration gone
Tabula rasa.
Then random images rush past
Bland thoughts float by.
Most nights are like that
Then, once a month . . .
No, I exaggerate
Twice every six . . .
A spark.
Pen skates on paper,
Soon a page is full,
A year's work done.
Was it the same for him?
Or did his words roar onto the page like Niagara?

Next week I will visit his grave once again,
Salute old Hegel's resting place as I pass
And on the cold new marble slab
Scatter red roses and pledge to fumigate our country.

18 Berlin, 12 August 1956

Before she could tell me what she thought of my little offering there was a knock on the door. Helge picked up her watch from the bedside table. Six o'clock. It had to be Gerhard, punctual to the point of irritation. None of the others would be there for at least another half an hour.

She took the poem next door and greeted Gerhard.

'What did you think?' I heard him asking her.

'Not bad. I'm not too sure of the last three lines, but it works . . .'

'May I read it, Vlady?'

She handed Gerhard the poem. He scanned it briefly and shook his head.

'Burn it, Vlady. No good. Too sentimental for a start. Brecht hated sentimentality.'

So did Gerhard. I just grinned, took the piece of paper from his hand, crumpled it in my fist, placed it in the ashtray and set it alight. Helge screamed at me.

'No, Vlady! You fool.'

Her cry was in vain. Only I knew that the poem was in my head and a better version would emerge one day. It didn't, as you can see, but I remembered. Your mother will confirm that what you've read is what I wrote all those years ago.

'Gerhard was right and you were wrong, my Helge,' I told her. 'We will only succeed in our tasks if we are ruthlessly objective. Self-aware and self-critical, unlike the men who rule over us.'

Gerhard nodded as he self-consciously lit his pipe. He was nineteen, a year older than Helge and me. The pipe was only a few weeks old.

'But, comrades,' Helge expostulated, 'both of you rush to the opposite extremes. For you, criticism has to be completely destructive, like air entering a sealed tomb.'

'Well spoken,' said Gerhard, without a smile. 'That is it exactly. We want to extinguish everything in this Stalinist tomb.'

'Everything?' Helge inquired plaintively. 'Everything? Including the foundations of the DDR?'

'Especially them,' mocked Gerhard.

Our discussion was interrupted by loud knocks on the front door, strange noises, and the sound of laughter. I was always fearful of the neighbours, zealots of the regime, so I rose hurriedly and opened the door. At first there was silence. Then Eric, Heide, Helen, Alexander and Richard, dressed in discarded army greatcoats, came to attention. They ignored me completely, looked above my head and goose-stepped neatly into the apartment. Safely inside, they discarded their coats and fell on the floor. Everyone laughed.

The room was large and solemn. The grey light coming through the windows had almost disappeared. On a table there were copies of the Italian Communist Party weekly, *Rinascita*, piled next to a small bust of Lenin. Next to it stood an old Russian samovar, now bubbling with tea.

Once the liquid had been poured into glass mugs and served, Gerhard called us all to order.

A collective earnestness gripped the meeting. I'm sure you know the feeling, Karl. In your case it probably happens when your leader addresses all of you on some solemn occasion. With us, it was the result of a belief that we were going to change the DDR and the world.

We were all members of the youth wing of the ruling party. We were aware that this small gathering was illegal; that, if discovered, we could all be expelled from the league and the university, sent into internal exile or to work in a factory. Everyone present was conscious that our futures could be ruined, our lives destroyed. Everyone knew the risks, but despite it all we were prepared to throw ourselves in the whirlpool of history.

We wished to reform and remake DDR communism, a communism that was hostile to our tastes, our hopes, our aspirations, and replace it with a humane socialism.

The crushing of the Hungarian revolt by Soviet tanks had only strengthened the feeling that the system could not carry on in the same old way for much longer. And yet the people had not completely lost their sense of fear, nor were they totally confident that they were on the right track. They were sure of only one thing. They could not remain silent and passive in the face of crimes that were being committed in their name. It was no longer sufficient to cover their ears and drone on, as children do, in order to keep out the lies of the regime.

'Comrades,' Gerhard's voice was trembling slightly, 'we are still few in number, but have no doubt, we will grow. All our lives, we have been held on a leash. Vlady was lucky. Unlike the rest of us he was not born in Nazi Germany. We are living in a sad century. The events in Moscow and Budapest make silence impossible. We have to make our voices heard, establish contact with like-minded comrades elsewhere in the DDR and work for the day when the DDR is truly democratic. The bureaucrats who blight our souls have erected a pyramid of lies and hypocrisy. If we do not shatter their world, other forces, more sinister, will arise . . .'

Talk of this sort carried on for nearly four hours, punctuated by a short break for beer, bread, cheese and ham. Each of us speaking bitternesses, combining personal knowledge of tragedy with the collective experience of the world.

Hardly anyone spoke with excessive passion that night. There was no thunder or lightning. We stirred each other calmly, without haste, giving ourselves time for reflection and speculation. This was not because we lacked emotions. It was a conscious rejection of the demagogy that had characterized the Nazi period, in which all of them had grown up. Nazism was a way of life they knew at first hand. Unending rants on the radio, forced attendance at carefully orchestrated Nazi rallies, the Horst Wessel song at school and the worship of blind hate against the enemies of the Reich within and outside Germany.

How do I write all this without boring you, Karl? Remember my Israeli friend, Joe Lotz? The thing he dreaded the most was his parents recalling the Polish town they left in 1936. No Jews there now. Joe didn't want to know. But you still live in Germany, Karl, and that's why I think you do want to know – or is it just that I want you to know?

After midnight we ran out of words. It was time for decisions. Should we set up a clandestine organization? Did we have the material and moral resources to circulate an underground newspaper? Or perhaps it would be wiser to confine ourselves to preparing and publishing a manifesto, a call to arms to a frightened and bewildered generation?

It was Helen Kushner who concentrated our minds on the world outside your grandmother's apartment.

'Walter Janka was arrested today!'

Shock registered on every face. Janka was one of the most respected publishers in the DDR. In his youth he had been in a Nazi prison. His brother Albert, a Communist member of the old Reichstag, had been beaten to death by the Nazis. Released from prison by accident, Walter had fled to Prague and made his way to Spain, where he fought with the Thaelmann brigade. After that defeat he had fled to Mexico with Anna Seghers; there he had founded a Communist paper. His past was well known. He was one of the DDR's élite intellectuals. He had resisted Ulbricht's attempts to make him conform to the current orthodoxy, and his publishing house was an oasis for critical minds.

The thought of Janka in a DDR prison outraged all of us.

'How do you know?' I asked in a choked voice.

'My mother was with Anna Seghers this afternoon. Walter was Anna's publisher. Someone rang to warn her.'

'Why Janka?' mused Gerhard in a puzzled tone. 'It would be hard to find a more loyal Communist in Berlin.'

'Because he published Lukács,' Helen replied. 'And because Lukács did not simply support the Budapest uprising with words – he became a minister in Nagy's government. It follows that Comrade Lukács is a traitor and an apostate. Ulbrichtian logic condemns his publisher.'

'And the poet who could have turned this twisted logic on its head is dead. Why is Brecht dead and Ulbricht alive? Lukács spoke at his funeral. Why don't they dig up Brecht's body and put it on trial?'

The thought cheered us up. Gerhard lay down on the floor. Richard and Alexander and I all stood up and posed as secret policemen.

VLADY: Comrade Brecht, we have orders to take you to prison.

GERHARD: I'm dead.

RICHARD: That's what they all say. Pick him up, boys.

[Gerhard's body is lifted and thrown on the sofa.]

VLADY: Now look here, Brecht. You know you're dead, we know you're dead, but the state has ordered your arrest.

GERHARD: It's a bit late, don't you think?

VLADY: It's never too late here.

GERHARD: Why has my body been arrested?

RICHARD: Ask your wife.

HELGE: They say that Lukács spoke at your funeral, Berty, and Lukács, as we all know, is a traitor.

GERHARD: I know that he wrote a book called *The Destruction of Reason*, in which he demonstrated how irrationalist modes of thought abetted the rise of fascism and reaction. Ulbricht did not comprehend the argument, but –

'Enough clowning. *Please*. Enough now.'

Something in Helen's voice made them all stop. They looked at her.

'I told you about Janka's arrest so that you would understand what we are up against. Instead you start play-acting. Don't you realize the risks we run?'

'Nobody is here under false pretences. We've been talking for weeks. Something has to be done. If you've changed your mind, Helen, we understand. You can go.'

'Don't be a dumbhead, Gerhard,' retorted Helen. 'I want to discuss what we should do. Since none of you have come up with a concrete proposal could I suggest that we draft a brief manifesto? Something that can be read and understood by anyone. I propose that Vlady prepares a draft and we meet next week to discuss and approve. Agreed?'

Everyone nodded.

'Excellent,' said Helen. 'Now we can all go home.'

'Just a minute,' said Helge. 'Next week is New Year's Eve. Some of us have persuaded Vlady to throw a party. Why don't we meet that morning to discuss the manifesto and then all of you can stay and help to organize the evening. Agreed?'

'Yes,' they muttered unenthusiastically.

For a long time that night, hours after my fellow-conspirators had left, I sat at my desk, face cupped in my hands, and stared at the blank sheet of paper in my typewriter. Helge was fast asleep next door.

'We have begun a long and dangerous undertaking,' I said to myself. 'If the local bosses don't crush us, Moscow will, and then ... ?' Slowly my fingers began to move and a title took shape on the blank sheet:

MANIFESTO FOR THE BIRTH OF A REAL DDR

A decade of totalitarian rule and iron discipline has robbed our people of their capacity for self-expression and self-organization. Coming as this does on top of what German fascism did to our nation, the results can only be tragic. This nation is longing to manage itself, to master its own destiny, free from both the stranglehold of bureaucratic rule and the dead hand of consumer capitalism, which rules in the Western part of our country.

At the end of the war, the citizens of the DDR entertained high hopes of freedom, equality and international brotherhood, but these, right from the beginning, clashed with the bureaucratic aims of Moscow and the men it sent to run this state.

The workers then discovered that their so-called socialist conquests were a sham. In 1953 we clamoured for reforms: a multi-party system, trade-union rights, freedom of the press, but DDR 'socialism' could not grant its citizens the rights that all West German citizens enjoyed as a matter of course, and rights which Rosa Luxemburg had argued were vital for the health of any system calling itself socialist. The workers uprising was crushed. People became cowed and sullen. Apathy reigned supreme.

It was this failure that made the rantings of our propagandists so much hot air...

By the time I had finished the first draft of the manifesto it was almost three in the morning. The freezing cold outside had penetrated the apartment. While I was working I had been unaware of how cold my body had become. Now I shivered as I undressed and crept into bed. Helge was in a deep sleep, breathing evenly. The heat radiated by her body was irresistible.

She's my lover, my comrade and my friend, I thought. She's loyal and she's passionate. I can rely on her. I tell her about things I've not confessed to anyone else. Perhaps my mother understands this instinctively and, for that reason, does not like her. Stupid Gertrude.

I embraced her. Still asleep, she turned and hugged me. Within minutes her warmth had spread to me. Before I could think back on the events of that day, I, too, was fast asleep.

A week later, on the morning of New Year's Eve, the meeting approved the Manifesto, finalized arrangements for having it mimeographed, and compiled a list of likely sympathizers in all the major cities to whom it should be sent, though, naturally, not in the post. For months we had discussed endlessly. At times, our own chatter had seemed to us to resemble a meaningless din. Workers, democracy, freedom, bureaucracy, dictatorship, intelligentsia. Words. Now we had decided to make use of them in order to do something, to move forward, to act, to confront history, to uncover the clear blue sky underneath the leaden clouds.

People had started arriving early and by ten the apartment was already overflowing. Young bodies were sprawled everywhere. Youthful spirits, helped by Gertrude's supply of Russian vodka, were robust and carefree. In the sitting room, a cultivated satirist was standing on a table and mimicking Ulbricht. His audience was laughing uncontrollably without a trace of nervousness. A self-satisfied smile on my face, I was whispering to Gerhard.

'Last year they would not have dared. It's the spirit of the Twentieth Party Congress!'

Gerhard, smoking a pipe and trying hard to strike an elegant posture, nodded in agreement.

'The auguries are good as far as our little endeavour is concerned.'

In the kitchen where guests were helping themselves to mulled Moldavian wine, a woman in her late forties was in full flow.

'You think I place my art too high. I disagree. My only function is to take my readers into confidence by relating *my* dreams to them. Not yours or those of the DDR or of the goat who rules over us. Collectivist art has no aesthetic value. Literature has an intrinsic value independent of everything else. *Everything* else.'

Her white-haired companion, a decade or so older, laughed at her.

'Wrong again, my dear. What you say applies to masterpieces. Exceptions. As for the rest, art is a product, like much else, of the human mind, destined for hurried consumption. It is a perishable commodity. Socialist-realist rubbish is neither better nor worse than capitalist rubbish. When I realized that the public for which I wrote had ceased to exist, I stopped writing.'

'You were full of shit then and you're full of shit now,' retorted his friend.

They were interrupted by shouts from the next room alerting all the guests that midnight was two minutes away. As the bells on the radio rang in the New Year, everyone burst into song. Then Gerhard called for silence.

'Comrades, let us drink to the memory of Bertolt Brecht.'

'Bertolt Brecht!'

'To freedom!' suggested someone else.

'To freedom!' the apartment echoed.

Just before the clock struck two, Helge and I announced our engagement.

'Comrades!' I informed them. 'Why make one commitment when you can make two?'

Laughter and several toasts followed, but I forgot everything the next morning when Gertrude returned. I told her everything. She started addressing me as Vladimir, a sure sign that she was angry.

'I am not a solitary sorceress, Vladimir. I am your mother and I am already half an hour late for my meeting. Surely you've insulted me enough for one day. Can we not continue tomorrow morning over breakfast?'

Before I could reply, she had walked out of the room and left the apartment. My aim had been to provoke an angry response in the course of which some hidden truths might be revealed, but my hopes remained unfulfilled.

Weeks passed and she continued to sulk. Relations between us had become frosty ever since I had presented her with a daughter-in-law of whom she disapproved. I defended Helge's integrity with great vigour.

'It's not Helge's fault that her father's a Lutheran pastor. Your father was a bourgeois. You still loved him.'

'My father perished in Belsen.'

'So if Helge's father was dead it would be fine.'

'Why did you have to marry her?'

'It was necessary.'

'Why? Is she pregnant?'

'You mean that would be sufficient reason?'

'Is she?'

'No.'

'Good.'

Helge's attempts to normalize relations had also failed. Gertrude was never rude, but she insisted on preserving a painful degree of formality. She also made it clear within a few days of her return that it was her apartment and that it was she, not Helge, who retained overall control.

Till now, despite all our arguments, I had thought of Gertrude, despite her flashes of temper, as charming, intelligent and sensitive. Now I saw a side of her which took me by surprise. One afternoon, I took advantage of Helge's absence and asked Gertrude to talk over things frankly with me. She looked at me as if I were a total stranger and refused to respond.

Why was she in such a state? I could understand that, like a good Jewish mother, she resented the intrusion of another woman in my life. Or that I had gone behind her back. It could be that the thought of sharing her apartment with a young couple permanently ensconced in the tiny bedroom next to her own made her furious. Our nocturnal whispering and passions might have made her feel an outsider in her own home. That would be normal, but was that all? Or were there some subterranean reasons as well? Something that had more to do with her own past, something that frightened her.

It could not have been a matter of ambition. She had no career planned out for me and the last thing she wanted was for me to follow in my father's footsteps. I was her link with a past infected by loss and deprivation. It made her unhappy, but it also made her strong. She might regret the price she'd paid for her own determination, but she had it and she used it. She gave me a hard time about Helge. Sometimes it felt eerily like an interrogation rather than an argument. Her physical stillness was a weapon, body armour. I'd stare back into those pale grey eyes and wonder what sights they'd seen...

When Gertrude remained obstinate, refusing resolutely to engage with me, I unburdened myself of everything I'd been storing up for the last six weeks. I defended my love for Helge. Gertrude had never seen me so passionate. It confirmed her prejudices against Helge. Her son's innocence had been wrenched from him by this blond-haired seductress. She said something like that and I replied in kind.

'I lost my virginity when I was barely seventeen. To a friend of yours, Mother, a loyal comrade. She was staying with us. Remember?'

'You're lying, you bastard!'

At last I had got to her. Pleased with myself, I became very calm.

'Since you've now raised the question of my legitimacy, Mother, won't you tell me more about my own? What was your real relationship with Ludwik? What happened to him?'

'I've told you a million times. He's dead.'

'Who killed him?'

'Why are you looking at me like that?'

'Who killed him?'

'Yezhov. He ran the NKVD in 1937.'

'Playing games again. Stalin had him killed. Who pulled the trigger?'

'I don't know.'

'Someone must know in Moscow. You never tried to find out?'

'Those who knew are also dead.'

'The whole system is dead, Mother. Khruschev's revelations have —'

'Some of us did not need Khruschev's speech, Vladimir. We knew.'

'Yes, of course. You knew, but you carried on regardless. Nothing mattered except saving your own skin.'

'Have you forgotten Victory Day in 1945? The big parade in Moscow? You and your friends cheering the victorious Red Army? Clapping your hands like a clockwork toy? And when they hurled those captured Nazi banners at the foot of Lenin's mausoleum, Vlady, everyone watching began to cry. Fascism had been defeated. Even though to achieve it, many Communists, like myself, had to make a pact with the Devil. Why do you think we cried that day, Vladimir?'

Despite myself, I was moved by the memory of that day in Moscow.

'Grief for all our dead comrades.'

'Yes, of course. But relief that the Soviet Union had survived. Maybe my skin was not worth saving, but the Soviet Union had to survive if Hitler was going to be crushed. Without the Red Army who knows what might have happened? Europe would have fallen for sure.'

I wished Helge had been there to witness this quarrel. I found it difficult to convince your mother that mine was much more than an embittered party hack, who had sold her soul to Stalinism. I wondered, though, what Helge would have made of any argument that equated Stalin with the Soviet Union. Your grandmother had a nerve, Karl. I mean, even if she wanted to defend the DDR, how the hell could this translate into telling me how and whom to love? If all the means are vital to your ends, do you have *carte blanche*? Unacceptable.

She reminded me of Gerd Henning, a creepy professor of German literature at Humboldt, a loyal Party member and a dedicated rapist. A few years ago, a young woman actually complained to the authorities and provided a graphic description of his method, the 'come back to

my room after lectures while I recite Goethe as he should be recited'
routine. When she did, he wanted her to shake hands with his penis.
She kicked him hard and ran.

The student's father was a high-up in military intelligence. There
was an investigation. Henning was cautioned. Can you imagine what
he told his colleagues, Karl? He put on his most pious voice and
declared: 'You must excuse me, comrades. My background is different
to yours. I was brought up in a proletarian family in Wedding. My
parents were underground Communists during the Nazi period. Both
died at Ravensbruck. I was hidden by a metal worker and his family.
We used to drink and swear and fuck throughout the war, but we
survived. Please excuse my insensitivity. Perhaps if I had gone to
Moscow or Los Angeles or Geneva my behaviour would have been
more refined, but here in Berlin, under Hitler, we lived roughly.'

He refused to reply to questions and left the room. He never
changed. I hate that sort of demagogy and despise men like him. It was
Gertrude who told me that story, but her thinking wasn't all that
different from Henning's.

At the university that year, I was trapped into a massive row with
Gerd Henning. I tried to persuade Henning to use his influence on
behalf of Eva Sickert, a brilliant young lecturer, who had fallen prey to
a harassment campaign organized by the Party and had, as a
consequence, been removed from her post. Sickert was accused of being
a follower of Lukács and 'prettifying the novels of the reactionary
English (*sic*) novelist, Sir Walter Scott', a charge she did not even
attempt to deny.

Sixty students, including me, signed a letter of protest. Henning,
with a patronizing smile on his face, told me: 'This may be appropriate
for you, Meyer, but not for me. My job, as a professor of German
literature, is to educate all of you, help you develop a critical
understanding of our language and literature and precisely for this
reason we should keep politics out of the university.'

'The state has introduced politics, Professor Henning, by demonizing
certain thinkers, and by the dismissal of Eva Sickert.'

Henning smiled, shaking his head in disbelief at the naïvety of the
student who stood before him.

'If a house was on fire,' I asked, refusing to give up, 'surely you
would help to put it out.'

'Not at all, my dear Meyer. I would rush to the telephone and call
the fire department. I am a professor, not a fireman.'

'You are a shit, Henning,' I began to scream, 'a swine without
honour, without shame, without integrity. Your sort really knew how

to survive under the Nazis. Didn't they, Herr Professor?'

Henning remained calm, though his eyes had filled with hate.

'Leave my room, Meyer.'

As I was leaving, he added an afterthought. 'And, by the way, Meyer, there is no reason for such bitterness on your part. I never fucked your wife.'

When, later that evening, Gertrude returned home, she was surprised to find me clean-shaven – in a fit of pique against nothing and everything I had shaved off my beard – but she was in too much of a state to worry about my appearance.

'What's wrong, Mutti?'

'Vlady, is there something you haven't told me?'

Panic. Till that fateful New Year's Eve, I had no political secrets from Gertrude. The dispute over my hastily concocted nuptials was, in part, a semi-conscious attempt to cover up the fact that Helge and I were engaged in clandestine political activity. Many times I'd been tempted to tell her everything, but something held me back. And then the intensity of the row over Helge convinced me that she was a dreary old Stalinist after all, and I was glad not to have revealed our secret.

'Vlady?'

'What could I possibly have hidden from you?'

'Listen to me, Vlady. These are not joking matters. You could end up in prison or dead. Now tell me everything.'

'How much do you know and how?'

'Forget the "how". It does not concern you. What I do know is that you and some others have distributed a manifesto calling for the overthrow of the DDR.'

'Not true, Mutti. We have called for a democratization of the DDR and the end of the one-party state. Far from being a call to "overthrow the DDR", it is the only way to strengthen and stabilize the DDR. The workers realized that instinctively in '53.'

'Did you draft the manifesto?'

'Yes.'

'Every single word?'

'Every single word.'

'Let me read it.'

I was trapped. I had no alternative but to give her a copy. Later she told me that a part of her had felt proud of me. The incident had brought back memories of Ludwik and his gentle eloquence, of conversations which, if reported, would have led to their immediate imprisonment and probably death in the Siberian camps. Those were much worse times, and yet many veteran Communists had risked their lives and denounced Stalin. What would Ludwik have made of her boy?

I handed her the manifesto and hovered round her chair as she put on her spectacles.

'Sit down, Vlady. Better still, leave the room till I've finished. You're not ten now, waiting to see what I think of your homework.'

I was relieved that she had calmed down. I smiled to myself and walked away. She saw me smile and it irritated her.

She put the manifesto on the table and stared at the photograph of me and Helge on the mantelpiece. 'I would love to have a good talk with her. To tell her that I love you so much that I can't help being jealous. To encourage her to give me a grandchild...'

I couldn't believe my ears. Peace at last. Our little civil war was over. As Gertrude resumed reading the manifesto she could not conceal her delight. Later that night she told Helge how she appreciated my political intuition and the crisply formulated sentences. There was a clarity of thought here, a euphony, which she found incredibly refreshing. Similar thoughts, she told us, were being whispered openly in Moscow, where Party members were slowly beginning to lose their fear.

Gertrude had looked up a few survivors from the twenties, two men and a woman who had never been uncovered as part of Ludwik's circle because they had left the Fourth Department and become school teachers several years before the Terror. Remarkably, they were still alive and delighted to see Gertrude. A whole evening was spent talking about Ludwik and the other Ls.

The two teachers had been part of a delegation of old Bolsheviks, which had included Bukharin's widow, who met Khruschev and pleaded for the freedom of all those who had been wrongfully imprisoned. Khruschev had given them his word that the prisoners would be released and, the day before she left Moscow, some of the newly released prisoners had arrived in the capital. In those days, Karl, the term quite matter of factly used was 'rehabilitation', as if the prisoners had simply been ill and just got better or maybe they were a set of old, rickety chairs: a bit of glue and some loose covers and they'd be quite serviceable. The same would have been done for the rest of the chairs had they not been found surplus to requirements in 1937...

Had it not been for her Moscow journey, Gertrude would have been petrified and would have done anything to protect her son. Yes, anything. Now she knew that it was only a matter of time. What Moscow did today, the DDR would ape tomorrow. Vlady might even end up a member of the Politburo.

The voice of the future member of the Politburo interrupted her dreams.

'Well?'

She looked up at me and smiled.

'What do you think, Mutti?'

'I agree with almost everything. If you remove the reference to a multi-party system I could even sign it myself.'

'But that is crucial. Rosa was right on this and Lenin wrong. Anyway, if you accept the right of a minority to exist inside a party, how can you challenge their right to form a separate party? You see, Mutti . . .'

'I do see, Vlady, but I disagree.'

'Fine. No problem. The debate will continue.'

'Excellent. Now tell me something. How many of you are involved? Who are the others?'

I hesitated. I did not want to tell her.

'Vlady?'

'I cannot betray their trust. We pledged secrecy. Who told you about the manifesto?'

'A very senior Party member. Like me, he was impressed. He thought it was the work of students. A few inquiries at Humboldt indicated that you might be involved. Nothing definite, you understand. But I knew straight away that you must be implicated. Instinct, I suppose. Who are the others?'

'Why do you want to know?'

'So I can make a few inquiries. What if one of your fellow-conspirators is working for the Stasi?'

'Outrageous.'

'Perhaps, but necessary for the success of your project. Please be a bit realistic, Vlady.'

I rose and began to pace up and down. She saw me stroking my forehead, which had always irritated her, a sure sign that I was nervous. I couldn't understand my own nervousness. Only six months ago I trusted her completely, told her everything she wanted to know and retired to bed with a light heart. This trust of an only child for a single mother may help you understand why I often berated myself for doubting her word that Ludwik was my father.

Before I could explain my refusal, I heard the noise of a key turning in the front door. My heart began to beat faster. It had to be Helge. She had returned. My mother would stop pestering me in Helge's presence. I had underestimated Gertrude.

Just as Helge entered the room, Gertrude stood up and greeted your mother with a cordiality that left us speechless. She took Helge's coat and pushed her on to the sofa.

'Go and make Helge some tea, Vlady. Can't you see she's exhausted?'

Astonished and speechless, I rushed into the kitchen. In my absence there was a remarkable development. Gertrude sat next to Helge and kissed her on the head.

'You must forgive an old mother her bad manners, my dear,' she began in her most charming tone. 'This boy is the only thing of value I have left in this world and I did not want to share him with anyone, not for another few years. I see now that you both love each other very much. Will you forgive an over-protective mother her psychic frailties? Shall we be friends?'

Helge was thunderstruck. Gertrude had, with one simple stroke, completely disarmed her. She hugged Gertrude and the older woman sighed and began to stroke Helge's hair. This was the incredible scene that greeted me when I returned with a glass of tea for Helge. Naturally, I was deeply touched. I thought it was my political *démarche* that had won Gertrude over.

Later that night Helge and I sat with Gertrude and recalled the old times. Without much prompting, we told her everything she wanted to know. Gertrude made a mental note of the other names and gave the project her blessing.

That night was the first time Helge and I felt at home.

Nineteen

WHILE RUMMAGING in Gertrude's desk one day, I came across an envelope with a set of unusual black and white photographs of her. In one of them, she was standing on a flat empty beach, but it was her clothes that struck me as odd. She was wearing a matching skirt and jacket, a beautiful straw hat and was laughing. She really looked happy. In another photograph she was with another woman, whom I did not recognize. In yet another, she was standing arms linked with a young man with a hard, beaming face and spectacles. He looked vaguely familiar; perhaps I had met him in Moscow. When I showed her the photographs, she snatched them from me angrily and left the room. I kept pressing her, but she remained tight-lipped and unfriendly whenever I mentioned them.

I had virtually forgotten the entire incident when one Sunday afternoon, she volunteered the story of those photographs. During her early years in Moscow, Gertrude had been especially close to Zinoviev.

Perhaps they were lovers, though I have no evidence to sustain this speculation. News of his execution in 1936 had unhinged her. Ludwik had to use all his powers of persuasion to prevent her taking her own life. If she was not allowed to commit suicide, she asked him, why could she not denounce Stalin and his tyranny and break publicly with Moscow? Ludwik was not unsympathetic to this particular request, but he persuaded her to wait six months and then they would discuss the matter again. He sent her off on a long rest cure to the Norfolk Coast in England, where she would be isolated from Moscow's prying eyes.

She had no idea where she was going or with whom she would be staying. She had barely arrived in London when the Dutchman who met her at the station had fed her and then driven her to another station where she caught the train to Norwich.

To her astonishment, the person waiting to meet her at Norwich station was Christopher Brown, her old lover from the Moscow days. He smiled and shook hands. Then she was driven away to the beautiful, large, Brown family house situated in the heart of Wells, a quiet, coastal town. It was an idyllic three weeks. Listening to her talk always made me want to go there just to have a look at the house and the beach. I still haven't managed to make the trip, but perhaps you will, Karl.

Brown was married to Olga, an *émigré* Russian; both were working for Ludwik. Olga was the niece of a Russian grand duke, a cousin of the Tsar. In 1917 her family had dragged her away from Moscow against her will, but not before she had left her jewels and a letter in a thick brown envelope marked 'For Lenin and the Central Committee of the Bolsheviks'. She was on the side of the Revolution from the very beginning. If she had stayed on and joined the Bolsheviks, Stalin would probably have had her killed like all the others.

In Britain she followed Ludwik's advice and never declared herself in public. She died recently, in 1982, at a ripe old age. After Ludwik's death both she and Brown broke all connections with Moscow and threatened to expose their agents if they ever tried to contact them again.

I don't think Gertrude liked or disliked Olga. As you can imagine, Karl, on hearing all this I was completely fascinated and obsessed by Olga. What was it that had made this young woman break with her family and support those who had had her uncle, the Tsar, and his immediate family executed? I plied Gertrude with questions, but she could tell me very little except that, on the one occasion when she had asked Olga what she felt about the Tsar, Olga had snapped back, 'The English and French killed their kings. Why should we have done it differently? In any case their lives would have been saved had our English cousin, George V, offered them asylum here, but he declined and they perished.'

Gertrude was struck by the tranquillity of England. Germany, Italy and Portugal were under the fascist heel; Spain was in the throes of a civil war; France often seemed on the verge of its own war with the republic under a popular front government, constantly in fear of Hitler and his fifth column inside the country; Russia was exterminating the men and women who had made the Revolution, the 'cadres who could only be exterminated through civil war', in Stalin's chilling phrase. Turmoil everywhere, but England, no provincial backwater, this, but the hub of a mighty empire, remained calm. Away from it all, Gertrude recovered her poise.

She had no news of her parents or Heiny, her beloved brother, except that they were alive and trying to get out of Germany. She thought of them a great deal and wished that she had utilized the Fourth Department network to rescue Heiny, but Livitsky had vetoed the idea as dangerous and mistaken. It would establish a bad precedent. She agreed with him, but wept when she was alone. It was on a Norfolk beach that she realized that, for her, the most important thing in the world was to defeat the Nazis. If this meant putting everything else aside for the moment, then it had to be done. Hitler must be defeated. Stalin would have to wait till later.

Christopher and Olga entertained a great deal and one weekend Gertrude was shocked by the talk she heard during lunch. The Browns were entertaining a dozen guests, men of influence and their wives. Gertrude was introduced as an old friend from Berlin. The Englishmen suddenly became very attentive, firing sympathetic questions to her about the glories of the Third Reich. They were all, without exception, extremely impressed by Hitler's achievements. They were also convinced – as Olga had reported to Ludwik on a number of occasions – that the English ruling élite would do a deal with Hitler to isolate the Soviet Union.

The next morning Brown told her they were expecting new visitors, but this time from our side. Gertrude was scared. She had been in the game long enough to know that the Fourth Department was being purged. Could the men who were on their way here be her executioners? Or were they bringing her a message from Ludwik? She could not explain her fear to Olga or Christopher. She did not know what they really believed and Ludwik had warned her not to share her doubts with anyone.

The two men arrived in the afternoon, were shown into the garden where tea was being served. They introduced themselves as Michael Spiegelglass and Klaus Winter. Of the two, Winter was easily the more presentable. A German Communist in his early thirties, he was of medium height, pleasing appearance, and dressed casually in a white shirt and brown trousers. He was much more at his ease than Spiegelglass, who was wearing a badly tailored dark brown suit, a white shirt and a nondescript tie. Regulation issue for secret agents on their first foreign assignment, the new men from the Fourth Department. Speigelglass was the same height as Winter, but he looked shorter because of his plumpness. He wore thick-lensed, gold-frame spectacles.

Gertrude didn't tell me much about him, but it was obvious from the way she talked that she had fallen in love with Winter. Yes, I had been right. The face in the photograph was familiar. Winter was still a friend, and when I was a child he would sometimes accompany us to special events like the Moscow State Circus.

The two men had travelled from Paris to Norfolk just to see Gertrude. Spiegelglass questioned her for two hours about Ludwik. His views on the Moscow Trials, the war in Spain, the situation in Germany, and so on. He denounced Stalin, but it was such an obvious trap that far from responding in kind, Gertrude reprimanded him and threatened to inform the Department in Moscow. Both men left the same evening, though Winter returned and spent a few days with them in Wells.

It was then that Gertrude realized Ludwik was in danger. She sent him a message and within forty-eight hours had received her authorization to return to Paris.

The story as Gertrude told it sounded tedious. I knew the tone well. It was the voice she usually put on for outsiders when she decided to regale them with stories of her heroic past: her voice slightly raised, her nostrils slightly expanded, her eyes shining with a slightly fanatical gleam, but it was a mask. I knew that from old because a tale told in this mood was never the same. The events, the people and her own role were always different depending on the audience. This time it was just her and me, but she had slipped on the old mask and I knew she was concealing the truth. What memories was she trying to suppress, and why? I tried, but it was never easy to extract her real self from the shell. I never found out the truth. Perhaps there was nothing to discover. Perhaps it was her affair with Winter that cast a special light on that idyllic period in England. Perhaps.

Twenty

LUDWIK WAS ALONE in his Paris apartment. A solitary existence was nothing unusual for a spy. Often he had gone to dangerous places for a long time and at times had thought he might never return, but here in the kitchen he missed Felix and Lisa. The stillness of the morning made him uneasy.

He gazed with keen tenderness at a photograph of all three of them on a skiing holiday; in it, he was disguised as a polar bear. The memory brought a smile to his eyes, but it faded quickly. In their absence, the sadness of his life became even more noticeable. This place was their little home, a retreat from the grim world. They felt happy and warm when they were here together. He sat staring at the white ceiling while he sipped his coffee. The truth, blinding and transparent, was clearly visible.

Ludwik was thinking. For nearly twenty years, he had believed that they were engaged in a planetary civil war between the forces of good and evil. If the world revolution did not triumph, then counter-revolution was inevitable. The Soviet Union would not survive unless Spain, Germany and France – and that was just a start – broke just like the Russians had done from the chain of world capitalism.

Since 1928, when the opposition had been crushed, Ludwik had realized that the Revolution in the former Tsarist Empire was beginning to degenerate. He was a veteran of the civil war. He knew all there was to know about difficult conditions. He had observed deserters being punished and watched the swift and summary execution of White prisoners. Neither was morally justifiable, but *in extremis* even those who considered themselves on the side of justice committed atrocities. The revolution had to be saved at any cost, and the traumatic experiences of the First World War had, for both sides, reduced the worth of human lives.

That phase was long over. Trotsky's armies had won the civil war. There was no reason for continuing the restrictions on democracy inside and outside the Party, and yet the situation had become much worse. Stalin's terror was destroying the old Bolshevik Party. Why had Ludwik, the master of strategy, the dialectician whose grasp of logic was the envy of the Fourth Department, failed to realize that sooner or later his own mind would be thrown into disorder?

Why? Because he did not have the courage to become an unattached citizen, condemned to silence or even death, held in contempt by his colleagues, who would impose a moral quarantine on him. To cut the umbilical cord that tied him to the Fourth Department was a fearful prospect, a leap into the void, and yet he could delay no longer. He was losing all sympathy for the official character that he embodied.

The final blow had come not from Stalin, but from Leon Blum. The French Socialist leader's refusal to help the Spanish Republic had, on one level, depressed Ludwik much more than Stalin's criminal activities in Catalonia. 'Non-intervention' was the name they gave to their cowardice. What else could one expect from the English, whose ruling class was dominated by secret and not-so-secret admirers of Franco, Mussolini and Hitler? The English ruling gentry were desperate for the Axis powers to wipe out Bolshevism, but Blum was a decent man, a Socialist. He had become the Prime Minister of France at the head of a popular front which the French workers had swept to victory in last year's elections.

If France had aided the Spanish Republic to exactly the same extent as Hitler and Mussolini were supporting Franco, the Spanish Republic would have won. It was too late now. Blum had supported non-intervention. It was a bitter, bitter blow. Did not Blum understand that he had unwittingly signed the death warrant of the French Republic as well?

Ludwik was sure that this would be the outcome. A strengthened fascism would not be held up by the Maginot Line. French passivity on Spain had demoralized many popular front supporters. Ludwik banged the wall with his fist. Filled with rage, he realized how impotent he had become.

It was Sunday morning and the streets below the apartment were quiet. The continental sky was blue and the sun was pouring into the sitting-room. On his own, he preferred the modest hotel in Clichy from where he had organized so much almost twelve years ago. Slowly, as he continued to stare at the white ceiling, two lists emerged in his mind. The first detailed the reasons for pulling out. (1) The Revolution has degenerated beyond repair; (2) The Spanish Republic is losing the civil war and Blum will not intervene; (3) If Spain loses, Hitler will invade the Soviet Union and Stalin will be incapable of defending it.

And the second list? His mind registered a blank. He could think of no political reasons to stay in any longer. The thought frightened him.

His eyes descended to see another framed photograph of Lisa and Felix that stood on his desk. Both of them were dressed in their smartest clothes. It made Ludwik laugh. Then he fell silent thinking of them in Moscow. He had received a message from Freddy saying that 'all was well', but nothing more. How could 'all be well'?

It was such a beautiful morning that Ludwik gave up the thought of making himself some more coffee and decided to walk down to his café for breakfast. He had just slipped on a jacket when the phone rang, then stopped, then rang again, stopped again, and Ludwik sat down with a sigh. The Department was trying to call him. The third ring he would have to answer and it was probably Michael Spiegelglass, the new boy at the embassy. An eager young terrier. The very sight of him made Ludwik nauseous. But it was not Spiegelglass. Instead he heard the light tones of one of his oldest agents.

'Ludwik?'

'Good. You're back. Same place in an hour's time.'

The meeting with Gertrude would be painful. He had managed to isolate her from prying eyes, but how would she react if he told her that he had decided to break with Stalin, to do what he had stopped her doing only a few weeks ago? He decided to remain silent for the moment.

As he approached the rendezvous point near Saint-Michel, Ludwik smiled to himself. He was sure she would be wearing her faded blue blouse and her round silver-rimmed spectacles. He was proved wrong on both counts. The woman who greeted him was attired in a smart, cream-coloured skirt, a matching jacket and, to his amazement, a navy blue straw hat. The old spectacles, too, had been replaced with something that must have come straight from the latest fashion magazines.

'Do you approve my disguise?' she asked him after they had embraced and kissed each other on both cheeks.

He nodded.

'The first time I met you, Ludwik, you were dressed in a three-piece suit, prominently displaying a watch, with a gold chain which was safely attached to your waistcoat. Your businessman look.'

'Wrong. I was Professor of Modern Languages at Charles University. My businessman costume was really vulgar. But your clothes are good. Olga or Christopher?'

'Christopher!'

'I thought so. The sun is still out. Should we walk by the river for a while?'

'Of course.'

Ludwik was somewhat distracted by the new-look Gertrude. Could this be the same woman who had threatened suicide a few months ago? She appeared far too jaunty and self-confident. He decided to proceed slowly.

'Tell me about England.'

'Olga said you know England very well. She said you were first in London in 1921, helping the Irish. Is that true?'

'Yes. That was Lenin's idea. You know he followed their Easter Rising in 1916 very closely. Felt sympathy with Connolly's revolutionary defeatism. I offered help. Yes, that's when I first met Olga. She was eighteen and very beautiful.'

'I know. She told me her story. So you recruited the niece of a Russian grand duke to the Bolshevik cause.'

'It wasn't so remarkable. She was already on our side. She was an obvious candidate. Do you trust Christopher?'

'Totally.'

She coloured slightly.

'How so sure?'

They walked on for a few moments before she replied.

'I am. I just am sure.'

'Did you sleep with him again?'

'Ludwik!'

'Answer me, Gertrude.'

'Once. It was a beautiful sunny day and the beaches were totally deserted and —'

'Spare me the details. Does Olga know?'

'He told her.'

'And?'

'She came into my room one night. We talked. It was OK.'

'What did she say?'

'She said "Ludwik sent you to us for a rest and a cure. You have now had both. I think you should leave us." I'm really sorry, Ludwik. It was all spontaneous. I had not planned anything. Neither of us had forgotten those weeks in Moscow after Lenin died.'

'Forget it. Did anyone from Moscow come to the house while you were present?'

'Yes.'

Ludwik froze. He had forbidden Olga and Christopher to contact the embassy while Gertrude was there.

'Why?'

'Olga said she had a message from someone. She said it might even be you. We had to see them.'

'Who was it?'

'Someone at the embassy in France. Spiegelglass? He said he was a friend of yours. That you went back to the twenties. He hadn't seen you for years. Just wanted to know how you were. Asked hundreds of questions about you. What you thought about the trials, about Spain, Germany, everything.'

'Including Stalin.'

'Of course.'

'Did you tell him anything?'

'No, but he tried to make me. He denounced Stalin, but neither Olga nor I responded. That was all. He was accompanied by a very nice, young German comrade. He was genuinely very friendly. Didn't mention you at all. Just talked about the world situation and his great passion for cooking. Christopher was quite impressed with him.'

'And you?'

'The German, Klaus Winter, cheered us all up. Ludwik, I'm getting tired. Can we sit somewhere and have something to drink?'

'Madame is missing her afternoon tea?'

She laughed, unaware that Ludwik was in a vicious mood. He knew that something had changed in her, that she was not telling him the whole truth. This only made him determined to delve deeper. It was while they were sipping their iced lemon drinks that he understood. He put her through a very simple test. In the course of a conversation about Lisa, he casually referred to Stalin as the gravedigger of the Revolution. For Ludwik, this was a very mild remark. None of his close friends would have given it another thought, but Gertrude appeared slightly shifty.

He kept looking at her till she felt obliged to speak.

'Our heroic age is a thing of the past, Ludwik. I've understood that now. We were utopians. This is no time for lofty sentiments. Fascist terror has to be defeated. Christopher and Olga are convinced that the English ruling class will do a deal with Hitler. That leaves the Soviet Union. It's all we've got, Ludwik.'

'So the choice we are offering the workers of the world is barbarism or barbarism, fascist terror or Stalinist terror?'

'There is no equation between the two systems.'

'For you perhaps, but for its victims? Would you prefer to be despatched by Stalin's executioners or Hitler's assassins? Come on. Answer me.'

'There is sometimes a similarity between opposites. It is the weakness, the pathetic philosophy that lies between them, a philosophy that can never decide that of the two opposites is good or evil; it is this that is unacceptable.'

Better to be the scissors than the paper, Ludwik thought. All this nonsense she was spouting came straight from the new machine-men in Moscow. She had been penetrated by official bureaucratic memoranda.

He had heard similar talk in Spain. How deeply the stench had invaded the consciousness of even veteran revolutionaries! He looked straight into Getrude's eyes. She looked away.

'I know, Gertrude. It's difficult, but now tell me everything. No need for evasions and half lies. Or have they told you that I'm really an enemy and that you must report back to them after every meeting with me? I thought so. Well, best of luck, my dear friend. I hope you stay alive.' He rose as if to leave. A half-throttled cry rose from her throat.

'Ludwik!'

Gertrude had begun to weep. She thought of the past, their shared perils, their harrowing conversations, of how he had saved her life more than once and how important he had been for her. He had not changed at all. A poet-philosopher caught up in dirty business. History had forced them all to make choices. She could not bring herself to break with him.

Ludwik sat down and patted her hand, though inwardly he was furious with her for capitulating to Moscow. He always took it personally when one of his people, someone he had trained and educated, underwent a moral collapse. Usually he blamed himself.

'I'm truly sorry, Ludwik,' she spoke, trying to conquer her tears. 'He never said everything in front of Olga. Once when we were alone, he said all those horrible things about you.'

'Did he say they suspected me of working for the Germans?'

'Yes!'

'Then it's serious. Now, please don't panic. Just try and remember everything.'

For the next two hours he systematically debriefed her. At the end of the session, he smiled. His enemies in Moscow were floundering. They must have been desperate to try and win over Gertrude.

'Did you tell Olga any of this?'

Gertrude nodded shamefacedly.

'I was so shaken, Ludwik. I had to talk to someone.'

'The first lesson I taught you was to overcome the desire to talk to someone. In our trade, such a weakness is fatal.'

'Olga was outraged. She said: "I trust Ludwik with my life. He is no more a German agent than you or me. This is Stalin's method and one day it will bring everything to an end." She was very helpful, Ludwik.'

'In her case, your indiscretion does not matter. I have trusted her with my life more than once, but you were wrong to talk. You should not have talked to Spiegelglass. You should not have talked to Olga.

Never do it again.'

'I never will. I do love you, Ludwik.'

'Another mistake.'

Ludwik's face took on a grim appearance, the look of a man with a troubled soul. Later that evening he was due to meet Spiegelglass. He arranged to meet Gertrude the following day and walked back slowly to his apartment.

Why, thought Ludwik, am I too much of a coward to look history in the eye? For over a year I have been oppressed by the same question. How can we live when our dreams are dead? And with them the dreamers. Except Trotsky, who continues to dream in his Mexican exile. Working for Stalin is no longer a serious option. He thinks and behaves like a gangster. He is systematically destroying all possible alternatives to himself. All the new thought processes have debased the old.

This is the worst year in my life. In many ways, for us, it is worse than under the Tsar. Stalin has already imprisoned and killed more revolutionaries than Nicholas. German comrades who fled from Hitler have been executed by Stalin. Now the GPU[*] have asked the police in Prague to arrest the German political exile Grilewicz as a Gestapo agent. Grilewicz, a former Social Democrat deputy, is now a dissident Communist and chairman of a committee of intellectuals in Prague set up to challenge the Moscow Trials. Stalin wants him destroyed.

Who is Spiegelglass?

Twenty-one

'IT IS AN HONOUR to meet a legend, comrade. You have been an inspiration to us from afar for so long that one wondered whether you really existed. One needs steady nerves for our kind of existence and revolutionary zeal by the bucketful. Don't you agree?'

They were seated in a crowded restaurant. Ludwik was trying to look into Spiegelglass's eyes, which were distorted by the thick lenses of his spectacles. Ludwik had been warned by Slutsky and Freddy not to underestimate the monster. Spiegelglass was still in his NKVD[†] travel gear, which amused Ludwik. German Intelligence would have no difficulty in recognizing his occupation.

'I exist.'

Ludwik, who knew that Lisa and Felix had left the Soviet Union a

---

[*] The secret police, which was integrated with the NKVD in 1934.

[†] The Commissariat of the Interior.

few days ago and were now safely in Prague, was not in a cautious mood.

'Tell me something, Spiegelglass,' Ludwik spoke in his most condescending voice as he replenished his colleague's glass with wine. 'How many attempts have there been on Comrade Stalin's life?'

Spiegelglass trembled slightly, but without losing his composure. It was Ludwik's favourite trick question for the machine-men. Spiegelglass was flummoxed.

'Come now, comrade. You have just got here from Moscow. I assume you were briefed by Yezhov. Good. Then I want to know how well you people are guarding our great and beloved leader. Our ship would crash without the great helmsman. Now tell me. How many attempts?'

'None, to my knowledge. Comrade Stalin is at the peak of his popularity.'

'What?' Ludwik exclaimed in mock anger. 'I have read internal reports of dozens of executions. Traitors who attempted to murder Stalin and you sit here calmly and tell me that none of this is true. Be careful, Spiegelglass.'

'I think you misunderstood me.' There was an icy glint in the machine-man's eyes. 'I did not say there were no plans. I repeat. There have been no actual attempts.'

'And why did these plotters plan to kill him?'

'Gestapo agents. Trotskyite infiltrators.'

'I see. Did you come here directly from Moscow?'

'Yes, of course.'

'Why are you lying?'

Spiegelglass paled, but did not avert his eyes.

'You visit London,' Ludwik's voice was rising, 'you tell one of my oldest operators that I am a Gestapo agent. You breach discipline by bursting into one of our safest houses in England and you think our operation is so flimsy that your squalid enterprise will remain secret.'

Spiegelglass removed his spectacles and rubbed his eyes. 'We all do what has to be done. You know that well.'

'Of course. Orders must be carried out and your orders no doubt include the recruitment of White Russian mercenaries. You need them to destroy old Communists. When did you join the Party?'

'Nineteen-twenty-eight.'

'So you still remember the time when Party members could argue with each other. Just before the converts, informers and arrivistes joined the party *en masse*. The Stalin levy! "New Bolsheviks", they called themselves as they loaded their guns to kill those who had made the Revolution.'

Spiegelglass was silent. He knew Ludwik spoke the truth, but he could not fully understand the motives of the man Moscow had told him to eliminate. The condemned man was speaking again.

'What are your orders regarding me, Spiegelglass? Surely if I am a Gestapo agent I should be shot without delay.'

'Please, comrade, try and understand. My orders have come from the very top. All they want is for you to return to Moscow. A simple transfer. Nothing more.'

'I know. Why not transfer me six feet below the ground here rather than the Lubianka?'

'Comrade, please. I must now ask you formally to introduce me to your network of agents in Europe, particularly, in Germany and Spain.'

'The Fourth Department knows what Moscow needs to know.'

'We need the information to fight fascist barbarism.'

'Yes, yes. I know. Moscow has the information. If Yezhov wants it he should go to Slutsky.'

'You're very arrogant, Comrade Ludwik.'

'When we started this enterprise, Comrade Spiegelglass, we knew what we were fighting for. The victory of socialism all over the globe. Some of us still believe in that. You and your White Russian cronies are nothing more than a bunch of killers. I have brought for you a little clipping which the Tsarist rag they produce here in Paris, *Voz rozhdenye*, published after the trial and execution of the Sixteen, Zinoviev and Kamenev among them, last year. Remember the trial? A copy was, as usual, sent to Stalin's office. Were you shown this in Moscow?'

Spiegelglass shook his head.

'Then I'll read it for you:

> We thank thee, Stalin!
> Sixteen scoundrels,
> Sixteen butchers of the fatherland,
> Have been gathered to their forefathers.
> But why only Sixteen,
> Give us forty,
> Give us hundreds,
> Thousands,
> Make a bridge across the Moscow river,
> A bridge without towers and beams
> A bridge of Soviet carrion
> And add thy carcass to the rest!

With the exception of the last sentence, my dear Comrade Spiegelglass, that is exactly what your boss is doing, is he not?'

'And the Party?' asked Spiegelglass in a flinty voice. 'The Party? What of our Party?'

'The Party that made the Revolution is dead. Your leader is busy murdering all of Lenin's comrades. What you call the Party is a giant bureaucratic machine, built so it can be manipulated by a few people – and even this machine is severely damaged. There were over three hundred thousand arrests in the first four months of this year alone. Did you know that, Spiegelglass? All you new boys think you're really clever. Others might perish, but you'll survive. All of you think that but very few survive. I've talked for three years now to eager and enthusiastic Stalinists like yourself. Most of them are dead.'

'Why are you still a member, Ludwik?'

'Good question. I thought that a victory in Spain might turn the tide throughout Europe, but Spain is lost. The Red Army stands between Hitler and the conquest of Europe. Yes, the Red Army. Denuded of its most brilliant generals by your great leader, but still a powerful bulwark against fascist advances.'

'What makes you so sure that Stalin won't do a deal with Hitler to isolate France and Britain?'

'He is trying hard, as we both know, but he will fail. Stalin has never understood the real meaning of fascism.'

Despite himself, Spiegelglass gave his opponent an admiring look. Ludwik sighed.

'And don't think they will leave you alive after you've done their filthy work. The whole pattern is now very clear. Yagoda gets rid of one set of old Bolsheviks, then is tried himself for being a fascist agent. He's replaced by Yezhov who wants to kill more mad dogs. But soon Yezhov and his assistants will also be executed. Pray for a war, Spiegelglass. It's the only thing that might save your skin. Pay the bill. I'm going.'

Ludwik left and Spiegelglass sat waiting for the waiter to bring him the bill, his eyes shining with excitement. In Moscow they sometimes brought prisoners before him who had been beaten so severely that they could no longer speak. Blood poured down their faces. Spiegelglass was jubilant. The vision had excited him. Fireworks burst inside his head. He began to fly. He wanted to see Ludwik in that position, wanted to hear the swish of the whips, wanted to humiliate the man who had just walked out on him.

'There is no hiding place for him on this planet,' he told himself.

Twenty-two

SAO RETURNED TO HIS APARTMENT in the rue Murrillo a poorer man, saddened by the loss of two irreplaceable friends, but also shocked by the knowledge that they had become flesh-peddlers on a gigantic scale. The president's entourage had given him the name of a policeman who knew who was killing who for treading on toes in the new Russia. Before he left Moscow he had been given the name of the killers. For a couple of thousand dollars, he was told by the same police officer, they could be found and executed. Sao had shrugged his shoulders.

'Two more murders won't solve the problem. Why were my friends killed?'

At first Sao thought the policeman was trying to evade his question, but this was not the case. He was simply explaining to Sao how Moscow functioned.

'Everything is for sale, Mr Sao. Should I tell you something that will make you laugh? There's an American film producer in town. He's got hold of some old KGB uniforms and he's asked for permission to film in the Lubianka. At first my bosses thought it was political and refused. The American then showed them the script. It was a porno movie. Everyone laughed, but they have been negotiating for three weeks now on the money.'

The real story finally came out. The killers belonged to a group of free-marketeers, shock-therapists who had built up a gigantic trade in human flesh. They exported Russian prostitutes to Thailand and the Gulf States; Baltic call girls were in great demand in Northern Europe and Romanian boys were at a premium throughout Western Europe.

Sao's murdered business partners had a rival enterprise, which was more multicultural in character. They were using the old Vietnamese network and engaging in flesh-exports from all the former Soviet Republics. The contradictions had become explosive and instead of relying on the needs of the market, the Russian entrepreneurs had taken the law into their own hands.

Sao's spiritual loss, however, had been more than amply compensated by the profits that had accrued to him as a middleman in three immensely lucrative deals involving Russia, China and Iran. All of these had involved the sale and purchase of missiles. Sao's share, which had come to nearly two million dollars, lay safely in a Lausanne bank.

He had come in to find a note from Marie-Louise, his divorced wife, informing him that she had taken the children to her parents' house in Brittany. He was instructed not to linger in Paris, but to join them as soon as he had recovered from jet lag. Sao had rung her, spoken to the children and promised to be there within a few days. Even though they were divorced, relations remained friendly, not least because Sao's father-in-law, once a senior officer in French Military Intelligence, had been instrumental in helping Sao gain a foothold in the arms trade.

A week later he still could not tear himself away from Paris. He had started going to his old bachelor haunts in search of old Vietnamese friends, but had been singularly unsuccessful. Instead he sat silently in an old Vietnamese restaurant and chatted to the waiters.

He had tried ringing Vlady on several occasions, but never found him at home. Sao was sorely tempted to hop on a plane and fly to Berlin, but he felt duty-bound to go to his family Brittany. Just before leaving for the station he tried Vlady again. This time he was lucky.

'Greetings, my friend.'

'Sao! Where are you?'

'Back home. I have the files you wanted, Vlady. They did not come cheap, as you know. I think it's what you need. I have them here. I wanted to come to Berlin, but Marie-Louise and the children are waiting for me in Brittany.'

'No hurry. I was thinking of coming to Paris next month, and –'

'Good idea. Spend Christmas with us. My father is coming from Hue. He has always wanted to meet you. Is that settled?'

'I'm writing it in my diary.'

'Vlady?'

'Yes.'

'Remember our early days in Dresden?'

'Yes, of course.'

'Once in my ultra-nationalist mood I was telling you about the Truong sisters and how they led a resistance in 40 AD and expelled the Chinese aggressors. I remember you laughed and said: "You Vietnamese always go on about the wretched Truong sisters. Why don't you ever talk of the year that followed, when the Chinese came back?"'

Vlady laughed at the other end and interrupted his friend. 'And why do you cover up the fact that two years later the sisters threw themselves into a river and perished? I remember at first how shocked you were and then, suddenly, you started laughing. Anyway, why did you start talking about all that now?'

'I was thinking about you and the Truong sisters a few days ago, when I was on my own, eating in a Vietnamese place, and I found myself laughing.'

There was something in Sao's tone that alerted Vlady that his old friend was not his usual ebullient self.

'Sao? Is something wrong?'

'I don't know, Vlady. I'm a bit tired of being so readily adaptable, so mentally receptive. I no longer enjoy being a wandering Vietnamese.'

'Meaning?'

'I've made enough money here. I could return to Hue or Hanoi and live the rest of life in peace and comfort. Do you understand?'

'Of course. What stops you?'

'The children.'

'Are you sure you're not deceiving yourself? You want to return and you don't want to return. After Paris, could you really live in Hanoi? Be honest with yourself.'

'Perhaps you're right. But I don't want to be buried here, Vlady. I want to return to my ancestors.'

'Ah! Now I understand. You want to go back to the Truong sisters. But they buried themselves in a river.'

'Why are you laughing at your old friend, Vlady? You cannot understand me because you people who live at home do not know what it is like.'

'How wrong you are, Sao. I am a totally rootless phenomenon. Born in France, I think. Early childhood in Russia. Transplanted to the DDR when I was eight. And now the DDR has gone. Am I a German, a Russian, a non-Jewish Jew or what? You have no such problems. I don't know what you're complaining about. If I were you I'd spend half the year in Vietnam and the rest in Europe. Don't pretend you're a great family man, Sao. You're never in Paris.'

'I have a son in Hanoi.'

For a few seconds Vlady was stunned into silence.

'How old?'

'Three years.'

'And the mother?'

'What about her?'

'Who is she?'

'A Vietnamese woman. I love her, Vlady.'

'That does complicate matters. Let me reformulate my advice. I think you should spend most of your time in Hanoi and a few months every summer in what will by then have become Marie-Louise's villa in Provence. That is, of course, if she still wishes to be friendly. Otherwise hang on to your apartment in Paris.'

'Don't be cynical.'

'I'm being realistic, Sao.'

'Do you think I should tell Marie-Louise now?'

'Of course. Why delay the agony? You'll feel much better.'

'You never liked Marie-Louise. Did you Vlady?'

'I only met her once.'

'Answer my question.'

'No.'

'Why?'

'I was never convinced that she really cared for you. She was your secretary, Sao. You took her to Indochina on business trips. Showed her the sights, including the sight of your oversized Swiss bank accounts. What had to happen, happened. She first became your fucking secretary, then your wife. The pattern is not original. Of course, there are some cases where the new arrangement works beautifully.'

'I think you're wrong, Vlady. She was initially very reluctant. I had to work hard. I had to pursue her like...'

'Like flies pursue dung.'

'Vlady, you are being unfair to her.'

'You've fathered a child in Hanoi. Fallen in love with its mother and I'm being unfair to your French wife. Please, Sao. Don't lose your sense of perspective.'

Sao started laughing. 'You have cheered me up, you know. I wish I could fly to Berlin.'

'Don't be a coward, Sao. Go to Brittany, my friend, and make it your Dienbienphu.'

'I love my children, Vlady.'

'And they love your presents. Since they hardly ever see you, they can't feel that close. But fathers who play Santa Claus throughout the year do become an obsession for their children, so I may be wrong. When you leave they will go crazy and want to live with you in Hanoi. It's possible. Is your new love in Hanoi prepared to mother these two as well?'

'I don't know. I haven't asked her because the thought never occurred to me. I'm sure it will be fine.'

'Good. Then off you go to Brittany.'

'Have you ever been in love, Vlady? I mean really in love. Or is it still an abstract bourgeois concept?'

'You're a fool, Sao. I loved Helge. Still do.'

'Then you know how I feel about Linh.'

'So that's her name.'

'Yes. Even as I talk to you, Vlady, I can see her in front of me.'

'Why have you never told me before?'

'I don't know. I didn't want you to think my relationship with Linh was sordid in any way and you might have ... well, you know what I mean.'

'I do, and I think you're a very big fool. You'd better go and catch your train to Brittany. Ring when you come back, and tell me how it all went. One more thing, Sao.'

'Yes?'

'You're still in the grip of the love disease. Yes?'

'Yes.'

'Then just wait a minute. I will read something out to you ... Sao?'

'Yes.'

'Listen to the song of the poet.'

'I'm listening.'

> Does the imagination dwell the most
> Upon a woman won or woman lost?
> If on the lost, admit you turned aside
> From a great labyrinth out of pride,
> Cowardice, some silly, over-subtle thought
> Or anything called conscience once;
> And that if memory recur, the sun's
> Under eclipse and the day blotted out.

'Brilliant, Vlady. Who is it? Brecht?'

'No, no, no! It's an Irish poet, Yeats.'

'Do you think he's been translated into Vietnamese?'

'Not sure, but the Chinese translation is good.'

'I will send Linh his collection in English. She will translate it into Vietnamese for our new publishing house.'

'Sao! I order you to stop dreaming. To Brittany, my friend. Adieu.'

'Ciao, Vlady, and thanks.'

For several minutes, Sao did not move from the chair on which he had slumped while talking to Berlin. He was annoyed at Vlady's suggestion that Marie-Louise had married him for his money. Vlady had no idea of the good times they had enjoyed together. He could not know of how well they had bonded in bed. Something was lacking in their relationship. Marie-Louise saw Sao as a successful businessman, nothing more. Sao felt that she never really understood the depth of his inner revulsion as far as his work was concerned. When he complained of the life that circumstances forced him to lead, she showed little sympathy. She had no idea what he was talking about. It was this that had led to an amicable divorce and an equally amicable financial settlement. Marie-Louise's father had made sure that his daughter would live in comfort.

Twenty-three

I NEVER WANTED TO BE a dead-weight in your life, Karl. That's the reason I deliberately kept you aloof from what had become a way of life for Helge and me. After we had founded the Committee for Democratic Germany (KDD), it was difficult to settle down to a normal existence. In the seventies my book, *A Manifesto For a New Germany*, had become an underground success, thought not as popular as Bahro's *The Alternative*. I seemed to have developed an instinct for how far this wretched regime could be pushed – and it was always a little harder than people imagined.

Our life became discontinuous even though the irregularities and dislocations tended to repeat themselves and a pattern began to emerge. Our lives seemed to be obeying cycles of chance, but were, in reality, acquiring an odd coherence. We became expert actors. Much to the surprise of my apolitical colleagues and students at Humboldt, I appeared to have changed. My behaviour, so they told me, had become much more conformist.

Your mother and I made trips to the West. Remember? I don't think you enjoyed them much. You wanted to be like the other kids. Am I right, Karl? Or were you secretly taking everything in and becoming desperate to be a normal citizen in the West? There are times I wish we could talk about all this while I'm still alive.

It was in March '84 that your grandmother took a turn for the worse.

'I feel wretched, Vlady. I am ready to die.'

Gertrude was lying in bed. Outside the first buds of spring had appeared on the linden trees. The doctor had been and injected her with painkillers. Helge and you were in Dresden for the weekend. I sat on a stool and looked at the shrivelled little woman. She had been confined to her bed for nearly a year and the old Gertrude was barely recognizable.

'I know, Mutti.'

Ever since we had made peace nearly thirty years ago, the truce had held. Did you realize that she was an active supporter of the KDD and much loved by all the new members? We had a network of nearly four hundred supporters dotted throughout the country. Most of them were Young Communist defectors from the Party. Some of them were children of leading Party officials.

Gertrude made it her business to know them all. She had written their most popular public manifesto, which had won them notoriety within the ranks of the Stasi and a great deal of respect in the other Germany from the Greens and groups to the left of the SPD, which, of course, cultivated good relations with Honecker and the bureaucracy.

When we congratulated her for the fine polemical tone of her writing, her face assumed a heroic and magnanimous expression. To tell you the truth, Karl, there were occasions when I felt the KDD would have collapsed through sheer inertia and fatigue. She always came to the rescue, with her uplifting speeches, her ability to find and approach print shops prepared to publish contraband in return for West German currency, her refusal to accept defeat.

'I won't be here much longer, Vlady. Think of me kindly, my son. Don't forget me.'

'How can you even think such a thing?'

'Everything I did was for the cause, Vlady. This is something which you must never forget.'

A sudden clap of thunder, followed by a squall of rain beating against the window-panes, gave divine emphasis to Gertrude's message. The morning sunlight had been replaced by a dull grey light, which had slid into the bedroom. Suddenly her eyes became alert and I saw her staring at me.

'Spring showers, Mutti. They always remind me of Moscow.'

'Yes,' she mumbled. 'Moscow. You know something, Vlady. Moscow always reminds me of young Ludwik. He used to listen, console, support, give advice, find out what had happened at a secret session of the Politburo, and then we used to laugh. I can still see his eyes twinkling. Outside the snow is falling, but inside . . .'

She shut her eyes and I tiptoed to the other end of the room. She opened them immediately afterwards and began to talk to me before she realized I had disappeared. It took her back to my childhood, and wartime Moscow, when everyone knew that the most important thing in the world was the defeat of fascism. Nothing else had mattered. Her mind would not stay fixed on any one episode, but began to wander. Ludwik's smiling blue eyes. Gertrude began to weep at the memory.

'Forgive me, Ludwik. Forgive me.'

'Mutti? I thought you had gone to sleep. Who should forgive you?'

'Your father.'

'Why?'

'I should not have stayed alive.'

'Mutti? Will you tell me something?'

She nodded.

'Was Ludwik really my father?'

I could see that I had stung her. The old face came to life for the last time.

'Yes. Why ask me now?'

'When I looked in the mirror this morning I saw you, but not Ludwik.'

'Stupid boy. For all we know, you may be the exact image of Ludwik's father. You have my father's eyebrows. On the day you were born I looked into your face and saw Ludwik looking back at me.'

I believed her. There was something in the way she spoke that convinced me she was telling the truth. I held her tiny, withered hand and kissed it, but this time she really was asleep. When I put her hand back gently on the bed I felt life ebbing out of her. I rushed to phone the doctor, but it was too late. She died exactly two weeks before her eighty-fourth birthday.

I stared at the bare room, devoid of colour except for the dark blue curtains which draped the window-frames, curtains she loved because they reminded her of her bedroom in her parents' house in Munich. They were exactly the same age as the DDR and they had faded a great deal, but she would not be parted from them.

It seemed hours since the doctor had left. I was sitting in her room looking at her dead body. Images of my childhood and the good times we had enjoyed together flashed past me. I felt guilty. Perhaps it had been cruel to question her about my father, to lacerate her wounds. I was desperate for the truth. I began to doubt her again. Gertrude was not a believer in death-bed confessions. She might not have told me the truth.

I stared at the photographs on the wall. There was a large one of me in Gertrude's arms. The one that used to make you laugh, Karl, when you were a boy. I was three months old, just before she came to Moscow. I loved the old family portrait, from her childhood days in Munich. The grandparents and uncle I had never seen. One of me aged twelve, looking sharp-faced and cheeky, wearing a necktie and a smart jacket.

Later that afternoon the undertakers arrived and took Gertrude away. Alone in the flat, I wept for the first time. I couldn't fall asleep that night. I got out of bed and began to pace up and down the whole apartment. Helge and you were on the way back from Dresden, but wouldn't arrive till the morning. I went back to Gertrude's room.

An hour later I was still slumped at Gertrude's cramped and fragile writing desk. I tried opening the secret drawer of the desk, but it was still locked. It was always locked. Forbidden territory. I forced it open and my heartbeat quickened. What treasures would I find?

I was greeted by one old photograph and letters whose envelopes had browned with age. The photograph was unfamiliar. Gertrude and Ludwik arm-in-arm outside some old café. The late twenties? Berlin or Vienna? Impossible to tell. Slowly I began to look through the letters. A few from Gertrude's mother, one from Lisa dated Moscow 1925, but nothing of interest. Then I saw a letter addressed to me. It was her handwriting. She had written it six years ago.

My dearest boy,

You will find this after I am dead. Everything that belongs to me is in this apartment. It is now yours. The only object I value is a little brooch which used to belong first to my grandmother and later my mother. If you have a daughter I would like you to give it to her. Otherwise it should be kept for Karl's children. I would not like it to go outside my family.

Sometimes I think my life was a total failure. Everything went hopelessly wrong. I used to believe that life after the war would be different. It was to a certain extent, but not enough. When I think now of the years after the Revolution, the years when I was a fugitive in other lands, the years that were a painful testing-time for all socialists, when oppression and hunger was dominant ... those were the richest and most fruitful years of my life. Do you understand, Vlady? I'm talking now of when I was in my twenties. No matter how awful our conditions were, our spirits were resilient, our vision was impassioned. Now our world is grey, and yet I prefer this grey drabness to what lies on the other side of the dreadful Wall. I can never reconcile myself to the laws of the capitalist jungle and the survival of the richest. Perhaps the greyness will go one day and you and your friends in the KDD will build a better world. I say perhaps, because I don't know. I'm not sure any more. The blind faith in the future has gone, leaving in its place a vacuum, a big hole, which could be filled by anything.

The socialist cause has done so much harm to itself and to others that the wound has become our most pertinent symbol. Do you remember those words? You spoke them at one of the KDD meetings and I disagreed with you in public, but secretly I was proud of you. Your father would have been so pleased. I suspect you're right, but I hope you're wrong. Anyway I know you'll do what is best for the movement.

I've already told you how close I feel to Helge and young Karl. You were right about her and I hope she has forgiven me all my early trespasses. She is a wonderful person and I hope that all of you remain happy regardless of what happens in the grey world outside.

Karl is a very intelligent boy, but I think he is intimidated by your presence. He is not interested in your politics and for this, I feel, you tend to punish him. I never interfered when I was alive, except for one occasion. I told Helge that she should speak to you and tell you not to crush Karl too much. She just smiled. I suppose she saw me as an interfering old fool. She never really got to like me, did she Vlady? But I don't blame her. I remember once, when I had come into the apartment quietly and neither of you were aware of the fact, I heard you defending me and Helge said: 'Gertrude will die with the Wall in her head.' And you laughed, Vlady. You laughed softly. Now that I have gone you can laugh loudly without fear that I might hear you.

I don't want this letter, my last communication with you, to become full of bitterness and recriminations. I have always loved you very much and everything I did, I repeat everything, was to protect you and make sure you lived a decent and healthy life. If I hadn't been pregnant with you I might have behaved differently and I might have died with Ludwik or soon after they got him, but I had to live because you were in my stomach. What do you think, Vlady? Would you rather not have been born?

I know you and Helge always saw me as a Party hack, but I was not uncritical. I was never a hundred-per-center. What you demanded was the total rejection of the spirit, logic and practice of the Party. That I opposed very strongly, and now I will tell you why. Ever since the formation of the DDR and the re-foundation of the Party, there were two layers battling for its soul. The 'cosmopolitans', as we were called, by which they meant Jews, Germans from the Soviet Union and Eastern Europe, returning German exiles, cadres who had fought in the Spanish Civil War or served in the Red Army. The second group saw themselves essentially as German national Communists.

Even inside the Party their nationalism sometimes frightened me. Deep down they preferred Franz Joseph Strauss to Brezhnev. I can see you laughing when you read this and mocking me: 'Mutti, what a choice. Cow dung versus horse dung.' That's what you would say, isn't it my Vladimiro? But now that you are beginning to take the Lutheran pastors seriously, let me remind you of what Albrecht Schonherr told his flock as Bishop of our Berlin: 'We do not wish to be a Church alongside Socialism, nor a Church against Socialism: we wish to be a Church within Socialism.' Within, Vlady! Within. Understand?

The seeds of nationalism are sprouting everywhere, while the dragon seeds of fascism lie dormant. When the beast rises again we will need a balancing force as disciplined and ruthless to crush it. It can only come from within . . .

I have written too much already. Long life to you and yours, my son.
Gertrude

As I read her letter, Karl, I was convinced that I was listening to a cracked bell. The secret wasn't there, and I knew she had one. I knew now for sure because she tried to justify herself through my embryonic presence in her womb. For her to write that could only mean that she was aware of the magnitude of the crimes she had committed. She knew what she was doing. Why had I not pursued her for it while she lived? You may think I was afraid of what I'd learn, and I can't prove you're wrong, but perhaps there was a skill Gertrude had learned in the dangerous places she lived in, a chameleon talent to pass unseen, or at least to hide what she was determined not to show. I think it worked on Ludwik too, even though he knew her better than most.

They buried her in the old cemetery behind the theatre, not far from where Brecht lay. There were over a hundred people at the grave-side, which was festooned with flowers and two red flags. Helge, you and I stood in a row shaking hands as we bade farewell to Gertrude's friends.

Most of the faces were familiar. There were present old comrades, veterans of the pre-war German party who had returned with Gertrude from Moscow after the war. These included Walter Ulbricht's widow, who kissed me. Did she realize who she was kissing? A few of my colleagues from Humboldt had turned up with black armbands. But who were the strangers? There were about two dozen men and women I had never seen before. They were dressed in civilian clothes, but their bearing indicated the organs of state security. The Stasi and Foreign Intelligence units appeared to be well represented. Amongst them was Winter, now an old man in his seventies. His shock of white hair distinguished him from the others, but he was also dressed differently. Gertrude told me he was the curator of the art museum where she worked.

He walked towards us, and introduced himself to Helge. 'Klaus Winter. I was one of Gertrude's colleagues. We go back a very long way. Please accept my condolences. Perhaps one day you and I can meet for a coffee, Professor Meyer?'

'That would be very nice, Herr Winter. Did you work with my mother at the museum?'

He smiled and nodded.

'We will talk about all that when we meet.'

As he walked away Helge tightened her grip on my arm. 'I don't trust him, Vlady. Did you notice his eyes?'

'Not really. Why?'

'A killer's eyes.'

'Helge! Your instincts are really going crazy this time. You're becoming like your patients!'

Before she could reply, you took charge of us and prodded your parents gently towards the exit. Do you remember what you said? 'Please, both of you. Let Grandma rest in peace. Wait till you get home before you start an argument.'

I hugged and kissed you on both cheeks. You looked embarrassed, as a fourteen-year-old boy would, but I think that deep down my public show of love pleased you.

A meeting of our underground group had been scheduled for the evening of the funeral. Helge wanted to cancel the event, but I insisted that Gertrude would have hated a political meeting being cancelled on her account. The apartment was crowded; over forty activists were present.

'Comrades,' I told them, 'we have messages of support from Wolf Biermann and Rudolf Bahro, messages they want us to print and distribute in the DDR. I will pass them around and at the end of the meeting, when all of you have read them, we can vote. OK? Good. Now Gerhard has the floor.'

Gerhard, who had been seated on the floor, stood up, took off his spectacles and began to speak. He informed the gathering that they had received an invitation to participate in the Friedensdekade, the ten days for peace initiated by the Samariter Parish, and to help with the Berlin Appeal to transform 'swords to ploughshares'. This was the beginning of our peace movement, which annoyed East and West alike.

'Stephan Krawczyk, Stefan Heym and Rolf Schneider have signed the appeal and...'

'Just a minute, Gerhard,' Gisela interrupted. 'Before you carry on we must clarify our attitude to the Church. Are we going to work with them? I mean, us? We're all non-Party socialists or Marxists. To link up with the Church at this stage is morally unjustifiable!'

'Why?' I asked her.

'Because the Church hierarchy is complicit with the regime. They made their peace a long time ago with the bureaucrats.'

'Gisela!' said Gerhard. 'The Samariter Parish people have the same relationship to the Church as we do to the Party: they're dissidents in search of a critical space. They want freedom, humaneness and tolerance. I know. I know what you're going to say. Of course we want much more, but we also want what they demand, do we not? We will never win this battle on our own.'

The debate raged for nearly three hours. Finally when the vote was taken even Gisela did not vote against, but simply abstained. A letter was drafted supporting the Berlin Appeal.

'Gertrude would have fought you all the way on this question,' Gisela shouted after they had voted. Everyone laughed. Then Gerhard stood up and proposed a toast.

'To Gertrude, who is no longer with us, but from whom we learnt a great deal and in more ways than she ever realized.'

The apartment echoed to her name.

'Gertrude!'

Later that night, not wanting to wake your mother or worry you, I wept softly to myself. Helge was not asleep. She stroked my head and encouraged me to talk.

'I was thinking of her. Trying to remember what she was like when I was a child. I can't remember a single occasion when we laughed together. I mean on our own. She laughed with friends, but never with me. Why?'

Helge sighed and held me close. 'I never got to like her, Vlady. I'm sorry. I always felt she had a terrible secret. Something in her past of which she was so ashamed that she repressed everything, including your birth and childhood.'

'But she was a very strong woman,' I argued back. 'You know that well. She could transcend most problems that were served up to her by life, by history . . .'

'Yes, but her strength lay precisely in her artfulness, her capacity to deceive herself and you and others. She was always keeping something back, not even telling you everything to your face and often parrying your questions with a light-heartedness that was so fake it must have hurt her inside.'

Helge was right. I confessed my own worries to her.

'I always felt she lied about my father, except this last time. She knew she was dying. When we discussed the matter she almost convinced me that it was Ludwik.'

'More likely she convinced herself, Vlady.'

'Perhaps.'

A fortnight after Gertrude's death, I received a phone call from Klaus Winter, the man with white hair who had introduced himself at the funeral. We agreed to meet outside the museum where Gertrude had worked. Winter did not invite me to his office. Instead we went down a side street and entered an unmarked apartment block, a post-war confection built in the Stalino-classical style. He smiled at me, but did not say a word till we had come out of the lift on the tenth floor, walked down a carpeted corridor and entered his apartment.

I was amazed. The place was packed with antiques and paintings and comfortably furnished.

'Not bad, eh?'

There was one large canvas — it must have been eight feet by six feet — that caught my attention. It was a modern canvas, an interesting copy of the old socialist-realist style, but with a remarkable twist. It brought together an interesting group of men.

Seated around a table from left to right, in a manner of speaking, were a uniformed Cromwell, Robespierre in his powder-green jacket, Trotsky in a tunic, with his stretched arm poised over the telephone waiting for the call which never came, Danton in seventh heaven after draining his glass of claret. The claret bottle is labelled Chateau Bastille 1791. Lenin was sitting on an armchair at a slight distance from the table, making notes.

On the wall behind this motley collection were portraits of Marx and Milton, while a bust of Voltaire rests on a nearby shelf. Sitting on the floor was a late-twentieth-century intellectual in blue denims, a black leather jacket, gold-rimmed spectacles, his two hands clutching his head as if he were trying to make sense of the old Revolutions. The unsigned painting is titled *History*.

'Where did you find this? Who painted it? I've never seen Trotsky in a socialist-realist painting...'

'Nor had the painter,' replied Winter. 'That's why she started the work. She lives in Moscow. A friend saw the painting at her flat and bought it immediately. I made him an offer in dollars. Gertrude liked it a great deal. Do you?'

I nodded.

'Take it away. It's yours.'

I was surprised by the casual generosity, but declined his offer. 'Very kind, but, alas, it is too big for our apartment.'

He smiled and said nothing for a few minutes. Then he spoke in a slow and measured drawl. 'Your mother and I used to look at it often and talk about old times. Can I get you a drink?'

'Coffee would be fine.'

While Winter was in the kitchen, I inspected the room, starting with the bookshelves. It was a thirties' library, to which a great deal had been added, not dissimilar to Gertrude's collection at home. Winter returned and saw me looking at the books.

'Here, let me show you what was our bible in the thirties.' He took out the first Russian-language edition of *A Short Course History of the Soviet Union* by J. V. Stalin and handed it to me.

'The devil's own work?'

'Don't be so naïve. It was written by a committee of people, Soviet historians who had sold their soul to the devil.'

'Why?'

'Something happened to us after we had defeated the Whites in the civil war. Lenin's death, Trotsky's incompetence in the face of Stalin's manoeuvres ... you must understand one thing. Stalin was a very able organizer of the Party. He took some of Lenin's less attractive ideas to their ultimate logic. He understood that to secure power he had to secure the Party and he did so with a ruthlessness that brooked no opposition. The people who made the Revolution were either dead or exhausted. What happened to us was like the melting down of our very being. We were lashed with the devil's whip. We lost control of our senses. Stalinism gave us insights into ourselves and other human beings. We plumbed the lower depths of our souls and the brand marks are still there – a sign of our collective shame.'

'Not everyone fell. What about the political prisoners in Vorkuta who went on strike against Stalin? What about Ludwik? He had the courage to resist.'

'Of course, of course. I do not deny that there were some who preferred suicide. The decision we took was to remain alive, and in order to remain alive we had to surrender our dignity, our self-respect.'

'Was it a price worth paying, Herr Winter? Look at the Soviet Union today or the DDR. Some of us are trying to fight for a new beginning.'

'No more Herr Winter, please. My name is Klaus. To speak of new beginnings is very noble, but we must learn to be dispassionate. I cannot succumb to the false pathos and believe that if people like you were in control, everything would suddenly became great and glorious and good and we would be transformed overnight by wonderful circumstances into becoming wonderful human beings.'

'Your cynicism is corrosive.'

'Cynicism? Remember those who succumbed to similar illusions in 1917 only to become the monsters who scared us so badly twenty years later? That form of self-intoxication is impermissible.'

'The world is bad, human nature is governed by selfish genes, we are all inherently evil. So, according to your logic, we should just sit back and cultivate our own minds. I disagree.'

'That is your privilege, but please don't distort my views. All I am advising you against is any sense of triumphalism. If I believed that human nature was static, incapable of change, I would not be a Communist today. But I must tell you that there is something in our psyche, probably something related to our biology, that allows our animal instincts to override, to jam the transmissions from our brain-cells. We humans have done more mischief to each other than the entire species from which we claim our descent. Do you agree?'

I was beginning to get annoyed, Karl, and I rose as if to leave. 'I've heard some of these arguments before, but despite everything I still believe –'

'Belief! That was always a big problem. Marxism as a surrogate religion with its prophets and popes. Look where it has got us. You believe? You have no right to believe. You must not believe ... Why are you standing up? I did not call you in for a discussion on philosophy. Please, sit down.'

I did as he asked me, but I felt I was being manipulated. Who in hell was Winter?

'Who are you, Klaus?'

'One of your mother's oldest comrades.'

'But you're somewhat younger than Gertrude. She would have been eighty-four this year.'

'True. I'll be seventy-nine this October. We were in Moscow together during the war. We worked in the same building. I remember you as a little boy.'

'So you worked for Soviet military intelligence as well? And you went to see her in Norfolk before the war. What were you doing then?'

For the first time that afternoon his face paled and he lost his composure, but only for a few seconds. 'Yes,' he replied in a slightly choked voice. 'I did meet her in England. It was work. What did she tell you?'

It was my turn to smile. 'Everything,' I lied.

'Now listen to me, Vladimir. Gertrude told me everything too. I know about the KDD and your political work. I'm very impressed. I circulated some of your pamphlets inside the Party. At the highest levels.'

I was stunned. I shouted at him. 'You did *what*, you crazy old man? How dare you? You had no right and she was wrong to tell you. She promised us that ... Who the hell are you, Winter? Tell me!'

'Why does it matter?'

'Because I'm beginning to feel nervous.'

'Did you ever ask your mother who she was?'

'She was my mother.'

'Listen, Vladimir. Your mother and I worked together. In the Soviet Union and in the DDR.'

I was beginning to understand, but still could not believe Winter's insinuations. 'Gertrude worked at the museum. Did you?'

Winter smiled, but did not speak.

'Well?' I asked in a tone that was becoming more aggressive.

Winter shrugged his shoulders.

'Look, Herr Winter. You invited me here. You wanted to talk. I want to leave because there is nothing more I want to say to you, but what are you trying to say about my mother?'

Winter's eyes narrowed as he looked at me. Helge was right, I remember thinking at the time. This man has blood on his hands.

'Vladimir, either you were very naïve or your subconscious instructed you to maintain the pretence. Did you not know that once you work for the intelligence you can never break free?'

'I knew she had worked for the Soviet Union, but...'

'You mean you really have illusions about the DDR? If Moscow leaves we will collapse overnight. We were Moscow's German extension and, naturally, those of us who had worked for them elsewhere in Europe were now sent home. Neither Gertrude nor I ever left. You're trembling, Vlady.'

'Are you telling me that my mother worked for the Stasi?'

'No! She worked for me, and I head a special section. We act as a liaison between the Foreign Intelligence, the Stasi and various under-cover operations inside both these organizations. We report first to Moscow, then to Berlin.'

I felt nauseous. I rushed to the bathroom and vomited. My eyes filled with tears. I tried to recover myself and returned to Winter's study.

'Have a drink, Vlady, if I may call you that now. I think you need one.'

'I'm fine. I drank some water.'

'You hate her now? You think she betrayed the KDD?'

'What I feel about her is between me and my memories of her. But what do you want of me?'

'Nothing much. I just feel we should meet once a month. I am not asking you to become a spy, Vlady. There's no need. We have a complete file on the KDD, its membership, its documents and much more detailed minutes of its meeting than you ever see. In short, Vlady, we know everything. We have a few dozen informers inside your group who are paid to write detailed and regular reports. Do you want to see them?'

I wanted to strangle him and burn his flat. I'm serious, Karl. It was the only time in my life that I felt really violent. Nobody knew I was there. If I killed him and destroyed all the papers, who would ever have found out? But it was a momentary madness, which scared me. I was now desperate to know the names of the informers. I said so to him.

Winter walked to a desk, picked up a file from which he removed two single sheets of paper and handed them to me. I devoured them like a man possessed. I was shaken to my very core. What I had read was a totally accurate account of a meeting that had been held two nights ago. I slumped in the chair, speechless.

'Sometimes we get contradictory reports. Gertrude would then clear up the problem. Now she is gone. By the way, I'm very pleased you've established close links with the Pastors. Some of them, as you would expect, are working for us. Your lot are different, they want the DDR to disband its standing army. Their simplicity is dangerous. It threatens our state.'

I was speechless, overwhelmed with shock, rage, despair. They knew. They could arrest us all any minute. I thought of you, Karl, and what would happen if both Helge and I were locked up. A state orphanage for you? The very thought made me scream.

'What do you want of me? I do not wish to see you every month or ever again. I will tell you nothing. Are you going to give me the names of the informers in our group?'

'No. Listen to me, Vlady. I happen to agree with your aims. If I were not working for the state I would be a member of the KDD. I think we do need to democratize, have elections, free the press and everything else, provided that in the last analysis the present state remains in control, just like in the Western countries which your friends admire so much. Our counterparts in Bonn, Paris and London are every bit as ruthless as we are. The difference is they have hundreds of years of experience.'

I agreed with him, but refused to give him the slightest satisfaction. 'I still don't wish to see you again.'

'But who else would tell you that a big debate is taking place within the Soviet politburo along lines not unlike some of the demands in your pamphlets?'

'You mean that there is . . . ?'

'A reformer in the Kremlin? Not yet, but soon. Very soon. My equivalent in Moscow, the late Yuri Andropov, decided that reform was the only way.'

'So if Moscow shifts gear, you will need a few supporters in the DDR.'

'You're an intelligent man, Professor Meyer. You might win sooner than you think.'

'I'm not sure that I believe you.'

'Wait and see. Patience is the noblest of virtues.'

I walked back to the apartment in a daze, oblivious to the spring sunshine, oblivious to the almond blossoms, oblivious to everything except Winter. My mind played and re-played the events of the afternoon. I wanted to run down the Unter den Linden, screaming to the world that my mother was a spy, that she had spied on her own family, that her crippled mind had totally destroyed any sense of honour. Morality was a concept Gertrude had never understood.

The apartment was quiet when I returned. You were away in Czechoslovakia with a group from your school. Helge was working late; it was Tuesday, when she saw extra patients in her rooms at the hospital.

'Come home, Helge,' I shouted at her photograph. 'Come home and analyse me!'

I walked from one room to another, removing every photograph of Gertrude I could find. There was one I had always liked: Gertrude holding you when you were three years old. She was smiling at you, a genuine smile. I loved that photograph. It was on my desk, but now I lifted it and smashed it on the floor. I hated that smile. It couldn't be real. Nothing about her was real. Her face, her emotions, her life – everything had been a mask.

When Helge returned that evening, I told her everything. She was shaken, too, but not completely surprised. For her it was as if a puzzle had been solved. For an hour we sat silently next to each other, buried deep in our thoughts.

Twenty-four

IF THERE WAS A SINGLE PERSON who could have told Vlady what he wanted to know about Ludwik, it was Felix, who knew him from a child's perspective. Felix, who was born out of the great love his parents had felt for each other in the heroic days of utopia. Felix, who understood more than his parents realized and who was alert to even the slightest change of mood on the part of either of them.

When Felix woke up on that beautiful July day in 1937, he tried to understand why he was feeling so happy. He frowned, struggling to remember the dream, but shrugged his shoulders and gave up. One reason for his happiness was that the three of them had been together now for nearly a month. Ludwik was no longer travelling.

Felix tiptoed to his parents' bedroom and turned the brass door-knob

TARIQ ALI

as softly as he could. The door creaked as he pushed it open. There they were, lying fast asleep in each other's arms. Felix smiled and walked out backwards, pulling the door shut behind him. It creaked again, making him shudder and stop, but there was no sound from the room.

Paris in summer. He leaned out of the kitchen window, shutting his eyes as the sun hit his face. The streets looked crisp and dry. The parquet of puddles appeared to have vanished. The noises on the street were getting louder and soon he began to see familiar figures.

In his daydreams, Felix would look at the shopkeepers and put different features on each of them. Then they began to remind him of people he loved, but who were now far away in the Soviet Union. Despite the strain on his mother, Felix had enjoyed their trip to Moscow. Old friends were fresh in his mind. Often he would start imaginary conversations with the imaginary characters below. Sometimes he would get so involved in the intricate details of his make-believe world that he would fail to see his mother, standing at the edge of the kitchen, drinking in every word he spoke. Occasionally he was embarrassed, but it never really bothered him.

Today he was happy, waiting for his parents to wake up. He made himself some breakfast, but he could not relax for long. An old civil war fantasy, which had first taken hold when he was five or six years old, had marched into his brain again to the strains of the 'Internationale'. He could already hear Marshal Tukachevsky's voice, soft and gentle, not like the generals he saw in the cinema.

'You can bring my breakfast now, comrade. I'm ready!'

Felix picked up the tray and took it to the Marshal, who smiled as Felix gave him the red-fist salute.

'Any news from the front, Comrade Marshal?'

'The Whites are in total retreat. Kolchak's forces have been defeated. Denikin has disappeared. Good news, eh?'

'Yes, of course, Comrade Marshal, but the foreign armies. There are twenty-two of them on Soviet soil. Can we defeat twenty-two armies?'

'Of course we can. Comrade Trotsky is arriving today. Would you like to meet him?'

At this crucial point the telephone began to ring. Felix cursed the caller and lifted the receiver.

'Yes. Yes, it's me. Mama is still asleep, Uncle Shmelka. I'll tell her you called. Sure. I hope so. *Au revoir.*'

Ludwik was never at home to callers unless he chose to answer the

202

phone. This house-rule was so deeply ingrained in Felix that it came to him automatically. Felix liked Livitsky. He was the only old face from home who was in Paris at the moment. He had been to see them twice last week, but they had all looked extremely tense and, surprise, surprise, they had stopped talking when Felix had entered the room. He hated it when grown-ups did that to him. He was no longer a child.

He had surmised that both his parents did some secret work for the Soviet Union. Neither of them had told him anything, but the house-rules were odd. Family travel plans, for instance, were never to be divulged to anyone. Lisa's explanation for this had been so unconvincing and stupid that Felix could no longer even remember what she had first told him. He frowned. Only yesterday, one of his friends, André, had asked him to come and spend a few weeks with him and his family in the Pays-Basque. Felix had declined. When André had persisted, wanting to know the reason, Felix had mumbled something incoherent to the effect that his parents were planning to take him on a long trip somewhere or the other.

It was the first day of the school holidays. He clapped his hands. That was one of the reasons why he was feeling so happy. How could he have forgotten? He was glad school was over. At first they had mistaken him for a Spanish refugee child seeking sanctuary from the horrors of the civil war. He had been given special attention and had begun to learn French at a surprisingly quick pace. Most of the teachers were Socialists or Communists and Spain was always close to their thoughts. The chemistry teacher's brother had died at Teruel. It was only later that the teachers had discovered that Felix did not speak a word of Spanish. They had deceived themselves, but their anger percolated through to Felix.

'I speak Russian, Polish and German,' he had declared, his eyes ablaze with anger.

'Russian!'

Even better than Spanish for some of the teachers and he had received even more care. His French continued to improve.

'What does your father do?' a friendly young maths teacher asked him one afternoon.

'He's a businessman,' Felix replied, as he had been told to do on numerous occasions and in numerous cities. The look of horror on the teacher's face made Felix blush.

'When did he leave the Soviet Union?'

The tone was now so hostile that Felix defiantly shrugged his shoulders. Was it Felix's imagination, or had the teacher actually muttered 'White scum'?

Since that day school had become an unendurable misery. A few kids had teased him about being 'a White', a gibe which, on one occasion, had led to fisticuffs. What had annoyed Felix even more was that when he told Ludwik and Lisa, they had laughed. Subsequently Lisa had spoken to the teacher, and the tension had eased, but school was no longer fun.

André was his only friend. They talked to each other about almost everything. Felix loved going to André's house. His father was an engine driver who worked shifts. Whenever Felix had gone home with André after school, his father was just getting out of bed, ready to go to work, but he always chatted to them, treated them as adults. On Sundays, André and his dad played an intense game of chess. Felix would have loved to go with them to the Pays-Basque for a week next month.

The sound of familiar voices reached him and he ran into the bedroom. He thought Lisa would be in an ebullient mood, exhilarated, just as he was, by what Ludwik had told him last week about never having to go away again. But her face was tense. It was a look Felix knew well, but in the past it had always been associated with Ludwik's absences. Today it was inexplicable. He hugged his mother and she held him close, stroking his face all the while. Words became redundant. These mute, emotionally charged exchanges always conveyed a special signal. It had been like that for as long as he could remember. Felix realized that his father's decision not to travel meant some threats that might be even more dangerous. Where did the danger lie, and why?

'Why is Mama so upset?' Felix and Ludwik were walking through the Latin Quarter. Ludwik had first seen Paris in 1923 and fallen in love with this city within a city. Napoleon III, he explained to Felix, had ordered the construction of the Boulevard Saint-Michel, but there were enough narrow streets to preserve the old Bohemian flavour.

Ludwik looked at the boy's hair, which was reflecting the sun and smiled to himself. How tall Felix had grown and how good-looking, just like his mother. He remembered the arguments with Lisa about bringing a child into a world torn by dissension and wars. Thank heaven she had won the argument. He put his arm round the boy's shoulder. His profoundest moments of agony concerned Felix. In the early days he used worry about what would happen to his son if he himself fell into enemy hands. As the years had passed, Ludwik had become more settled in his mind. Now Felix would at least remember his father.

'I'm not a baby any longer. I know more than you realize. She's upset because she's worried about you. Why, Papa? Please tell me. Please.'

'I'll tell you when we're on holiday. I promise. We'll sit down together in a café and have a long talk.'

'So we are going away together?'

'Not exactly. You and Lisa will leave tomorrow, and I will join you within a few weeks. I promise.'

'Is that why Mama is upset? Because you won't be going with us?'

'That is certainly one reason.'

Felix's face clouded, but he did not say anything. Why did Ludwik have to stay here for another few weeks? They had now crossed the rue de l'Odeon and reached the kingdom of literature. Felix loved the Galéries and had intimate knowledge of the arcade. Even when Ludwik was away on his travels, Lisa would often bring him here, leaving him alone to browse for hours.

While Felix looked at the newest books and longingly eyed the stationery, his father strolled casually to a second-hand stall, behind which an elderly woman was constantly rearranging books. Her eyes lit up when she saw Ludwik, but not a word was exchanged. She went away and returned with what appeared to be a very old book and handed it to Ludwik. This time her eyes expressed concern. Ludwik noticed, and gave her a reassuring smile and a nod as he took the book from her. As he walked away she looked around anxiously to see if they had been observed by any strangers, but everything seemed normal. She knew most of the old customers. 'Be careful, Ludwik,' she muttered to herself.

Ludwik went in search of Felix and found him at the stationery stall. As he did so he removed a piece of paper from the book and put it in his pocket. Felix took the book from his father, a first edition in Russian of *War and Peace*. Felix shook his head and smiled. Ludwik laughed. His collection of antiquarian books always amused Felix, who could not fully appreciate the point of having several editions of the same book.

When they got home some hours later, after detours via the Café Voltaire and to buy a pair of tough climbing boots for Felix, he got a terrible shock. The apartment was completely bare. Everything had been taken down from the walls. Suitcases full of clothes and books covered the floor. They had lived here for nearly two years and Felix, unlike his parents, had become quite attached to this apartment. Ludwik saw the look on the boy's face and squeezed his shoulders affectionately.

'Your mother's already done the packing for the holiday!'

'But she's packed everything. Aren't we coming back here?'

Felix's distressed voice upset Ludwik; he was hurt. Ludwik knew only too well that the nomadic existence they led was psychologically destabilizing for Felix. Till now there had been no other alternative, except, of course, for Lisa to move permanently to Moscow with Felix, and that was impossible.

'Felix, we will never return to this apartment. Tomorrow you're off to a place far away from here. No letters, no telephones, no messages. And from now on we'll all be together. Always. Happy?'

Felix hugged his father.

'Are you getting a new job? Are you tired working for the Soviet Union?'

'Very tired.'

'Hmm. Soon you'll be totally bald.'

Ludwik smiled as he sighed. If only he could be let off so lightly. He took out the crumpled note he had been handed at the bookstall.

Some men, definitely Russians, were asking about you today. When you had last been and did I expect you to call on any particular day. I pretended not to know you and not to understand them. They had no idea I spoke Russian so they cursed you, but believed me. Must be the wrinkles on my face. Take care, Ludwik.

That evening as he was preparing to go to bed, Lisa told her husband not to keep the boy up for too long. 'He must sleep soon. We've got a long day tomorrow.'

As Lisa rose to clear the kitchen table, still littered with the remains of their supper, Ludwik lifted his son on his back as he used to when Felix was much younger and moved towards the tiny, enclosed space – more a cupboard than a room – where Felix's bed was situated.

'No Spanish stories tonight, Papa. They've got too sad.'

Ever since his third birthday, Felix had insisted on special bedtime stories whenever his father returned from a long trip abroad. These had always involved an animal in the central role. Ludwik always ran into a talking seal in Amsterdam; a distraught lion in London; a lost polar from Siberia in Vienna; a disorientated bison in Geneva; a python in Munich, and so on. Around these animals, Ludwik developed a style of explaining to his child what was going on in the world outside.

As Felix grew, the animals slowly disappeared and were replaced by imaginary superhumans and then, for the last three or four years, Ludwik had recounted true stories culled from his experiences in the Soviet Union, Germany, and lately, the civil war in Spain.

The war in Spain was talked about endlessly everywhere Felix went. He was proud that his father was helping the republic against the fascists and one summer, he and Lisa had joined Ludwik in Collioure for a week. He had loved the town so much that he wanted to spend more time there and his parents had agreed. Everyday, while Ludwik visited his republican village in the mountains, Felix would drag Lisa to explore the medieval castle.

But it was not just castles, ice-creams and cakes. Nor the timeless hours spent playing on the beach. The fact was that Felix had made friends with a boy his own age. The two had become inseparable. Lisa was delighted to see her boy so happy. It took her a few days to realize that Felix's new friend had a sister, a year older than the boys. Felix developed a crush on her and began to follow her everywhere, much to the irritation of her brother, not to mention her more serious suitors.

And then came the day when the brother and sister departed. The holiday was over. Felix was heartbroken. He wandered around the battlements of the old castle feeling sorry for himself and imagining situations in which he rescued his beloved from the forces of evil. He even went off food for a few days. Lisa and Ludwik had observed everything in silence. Any attempt to talk about it with Felix would have been fatal. Before the week was over Lisa had nursed her son back to reality.

Ludwik had told him dozens of stories about Spain. Of how the Spanish workers were fighting against Franco, Hitler and Mussolini. Of how Americans, Russians, Englishmen and yes, Germans as well, had come to the aid of the republic. Tales of heroism, days of hope. After a time, Felix began to find Ludwik's stories repetitive and predictable. Heroism can become incredibly dull. But there was something else as well. He wasn't getting the full story. He had heard his parents talking in whispers about the poisonous undercurrents, the war within the war, the killings inside the republican camp. Felix did not understand much of this talk, bur he knew that whatever it was, it upset his parents a great deal.

'Tell me about when you were a boy, before the Revolution. Uncle Shmelka said you were always arguing with everyone.'

The boy lying in the bed in the shadows of a summer night looked adoringly at his father. Ludwik bent down to kiss Felix's eyes.

'There was a whole gang of us in this tiny town. We all went to the same school. Outside school we spent most of our time together. Our summer headquarters were on the river bank. We would swim, compete with each other to see who could catch the most fish, light a fire and grill the fish. Nothing like that taste.

'During winter we used to hang around the railway station. A border town has many advantages. We were part of the Austrian Empire. The other side of the river was the Tsarist Empire. Personally, I preferred the Austrians. We used to watch the trains go by and dream of seeing the big towns. St Petersburg, Berlin, London, Paris and Vienna. Our world did not extend beyond those places. We used to watch the people returning to Lemberg from Vienna. For some reason, which we never understood, all the beautiful ladies from the Russian nobility used to discard their flowers at insignificant little Pidvocholesk. We used to pick up the flowers, sprinkle them with water, tie them with new string and sell them to people going in the other direction or to Shmelka's mother. She always bought them from us.'

'Were Uncle Shmelka's parents rich?'

'Not really, but compared to the rest of us they appeared wealthy. He always wore clean clothes, had music lessons and the ultimate luxury: a room to himself at home.'

'Ludwik! Enough. Let the boy sleep.'

They smiled on hearing Lisa's voice. Ludwik kissed Felix on both cheeks.

'Sleep well, my son.'

The next morning, Ludwik moved to a small hotel in Clichy, while Lisa and Felix boarded a train that would take them to Switzerland, but via an elaborate detour which Ludwik had worked out to throw any hounds off his trail. His own future was uncertain, but he was not prepared to take any risks with their lives. Better that they reached their destination totally exhausted than not at all.

Lisa is dreaming: *Gigantic waves, like thick sheets, pure white like washed cotton, have enveloped her senses. Ludwik's head keeps bobbing up and down. Is he trying to swim? No. He's disappeared again. The waves have settled down. It's not the sea at all, but snow. A snow desert. She recognizes the familiar polar landscape. Siberia. And there she is herself, walking towards a stream which is flowing, but in slow motion. She reaches the edge of the water and is suddenly confronted by a gigantic tree trunk. A man is chained to it, but is not struggling at all. She recognizes Ludwik and runs towards him shouting 'Ignaty! Ignaty!', but the trunk and the man tied it keep receding as in a mirage. Then she is stuck to the ground and cannot move. Paralysis. The tree trunk has stopped as well. Blood is pouring out of Ludwik's face and dripping into the stream, like candle wax on water. Pearls of blood. He is dead. No. He is still alive. A smile appears on his face and he begins to speak, but the voice does not belong to him. It is a deep voice and every word is crisp and clear. It's the voice of the Jewish actor Mikhoels on the Moscow stage. Ludwik in Mikhoels's throat mask. He is reciting a poem which is reassuringly familiar:*

I have outlasted all desire,
My dreams and I have grown apart;
My grief alone is left entire,
The gleanings of an empty heart.
The storms of ruthless dispensation
Have struck my flowery garland numb —
I live in lonely desolation
And wonder when my end will come.

Shadowy figures are moving behind Ludwik, axes raised high as they prepare to execute him. Another voice. Disembodied. Eerie. Who can it be? Felix. Repeating a phrase over and over again: 'Our own people ... our own people ... our own people...' The axes are about to fall.

Lisa woke with a jolt, the dream fading away as the train lurched slightly and began to wind its way up the final stretch to the Swiss mountain village of Finhaut. She felt the wetness on her cheeks with her hands. The Pushkin poem was really odd. She had learnt the verses at school, when she was nine or ten years old. Never read or recited it since that time. One of memory's surprises.

Next to her, Felix was still fast asleep, his head leaning against the window, the afternoon sun printing shadows on his face. Lisa combed his hair with her fingers and looked out of the window. It was a stunning picture, the Valais in its summertime glory. Alpine flowers in full bloom. The primrose-yellow stars brought a smile of delight to her face. For a moment everything else was forgotten as she inhaled the surroundings.

The compartment was filled with the rich odour of roses, which had been brought on board with the rest of their honeymoon baggage by a young German-Swiss bride and her French husband. A hundred creamy white roses. They were the only other people in the compartment.

Felix, unused to such sights, had been amazed by the size and beauty of the bouquet. The young bride, touched by the obvious pleasure on the boy's face, had removed a rose from her collection and pinned it on to his pullover. Lisa smiled at the sight. The rose lay on Felix's chest, drooping slightly as if parodying the posture of its new owner.

Ever since last night, when Ludwik had told her of his decision, she had been mute with fear.

'I've decided to retire,' he had said with a strange, sad smile. 'I've had enough. I will write and tell Moscow next week.'

She had held him close, but he could see from her eyes that she was petrified. Both of them were aware that the chances of survival were slim. Even a very minor flunky was not allowed to leave without a severe interrogation. What would they do to her Ludwik? The man who had established networks in over a dozen European countries?

'Why are you thinking, Mother?' Felix, wide awake and excited by the sights and smells of the mountains, was looking straight into his mother's eyes. They were alone again, the newlyweds having disembarked at the last stop, and the train was climbing slowly and painfully to Finhaut.

Lisa hugged him, but did not reply. She and Ludwik had decided even when Felix was three and had the knack of asking awkward questions, that it was better to remain silent than to tell lies – except, of course, in very special cases. It had been the only way. The nature of Ludwik's work would otherwise have meant creating a totally false universe, a kingdom of untruths, and this was unacceptable to both Felix's parents.

Felix, for his part, grew to accept that in this world there were many questions to which he would never receive an answer. He thought it quirky, but accepted it as a fact of life, the way children often learn not to challenge adult decisions.

The train pulled into the station. Lisa and Felix stepped down on to the platform and breathed the mountain air. A porter helped with the luggage and within half an hour they had reached the chalet Ludwik had selected as their retreat from the world. Both of them were thinking about him.

'When will he come?'

Twenty-five

L UDWIK WAS ALONE in Paris. He spent very little time in his hotel room and avoided all his old haunts and contacts. One night, he was returning to his hotel well past midnight when he saw a stranger watching his hotel bedroom from the street. He waited till the man left and checked out at three in the morning.

It was well past midday when he woke the next day in a safe apartment on the top floor of an old block in the rue de Condé. There was nobody else in the whole world, not even Lisa, who knew of its existence. Ludwik strolled out soon after two that afternoon, ordered a coffee and a croissant at the nearest café and used the telephone to ring Livitsky as pre-arranged. Within half an hour Livitsky was at the café. He took out a three-day-old copy of *Izvestia* from his briefcase and handed it to Ludwik. They had not yet exchanged a single word.

'Are you sure you weren't followed, Shmelka?'

'Positive,' replied Livitsky.

As Ludwik read the newspaper his face filled with anger. 'The killers of the old Bolsheviks are being given medals! We can't stay on, Shmelka. This butcher is killing everyone. Why the hell did you let Bukharin go back? He should have stayed and linked forces with Trotsky.'

'He was frightened. Trotsky, too, will be killed. Spiegelglass boasts about it already.'

'We must warn Trotsky. Have you any contacts? His son is here.'

'Would he trust us?'

'I cannot wait any longer. I have written a first draft of my letter to the Central Committee, returning my Order of the Red Banner. Tomorrow I will send it to Moscow as well as to friends in Amsterdam and London with the instruction that it should be made public. Once that happens we will be able to see Trotsky and warn him of what we know. Why are you looking at me in that way?'

'You don't want to live any more, do you?'

'I do. I have a son. I want to see him a grown man.'

'But your letter is an invitation to murder. They'll kill you, Ludwik. You know that better than me.'

'There is a risk, but...'

'No buts, Ludwik. The only people who could protect us are the state intelligence agencies of Britain and the United States.'

'Not Britain,' Ludwik laughed. 'We have too many of our people in there. I put them there and now I'm scared of them. In any case, we must never sell ourselves to the bourgeoisie. Better to die.'

'Perhaps I should sign your letter as well. Both of us quitting together might have a bigger impact.'

'I disagree. We should spread it out. Who knows, a few others might join us as well.'

'Will you give me a phone number?'

Ludwik handed him a piece of paper. Livitsky memorized the number and destroyed the note. The two men shook hands warmly.

'Who would have thought all those years ago in Pidvocholesk that we would end up like this...'

Ludwik embraced his friend as the two men parted. Livitsky was frightened. He felt empty inside. He knew that he would never see Ludwik again.

Ludwik climbed the stairs back to his refuge and began to re-draft his letter.

When he had finished he felt at peace with himself. He was free again. He opened the window to let in the fresh air and looked down at the people on the street. He smiled at the clear blue sky. Life was flowing smoothly in Paris that day. If only he had been feeling so happy in a Leningrad apartment as he looked down on the Nevsky Prospect.

At the corner of the street he saw a group of young men in army uniform, but he could not sight any NKVD operatives. Ludwik sat down at the typewriter and began to type out his letter.

16 JULY 1937
TO THE CENTRAL COMMITTEE OF THE COMMUNIST PARTY OF THE USSR

I should have written the letter I am writing a long time ago, on that day when the Sixteen – each of them a veteran Bolshevik – were massacred in the cellars of the Lubianka on the orders of the 'Father of the People'.

I kept quiet then and I did not raise my voice at the murders that followed, and as a result I bear a heavy responsibility. My guilt is grave, but I will try to repair it, to repair it promptly and thus ease my conscience.

Up to this moment I marched alongside you. Now I will not take another step. Our paths diverge! He who now keeps quiet becomes Stalin's accomplice, betrays the working class, betrays socialism. I have been fighting for socialism since my twentieth year. Now, on the threshold of my fortieth, I do not want to live off the favours of the NKVD. For sixteen years I learnt to work illegally. I have enough strength left to start all over again in order to save socialism.

Your self-congratulatory noises will not succeed in drowning out the moans and cries of the victims tortured in the cellars of the Lubianka, in Svobodnaia, in Minsk, in Kiev, in Leningrad, in Tiflis. You will not succeed. The voice of truth cannot be drowned out for ever by corrupt and dislocated men like yourselves, devoid as you are of all principles and, with your mixture of lies and blood, poisoning the workers' movement throughout the world . . .

He warned Stalin not to take at face value the multitudes who acclaimed him. A terrible hatred lay hidden beneath the adulation. He explained his own political evolution and why he could no longer serve Moscow. He signed himself 'Ludwik'. Then, almost as an afterthought, he added a paragraph:

In 1928 I was awarded the Order of the Red Banner for services to the proletarian revolution. I am enclosing the decoration. It would be beneath my dignity to wear an order also worn by the executioners of the best elements of the working class in Russia. In the last two weeks Izvestia has published the names of those who recently received the award. Their achievements have been discreetly kept quiet: they are the men who have carried out the death sentences on the old Bolsheviks.

Ever since he had built his network, Ludwik had also devised a plan for getting urgent letters to Moscow within twenty-four hours. He put the letter to his former employers in a brown envelope and marked it for the urgent attention of the Fourth Department. Then he walked to the Soviet Embassy, posted it in the special letter box and left without saying a word to anyone except the doorman, who smiled at Ludwik and gave him a wink.

After several detours, he returned to the rue de Condé, convinced that he had taken them by surprise. The last place they would have been expecting him was at the Embassy. Ludwik thought he was now safe for a few days, till the letter reached Moscow.

He had underestimated the enemy. Within an hour of the letter being delivered, Spiegelglass had used his authority to open it, read it and call a meeting of his top operatives.

'Ludwik has betrayed us and gone over to the Nazis. I want him and his family found and executed. That's all. Any questions? Good. Don't come back till you have carried out this task. And send in Livitsky.'

Livitsky walked into the room ashen-faced.

'Where is your friend Ludwik?'

'I have no idea.'

'Is he still in Paris?'

'I really don't know. We have not been in touch for several weeks. As you know I returned from England only yesterday.'

'I don't trust you, Livitsky. You cosmopolitans are all the same. Slowly we are cleansing the stables. I'm warning you. If you don't help us find him you will be returned to Moscow, where they will question you in the Lubianka.'

Livitsky gave a weak smile. 'Thank you for your trust, comrade. Now I have work to do against the real counter-revolution.'

'Get out Livitsky, and have no doubts. Ludwik is finished.'

Livitsky went to a café and ordered two large brandies. After he had consumed them, his hands stopped trembling. He went to the bar and rang Ludwik. Two short rings and stop. Then three short rings and stop. The message was simple. Run for your life. You've been discovered. His task accomplished, Livitsky returned to his own apartment and was reassured to find an NKVD operative trying hard to look normal on the opposite pavement.

Ludwik was staggered by Livitsky's message. How could they have been so quick? Then, angry with himself, he banged his fist on the table. Spiegelglass must have opened the letter. Ludwik cursed himself for not having used another channel to Moscow. He packed his typewriter and his clothes and walked out of the apartment. He knew that the railway stations in Paris would be unsafe for the next few days. There was no alternative but to take the car. His black Citroën was parked outside the house of a friend, the old woman who had handed him the warning note a few days ago. She was his most reliable and oldest letter-box in Paris. He was tempted to go to her apartment to say farewell, but his instinct was overridden by the years of iron discipline. There was no room for sentiment in this wretched business.

He made sure that the car wasn't being watched by walking up and down the side-streets. The day had been quite hot and Ludwik welcomed the evening breeze, wishing that he had not had to dress himself in a suit and tie. Only after he had made sure that he could not possibly have been watched did he enter the Citroën.

Within half an hour he had left Paris behind and was heading towards Dijon. The roads were pitch black and Ludwik had no option but to drive slowly. For three hours his was the only car on the road. By the time he reached Dijon it was early morning. The station was not too difficult to find. He dumped the car and found a workers' café, where he ordered a cognac with his coffee. At the station he was lucky. There was a morning train for Lyon and from there he could get a train for Lausanne.

It was late afternoon when he reached Finhaut. Lisa and he had passed through here once before, many years ago, and wondered why this exquisite mountain village had neither a hotel nor a restaurant. Lisa had found rooms in the mayor's house and Ludwik was directed there by some children, who had already befriended Felix.

It was Felix who saw him first and came running down a hill shouting at the top of his voice.

'Papa! Your hair's gone white!'

Ludwik lifted the boy off the ground and kissed him. Together they went to the mayor's house. Lisa saw them from the window and rushed down to greet him. She, too, noticed how his hair had changed, but did not say anything.

All three were sharing a room, thus limiting the conversation between the two adults. Ludwik, in any case, was exhausted and went to bed immediately after a spartan supper consisting of bread and

cheese washed down by a glass of hot milk. He was asleep long before
Felix that night.

When Ludwik awoke the others were still fast asleep in their tiny
cots. He went to the window and stood there, looking for calm in the
alpine landscape. He knew he was standing on the edge of an abyss,
but compared to the world of mirrors, masks and tortures from which
he had just freed himself, even the abyss was enticing.

His whole adult life had been spent playing chess with death. His
generation was not frightened by the thought of death, but what made
it acceptable was the thought that one might die for a cause, in the
course of a titanic struggle for power.

Now he realized that the Revolution in which he had played a small
part had degenerated beyond recognition, and that people who had
once worked under him would now be recruited for the hunt. They
would try and corner him and, if they succeeded, he would be shot.
How long could he wander restlessly, looking over his shoulder every
few minutes to see if the executioner had arrived?

He recalled last night's dream. Memories of his childhood. A moon
seen through the mist, the wet mud on the roads which used to splatter
his clothes, the sun coming through the trees, his father playing the
piano night after night, his elder brother, whom Ludwik had not seen
once since the Revolution. Was he dead or alive? His renegade
brother, who had fought with Pilsudski against the Red Army in 1921.
Freddy had told him that his enemies in Moscow were trying to use
that fact to discredit Ludwik.

Lisa came up quietly and put her arms around him. 'The living
conditions here are primitive,' she whispered, and they both giggled.

'Shhh,' said Ludwik pointing to their sleeping boy.

'His presence makes it worth while. Our reward for years of pain
and trouble,' said Lisa.

'I hope I haven't brought disaster to the two people I love most in
this world. Perhaps you and he should go away...'

'No.'

The first week passed quickly. Ludwik began to unwind. They went
for long walks. Ludwik told Felix stories of the past, the days before
the Revolution. When he and Lisa were alone they would discuss the
future. Ludwik was desperate to contact a few of his trusted friends in
Amsterdam, in particular the Dutch dissident Communist Sneevliet.
Through him Ludwik wanted to offer his services and his immense
knowledge of the inner workings of the system to Trotsky.

'I think you should publish your letter now, Ludwik. It will make it
more difficult for them to kill you.'

'True, but it would alert every other intelligence service in Europe and things will become difficult. I need someone to carry out little tasks for me, someone I can trust. Gertrude?'

'Why her? Do you still trust her after the English affair?'

'She confessed everything. These men may satisfy her physical needs, but she does not respect their intellects. You know she was suicidal a few years ago. I'm worried that if she thinks I've disappeared without trace she might try to kill herself again.'

'I'm not convinced,' said Lisa and frowned.

'You never liked her?'

'No.'

Ludwik laughed.

Twenty-six

IT WAS IN NOVEMBER 1992 that I plucked up enough courage to talk to your mother. She was sitting in the kitchen in our flat, sipping tea. I knew I had to tell her before she read it in some newspaper. We had both been active in the movement that had finally toppled the regime. In 1989, we were part of the human stream rushing past the buildings where once the bureaucrats had held sway and then through the Wall to the other Berlin, only to see the fruits of their victory stolen by the Christian Democrats. I lost my job exactly one year later.

My throat was tight with fear. 'Helge.'

She knew immediately from my tone that it was serious. 'Have you murdered someone, Vlady?'

'Worse.'

Her voice became subdued. 'You'd better tell me.'

I sat down opposite her and confessed. I told her that I had seen Winter several times without telling her. She frowned at that, but when I told how Winter had actually drafted the last three letters the KDD had sent to the Politburo, she stared at me in disbelief. I told her that I had never named names. Never. I was seduced by Winter's inside information from Moscow and his detailed knowledge of our own Politburo. Winter was a supporter of Gorbachev, a reform Communist. She stopped me at that point.

'Vlady, are you telling me this to test our relationship? Is this some stupid game you've devised?'

'No. I've told you the truth.'

She slapped my face, pulled my hair and aimed a glass at my head.

'You betrayed us, you bastard. You deserve to die! You should die! I hate you. I must have misjudged you. How could I have thought that you had integrity?'

'Listen, Helge. Please listen. He threatened me. Told me if I didn't see him they would let it be known that Gertrude worked for them. They would award her a posthumous medal.'

'I hope they'll award you a posthumous medal after you've hanged yourself.'

'Helge, I told them nothing. They knew everything.'

'What are you really saying? If you gave them no information, why did they need you?'

'I've told you about Winter. He's an old Communist. He wanted to save something from the wreckage – we all did in our different ways. He needed an organization to pressure the Party leadership, and we obliged. One-third of our members were planted by the intelligence services.'

'And our leading ideologue was getting tactical advice from the top intelligence chief in the DDR. Aren't you at least ashamed, Vlady?'

'I felt that Winter was on our side. His intimate knowledge of world politics and of the developments in the old Soviet Union was very useful for us. I felt I was using him as much as he was using me. Where do you think I got the transcripts of Gorbachev's talks with Honecker? Have you forgotten their impact? It gave us the courage to come out on to the streets. We knew that Moscow would not send in the tanks like in '53.'

'If it was all so innocent, why didn't you tell me you were seeing Winter?'

'I would have if I didn't know you so well. You would have disapproved and executed me morally. I need you, Helge.'

'You're lying again, Vlady. Why not admit you were ashamed because you knew what you were doing was wrong. Morally wrong, certainly – but much more. It was a betrayal of your comrades, who were taking risks with you and for you. Have you forgotten the way the younger comrades looked at you when you spoke? Hope was written on their faces. And now you tell me that the words you spoke were not your own; Comrade Winter wrote your script. Look at yourself in the mirror.'

I could not reply to her. I just sat there, sat motionless, benumbed and crippled with remorse. She looked at me with pity and contempt.

'Why are you telling me all this now?'

I remained silent.

'Are you scared that Winter or someone might grass on you? That we would read all about in the newspapers?'

I nodded.

'Is that a real possibility?'

'Yes.'

'How do you know?'

'Winter told me that a journalist was asking him questions about me.'

'You still see Winter?'

'He's very active in the PDS, Helge. We were all thinking of joining at one stage, weren't we? For heaven's sake, Winter was amongst the best of them.'

Helge could take no more. She walked out of the apartment in a rage. I rushed out after her, trailing her like a dejected dog. Finally she stopped, and turned round to confront me.

'Vlady, I cannot live with you any longer. I need to be with other people. The very sight of you sickens me. Really. How will I face them after this? Please stop following me.'

'Where will you go?'

'To my friends. I might stay in the hospital tonight. As for tomorrow . . . ?'

I returned to the apartment not knowing which way my life would turn. Could I begin afresh, renew myself, win back Helge's love and, later, her trust? Every half hour I would ring her room in the hospital. No reply. At three in the morning I fell asleep.

The next morning you rang and told me that Helge had told you she was going to leave the apartment, move to New York and live on her own, but without giving any reason. You automatically assumed that I had been unfaithful. I did not correct you, my son. I felt you would not have understood anything else. There was not a drop of politics in your blood. Forgive an old man his stupid pride – I should have told you everything at the time.

What stunned me was the speed with which Helge left for New York. I was hurt, assuming that she must have made plans to leave me long before I confessed my guilty secret. I even thought she might have a lover and they had both run away together. Months later I discovered by pure accident that a colleague at the hospital had been offered the New York job, but had been unable to go because her mother was seriously ill. She had recommended Helge, who flew over and was offered the post the same day.

So your mystery is solved, Karl. What I have written is the real and only reason for our break-up. Do you think she was right? I do. I often think of how I can redeem myself in her eyes. I need her, son.

Twenty-seven

S AO HAD LEFT ME ALONE in his apartment on the rue Murillo. He had left for Hanoi to bring his Vietnamese lover and their son back to Paris. I hated being alone. I wanted Helge at my side. Sao had brought me everything I had asked for from Moscow. It was next door in his study. I delayed the inspection, Karl. I felt uneasy, as if on the edge of an abyss. My cursed instincts warned me that something unusual awaited me.

I made myself a large pot of coffee and returned to Sao's study. Ludwik's suitcase filled with clothes and books lay on the floor. The two files Sao had bought for me were marked 'Gertrude Meyer' and 'Ludwik': a smell of stale Russian cigarettes, bundles of documents with marks where rusty paperclips had been removed, and Ludwik's passports.

I turned first to Ludwik's file, so bulky in comparison to the other one, and was surprised to find a collection of snapshots. I had no idea who most of the people in these photographs were, but there were some recurring images. Ludwik with a woman. She had a strong face with striking features. Then a child began to appear in the photographs. I sighed. My instincts had not been so wrong.

The woman in the photograph was Ludwik's wife or companion and the boy with the intelligent eyes was their son. Of that there could now be no doubt and so Gertrude had either been living a fantasy or had deliberately lied to me. The third option, that she had indeed had a short-lived affair with Ludwik, of which I was the consequence, seemed unlikely. I was now fairly certain that Ludwik was not my father. There was not a single photograph of Gertrude with Ludwik.

I saw the original of Ludwik's famous letter to the Central Committee which my mother had memorized and recited to me a number of times. There had also been the memorable occasion when she had retold the story of Ludwik's letter to the assembled ranks of the KDD, no doubt after obtaining permission from Winter and in order to enhance her own credentials as a dissident.

I flicked through the documents, many of which were trivial and uninteresting, till I came across an envelope marked:

TOP PRIORITY: For the special attention of Comrade J.V. Stalin.
The Execution of the Arch-Traitor 'Ludwik'.

My hands trembled as I removed the typewritten report from the envelope. The paper had faded and was on the verge of disintegration. I spread each of the pages carefully on the table. Then I carried every sheet individually to the photocopier. The task completed, I sank into Sao's leather armchair and began to read.

From: H. Spiegelglass.
6 September 1937

From the very first time I met Ludwik, I understood that we were dealing with a traitor and a criminal of the very highest intelligence. Once he had handed in his so-called 'Letter to the Central Committee', our agents were on his trail. We knew he was in touch with Western intelligence agencies. Either Berlin or London could have taken him, but it soon emerged that he was playing off one against the other, presumably to see which of them offered him more money.

Having studied this man's record and character very closely, it soon became clear to me that his sentimentality and his weakness, which led him often to blur the frontier between friendship and professional work, would enable us to trace his whereabouts. This judgement was vindicated much sooner than we expected.

We knew that Ludwik had several women working as agents in Europe. I had already established contact with two of them in Britain. There were others in Germany and Austria. One of these, G.M., a German Communist I met in Britain, was particularly close, if not intimate, with Ludwik. I took another German agent, K.W., to see this woman.

K.W. began to cultivate G.M. in June of this year. Soon he declared himself as a fellow German Communist working for us and told her that he was in love with her. She, in fact, had genuinely fallen for K.W.'s charms and they became intimate. K.W.'s report on the details of his seduction are appended to this report. From it you will see that physical love, of which G.M. had been deprived for far too long, played a central role in our victory. Her loyalty to Ludwik was based on hero-worship and her love for him. His refusal to countenance sexual relations with her had, as K.W.'s report shows, built up certain resentments. I am only adding these details because I was told by Comrade Yezhov that Comrade Stalin wanted a complete report with nothing left out, no matter how small and insignificant it might appear.

Once K.W. had succeeded in winning her confidence, he told G.M. that Ludwik had betrayed our movement and had to be captured and

executed before he was taken by Berlin. She resisted this line of
argument, but K.W. told her that even if Ludwik did not go willingly
to Berlin, they would find him and make him talk. The future of our
German operation could be threatened.

It was at this juncture that she confessed that Ludwik had been
in touch with her and she was going to meet him and his family.
Accordingly, we moved our operation to near the Franco-Swiss border.
We sent her with a box of poisoned chocolates for the whole family.
That would have made it easy, but the sight of Ludwik's young son,
Felix, unnerved her, and she snatched the chocolates away from him.
Her behaviour was odd, but Ludwik's suspicions were not aroused. She
said she had to rush off, but made an appointment to see him a few
days later.

All our operatives were on a state of alert. She met him in a café
near the station at Territet. They took a walk and our car drove near
them and stopped. Both of them were bundled into the car. Then he
realized that she had betrayed him and started struggling. He
grabbed her by the hair on her head and she began to scream. It was
4 September, 1937. Our team was on the Chamberlandes road, not far
from Lausanne. We stopped, threw him out of the car and executed him.
He was treacherous to the last. He shouted: 'Stalin's system is built
on terror. It will not last. Long Live the World Revolution...'

At this stage we had to make a choice. Should we go to Finhaut and
execute the traitor's family and risk being captured ourselves? I
was contacted by phone and ordered to return the team to Paris.

The military precision of our operation...

I could read no more, Karl. My stomach was gripped by a horrible
fear. I felt sick. The accounts I had received from Gertrude of
Ludwik's capture had been remarkably short of detail. She was the
woman who had led them to Ludwik? Was it ... could it be? I
wanted to jump out of Sao's top-floor window.

Then I opened the file marked 'Gertrude Meyer'. Nothing of interest
here, unless something had been removed. There was a dull,
departmental report commending her loyalty and a note reporting her
safe arrival in Berlin and the setting up of the new liaison group under
Winter in Germany. I assumed that her post-war crimes would be
recorded in the DDR archives. I went back to Ludwik's files and found
a letter from Lisa to Freddy in Moscow; it had been written just before
Lisa and Felix, helped by Belgian friends, left for the United States. It
made me weep, Karl, and I wondered how you would react. I weep for
Ludwik and Lisa and Felix and for ourselves. My mother was an

assassin. How does that sound to you, my boy?

My dear, dear Freddy:

I don't know if this letter will ever reach you, but I am sending it to our old safe address. It will go to Vienna, then Prague and reach you from Kiev. It must reach you, Freddy.

You will receive no further news of Ludwik. He is dead. They killed him last week. His body was discovered riddled with machine-gun bullets. They carried on firing even after he was dead, as frightened hunters do when they cannot quite believe that they have actually shot a tiger.

Ludwik was preparing to go to Rheims where he had arranged a meeting with the Dutch Socialist leader, Sneevliet, but before that he had an assignment with Gertrude Meyer. Remember her? It was she who betrayed him to the NKVD.

Felix was worried when I returned from Territet without Ludwik on Saturday. For the next two days he kept asking about his father. I read about it in the first edition of a Lausanne newspaper on Monday morning. I told Felix a few hours later and we both sat on the side of the road and wept.

Ludwik knew that they would not let him live for too long. Every morning he was still alive he would smile grimly as if to say 'I've lasted another day.' Every day brought fresh hope and fresh fear. He said once: 'Now I know what it must be like for all the others in Moscow.'

He was desperate, with the backing of independent-minded socialists, to tell the world of Stalin's crimes and to warn Trotsky that a special unit had been working on his assassination for quite some time.

The last week we were together, Ludwik began to imagine things. He began to see all of you; on a train, he thought the conductor looked like you. On a bus he imagined that the driver resembled Larin. He had never felt so alone in his life, and so cut off from his friends and comrades. One day when I was more depressed than usual, we started talking about the old days in Vienna and about all of you and Krystina, and one memory followed another. The only time he really laughed was when talking about all of you in Pidvocholesk.

'When we were young,' he said, 'we were desperate to leave Pidvocholesk. Each of us had a burning desire to see the world, to turn our backs on Galicia. And now here I am in the midst of splendid scenery, and I would give anything to taste the scalded milk my mother used to give us on cold winter nights. It was burnt till it had turned the colour of oats.'

Another time he reminded me of Leviné's speech in the dock at Munich: 'We Communists truly are dead men on leave, but who would have thought that we would be hunted down and killed, like Misha in

*Kiev, by people who call themselves Communists and are carrying out the
orders of the Communist Party?'*

*Last month we went to Vevey, a picturesque little town by the side of
the big Lake Geneva and found ourselves admiring St Martin's church.
As we were looking at the gravestones in the cemetery, we found two
English names, Ludlow and Broughton. Who were these seventeenth-
century Englishmen? We went into the church and asked the Pastor. To
Ludwik's amazement, the Pastor knew their entire history. The two
Englishmen were revolutionaries. Edmund Ludlow was one of the judges
who tried Charles I; Broughton had read the sentence of death. By pure
chance we had stumbled on the graves of two of Oliver Cromwell's closest
comrades. They had fled here after the Restoration to escape execution.
They had been alerted by Thurlow, Cromwell's chief secretary, who
warned them that their lives were in danger.*

*In Vevey they had been greeted as heroes and the local villagers had
prevented any suspicious strangers from coming near the village.
Lieutenant-General Edmund Ludlow's house had been fortified and
guarded: every boat approaching the beach was carefully scrutinized.*

*Any tramp who wandered into Vevey was seized and thoroughly
searched. Innocent tourists were viewed as suspicious characters. Ludlow's
chamber had a bell at the sound of which all the citizens were ordered to
arm and rush to the Englishman's house. The two men had married
again and died natural deaths. The tablets in their honour spoke of them
as 'the defenders of the liberties of their country.' Their descendants were
still in Switzerland.*

*Ludwik and I stared at each other in amazement. Both of us were
thinking the same thing. If only the three of us could be protected by the
Swiss villagers of today and live out our lives in peace. Ludwik said, 'It
was a more civilized century than ours. We only know how to produce
orphans.'*

*Felix, too, knows that his father was killed by 'our own people' –
that's how you referred to them in Moscow, Freddy. Felix asks difficult
questions and he wants answers. Yesterday he asked me casually: 'Mutti,
where did Stalin spring from then? Wasn't he a close follower of Lenin?'*

*I think Ludwik's son will never become a professional revolutionary.
He is filled with hatred for the people who killed his father.*

*I wish you were here, Freddy. You and all the others. I need you. I
miss you. I'm frightened for you. No one who ever worked with Ludwik
is safe. Run, Freddy, run. Save yourself while you can.*

Lisa

So, my son, you have lost one grandfather and gained another. I think Winter must be my father. Only that can explain how my name was not on the Stasi files. He must have made sure. If I had known that, I might not have told Helge and she would still be here and I would not feel so fragile or emotionally destabilized. I was stupid and cowardly, but not a criminal like your grandparents. As at other times, but in a more obsessive fashion, a blind force now drove me to meet up with Winter.

Twenty-eight

JULY 1945. Berlin was drenched in sunshine. Everywhere the wreckage of war. Hordes of women were clearing the rubble. Underneath it lay thousands of dead bodies. It had rained for the last two days and the appearance of the sun had brought with it the stench of decaying flesh.

A group of newly arrived American officers was walking down the Ku-Damm, when one of them heard his name called.

'Felix! Felix!' The voice was loud and spoke Russian. 'Can it be? Is it you?'

The young American officer stared at the figure in a bedraggled Red Army uniform who was shouting his name from an open jeep. Felix had been told on arrival that a Red Army officer was searching for him, but he had pretended not to hear. He hated everything Soviet.

Felix could not see him properly, but as the jeep drew closer, recognition dawned. It was Uncle Freddy's son, Adam, his old school friend from Moscow days. Adam, a major in the Red Army, jumped out of his jeep. The two men embraced.

Felix introduced him to his fellow officers, who were very impressed at their shy young colleague's range of contacts. He arranged to meet them later, and was pushed into the jeep by Adam, who instructed the driver to take them back to his billet near the temporary barracks.

They did not say much to each other in the jeep. The driver was instructed to go and find some food and drink and bring it back within an hour. Adam and Felix found a makeshift bench in the clearing outside the barracks.

'Uncle Freddy?'

'Dead.'

'How?'

'Once they had killed your father, it was only a matter of time. We got your mother's letter. Freddy wept like a child. He told my mother that he would never be taken alive. When they came to arrest him he jumped out of the window of his room. You know he worked on the top floor of the Fourth Department.'

'Your mother?'

'Survived. Fortunately for her, she had been separated from Freddy for many years. They questioned her about Freddy and Ludwik. She told them all she knew, which wasn't much.'

'You feel no bitterness, Adam?'

'Bitterness?' He gave a hollow laugh. 'I used to feel a burning hatred. When I first joined the Red Army I used to dream of killing Stalin. Really.'

'And now?'

'The war changed everything. You know some of what we've been through. In my unit there were men whose entire families had died during the collectivization campaigns. There were officers, including a general, who were released from the camps because their skills were needed. They loathe Stalin and everything he represents. Like me. But we hated the Nazis even more. Freddy's entire family, all my aunts and uncles and grandparents, were wiped out in the Babi Yar massacre: several hundred women, men and children of Jewish origin taken to the woods, forced to dig their own mass grave and shot dead. The Germans saw it as target practice. This wasn't just the SS, but ordinary soldiers. Dehumanized monsters. It wasn't just the Jews. The Germans treated all our people worse than animals.'

'Is that why you let them rape and loot Berlin?'

'*Let* them? Orders came from the very top. Stalin instructed the high command to encourage the men who had fought a hard war to "have a bit of fun". His words. When the high command ordered a halt to the rapes they stopped. Our army is very disciplined. The logic was simple: they treated us like animals and in Berlin we showed them we were animals. The day we entered, there were households who flew the red flag. Women rushed out with their old Communist Party cards which they had hidden during the Nazi years. They showed them to us with tears in their eyes as they welcomed our units. Imagine the horror when Red Army soldiers raped them.'

For some moments neither of them spoke. They had both heard their fathers talk of how the cataclysms of war might change everything. Existing mountains would be flattened and little hillocks rise to new heights. They had thought that this war would transform the world for the better just like its predecessor.

As their faces began to grow familiar to each other once again, and disused memories stirred, they started to talk. Felix told Adam of how they had arrived in the United States with the help of friends in Paris, where they had stayed for several months after Ludwik's assassination. Lisa had met Shmelka again, and later Trotsky's son, Sedov, who had so much wanted to meet Ludwik. She had also met the writer Victor Serge. Each of them had helped the move to the United States.

He described how in New York, Lisa had been interviewed by the intelligence services about Ludwik. She had told them that she knew nothing of his operational secrets, least of all where and how he had infiltrated Western agencies. They appeared to be satisfied. Felix himself had gone to school and graduated just in time to be conscripted.

'When I told them that I spoke Russian, German, French and Polish, they assigned me to their Special Services unit, which is like the Fourth Department used to be. We provide military and political intelligence to the top brass.'

'And your mother?'

'She's on her way back to France. We have decided to live in Paris after I'm demobilized. I studied mathematics and want to return to it after this is all over. You?'

'I was studying physics when the war started. I will return to Moscow University after all this is over and start again. Will you ever come to Moscow again, Felix?'

'No. For me Moscow means murder, human beings swept away as if they were autumn leaves. No, I won't return to Moscow.'

'I understand. In this war we sacrificed many lives foolishly. Most of our generals have no respect for human life. Zhukov used soldiers as mine detectors! But I live in Moscow, too, Felix. And there are many others like me. We have no other country. Will you never come back? Not even for a short visit?'

Felix shrugged his shoulders. 'Ludwik always used to say there is no such thing as never because, like the world we live in, we too, are constantly in flux.'

Lunch had now arrived. They feasted on stale black bread, tinned herrings and a bottle of vodka – nothing else. Better than what Adam had eaten last night: croquettes made of turnip greens, which tasted as if they had been stuffed with horse manure.

It was the black bread that reminded Felix of his last visit to Moscow. Lisa and he had gone as a diversion, to make them think that Ludwik was as loyal as ever. He held back the tears. Seeing Adam had brought back painful memories. He remembered conversations between his parents and their friends. Talk would often turn to the Tsar and Stalin. They would compare notes on repression. Under the Tsar, it was generally agreed, they had been driven close together, there had developed a sense of solidarity and community. They had made sure that families of the prisoners sent to Siberia did not starve. In Siberia itself they had helped each other. But Stalinist terror had destroyed the basic bonds of human solidarity. People had become scared of their own shadows. They had grown accustomed to living in a void.

'Did Freddy tell you who betrayed Ludwik?' Felix asked his friend. Adam nodded.

'She's here in Berlin. I found out through our network. I have her address here in my pocket. I walked outside her apartment block several times yesterday, but –'

'What?' roared Adam jumping up in a rage. 'What are we waiting for?' He began to drag Felix towards where the jeep was parked.

'Stop, you madman,' Felix protested. 'Where are we going?'

'To execute her,' replied Adam. 'To avenge our fathers. As a Soviet officer I have the authority to –'

'She's a pathetic woman, a tiny cog in the giant murder machine. She has a boy. But come with me. I have some questions to ask her and I need a witness.'

In normal times, Adam would have requested permission from a superior, but he had fought hard to reach Berlin, and faith in authority was at its lowest ebb since Stalin's accession to power. Senior Soviet officers were only too well aware of this phenomenon and rarely interfered.

Felix guided his friend to the block. They found her alone. When Gertrude saw Felix, she became very agitated, turning her face away, trying to sink back into the corner of the room. Her hands began to tremble. She seemed to be having a fit. Felix looked at her and images of Ludwik flashed through his head. He gasped for air for a few seconds, as though he were suffocating. He felt as though he had plunged off a precipice. His jaws alone moved; his lips seemed still and white. His head was split by an anguished scream. He was benumbed. The blood drained away from his face. Adam saw the transformation in his friend and grabbed him by the arm.

'Felix. What's wrong? Are you feeling ill? Get him some water.'

Felix regained his composure and saw the fear on her face.

'I have a young son,' she whimpered.

'And we both had healthy fathers,' replied Adam.

'What are you going to do? Are you going to kill me?' she pleaded with Felix.

'I just want to ask you a few questions. I want the truth, Frau Meyer.'

'If you lie,' Adam interrupted, 'I might just decide to –'

Felix stopped him with a gesture.

'Frau Meyer, you know who I am? Good. Why did you betray Ludwik to the killers?'

Gertrude began to weep.

'They threatened me. That didn't work. Then they promised they would get my parents and Heiny, my little brother, out of Ravensbruck. I believed them. I never believed any of the rubbish they told me about Ludwik being a Gestapo agent, but I did believe they could save my parents. Spiegelglass said my parents and brother would be exchanged for some Germans Hitler really wanted.'

'Were they?' asked Felix.

'No,' replied Gertrude. 'It was a trick.'

Felix looked into her eyes, but Gertrude turned away. 'I have a little boy, Felix. If it weren't for him I'd kill myself and spare you the trouble. I would have done after Ludwik's death, but I was pregnant...'

'Enough,' said Felix. 'Tell me Frau Meyer, was it easy to kill him? Did he say anything to you? Your hairs were found in his hand.'

She began to weep again.

'Talk, you bitch,' said Adam reaching for his revolver. He felt nothing for this woman, and would have shot her without a second thought. Gertrude understood that Felix was her protection. She fell on her knees before him.

'I will never forget Ludwik's face that evening as long as I live. He was angry with himself for having trusted me. I thought he was dead and bent down to kiss him when he grabbed me by the head and shouted "Traitor!" To the others he shouted "Long Live the World Revolution!" They pumped all their bullets into him after that, and at that stage I lost consciousness.'

They left her apartment without looking at her again. As they were about to enter the jeep, they saw young Vlady with two Germans in Russian uniform being taken back to his mother. Both the men stood to attention and saluted Felix and Adam, who nodded curtly and started the engine.

That night Felix started writing a long letter to Lisa in which he recounted the events of that day.

... She stood in the doorway and watched us walk to the lift. Do you know, the lift was actually working in the block she's living in. I saw her son — I'm sure it was him — as Adam and I were leaving. She is a pathetic creature, and I wasn't tempted by the poison of revenge, not even for a second. It was horrible seeing her again, but it had to be done.

Who knows what her real reasons were for betraying Papa. What she said didn't completely ring true . . .

But our day was not yet over. As we arrived back at Adam's quarters and parked the jeep, a column of German prisoners, guarded by Red Army soldiers, was being returned to a temporary prison camp behind the barracks. They had spent a long, hard day clearing the rubble from the side streets. The sun was still out and the prisoners asked for and were given permission to sit on the grass for a few minutes. They looked gratefully at their captors. One of the guards threw them a packet of cigarettes, which were immediately shared out.

We observed the scene in silence. They were walking past the prisoners when one of them stood up and looked at us in amazement.

'Felix! Adam! Don't you recognize me?'

We stopped and looked at the man who had shouted our names. Who was this wretched-looking bearded figure in the torn uniform of a Luftwaffe pilot?

'It's me, Hans. Remember? We played chess a few years ago in Moscow.'

Adam and I looked at each other. I rushed to Hans first and embraced him warmly. Adam followed suit. The guards had saluted Adam. He ordered them to release the prisoner into his custody. He hurriedly scribbled a receipt for Hans and the three of us walked away together.

It was an odd sight. Three men, clearly friends, but wearing three different uniforms, one of them German.

Adam insisted we return to his room. There we drank more vodka. I insisted that Hans shave off his stupid beard, and Adam provided the implements. After he had finished shaving I held the mirror up to his face. Hans began to weep. Adam hugged him.

'We're all the same now. It will be fine.'

After Hans had calmed down he told us his story: 'After the Hitler-Stalin pact, dozens of German Communists in Moscow were handed back to the Nazis. My mother was sent immediately to Ravensbruck. She was murdered by a Nazi doctor, purely for his amusement. I was sent to an orphanage where you automatically became a member of the Hitler Youth. They selected me for the Luftwaffe. I was a good pilot, so they sent me on bombing missions over Moscow and Leningrad, after which I would always dump the bombs over vacant fields before returning to base. I never identified Moscow with Stalin. If I had, it would have been easy to drop the bombs. For me Moscow was all of us and others like us. I often thought about you and my other friends. What happened to you, Felix? Why are you in American uniform?'

Adam and I told him our stories. Each of us had lost a parent thanks to Stalin and Hitler. We looked at each other in silence, thinking of old times. Then Adam took Hans back to the prison camp. Both of us were determined to obtain his freedom.

'If you can't get him out, Adam,' I told him, 'I'll have a try from my side.'

'Don't worry,' said Adam. 'My general was in the Polish Party with Freddy and Ludwik. He'll understand why Hans cannot remain a prisoner of war. But Hans, tell me something. Where will you live in a divided Germany?'

Hans thought for a moment. 'Germany is like a shell-shocked prostitute, not knowing who will take her next or how. She has been plundered, betrayed and sold out, first by Hitler and the fascists and now by the Allies. I wanted them to win, but I have no desire to live in any occupied country. I suppose I could go back to Dresden, where my father's family used to live, but I don't want to live under Stalin. On the other hand, I don't think I could bear living in Munich.'

'In that case you mustn't,' I said. 'Come and live with us in Paris. I mean it – and my mother would be very pleased to see you.'

Hans smiled. 'Don't forget I am a German. We bear the mark of the beast. It will take a long time for passions to cool.'

I hope you agree with me, Mother. I know you will. Seeing Adam and Hans reminded me once again of all those we've lost forever. Ludwik, Freddy, Misha, Uncle Shmelka, killed in his New York hotel after his flight from Paris. The five young boys who had grown up together in the tiny Galician town of Pidvocholesk, all poisoned by water from the same well.

Ever since Father's death, I've been grieving and angry. Adam made me realize that I was not unique. But it was Hans who renewed my faith in humanity. Hans, whose father had been killed by Hitler and whose mother had been handed by Stalin to Hitler to perish in Ravensbruck. This same Hans had refused to bomb Soviet cities. If discovered he would have been executed without ceremony.

Hans demonstrated that the good in us can never die. He proved that even when they put the gun in your hands and give you a good excuse to pull the trigger, you can still say no. Remember that poem Ludwik used to like: 'They that have the power to hurt and will do none...'? I feel that Adam and I got through that test today.

Twenty-nine

A GREY APRIL DAY. The rain is coming down. It is nine o'clock on a Sunday morning. Berlin is half asleep. Vlady, still drowsy from a late night, staggers to the window and draws the curtains. It is definitely not a spring shower. The clouds are thick. It could be autumn. The relentless rain spreads gloom and melancholy.

'I am not fit for anything any more,' muttered Vlady to himself.

After he had shaved he examined himself carefully and persuaded himself that he looked no older than he had ten years ago.

Ever since he had read the file marked 'Gertrude Meyer', Vlady had felt himself sinking. After Winter's revelations, he had thought nothing he learnt about his mother could surprise him, but the fact that she had actively participated in the killing of Ludwik had shaken him deeply. Depressed and despondent, Vlady felt his sorrows had multiplied. He was possessed by a feeling of alienation from everything. Sometimes he was overcome by savage desires; he wanted to disrupt his own life by an act of violence. He became morose and taciturn, someone his friends began to avoid.

What had hurt the most was the evidence that had finally confirmed what he had always suspected. Ludwik was not his father. That he had been prepared for, but the realization that his real father was an NKVD hit man, an assassin who had impregnated his mother with false smiles and made-to-order sperm, carrying out instructions to the letter – this had added to Vlady's torment. Was it Winter?

In despair, he had turned to Evelyne for some physical comfort. But whatever talent the woman may have had during her student days had dried up completely. She had become an egocentric mediocrity, a bore capable of discussing only herself and her brilliant films.

One night after she had made love to him – this, too, had become a soulless routine – Evelyne had announced that she no longer wanted him as a lover. They should simply remain friends. The news had cheered Vlady. He agreed, and they had gone to a café to seal the new pact. That's where Kreuzberg Leyla found them. They were quarrelling and she threatened to paint a second picture of them, sitting at the counter, each with half an apple, each with a bite missing. She would call it *After the Wall*. They laughed and all three decamped to see the uncut English-language version of *Blade Runner*.

When he got home, there were two messages on his answer-machine. The first was from Winter, confirming their date and suggesting a French restaurant in Kreuzberg. The second was from Sao in Paris, demanding that Vlady ring him immediately on a matter of some urgency.

'Greetings, Sao.'

'I'm glad you rang. Where were you?'

'Watching *Blade Runner* for the third time. Have you ever seen it, Sao?'

'Of course. Usual money-wasting Hollywood rubbish. What do you see in it?'

'Images of a decaying, authoritarian, polyglot capitalism and its state machine, which is depicted as totally coercive. Even the façade of democracy has been abandoned. It's a vicious critique of the system, Sao, a system that's now occupying your country. Boeing, Citibank, Mobil, Delta, Marriott, IBM, Unilever. *Blade Runner* is a masterpiece, Sao. Go and see it again.'

'A desperate person can read anything in nothing. That is the fashion these days, isn't it?'

'I'm not a post-modernist zombie, Sao. And if you think —'

'Vlady, stop all this nonsense. I did not ring to argue about some Hollywood movie. Listen to me. Something important has happened and I need you badly. This time you must not say no to me. I am owed money by an American shyster. You understand me?'

'No,' sighed Vlady.

'Yes you do. The deal does not concern you. This guy owns a small publishing chain in North America and Europe. I can't remember the German name, but listen. In return for the money he owes me, he has offered me his publishing empire, which he says is losing money, but could be turned round by an intelligent chief executive. Who cares? Now listen to me. I want you to run this enterprise. I'll manage the business side. I need someone who knows something about books.'

'Why?'

'What do you mean, why?'

'You don't need someone who reads books to run an empire. Hire an arms-dealer or some overpaid accountant. It doesn't make much difference the way our culture is going. I suppose Germany is still different, but the Anglo-Saxon end is a nightmare.'

'I know, Vlady, I know. I need you. Yes or no?'

'Let me think about it. I'll ring you tomorrow. If I accept, Sao, where will I be working from? I mean which city?'

'I think you'll spend most of your time flying, Vlady. I'll book you some office space on the Concorde.'

When Vlady did not react to the joke, Sao panicked slightly. 'You can work from wherever you want – New York, Paris or Berlin. Do you want to know your salary?'

'No!'

Sao laughed. 'Have a good day, Professor Meyer. Linh sends her love.'

'Is she settled now?'

'Sure, but she misses the old country. Her cooking is sensational, Vlady.'

'That must make you truly happy, Sao.'

Sao laughed. 'Come and see us soon and make sure you ring me first thing whatever your decision. And one more thing. You know my name for our publishing house?'

'No.'

'Five Tigers.'

'*Au revoir*, Sao.'

Outside it had stopped raining and large patches of blue sky had appeared as a prologue to the sunshine that now lit Vlady's study-bedroom. His mood had altered. He felt a sense of exhilaration. *Blade Runner* had reminded him that the culture was not without its critics. Sao had offered him a job. He could not sit still. He began to pace up and down in the apartment, whose walls were now bare. Every object associated with Gertrude had been removed. Vlady wanted to talk to Helge, to Gerhard, to anyone except Evelyne.

Some hours later, in desperation, he rang Karl to tell him about the offer he had just received from Sao.

'What do you think, Karl?'

'It is very good news, Vlady. You must do as you think best.'

'What do you think your mother would have advised me?'

There was a long silence.

'Karl?'

'Yes, I'm here. I don't know. Can I ring you later? It's just that there's a crisis on here. The Party is going to dump Scharping and go for Lafontaine which could be a disaster. He's too left for the present climate . . .'

'I disagree. He's the best you've got. I might be needed to write his speeches, and you could work for Sao. Karl? Are you there?'

'We'll talk soon, Vlady. I'll ring you tomorrow. I promise.'

What a desolate conversation, thought Vlady. He decided that this was the time to send Karl his manuscript. Let the boy read while he, Vlady, was still alive to argue with him. He packaged the manuscript carefully and enclosed a handwritten note:

*When I called you about the job Sao offered you were cagey as usual.
There's no point in our spending the rest of our lives at arm's length. I've
been putting together part of a family history, researching Ludwik and
Gertrude, looking at what happened between me and your mother and
debating whether or not to send this to you. Don't open it if you feel
you're better off just leaving the past behind you. I wouldn't argue with
that decision. But if you open it, promise that you will read it through
till the end. I hope you'll want to talk about what's in here.*

Thirty

HE WOKE UP just before noon, unprepared for the shock awaiting
him. At first he couldn't believe his eyes. It must be a dream. He
covered his head with the blanket and emerged slowly, sure that the
apparition had gone.

She was still there, sitting on her favourite armchair. 'Hi, Vlady. I
let you sleep.'

He jumped out of bed. 'Why didn't you warn me?'

'You might have run away.'

'*I* might have run away! Has New York made you crazy, Helge?'

He sat on the edge of the bed looking at her. Her eyes were soft
again, lacking the hostility of their last encounter. Her voice, too,
which had been full of tense, restrained anger, was back to normal. He
sat on the floor at her feet, burying his head in her lap.

Old recollections flooded back. They talked about themselves, about
Karl, about their lives during the separation. Helge confessed that she
could no longer stand living in the United States because she was
white. She regaled him with stories of her friends who went to
inordinate lengths to conceal their 'whiteness'. Even the Italians were
now referring to themselves as the 'Olive Nation' and a close friend of
hers, a fellow psychoanalyst, had returned to southeast Kentucky and
was now writing a book on the Melungeon people.

Vlady sat up in amazement. 'The what people?'

'The Melungeons.' Helge patiently explained that whereas mythology
proclaimed that everyone in the Kentucky mountains was of Scottish or
Irish origin with the odd splattering of Cherokee blood, the truth was
otherwise. Melungeons were the descendants of various ethnic groups
who came to the interior of the continent before the English. Many
were from Spain and Portugal. Thus, her friend had now demonstrated
the genetic linkage between Appalachian 'whites' and Spanish and

North African Moors and Jews. There was even evidence of links with Turkish communities.

Vlady was fascinated and bewildered. 'Why,' he wondered. 'Why the obsession, and why now?'

Helge smiled at his curiosity. It was like the old days, when she would recount some psychoanalytic discovery that had totally escaped him. 'I suppose they want to challenge the notion of a hegemonic northern European racial base in the American South and Appalachia.'

'Make sure your Melungeon friend sends us a copy of the book. I suppose it was difficult for you. Your genealogy can't be improved. A white Protestant from Saxony. I'm glad, because it's brought you back.'

'It wasn't just that. I missed you, Vlady.'

After they had made love Helge told him that she, too, had read the manuscript he'd sent to Karl.

'What did Karl think?'

'He was shaken by Gertrude's story. Even I was, Vlady, and I had no time for her. It must be unbearable for you. Karl arrives in Berlin tomorrow. He will tell you what he thinks himself. I'm glad you wrote it all down.'

It was when Helge suggested they eat at an old haunt that he remembered he had a dinner engagement with Winter. At first she was taken aback.

'A few minor and one major question still need to be answered, Helge. Come with me. Please.'

She shook her head. The thought of him dining with Winter on her first day back in Berlin had changed her mood. He detected this, but carried on pleading till she agreed to accompany him that evening.

Vlady had not been as happy as this for a long time. As they stepped outside, he took her arm and kissed her hair. The street seemed strange compared to earlier that afternoon. The wet pavements were dry and the sky had cleared. As they walked towards the Brandenburg Gate, he saw a flurry of colour. Groups of gays, in festive mood, were returning to the East after their day-long fest, ignoring the hooting of car horns as they crossed the Unter den Linden. Older couples dressed in their Sunday bests tried their best to ignore the revellers.

They exchanged smiles. This was the Berlin they both liked. Clouds were beginning to cross the sky again. Pleased that they had worn their raincoats, they quickened their pace, caught a bus to Kreuzberg, and by the time they reached the restaurant it had begun to drizzle again.

The place was crowded, surprisingly for a Sunday evening. Winter was seated at a corner table. They approached him; if he was surprised at Helge's presence he hid the fact remarkably well and immediately set about charming her.

'I just wish to warn both of you that there's a man present here who has not yet seen me. He's sitting in the other corner with his wife. If he does come and harass me, just remain calm, and do not attempt an intervention.'

'Who is he, Klaus?'

'A fool of no importance. Damn his soul. His wife has seen me. Fasten your seat-belt, my dear fellow.'

An elderly man dressed in a faded green silk suit was approaching their table. Winter's face turned to stone.

'Good evening, Klaus. It has been forty years. Have you still not forgiven me?'

Klaus Winter did not reply.

'Look at the menu, Helge and Vlady. What do you want to eat? This disturbance will soon pass.'

The stranger's eyes filled with sadness. He did not persist, but walked away slowly, his shoulders drooping.

'Klaus,' said Vlady, fearing the worst, 'I will not discuss anything with you or even stay here unless you tell us about him. Is he a former agent who betrayed you?'

'Much worse, Vlady. Much worse.'

'Like what? I insist, Klaus.'

After the orders had been taken and a bottle of claret uncorked, Winter told the story of his relations with the man in the green silk suit.

'His name is Walter. He's my first cousin – our mothers were sisters. He's a year older than me, but the bastard is much better preserved. We quarrelled nearly forty years ago.'

Slowly the story unfolded. The two cousins had grown up in the same house in Wedding and had become very close friends. The only time they had been separated was when Klaus had gone to Italy for a year to study art history. He had stayed as a lodger in Lucca, and while there he had learnt how to cook.

'And I became a fanatical cook. Everything had to be perfect. When I came to Berlin, I cooked for Walter and everyone else. They were amazed but delighted. One winter, Walter and I went skiing in the Swiss Alps. I was tired and stayed at home one day. I told him not to be late because I was preparing a special sauce for the pasta, my own invention, which would be ruined if overcooked. He came back after a whole day's skiing and demanded supper immediately. I told him it would be another five or ten minutes. He said "fine". I carried on cooking. The next thing I see is that Walter has surreptitiously unwrapped a large bar of chocolate and is eating it like a wild animal. Naturally, by the time my sauce for the pasta is ready, Walter has lost his appetite. I went mad, Vlady. I kicked him out. Nobody had ever insulted my cooking like that before. We have never spoken since that day.'

'I can't believe this, Herr Winter,' interrupted Helge. 'You've made it up.'

'Is that the truth, Klaus?'

'I'm warning you, Vlady. Don't provoke me on this subject. You know full well I have written a book on Italian cuisine. I'm working on a new one about food in the former Soviet Union. I take food very seriously, Helge. Walter knew that well. He chose to belittle my cooking. Now, tell me what's happening to you. And why haven't I seen you for over a year?'

Vlady told him everything. The discovery that Gertrude had helped murder Ludwik, that Winter had been involved in the affair, and that for that reason he wanted to ask him a few questions.

Winter's face did not register any surprise at the revelation.

'I knew about her. You know, till the end she was working for Moscow, not us. I knew that and one night – we were both drunk – she told me the whole story. She was crying like a child, Vlady. I was not involved in that affair, not that I did not commit other crimes, probably worse. You know that. She loved Ludwik, but he was not interested in her like that and this was her revenge. She told me that if she had not been pregnant she would have killed herself.'

'I wish she had. Strange way of showing her love for Ludwik!'

'Hell hath no fury like a woman scorned, Vlady. Surely you –'

'How long were you lovers, Klaus? I know you seduced her in England in the same year that Ludwik was killed. Did it last?'

Winter shrugged his shoulders, a frown crossed his face. 'I'm not your father, Vlady.'

'Then who?'

'She was sure it wasn't me, but the Englishman. He was an old lover before he married Olga. One day, or so she told me, he came to her bed at night and they revisited old times. She was convinced that Sir Christopher Brown, as he later became, was your father.'

'Is he dead?'

'Yes. For a time he served as their ambassador to the Soviet Union. Both Gertie and I laughed about that a great deal.'

'You mean that he and Olga were never uncovered.'

'Of course not. We didn't expose them, and the only Englishman who knew they were on our side was Philby. I think Christopher and Philby met in Moscow on more than one occasion.'

Underneath the table Helge clasped Vlady's hand. Nobody spoke for a while.

Winter tried to lighten the mood. 'Would you rather I had been your father, Vlady?'

'No!' The reply was abrupt and speedy. 'My preferred choice is still Ludwik, but failing that I'd rather Mr Brown than anyone involved in killing. I wish Gertrude had killed herself.'

'You're wrong, Vlady, very wrong. Just because history continues to commit outrages, you must not give up.'

'History's outrages are carried out by thinking human beings, are they not Klaus? Intelligent, cultured human beings like yourself. You were always a master-chef, weren't you, Klaus? Human meat. Animal meat. Same for you?'

'Calm down, Vlady,' Helge cautioned, even though she was pleased that he was angry.

'Human beings who profess to believe in noble ideologies,' Vlady continued. 'Look where it's got us now. The slate has been wiped clean.'

'Nonsense. Our time will come again. Not in the same way, of course. We've all learnt very bitter lessons, but we have not been wiped off the map. Can't you see what is happening in the world?'

'Only too well. Fascists in an Italian government, where the men who control the videosphere run the country. In Moscow the criminals run the politicians...'

'Straws in the wind, Vlady. Everywhere else the people are returning to the fold. They are not looking for grand designs. All they want is a decent welfare state and some degree of egalitarianism. Who else will give it to them? The Socialists are floundering everywhere. Post-Communist capitalism is like a steam-roller, crushing everything in its path. Is it capable of solving the problems that Communism failed to solve? Only ideologues driven mad by triumphalism can think that poverty or the thirst for justice no longer matters. In Europe it might be the two-thirds who rule and prosper, but on a global scale the nine-tenths are on the other side. Communism is dead, but something will rise from its ashes. This is the wrong time to give up, Vlady. You need a Party.'

'Your party's over, Klaus. Just accept it. That world has gone for ever.'

> I tell you what: your groping theorist
> Is like a beast led round and round and round
> By evil spirits on a barren ground
> Near to the verdant pastures he has missed.'

Winter chuckled. 'Mephistopheles to Faust. Good. Winter to Meyer: Too rash as always, my friend. At a time when capitalism is truly global the people will need new political institutions to protect them against its savagery. I've just returned from Beijing. My Party is not doing too badly there, you know. In Eastern Europe and Moscow we are rising again – not because we were good, but because the shock therapists are worse. The space is limited. But it's there all right. We're beginning to grow here again, without the dead hand of the DDR. Why don't you join the PDS, become active again? You mustn't wither away before the state, Vlady.'

'Fantasy politics, Klaus. Do you think I should accept Sao's offer?'

'Of course. Immediately. Without second thoughts. What's wrong with you, Vlady? It would be good to have you running a global publishing house. Who knows, I might even offer you my memoirs!'

'As long as I'm not in them, Klaus. Look, your cousin's leaving. Please make friends with him. He's really upset. Go on. If you do, I might seriously consider joining the PDS or something.'

'Walter!'

Winter's voice was heard by everyone. His cousin stopped near the door and turned round to look at him. Winter nodded. Walter rushed to their table and the two men embraced.

'By the way, this is my friend, Professor Vladimir Meyer, his wife Helge. Walter Nürnberg.'

'Happy to be present on this occasion Herr Nürnberg. We were both leaving. Happy reunion.'

Vlady and Helge walked out quickly. It was clear again and they stood still to observe the cluster of stars in the night sky over their city, which would soon be remodelled as the capital of the new Reich . . .

'Without you,' he whispered to Helge, 'I had begun to feel like a blown seed, floating on the wind.'

She did not reply, but took his arm and gently propelled him homewards.